*R*ose steadied her nerves with all the will in her soul. She would not react, would not give the advantage. This was simply another sort of attack, after all. Besides, she was much practiced in the art of concealing her emotions.

Except for that tiny portion of her that thrilled to his closeness, that noted the virile scent of well-warmed man, that longed to push that single dark lock back from his forehead, that was achingly aware of his near-nakedness . . .

Rose pulled herself from that fruitless world of fantasy with an exertion of will. "Having trouble finishing a sentence, Tremayne?" She affected a bored tone. "Then again, the aristocracy doesn't precisely breed for brains, does it?"

For a moment, she thought he might actually laugh. Then his expression returned to that manipulative smirk that swayed so many women but only left her cold.

"I have an idea. Why don't you wrap your hands around my thick . . . hard . . ." He plucked a weapon from the rack. "Staff?"

"A charming heroine and a dashing spy hero make *The Pretender* a riveting read . . . entertained me thoroughly from beginning to end."

—Sabrina Jeffries, *USA Today* bestselling author of *After the Abduction* on *The Pretender*

"With delicious characters and a delectable plot, Bradley delivers another enticing read."

—*Romantic Times* on *The Spy*

St. Martin's Paperbacks Titles
by Celeste Bradley

The Liar's Club

The Pretender

The Impostor

The Spy

The Charmer

The Rogue

The Royal Four

To Wed a Scandalous Spy

Surrender to a Wicked Spy

The
Charmer

(Book Four in the Liar's Club)

CELESTE BRADLEY

St. Martin's Paperbacks

THE CHARMER

Copyright © 2004 by Celeste Bradley.
Excerpt from *To Wed a Scandalous Spy* copyright © 2004 by Celeste Bradley.

ISBN: 0-312-99971-2
EAN: 80312-99971-1

Printed in the United States of America

St. Martin's Paperbacks edition / October 2004

St. Martin's Paperbacks are published by St. Martin's Press, 175 Fifth Avenue, New York, NY 10010.

10 9 8 7 6 5 4 3

This book is dedicated to Hannah,
who decided that one of the spies should be a girl.

Acknowledgments

Thank you, Bill, my wonderful husband and best friend, for bringing me flowers every week, even after 20 years.

Thank you, H & G, for already showing me the women you will someday be. I did good!

As always, I must thank Darbi Gill, Robyn Holiday, Joanne Markis, Jennifer Smith, Alexis Tharp, Cindy Tharp, and all the gang from Music City Romance Writers. Hanging with the girls keeps me sane.

The
Charmer

Chapter One

❖

ENGLAND 1813, AUTUMN

His naked, sculpted chest gleamed in the candlelight. His shoulders, broad and muscled, narrowed to a hard waist and flat belly. He was tall enough to make her feel small, although she wasn't, particularly. His gray eyes watched her as intently as she watched him. She didn't want to miss a thing—not the way his tousled dark hair hung over his brow, not the way his chest rose and fell with his quickening breaths. Especially not the way his sweat-dampened breeches clung to powerful thighs that were already braced to receive her advance. She knew his form well, knew the feel of him, the shape of him. Yet there was always more to learn.

Rose couldn't blink, couldn't look away. Her eyes became her only conduit to him as she shut out everything else. There was no London, no England, no war. There was only this man—this beautiful, half-naked man who gazed at her with such intensity.

She stepped closer. Careful. She mustn't seem too

eager, nor too nonchalant. If she was to fulfill her wish here in this dimly lit room, she must play wisely and well.

His chest swelled as he inhaled and the golden glow from the candles played like music over his hot and rippling body. He exhaled in a rush.

She almost smiled. It was a sign.

As he moved toward her, she spread her knees and readied herself. Her patience had repaid her, for as he wrapped his arms about her—

She rolled him cleanly over her shoulder and tossed him hard to the mat beneath them.

Collis Tremayne lay there, gasping back the breath that had been knocked from him by the fall. Rose Lacey, former housemaid turned spy trainee, only cocked her head down at her opponent and folded her arms.

The hand-to-hand combat trainer stepped forward and grunted. "Should have rolled out of that fall," Kurt said.

Kurt was the premier assassin of the Liar's Club, the band of Crown spies that operated behind the facade of a gambling hell that stood opposite the school. Who would ever have thought it? Assassins and spies had become everyday associates of Rose's ever since the day she'd been liberated from her former position and installed as the first woman ever to be trained to be a Liar.

Kurt, who also cooked for the mixed band of gentlemen and street thieves that made up the Liars, was very, very good with puff pastry and anything bladed and sharp. Ever a man of few words, the scarred giant turned his back and returned to his place along the wall.

The weapons training room, or the arena, as Kurt had dubbed it, was the largest portion of the cellar of an unassuming building in a not-quite-respectable area of London. Of course, it no longer resembled a place for storing root vegetables and casks of ale. Pity about that ale. Rose wiped perspiration from her face with the back of her forearm. She truly could use a pint about now.

Currently the stone walls were adorned with racks of weapons and other training accoutrements. Against one wall stood a rack of straw-stuffed canvas figures that served as the enemy for students too likely to kill one another accidentally. She herself had graduated from dummies very quickly, thank you very much.

Fortunately, there was plenty of room for errors, as the great space was broken only by six thick oak foundation pillars that supported the building above. Alarmingly painted targets adorned another wall, while above it all hung a rather medieval candle-holder that reminded Rose of the giant oaken cranks that had once lifted a castle's drawbridge. It held forty candles or more, which she knew because she paid her board at the school by cleaning it as well.

Most of the students lived at the school and did as she did. Tiny bedchambers had been carved from the top-story attic. A bit cramped, it was true, but Rose felt the charm of her very own room more than made up for the lack of space.

And Kurt lived there, when he wasn't tending the

kitchen of the other establishment. She glanced at
him, awaiting further instructions. The giant instruc-
tor made all the other students lined up against the
wall look like children. Some of them were, compared to her and Collis. They two were the oldest in
the group by several years, having both come late to
the school.

To the world, it was known as the Lillian Raines
School for the Less Fortunate.

To those few who knew better, it was the Academy,
the training ground for the most elite gang of thieves
and spies ever in the service of the Crown—the Liar's
Club. Rose and Collis, all of them, were the next gen-
eration of this mixed band of badness and bravery.

That is, if they didn't kill one another before grad-
uation.

A rumble came from Kurt. Rose nodded. She
looked back down at her opponent. Collis Tremayne,
the stuff of a maiden's dreams. Even with one arm
rendered useless Collis was a prime specimen of
manhood.

He was quite tall, making Rose feel like standing
as straight as possible to make up for her own mid-
dling height. Some said he looked like the younger
brother to his uncle, Lord Etheridge, and he did, in a
literal way. Collis had the thick, nearly black
Etheridge hair and the pale gray Etheridge eyes,
though not as eerily silver as his uncle's. Collis was
far more high-spirited and playful than his uncle.
Too playful by half, if anyone were asking Rose's
opinion.

Handsome, charming Collis was also the heir to

the great fortune and title of Etheridge—and the bane of Rose's existence.

He'd caught his breath at last. Rose offered him a hand up. He grinned up at her. "Now, if only you fought in skirts, being tossed to the floor might be a pleasurable experience. I might at least be paid for my troubles with a glimpse of those lovely ankles."

Rose snatched her hand back. "Oh, but trousers keep off the vermin and other *pests,*" she said pointedly.

"Again," came Kurt's order from the shadows. "You're two and two. Last fall." The great candle-bearing wheel above them hissed and flickered as Rose and Collis circled each other again.

"Don't give it away, lad." Kurt's rumbling advice seemed to come from all directions. "You're gusting like a bellows afore you rush her."

Blast. Rose wished Kurt hadn't told Collis that. It was her best clue. Collis was far stronger than she was, even with his disabled arm. She was perhaps a hair quicker, but that was only from years of dodging blows and gropes from her employer and his son, Louis.

Former employer, that is. Dead and gone now, and good riddance to the evil and traitorous Mr. Edward Wadsworth. No longer was she a poor little house-maid, beaten for every petty or imagined offense.

Nor would anyone ever beat her again. She was fast and she was smart, too smart to allow herself to be ill-treated evermore.

Rose pulled her mind from the past and set herself firmly into the present. There was only Collis. He tossed back the dampened lock clinging to his brow and she was put in mind of a sleek and spirited stallion. Magnificent, unbearable Collis . . .

He rushed her without any sort of warning. She had no time to sidestep, no time to react in any way but to shrink back. Old memories, old fears, old reactions took her over. She ducked wildly, without reason. His attack bowled her over, tumbled her back—

And rolled him directly over her and flat onto the mat once more. It took a moment before Rose realized what had happened.

She'd accidentally won. Collis had expected resistance, had expected a countermove. His speed and force had been so great that he'd done himself in, rather like swinging too hard at something that suddenly isn't there.

She looked up from her own crouch to see Kurt standing over them. Kurt's scarred and craggy face used to be difficult for Rose to look at directly, although now he seemed as familiar and comfortable as the shabby furnishings of the training arena.

The man only grunted once at Collis, although he sent Rose a piercing look that told her he had seen her instinctive cower.

But Collis hadn't, thank heaven. Rose raised her chin, defying her own weakness. She shouldn't think about Collis as if he were an ordinary man, who might take the fancy of an ordinary girl. She certainly shouldn't allow thoughts of him to distract her in the middle of training.

Collis rolled over to stand, using his good arm to

brace his rise from the mat. Rose took a step toward him, her hand out once more.

Collis's head came up as her next step rustled the straw-filled mat. She thought she saw struggle on his face before he dredged up a teasing grin. "Your match, Briar Rose."

Rose stiffened at Collis's reminder of her origins. Briar—a weed, a pest to be rooted out of any respectable garden. Her chin rose and her eyebrows crept to a haughty level she had learned from the finest of British butlers. "Imagine that," she drawled in her best upper-class mimicry. "Bluebloods still bleed red."

Collis brought his knuckles to catch the drop seeping from his split lip. His eyes widened comically at the smear of blood.

The other students were preparing for weapons practice. Gleaming pistols came from their boxes. Rags and oil emerged to clean the deadly things. Rose grimaced. She was good with the defensive weapons, good enough to deflect even Kurt's blows on occasion. Still, the servant girl within flinched from handling the pistols. Firearms belonged to the Quality. Mustn't touch.

She knew Kurt despaired of ever making her an offensive operative. Even with all the extra training he'd provided her, she could not bring herself to attack. It was just as well, for she had the feeling he'd wanted her as his own apprentice. He considered her servant skills a major advantage in getting close to a target, then getting away. Rose's stomach churned. Rose the Assassin? Ew.

But Rose the Spy . . . perhaps. If she could keep in mind the woman she'd become.

She'd been contrary enough as a child. When she went into service, she had learned that it would not serve her well to be so stubborn. Many lashings later, the rebel within had been mostly quelled.

Until Clara Simpson had happened upon her. Rose had been crying alone on her little pallet in the attic, where she'd been banished after one too many clumsy incidents. Many times she wondered why Mr. Wadsworth didn't simply sack her, but so many servants came and went in that household that she mused that he probably thought he already had.

After all, it wasn't as if anyone called her by name. She was addressed as "You there!" or "Girl!" so often that at night she would repeat her own name to herself in the dark, just to remind herself of the sound of it. Perhaps a tiny rebellion after all.

Widowed political cartoonist Clara Simpson had swept in like an avenging angel, with sympathy and stolen food and the outlandish request to take Rose's place. At first Rose had been only too happy to slumber away the hours when Clara worked as maid, for it seemed she could never sleep her fill. Then one day, her spirit strengthened by rest and the treats that now came her way, it occurred to Rose to wonder what it was that Clara found so fascinating within the Wadsworths' household.

Curiosity had stirred from some forgotten corner of Rose's mind, sharpening her wits and brightening her existence with the game of hide-and-seek-information. At first there was so much she hadn't understood, complicated concepts that rang meaningless on her ears—until she began to study at the Liar's Academy.

A great deal had come clear during her lessons in politics and history, dangling bits that only spurred her to further effort in order to provide the context needed for the information that she already held.

Wadsworth had been dirty indeed, leader of a group of treasonous plotters known only as the Knights of the Lily, a reference to the fleur-de-lis that was the emblem of French royalty. The group had been squelched once before, years before Rose's time there, but Wadsworth had been left untouched for reasons of political benefit. Untouched but not unwatched.

But the evil Mr. Edward Wadsworth was dead now, killed at the hands of Lord Etheridge himself while he was rescuing his beloved Clara.

Rose wanted to be like Clara more than anything in the world. Clara had a mission, a purpose in life. Her drawing talent had done more than support her in her widowhood; it had given her a way to strip the pretty veil away from the dirty doings of the Quality, to defend those who couldn't defend themselves.

Having a husband who was mad for her didn't hurt, either. Lord Etheridge was as aristocratic as any man Rose had ever seen, but she didn't hold it against him. No one who loved that much could be all bad. Odd how a bloke's armor chinks told you more sometimes than his strengths did.

At his urging, she'd been happy to flee the Wadsworth house to find refuge with the warm and gracious Lady Raines.

When she'd diffidently knocked at the service entrance of that fine house months ago, she'd had no hopes of anything but a meal and perhaps a position in the scullery where she wouldn't be worked too hard or fed too little.

She'd been welcomed, fed, and interviewed in the first hour. Agatha Raines had eyed her closely, asked her several pointed questions, then clapped her hands with glee and announced, "You'll do very nicely indeed."

Within days Rose had found herself installed in her own cozy room in the school attic and pressed into tutelage under various outlandish teachers. Kurt, of course, taught her hand-to-hand fighting and weapons. Feebles had shown her the ins and outs of picking pockets. Button had instructed her in costume and disguise and how to learn to play any character by observation and emulation. The shy and earnest Fisher had drilled her on codes and mapmaking. Lady Raines had taught her how to speak and move and conduct herself no matter at what level of society she found herself.

Entirely willing to be seduced by the kindness surrounding her, Rose had thrown her very being into improving herself in any way her teachers wanted, despite the oddness of the requests.

Rose felt as if she had been a parched and dying plant, suddenly blessed with all the water and care she could desire. She expanded—she grew—if she could have put forth flowers to reward her benefactors, she gladly would have.

So now, with a deep breath, she took up her pistol.

And promptly dropped it. She could hear Kurt's gusting sigh from all the way across the arena. She sent him an apologetic shrug.

Oops.

Collis slung a piece of toweling over his shoulder, watched Rose Lacey fumble her pistol, and grunted in sympathy. He knew how embarrassing clumsiness could be. His left arm would never be whole and his balance was still uneven without the use of it. Hence this afternoon's trouncing on the mat. He'd get better. All he needed was time.

Perhaps.

He looked away uncomfortably. Perhaps.

He himself wasn't required to sit firearms practice, thank the fates. He'd grown up shooting for pleasure on the Etheridge estate and knew his pistols inside and out.

Absently he rubbed the shoulder of his deadened arm. Although he had no feeling from the joint down, the muscles above there ached as badly as did the rest of his body from hitting the mat often and hard.

Briar Rose had enjoyed that, he just knew it. There was no hiding that spark of victorious light in her eyes when she bested him. Her lips would relax and quirk just a bit to the left and her lids would drop slightly to shield her triumphant gaze—and Collis would know she was crowing inside.

It was his secretly held belief that there was far more to Rose Lacey than met the eye.

Oh, she played the no-nonsense trainee well enough. She certainly looked the part, as serious and disapproving as a nun with her sensible braids pinned tightly about her head. The odd thing was, the more tightly she wound herself into the perfect student, the more Collis had to wonder what would happen when she sprang free.

There was potential for a most noteworthy springing free there, he suspected. A truly respectable eruption, in fact. No one was that industrious or that quarrelsome without something pushing them hard from behind.

Not that he was interested in her or anything of the sort. She wasn't his preferred variety of woman at all. He liked them pretty and round and bubbly. Rose was far too long of leg and far too short of bosom. Her features were austere, despite those deep hazel eyes. No one would look twice at her face—until she smiled.

Not that she often did. But by God, when she did . . . Collis had found himself breathless more than once, gone still and riveted by that radiant smile. Then it would be gone, and he would shake himself back to reality.

Of course, Briar Rose cared nothing for his opinion of her beauty. She cared nothing for him at all. She seemed completely consumed by her own aspirations. There wasn't a score he'd earned that she hadn't topped or come bloody close to, not a move he tried that she couldn't counter. The hell of it was, the more she competed with him, the more he looked forward to coming into the Academy every morning. Sooner or later, one of them was going to collect their winnings.

Winnings. Winnings always reminded him of

Ethan Damont. Never had a bloke taken more winnings than Ethan. And last night he'd been in the Liar's Club.

The public side of the club of course, which truthfully was rather exclusive in its own right. The gentlemen's establishment known to the world as the Liar's Club was limited to members only. Of course, the only membership requirements were those of being rich, bored, and vaguely bad.

Ethan was all that but rich. Unless he'd come into some fortune that Collis didn't know of, Ethan Damont worked hard for a living. Worked hard playing hard, that is. Ethan was a professional gambler, making his way through the world depriving rich and stupid young men of their—in his words—undeserved wealth.

And last night, there Ethan had been, raking in his winnings with that same wry, disinterested manner in which he'd taken every tuppence from the other boys at school. Collis watched Ethan light his cheroot from the cigar candle he held to its end. His old friend let out a puff or two, then finally flicked his gaze to Collis without a moment's surprise.

"Tremayne," Ethan greeted him laconically. He leaned back in his chair and stretched his legs. "Surprised to see you in this hole. Then again, you never did have any taste."

Collis laughed easily. Ethan knew very well that the Liar's Club supplied its members with all the finest in food, wine, cigars and gentlemanly entertainment. There was even a raised stage on one end of the clubroom for those less-than-gentlemanly entertainments, although there was a standard policy against any actual prostitution taking place.

Nodding to that velvet-draped stage, now standing empty, Collis took a chair. "You missed the show tonight. That python was the damnedest thing I've ever seen. Six feet if it was an inch."

Ethan shrugged. "I heard about it. My latest victim brought me here as his guest, but not until the fun was over. Can't say as I'm sorry I missed it. Why would any girl want to dance with a snake?"

"Same reason she'd want to dance with you, I suppose."

That finally got a chuckle from his friend, to Collis's relief. Ethan did not look as though he were thriving. Collis had not seen him for a long time.

Ethan and he had a long history. They had spent their years at school using their wits and their fists to get them in and out of trouble. Unlike Collis, Ethan was not highborn. He was the youngest son of a dour shipping merchant who had decided the irreverent young man was not fit to inherit any portion of the business, so after giving him an education had sent him out to make his own way. And so he had.

Ethan was a master of the cards. A cheat, yes, but the finest, most affable, infinitely challenging cheat about. The wealthy men of Society could not resist him. It had become something of a mark of social superiority to play against "the Diamond". He fleeced only the mighty, and he only took what was needed to continue his delightful lifestyle in the Polite World.

To have Ethan in your game was to experience the

height of the manly art of gambling. He never stole estates from lordlings too young to know they were out of their league. He never targeted desperate men out to restore fallen fortunes. He was a most ethical, honorable cheat. Most importantly, one could never prove the fact.

Collis never, ever played opposite him.

But the dashing and handsome youth from Collis's past had become a jaded, world-weary man, though he was no older than Collis. Ethan's eyes were flat, his gestures mechanical as he toyed with the deck of cards.

"How are you these days, Damont?" Collis leaned forward. "Really."

Ethan didn't look at him. "Better than you."

Rebuffed, Collis sat back with a snort. "True. At least you still have both wings."

"That is I. Fully fledged and nowhere to fly."

The words were quiet, almost inaudible, but they rang in Collis's head like a bell. Nowhere for an intelligent, wily, adventurous fellow like Ethan to fly? Excitement twined through him. Oh, had his friend come to the right club!

Still, nothing could be done without clearing the notion through Dalton first, so Collis had taken his friend's latest address and bid him a cheerful goodnight. Recruiting wasn't a trainee's job, but this idea was simply too brilliant not to pass along.

And admittedly, it had not been very comfortable being with Ethan last night. His old friend's presence had brought back far too many memories. Recalling the boy he'd once been, the man he'd become for a while . . . until that day on the battlefield when the cannon fire had blasted him from his horse, breaking several ribs and shattering his left arm so badly it had nearly been declared hopeless and amputated.

If not for one very observant surgeon, who had seen that the pulse in Collis's left wrist was still strong and had ordered the arm set and left to heal on its own, he would indeed be without one wing.

But healed did not necessarily mean recovered, so his soldiering days were over almost as soon as they'd begun. No more war, no more battles, no more music—

Don't think about it. Think about this day, this work.

It was worthy work, or would be as soon as he became a Liar in truth. He couldn't wait.

On the few missions he'd taken part in, he'd not been a real operative. He'd once helped James Cunnington attempt to locate an elusive prostitute named Fleur. Those had been interesting days, combing every place from the finest establishments, like Mrs. Blythe's elegant house of entertainment, to the lowest and filthiest corners of the stews—educational in itself, to be sure, but he'd only been along for the ride. He'd not even been told why they were searching for the girl.

Another time he'd donned the red vest of a Bow Street Runner to search for a traitor's daughter—but again, errands, not missions.

For now, Collis's mission was to graduate the Liar's Academy—and to enjoy provoking Rose, with her flashing eyes and snug breeches that showed entirely too much length of leg—

Rose turned just then and caught him looking. Collis blinked innocently under her questioning glare, until his grin turned to laughter. She was so much fun to rile.

He crossed the room to lean one hip against the wall near where she sat with her firearms class. "That was good work on the mat. You're going to be as good as me someday."

Rose sighed, then put down her pistol and cloth. She folded her arms, tucking her fingers beneath her rolled-up sleeves, and eyed him with raised brows. "Flirting again? It won't work, y'know. I'm immune."

He grinned at her, that easy smile that sent tiny shivers through her. "Flirting is so passé. I'm . . . beguiling."

She stiffened her spine against its traitorous tendency to melt. "Well, go beguile somewhere else. I'm busy."

"Oh, but I love to watch you work." He stepped closer. "You're so very . . . nimble-fingered." His voice went husky and his eyes seemed to go darker, from smoke to storm cloud. He moved a step closer, until her elbow was so close to his . . . um, hip . . . that she could feel the heat of his body on her bared arm. She ought to get up and move away. She ought to say something sharp, a rebuke for such ridiculous maneuverings.

Too bad her mouth was so dry.

She always could feel him near her, as if he were

surrounded by a wall of heat that seeped through her clothing to warm her skin. For once, he seemed to feel it too. The teasing gleam in his eye faded, to be replaced by something darker and much, much more intense.

Breathing was becoming a problem. She parted her lips for more air to her lungs. His eyes flashed at that small, moist sound. Oh, God, she could fall into those cloudy-sky eyes forever—

A sound came from nearby, a not-so-subtle clearing of a raspy throat.

The spell over Rose popped like a soap bubble. She spun toward Kurt in relief. "Yes, sir?"

With a grunt, the trainer jerked his chin toward the dismembered pistol before her.

Rose blinked. Right. The pistol.

She picked up the pistol, refusing to notice how her hands had that tendency to shake again. She was immune to blarney-bleating toffs with more looks than honesty. Immune.

Completely.

And as soon as her body stopped quivering with unreleased heat, she was going to prove it.

Collis watched Rose handle the pistol, unable to take his gaze from her quick, skilled fingers. Her hands were actually quite elegant, despite the short, practical nails. She cleaned the barrel, her touch almost caressing as she stroked the cloth up and down.

He was quite sure he was choking. What would it feel like to have those hands on him, stroking him in just that skillful way?

Rose never fluttered her hands like some women he knew. Every movement she made had a purpose, with grace and economy combined. She had very sensible hands.

Collis found himself suddenly convinced that anything else was just plain silly on a woman. Who wanted a female who couldn't keep a grip on her own fan, for pity's sake? Who wanted to be touched with weak, flaccid fingers when he could be held fiercely tight by a woman who meant it?

Elegant, sensible hands.

How intriguing.

Through the opening into the hall, Collis caught a glimpse of the proprietor of the Lillian Raines School—Sir Simon Raines himself—talking to Dalton.

Collis smiled and strode forward. Just the men he'd wanted to see.

Chapter Two

───────────── ❖ ─────────────

When Rose returned from helping Kurt lock away the pistols and kit—she suspected Kurt of using any excuse to accustom her to handling cold iron—she found that Collis was still in the arena talking to Lord Etheridge and Sir Simon. Sir Simon Raines had been the spymaster of the Liars before Lord Etheridge and now ran the Academy with his wife, Agatha. With a nod, Sir Simon exited the room, leaving the Etheridge men in deep conversation.

Collis had only thrown a bit of toweling over one broad naked shoulder. He looked entirely delicious. Rose forced herself to look away. The fighting dummies were looking very smart this evening.

She looked back at Collis. Yes, still delicious.

Side by side, he and Lord Etheridge seemed more like brothers. Dalton Montmorency the elder, more sober brother, and Collis Tremayne the younger, more dashing one.

"Rotter," the young ladies of the aristocracy whispered of Collis Tremayne with fascinated longing. "Rake. Heartbreaker."

"Charmer."

There were, unfortunately, many opportunities to watch Collis in the act of charming any and every woman in his path. Even her.

The first time had been when he'd first joined the Liar's Club a few weeks after her own arrival. Rose shook her head, thinking of the diffident creature she'd been only months ago. He'd been standing by his uncle, much as he was now, who was showing him about the place. Collis had turned to her with a smile that had transformed her knees to water, and had beckoned her closer with one lazy finger.

She'd obeyed out of habit and out of the deepest enchantment she had ever experienced. His cloudy-day eyes twinkled warmly at her, and his smile spoke of sweet intimacies she'd only dreamed of. He was so fine and handsome, so elegantly rugged, so—

"Fetch me some tea, won't you, ducky?" He'd smiled that patented melt-away grin at her.

Icy comprehension had doused Rose's thrall in a moment. She'd stood frozen, too indignant to turn and walk away. She'd only been in the club for a few weeks, yet already she had begun to expect the treatment of an equal. The bloomin' gall!

Lord Etheridge had won her heart and loyalty forever when he'd frowned at his nephew. "Rose is not the help. She is a trainee–second grade." His lordship's lips had quirked. "One grade higher than yourself, actually."

The grin had drained from Collis Tremayne's handsome face. The moment had been sweet indeed. She'd dipped a saucy curtsey and walked away, leaving Collis Tremayne slack-jawed and quite without his tea.

Unfortunately, Collis had soon caught up with her in rank. She began so far behind, after all. Now with both Rose and Collis standing at trainee–first grade, they ran neck and neck to achieve full induction into the club.

Rose had never struggled so hard in her life, not even for the demanding Mr. Wadsworth. Collis, however, seemed to hardly need to work at all, except for hand-to-hand training. There she surpassed him, at least defensively.

No matter that her new spectacles had allowed her to advance quickly through the reading and writing courses that Milady Raines had created. No matter that she had excelled at both subject identification drawings and mapmaking. No matter that even Kurt had difficulty laying hand or blunted weapon on her in the arena. Collis was always there, coming up behind with ease and that lazy teasing smile.

Now, seeing Collis with his lordship, she hesitated. She'd hoped to get in a few more hours of practice with the weapons before bed, especially after her backsliding cower earlier. She hung back in the doorway, waiting for Collis to leave.

"He was here last night playing cards," Collis was saying to his uncle with sure urgency. "And winning. He lives not far from here, in High Street. He's the perfect recruit, I tell you. Imagine the places a professional gambler can go—the people he can associate with all over Europe!"

The man Collis spoke of must have been spotted in the public rooms of the club, which actually stood on the opposite corner. The school was connected to it by a damp and unpleasant stretch of tunnel, so most trainees and Liars seemed to regard the two structures as one establishment.

Rose detested the tunnel. Give her a drafty old attic any day. Despite her freshly applied education, there were still a few cracks where her common upbringing showed. Underground was where bodies were buried. That was that.

Lord Etheridge noticed Rose hesitating in the doorway of the arena and beckoned her in. Collis was half turned away and didn't notice in his zeal.

"I've known Ethan Damont since school, Dalton. I'm sure he is to be trusted. He's a good man beneath that gambler insouciance. He's a smart bloke, very fast on his feet. We *need* more men like him."

Etheridge nodded, obviously considering the matter. Then he smiled at Rose as she came closer. "What do you think, Miss Lacey?" He always addressed her as a lady. "Do you think I ought to consider a gambler for the club?"

Rose didn't think the idea sounded profitable at all. Even she knew who the Diamond was. The Voice of Society news column mentioned him regularly and with great relish. "I wonder if someone so public would be a good recruit, my lord. Milady Etheridge and Milady Raines are hoping you'll be bringing in more girls for training, like me. After all, a chambermaid can go right into a suspect's unmentionables drawer in the middle of the day with no questions asked."

"Hmm." Lord Etheridge tilted his head and cocked a brow at Collis. "When your gambler friend can do that, I'll recruit him." Then he turned away with an approving nod to Rose and left. Rose stared after him. Was his lordship *chuckling*?

Rose began to remove the shawl she'd donned earlier against the cellar dampness. She looked up from untying the knot in front to see Collis, still half-naked, still delectable, gazing at her with his arms folded over his gleaming chest.

"I can't suss you out, Briar Rose." Disappointment was plain in his voice. "Ethan Damont could be a true asset to the club. One would think you were afraid of some competition once I graduate."

"You graduate before me?" Rose lifted her chin and crossed her own arms. "That's amusing, considering that I was here first. And who sent me here? . . . Why, I believe it was his lordship!" She smiled sweetly. "I would think it all depended on whom one knows . . . except I didn't know him at all, did I?"

She hit the mark with that arrow, she knew. Collis was very sensitive about being "qualified" by no means other than nepotism.

There was no reason to think that, of course. Collis was everything the club needed—brilliant and brave. But challenge flashed in his gray eyes all the same. Oh, no. Now she'd done it.

"Prove it," Collis taunted with a gleam in his eyes.

"Here and now. Prove that you deserve to be a Liar before me!"

Rose narrowed her eyes at him. "I have nothing to prove to you, Collis Tremayne. To Kurt perhaps and certainly to his lordship—but I could quite happily go to my grave without knowing or caring for your opinion of me."

He came closer—a bit too close for her peace of mind—and smiled seductively at her. "So you aren't a bit curious?" His voice was soft and deep. Oh, she was curious all right. Curious about the way his taut skin rippled over his hard belly. The way his training trousers hung just a bit too low on his lean hips, showing that intriguing path of fine hairs that led—

"No," she blurted.

"I doubt that. Don't you want to find out who the best Liar is, once and for all?"

Rose knew who the best Liar was, but she didn't think it would do him any good for her to give in to his outrageous bullying. If he ever decided to give the club his all, there would be no doubt in anyone's mind who was the best Liar who had ever lived.

Yet in the past months, the seeds of hope that she had kept protected all those years had germinated into a bright-blooming pride. He was good, but maybe, just maybe, so was she.

He grinned at her hesitation. "I double-damn dare you."

The childish dare only spiked her new self-respect. She was not about to let an arrogant, light-minded lout like Collis Tremayne take that away from her.

She raised her chin and gazed at him, keeping her expression cool. "Very well, then, blueblood. Have at."

The sabers were first. Rose had chosen them, to Collis's surprise. But doubtless Rose was aware that she would only be able to defend against his strength while she was relatively fresh. There were less heavy weapons to tackle later.

Collis had to admit to some surprise that she'd taken him up on his challenge. Rose's usual response to his teasing was to toss her head and pretend disdain, all the while coloring slightly in her fair cheeks.

Yet she had called his bluff, and now he was going to have to defend his masculine honor with a bout of swordplay. If his fencing master could see him now, challenging a *girl*! Collis grinned as Rose tossed him his saber, hilt first. He caught it absently, the metal pommel cool in his hand, while he watched her assume a defensive stance.

"Don't take it too hard when you lose, Briar Rose," he teased. "I won't tell if you won't."

Her eyes narrowed. "All mouth and no trousers, Tremayne."

Oh, that did it. Collis stepped forward to sweep his blade whistling through the air. She raised hers to parry, and Collis saw her eyes widen as she felt the force of his strike.

He still felt somewhat clumsy with the saber without the use of his left arm for balance. In any case, this was no elegant fencing match. Liars were taught to use weapons solely to stop or kill. There were no rules but that of prevailing for the Crown. Although

Rose was deadly quick, she was hardly a physical match for him.

Clumsy as his left arm might be, his right was as strong as it had ever been. He gave her no quarter, hacking at her with the dulled blade until she was very likely black-and-blue beneath the padded suit she'd donned. He finally hesitated mid-swing, beginning to feel sorry for her—

Until she disarmed him with a neat twist of her sword that pulled the sword hilt from his hand and sent his weapon spinning into the shadows. Collis froze in surprise, staring at his empty hand with jaw dropped.

Rose knew she ought to have moved in to riposte, but she only stood before him with blade sagging, her chest rising and falling rapidly. Kurt had shown her that trick only yesterday and she'd scarcely had the strength left to execute it after the pasting Collis had given her. He'd not given her an inch, openly using the advantage of his superior strength against her. She found herself obscurely hurt by that.

Rose went to the weapons rack to hang up her sword and kit. Only this morning she might have fetched Collis's to the rack as well, trying in some small way to lessen the sting of losing. Her shoulders straight despite her weariness, she turned to face him.

"Are we quite finished?"

He shoved his dark hair back with his good hand and grinned at her, his white teeth flashing in his tanned face. "What's the matter, Briar Rose? Worried you can't do it again?"

As quickly as the simmering anger within her

came to a boil, Rose reached behind her to the rack
and sent a throwing blade spinning through the air to
thud quivering into the straw-filled mat between Collis's feet.

He jumped back, clapping his hand protectively
before his groin. "Bloody hell!"

Kurt was going to glower frighteningly when he
saw that slit in the canvas. He was a demon about the
upkeep of the arena. Still, Collis's shock was worth
every minute that she would spend repairing the mat.
Her lips twitched at his defensive pose.

"I wasn't anywhere near the Etheridge jewels.
Honestly, Collis, you *do* have delusions of grandeur,
don't you?" She raised one eyebrow in a sterling imi-
tation of Sir Raines's butler, Pearson. She knew Collis hated that, which was why she had practiced it
before her mirror until she'd perfected it.

Collis saw that blasted eyebrow rise all right. He
felt his face flush as he bent to pull the knife from the
mat. "My turn to choose, Miss Thorn." He approached her slowly, never taking his eyes from hers.
It was beneath him to enjoy that flicker of apprehension he saw there. Low and dishonorable.

But sweet.

He came so close that he could smell the subtle
scent of her hair. Was that lavender? She didn't move a
muscle as he reached behind her to hang up the knife.
He smiled slowly. "And I choose . . ." He let his voice
trail off to a whisper as he stepped closer still.

To his surprise, Rose didn't so much as twitch.
Most women he knew would have giggled or quiv-

ered or otherwise reacted to him being so close. Rose, it appeared, was made of sterner stuff.

Rose steadied her nerves with all the will in her soul. She would not react, would not give the advantage. The Wadsworth men had done their worst and hadn't broken her. Collis Tremayne was a rank amateur in comparison.

Except for that tiny portion of her that quivered at his closeness, that noted the virile scent of well-warmed man, that longed to push that single dark lock back from his forehead, that was achingly aware of his near nakedness . . .

Rose pulled herself from that fruitless world of fantasy with an exertion of will. "Having trouble finishing a sentence, Tremayne?" She affected a bored tone. "Then again, the aristocracy doesn't precisely breed for brains, does it?"

One corner of his mouth twitched at that. For a moment, she thought he might actually laugh. Then his expression returned to that sly, knowing smile that swayed so many women but only left her cold. Well, at least hardly warm at all. Mostly.

"I've an idea," he said. "Why don't you wrap your hands around my thick . . . hard . . ." He plucked a weapon from the rack. "Staff?"

Dancing back a few steps, he assumed attack position with a six-foot oak quarterstaff in his hands. Rose barely had time to fumble behind her for another before the swish of his first blow went over her head and glanced off her shoulder.

Numbness shot through her arm and she almost

lost her grip on the staff. Unable to bring it up to block him, she took advantage of his next swing to duck beneath his outstretched arms and roll past him.

Of course, she couldn't pass up the chance to slap him across the backs of his knees with her own stick. His balance faltered, and he stumbled, although he did not go down.

Fry it, she should have hit him harder. Still, his stumble gave her the chance to stand matched against him, braced for attack, although her arm still tingled to the bone.

He was very good with the staff. This was one area where his wounded arm did not seem to hinder him at all. In fact, she had seen him turn to take a blow on that arm more than once, making his lack of sensation work to his advantage.

She hadn't a hope against him. The staff was not her best weapon against someone with longer reach and height—which included almost everyone.

The only way to win this was to back from his blows, making him waste strength until he slowed or made a mistake. The impact of stick on stick rang through the bones of her hands and arms as she tried to strategize. She only needed to be careful not to let him back her into a—

The rack of sparring dummies came up against her back. Bloody hell indeed. She twisted under Collis's unrelenting blows, trying to slip through the rack between the dummies. But some light-minded trainee had dressed the dummies in bits of stolen French uniforms. Rose's sleeve caught on the buttons of one jacket while her hair snagged in the pins holding the tattered epaulets in place. The rack of dummies came tumbling down.

Rose went with it. To add to her defeat, as she rolled into the disintegrating rack she felt Collis's staff give her a brisk wallop across her buttocks. "Point to me," he crowed.

As she sat up amid the wreckage, she wasn't sure what smarted more, her pride or her rear.

"Give up, O Thorny One?"

He was leaning on his staff like a shepherd with his crook, grinning at her. Rose felt her chest rising and falling like a bellows. Collis wasn't even breathing heavily.

The rat.

Part of Rose wanted to quit. Let him win, for what did it matter? His sort would always win in the end. Power and wealth won out, especially when paired with top-drawer lineage and dark-angel magnificence.

Then again, why should she let him win this? He'd been handed the world the moment he'd been born. Perhaps it was her turn.

"My turn." She stood and walked past him to the weapons rack. They'd used swords and staffs, and she didn't want to go hand-to-hand again. There were daggers aplenty, mostly dulled. The only weapons on the rack kept sharp were the small, gleaming throwing knives. Rose inserted her fingers between the hilts of the six remaining knives, lifting three in each hand like a circus showman. They were her best weapon and Kurt had taught her well.

She turned and nodded at Collis, her hands hidden at her sides. "Take a step to your left, if you please."

He only frowned at her.

She tilted her head and shrugged. "As you wish."

The knives flew past Collis with such rapidity that they thudded into the wall behind him with a sound like hail on the roof. After the first shining weapon had spun through the air between them, Collis had frozen. He had no choice but to trust to Rose's accuracy after he'd been too slow to realize he stood directly before the cork target mounted on the wall.

Come to think on it, it wasn't so alarming. Rose hadn't missed her target in a very long time. Collis knew if he turned now, he would see an outline of himself sketched in small, deadly knife hilts.

Instead of turning, he merely dropped his staff and took three steps directly backward until his back was pressed to the large target. Unlike the concentric circles on an archery target, this one was painted in the silhouette of a man with different regions labeled: KILL, MAIM, and DISARM.

Rose had ignored those grim designations, as Collis could tell by the knife hilts that rode on both of his shoulders, astride his hips, and—oh, *hell*—snugly between his thighs.

Only five. He raised one hand to reach over his head. Six. He plucked the sixth knife from the cork to settle the blade between his fingertips.

Rose had never moved from before the weapons rack. She stood there with that blasted arch look upon her face and spread her arms like the target painted behind him. *I dare you,* that look said to Collis.

Unfortunately, he didn't dare. He wasn't bad with the knives, but at this distance he didn't have Rose's accuracy. To be honest, he'd never truly applied himself to the knives, concentrating instead on more manly pursuits like the sword and hand-to-hand. He actually wasn't all that accomplished with the staff, either. He'd simply bludgeoned Rose out of that match.

So, as much as he would love to send the knives whizzing past her to wipe that expression from her smug little features . . . he couldn't risk it.

He might want to kill her, but he didn't want to *kill* her. Instead, he turned at the last moment to send the knife into one of the wooden pillars that supported the school above them. They weren't much wider than Rose, so some accuracy was required. The hilt sank deep. "One."

He sent knives into the next four pillars as quickly as he could pluck them from the wall behind them. Not bad. His pride rising with every thud, he stopped to grin suggestively at Rose before pulling the last knife from between his legs.

She wasn't even watching. She stood with her arms folded, staring at the floor with a bored expression, twisting the toe of one shoe into the mat.

With a growl, Collis tossed the last knife, barely glancing at his target first. Then he looked quickly back in horror as his blade flew with perfect accuracy—

Into the rope that suspended the chandelier.

The chandelier that must weigh eighty stone in all.

The chandelier that hung high over the head of Rose, who was now bending to look at the floor.

No time to cry out. No time to explain.

Collis flung himself across the room. *Oh, God, he was too far away—*

He took her to the mat in a ferocious tackle, rolling over and over with her in his arms. Behind them the giant oaken wheel crashed to the floor, sending up a whoosh of wind and hot spattering wax mingled with straw from the shredded matting, plunging them into total darkness.

Chapter Three

———— ◈ ————

Rose couldn't breathe. Couldn't see, couldn't move. For a single second, her mind went circling in panic. Then she focused with a will.

She couldn't see because the candles had gone out. Something heavy crashing to the floor—added to darkness permeated with the smell of smoking wick—equaled a narrow escape from Death by Chandelier. She'd been standing directly beneath the giant wheel if she recalled correctly.

Which meant that something had cut the rope.

Collis. And the reason she was lying here with the breath knocked from her lungs?

Collis. And the great warm weight that even now pinned her limbs to the floor?

Collis.

She forced her lungs to expand. The first painful breath was followed by another, less so. Above her she felt Collis sucking in a great lungful as well.

"Are you injured?" His breath brushed her face.

His arms tightened around her, pressing her to his hard, bare chest.

"No," she whispered. "I don't think so." Distracted, she realized that she seemed to be embracing him as well. Her arms were looped under his and her hands clasped the back of his broad shoulders. Broad *naked* shoulders.

His muscles flexed beneath her hands. Momentarily charmed, still dazed, Rose dug her fingertips lightly in response. *He's so strong. Holding me so close, as if I were as dear as dear could be.*

Breathing still wasn't easy. In fact, it was becoming more difficult by the moment. He covered her like a lover, with her breasts crushed against his broad chest and his knee pressed between her thighs. The firm pressure against her sensitive center made hot jolts of want shoot across her body.

When he shifted that knee slightly, she nearly whimpered at the sensation. Her thoughts faded for a moment as she merely *felt.* She felt her skin shimmer as the heat of his body penetrated her. In a moment she would puddle like melted wax beneath him. He smelled so good—man and sandalwood and just a hint of clean sweat.

Deep inside her a tiny voice sighed in pleasure. *Don't move.*

Collis couldn't move. Wouldn't move. His senses were full of sweet aromas, warm sensations, and tiny breathless sighs. His arms were full of supple female.

She was lithe and strong beneath him, not limp and compliant. Firm and lively and very, very arousing. His arms tightened. For a moment he forgot everything but his arousal and the feel of her hands spread on his bare skin.

His breath mingled with hers as their lips hovered, not an inch apart. He could have her. He felt it in the way she lay open to him, the way the vee between her thighs was heating where his knee pressed. He could have her and it would be fast and hard and hurried and so very good.

They were already alone, already lying down, already in darkness. . . .

She made a small noise. She writhed a bit in his arms. The squirm of her hips beneath him fired his erection further. He forgot his impairment, forgot that he couldn't feel how tight he was—

"Squeezing me!" Her voice reached a squeak. His arms loosened instantly. With horror he realized that he was as hard as stone.

Over *Rose Lacey*!

Quickly he scrambled backward, his feet scuffling in the scattered straw. He stood slowly, his hands fisting and releasing. *Think of cold water, man. Damp and snowy days when the fire only reaches so far and the water in the washbowl is like ice.*

His towering erection began to subside. Thank God the room was dark, although he suddenly realized it wasn't as dark as it had been. He blinked.

Rose was standing. "I can see you now. A candle must have survived, or perhaps a—" She stopped with a gasp. "Fire!"

Collis whirled to gaze at the wreckage in horror. She was right. The wax-soaked straw had smoldered under their inattention. Even as he watched, the tiny tongues of flame licked farther along the ruined mat as thickening smoke began to rise.

"Oh, God," he breathed. Not a curse. A prayer.

There was no time to run three flights of stairs to wake the other students—no time to run for help at all. The desiccated straw would burn like—like straw.

They ran to the flames and began to stomp them, but they spread too fast.

"The kitchen," Rose said. "Quickly—the pump!"

The school kitchen lay directly behind the arena. In a breath Rose and Collis were inside, fumbling in the dark. She pushed him to the left. "There, by the sink."

He felt around frantically. He'd never stepped foot into this kitchen. Kitchens were for servants and—at Etheridge House—for stealing a late-night bite from the larder. Right now he was wishing mightily that he had lowered himself to step foot into the school kitchen.

He found the rigid metal handle of the pump. He knew how to use a pump, thank God. It was like the one in the stables, and he knew how to care for his own horse.

Below the spout he found a small pot full of water that likely always remained there, just as in the stables. He primed the pump with a careless splash and began pumping with all his might.

Rose bumped him, shoving a large pot beneath the stream of water that gushed from the spout. In an instant it was full and she replaced it with another. Without a word, she ran with the two full pots into the next room. Collis continued pumping with his deadened arm, watching it closely in the unfortunately increasing light flickering from the other room. Now he could smell smoke, even in here.

They were going to burn down the school. Dear God, they were going to burn down London! With the other hand he reached blindly over his head for any container in reach that he could fill.

Rose came back, pushed the empty pots at him, and disappeared with the ones he'd filled. They worked like this in panicked and breathless silence for what seemed like hours. Collis felt the water run over the sink into his boots but never let up the pumping. Rose blew past him, tossing empty pots into the water with a splash that soaked them both and pulling full ones dripping from the sink.

Collis wanted to help but stayed where he was. Rose was faster. He was stronger. This was the best way to do it. He could only carry one pot without spilling it—his dead hand never seemed able to keep a grip unless he was looking at it.

Finally, he felt a small, cold hand rest on his good arm. "Stop," she breathed. "It's out."

Sure enough, there was no more dangerously flickering light, although the kitchen was choked with smoke. He reached out one arm to support her, letting his dead hand slide from the pump handle. She sank against him for a moment.

Now that they weren't in a panicked frenzy, Rose realized how cold and wet she was. Her clothing was soaked through, especially where she'd been forced to douse her own trousers to protect her legs from the heat of the flames.

But Collis was warm and he felt as solid as a tree in

the smoky darkness. She wanted to rest her head on his shoulder and shake with all the relief and leftover panic welling inside her.

Surely he wouldn't mind, after what they had just gone through together? To lean on someone strong . . . just for a moment . . .

"Bloody *hell*!" The roar came from the arena.

The smoke had roused Kurt.

Rose watched warily as Sir Simon Raines tapped a finger on his lips while he walked slowly about the room surveying the damage done to the Lillian Raines School for the Less Fortunate. The former spymaster turned headmaster was usually a cheerful man, quite willing to be teased by his pretty wife, Agatha.

This early dawn, he was not so merry. In fact, Rose had never seen the man so grim as he eyed them both. Collis was standing with his arms crossed, leaning against the very post that had once held the rope to the giant chandelier. His expression was one of buoyant unconcern. His knife still protruded from the wood above his head, just out of reach.

Rose couldn't decide whether to run screaming into the dawn or throw herself at Sir Simon's feet and beg for mercy. The devastation surrounding them was bloody phenomenal.

It had seemed bad enough in the darkness and panic. Now, in the bright light of the several carriage lanterns hastily hung about the chamber, it was much, much worse.

The giant mat was ruined. Not only had it torn

down every seam from the impact of the chandelier, but it also bore a great charred hole in its center. Rose tried not to think about the way it also squelched wetly beneath his lordship's every step.

In the middle of the room, the wreckage of the giant oak wheel looked like the last siege of some medieval fortress. Great spokes pointed skyward like broken spears raised toward the pall of smoke that still drifted through the beams.

Around the perimeter, the dummies lay sprawled like the dead warriors of that fortress. Dimly Rose remembered knocking them down a few hours ago—had it only been such a short time? Now they were ruined as well, soaked by the volumes of water she had thrown on the smoldering mat. They would never dry but only mildew and rot from within.

It was carnage, plain and simple.

Rose tried not to think about the additional damage they'd done to the swamped and smoky kitchen. It would take days for the hungry students to clear it.

Sir Simon stopped and turned to face them with his hands clasped behind his back and ire in his blue eyes. "Fire, flood, and famine . . . in one short night. I must say, I wouldn't have believed it could be done." His dry tone did not bode well.

Rose didn't move or respond in any way. It was time to think carefully. Although she would never lie directly to the headmaster, she'd long ago learned how to evade complete disclosure. Everything might still be passed off as an accident. She was clumsy, everyone knew that—

Sir Simon let his sapphire gaze pass over her for

one long moment, then turned it on Collis. "Here's what I see. You challenged Rose to a contest. You then carelessly sent a knife into the moorings of the chandelier. What have you to say for yourself?"

Rose blinked in dismay. How had he known?

Collis couldn't help his surprise. Rose must have sold him out. She hadn't seemed the sort, but then again, she was awfully keen on the rules. He didn't look at her but only kept his eyes on Simon. "I'd say you got the gist of the story, then." He shoved off the post with a grin. "It's just a bit of mess after all—"

Simon's sharply raised hand halted Collis's offhand apology. Collis subsided, glancing at Rose for support. She was looking down, her hands clasped tightly before her. Collis found himself disappointed that she'd obviously not felt the same sense of camaraderie after their struggle to douse the fire.

Oh, was that what you were feeling? And does camaraderie usually come accompanied by a raising of the old flag?

Collis squashed the thought. Lusting after Rose? 'Twould never happen again.

Simon was eyeing him now, but Collis didn't even bother to hide his impatience.

"What's all the fuss? It was nothing but a bit of healthy competition that got out of hand."

"You demolished the arena."

Collis threw up his hands. "I'll sew you another bloody mat, all right?"

Simon's gaze was cool. Too cool, really, for Collis's comfort. This wasn't going to go away, it seemed. For the first time it occurred to him that there might be serious consequences coming.

"What's it to be then? A scolding? A slap on the wrist?" *Expulsion.* The word began a nasty singsong in his mind. *No more Liars, lost it all, all adrift again.* He shook it off with a quick jerk of his head and forced a careless grin. "Probation?"

Simon didn't smile back. "You were already on probation."

Collis felt a shock go through his gut. Already on probation? He dropped his pose of unconcern. "Based on what offense, may I ask?"

"Lack of ability to play well with others," Simon snapped. "I've had my fill of the both of you, squabbling like children. You two are the best we have—the best we ever hope to have—yet neither of you has the slightest idea of what being one of the Liars truly means!"

Simon folded his arms and glared at them equally. "Hasn't it occurred to either of you that there may someday be a need for the bonds that you discount today? What of later, when you might be working Liars together?"

Uneasily Collis noticed that Simon said "might be"—not "will be." Collis opened his mouth to protest again, but there was nothing he could say in his defense that would not sound more asinine than what he had already said.

Simon gazed at him for a long moment, his frustration still very apparent.

Habit made Collis tilt his head at the old insouciant

angle, and habit kept his tone free of worry and pain. "So what do you propose to do with me?"

"Us," said a voice from beside him.

He glanced down to see a pale and obviously nervous Rose standing at his side. He frowned. Why would she be willing to do that when a moment ago she'd turned him in like a watchman after a bounty? She raised her serious hazel gaze to his. Her eyes were the color of the sea and as full of the unknown. He'd never noticed. . . .

The moment was lost in the wake of Simon's next words.

"I hereby assign you your first mission." Simon folded his arms. *"Together."*

A few hours after the debacle in the arena, Rose traveled the tunnel toward her customary stint helping out with the Liar's Club meal preparation. She was hoping the main kitchen would be empty but for Kurt.

Kurt was the biggest, hairiest, ugliest man Rose had ever seen, but she loved him dearly. Killer or no, he was the one she turned to when she felt she couldn't master the skills she needed, when she lost, and when she won. Clara was as dear as a sister, but Rose knew her friend still sometimes saw her as "poor little Rose."

Kurt wouldn't say a thing about this morning's embarrassment, she knew. Of course, Kurt wouldn't say three words together at pistol point, but he was always able to spare the time to give her a bit of extra training in the arena. His undemanding silence would be very comforting this morning.

However, when she entered from the tunnel door, through the storeroom, and up the short flight of stairs, she saw that Stubbs and Feebles were sitting at the worn oak worktable, having tea.

Feebles? She'd never actually seen the wiry little pickpocket inside the club before. Usually he hung about the street outside, a fringe member. Rose had heard some of the Liars jest about the ragged fellow not being quite housebroken.

Feebles was a curious sort of person. He was a small man dressed in tattered jacket and cap, yet he was an undisputed genius at sly information gathering and unassuming invisibility.

To Rose, Feebles was like the fog. He'd be right before you one minute and gone the next, sliding from your attention the moment you forgot to look at him. She'd never actually seen him come and go. He was simply there, or not. She wished he could teach her how to do it, but when she'd asked him once, he'd said he'd been born with it. Then—while she'd been distracted by the mind-bending picture of Feebles as a tattered, sharp-featured pocket-picking baby—he'd slipped away.

Even so, he'd always had a shy smile and a tip of his cap for Rose, and she liked him. More than once she had delivered something tasty from the kitchen to him as he held his chosen post outside.

Stubbs was a friend as well. The sturdy young doorman had struggled to learn to read ably, just as she had. Although Stubbs had already been a Liar when the school had opened and had not been required to train with the other students, he and Rose had spent many hours at that very table, sharing a candle and a set of books.

She'd not been completely ignorant of reading and writing, although she'd never managed to be really good at it. That is, until it occurred to Lady Raines to have her fitted with spectacles. Suddenly, the world came clear. Trees separated from blobby green masses into distinct and separate leaves. The city sharpened and enlarged about her—and best of all, the words on the pages flowed fast and beautifully beneath her vision.

It turned out that she was neither clumsy nor stupid, but merely near-sighted.

For his part, Stubbs was aiming to be a saboteur for the club. It was true he could dismantle any mechanism and put it back together with blinding speed. He'd been stalled by his inability to read, but once he'd taken it in, he'd progressed quickly. He was going out on his first mission soon with James Cunnington, as soon as James and his wife, Phillipa, returned from their honeymoon.

Phillipa was already expecting, just like Agatha, so Rose didn't expect she'd have much to talk about with the new lady in the club. She sighed. Babies were everywhere suddenly. She wasn't exactly envious, although she wanted children . . . eventually. First she wanted to see what the rest of the Liars saw—adventure, purpose, even danger.

First she wanted to belong.

The three of them, Kurt, Stubbs, and Feebles, now watched her expectantly. She stopped, nonplussed.

"Were you gentlemen waiting for me?"

Feebles grinned proudly at her. "You sound just like Lady Clara, you do."

Stubbs nodded vigorously. "Every bit."

Kurt only grunted when she took her own seat at the table. Instead of passing her vegetables to chop or dough to knead, Kurt slid a dish of her favorite chocolate biscuits before her. Stubbs jumped up to fetch her a cup of tea, and Feebles shyly passed her the cream pitcher and whispered, "Buck up, lass."

Oh, blast. Tea and sympathy? She wasn't sure she could bear it. "Thank you," she said somewhat repressively. Perhaps if she didn't begin, they wouldn't carry on. Her appetite was entirely gone, but she nibbled at a biscuit to spare Kurt's baking pride. It was delicious, of course, but the sweetness that she usually adored sat sour in her stomach. The tea was lovely and fragrant, but she couldn't swallow much past the growing tightness in her throat.

It would break her heart to leave the club. She'd never had a home like this, where she was so much more than an extra child or an invisible housemaid. Here, she was someone. Here, she belonged.

Or at least, she would soon, if her row with Collis didn't cost her everything she wanted so badly. She blinked away that black possibility to see that her companions watched her with doleful and worried eyes. She forced her spine to stiffen. There was no point in loading the cart before it was hitched.

Forcing a smile for her friends, she took a large bite of biscuit. Time for a change of subject. "Mr. Feebles, do tell us—what's the most revolting thing you ever found in someone's pocket?"

Chapter Four

Collis had spent only an hour in his rooms at Etheridge House, time enough to change and rid himself of the smell of smoke and the disquieting memory of brief attraction he'd shared with Briar Rose. Now he was clean, dressed, and entirely at loose ends.

He'd no more than trotted down the front steps of Etheridge House before he wished he could turn about and go back inside. Two young ladies, accompanied by their maids, were strolling slowly by. Young ladies tended to pass *very* slowly these days. Collis vaguely remembered that these two were neighbors to Etheridge and was fairly sure he'd been properly introduced at some point in the past. He'd been introduced to every unmarried maiden from Glasgow to Brighton, after all. All well-born, all fashionable, all alike. These two were as peas in a pod, pretty enough to be pleasant, yet apparently forgettable or he'd remember them better.

He tipped his hat and smiled dutifully. They slid their eyes sideways and slowed their pace to a bare crawl. Then, obviously having decided the moment was appropriate for a bit of friendly conversation, they stopped.

After three sentences of greeting, Collis began to wish they hadn't. The fluttering lashes and longing gazes didn't seem to carry quite the usual reassuring balm to his ego, and the friendly conversation seemed lacking. They did not retort provokingly to his male banter, nor did their eyes flash with challenge and intelligence.

Still, he smiled warmly at them. At least their company kept him from thinking about the conversation inside Etheridge House.

Rose was walking slowly toward Lord Etheridge's residence. She was in no particular hurry to face down his lordship's sentence.

"After the two of you make yourselves presentable," Sir Simon had said to her and Collis earlier, "we'll be expecting you at Etheridge House at noon."

As she approached the large, fine house, she took a deep breath. She was lucky, truly. She ought to have been cast out entirely after such antics. It was evident, although the spy-headmaster had not said so precisely, that this trial mission with Collis was her only chance to save the place she had made for herself. Her lovely, purposeful new life—depending on her working with a man she couldn't get on with for three minutes running.

Even as the thought crossed her mind, she spotted him. He was standing on the walk near the front steps of Etheridge House, apparently at ease while he passed the time of day with two fawning ladies doubtlessly out on their morning calls.

Her chin high, Rose approached the trio as they stood just before the steps. The two ladies were intent upon Collis, their eyes bright and their gloved hands gesturing delicately.

Rose had been taught by her training to interpret stance and expression and she could read quite clearly the message being cast: *You're handsome and manly and socially advantageous and I'd eagerly kill the lady next to me in order to gain your attentions.*

Well, perhaps not kill. Probably only slice and maim, in the social sense. Therefore, Rose prepared herself for the ladies turning scathing glances her way when she approached. She was not disappointed.

Collis turned her way when he noticed the ladies redirecting their attention. His lip curled slightly in a guarded smile. Rose's stomach ached at the thought that he believed she had turned the blame on him this morning. Of course, he'd been awfully eager to think it, hadn't he? Why, when she'd never given him a single reason to think her such a sneak?

Rose cultivated that indignant thought, for it afforded her spine more steel than did dwelling on silly and hopeless dreams regarding Mr. Tremayne.

But Collis's manner was all affability when Rose stopped before him. He doffed his hat very formally and bowed to her carefully mastered curtsey. "Good morning!" he said brightly.

He then turned to the other ladies and smiled. "Ladies, may I introduce a friend of the family?"

Rose barely kept her jaw from dropping at that.

The ladies ran discerning gazes over her simple but quality attire. Rose waited, but the young women obviously could not quite place her status by her appearance alone. Never had she been more thankful for Lady Agatha's insistence on excellent cloth and fit for the students' garb. Her ladyship's thinking was that quiet quality could pass in almost any environment, be it high or low.

The ladies finally nodded warily and Collis bowed again. "Then may I present our dear friend—" His smile was challenging. "Our dear friend, Miss Thorn."

Thorny Rose. She hid the sting and kept her chin high and her expression serene. Dropping another curtsey to the ladies, she accepted their greetings with composure.

Obviously miffed that their entertainment had been interrupted, the two ladies made their farewells to Collis and walked slowly away with many a longing glance back, punctuated by whispers and giggles.

Rose couldn't help rolling her eyes at such silliness.

Collis looked at her oddly. "What's wrong, Briar Rose? Envious that they know how to have fun?"

"Not at all," she snapped. "I pity them."

He blinked at that. "Pity them? Whyever for?"

"Because they likely think you truly give a damn about them now."

"You're being absurd," Collis protested. "I only passed a moment with them. We talked of the *weather*, for pity's sake!"

She folded her arms and glared at him. "It isn't what you say. It's how you say it!"

He matched her annoyed pose. "That is a ridiculous notion. What could it matter how I said it? I spoke to them the way I speak to all women."

She raised a brow. "Precisely." She dropped her arms to her sides and looked down for a moment. Collis watched her, bemused, until she raised her gaze to his. Collis found himself riveted. Her eyes had become deep seawater pools and her lids hung heavy, as if she was just rousing from her bed. "Why, Mr. Tremayne," she said throatily. "Tell me, do you think it might rain today?"

Collis forced himself to swallow. Her lips—had they always been that full and red?—had uttered the casual sentence slowly and fully, as if she were kissing each word. Her voice, suddenly low and dark, threatened to reach directly down his spine and into his trousers to create an embarrassing display. She took a tiny step closer to him. He very nearly backed away in dismay. "What are you *doing*?"

She halted and took a breath—and brisk Rose was back.

"Simply proving a point," she said. "It does matter *how* you say something, even something as benign as 'Nice weather today'."

"Well, I certainly don't talk like that! That—that likely isn't even legal!"

"That is precisely how you speak to women, as if you've been waiting all day simply to stare into their eyes and find out their secret opinions on precipitation!"

He glared at her, flustered and confused. He didn't do that—did he?

Looking Collis directly in his stormy-day eyes, Rose continued. "Why do you get their hopes up that way? You aren't interested in them any more than you are in me. Why do you put on such a show? Don't you believe anyone will like the man beneath?"

Collis blinked as her accusation hit home. The man beneath? How could he believe that when even he didn't know who that man was? That man died on a battlefield, flattened by cannon fire.

So he grinned widely around the pain. "Rose, how forward of you!" He leaned close and dropped his lids slightly, imitating her imitating him. "However, if you're determined to see the man beneath. . . ." She blushed outright and Collis laughed aloud. "You left yourself open for that one, Briar Rose!"

Rose's mind wasn't anywhere near the topic, for she'd had a sudden heated memory wash over her. Dark room, breathless heart-pounding silence, and Collis's half-naked body covering hers.

That had been the moment when she'd actually considered having him, right there, in the smoky dark cellar arena . . .

But he'd only been teasing again. She'd been breathless. He'd only been audacious. Rose bore briskly toward the door.

She almost hoped he'd continue to impede her. A glance down the way confirmed that the two ladies lingered nearby. Wouldn't it be lovely to drop him on his brazen arse in sight of his fawning admirers?

He obviously realized that she had no intention of stopping, for he stepped neatly to one side and bowed her through. The gallant action gave her the appearance of being rude, of course. She half-turned to him. "I pity the waste," she said with low intensity. Then she continued on to the door.

Fortunately, the Sergeant had been ready for her and had the door open before she could even lift her hand to the knocker. Lord Etheridge's majordomo was a small, spare man whose livery had been cut in a military fashion in keeping with his past services in battle. All in all, he cut a neat, impressive figure at the door.

He was a nice man as well. When Rose stepped over the threshold, he made sure to bow deeply and respectfully. "Her ladyship is waiting most eagerly for your visit, miss," he intoned just a bit too loudly.

However, it was just loudly enough for the ladies now eagerly returning down the walk to hear clearly. Gratitude made Rose's eyes burn when Collis's taunting had not. *Thank you,* she mouthed at the Sergeant, and strode inside with her head high.

Collis watched her go, aggravation twining with regret in his gut. He was well aware that his actions were beneath him. But damn it all, she was simply so easy to get a rise out of!

And never boring. Ever.

The Sergeant left Rose in the entrance hall for a moment while he went to announce her. She waited patiently, comfortable enough in the lovely surroundings from her many previous visits. Lord Etheridge was still a remote and authoritative figure to her, but Lady Clara was the nearest thing Rose had to a sister.

A taut sniff sounded behind her. Oh, bother. *Denny.*

Rose turned with a fixed expression of politeness on her face. Denny was Collis's valet, although Collis used him little, leaving Denny far too much time to work himself into fits of imagined dramatics. Denny had been general houseman for Sir Simon once, then valet for James Cunnington, before being passed on to Collis.

Apparently James's new wife, Phillipa, had too much sense to tolerate Denny's presumptions. Collis found Denny's displays amusing. Rose merely found him wearisome.

Denny was a smallish man, and although he claimed to be quite young, his reddish hair did not quite cover his shining pate. He was no taller than Rose, although he tried to look down his nose at her. She hoped this gave him a crick in his neck.

Denny was a right pest. His drawers were still drooping about her recruitment when he'd never been asked. She, a mere ignorant housemaid, had been chosen to train with the Liars, while he, trusted confidant of the former spymaster himself, was now nothing more than a bored valet.

She'd feel sorry for him if he weren't so bloomin' obnoxious about it.

"Good afternoon, Denny."

A petulant expression crossed his face. "Oh, hello, *Miss* Lacey." His upper lip curled. "I heard you caused quite a mess for my young master to clean up."

Collis, cleaning? The image boggled the mind. She opened her mouth to correct Denny, then stopped. There was no reasoning with those who wouldn't reason. Denny was simply Denny. She nodded instead. "There is indeed a mess."

Satisfaction shimmered in his flat blue gaze. He slid his gaze toward the parlor, where the Sergeant had yet to emerge. "They've been talking you round and round for hours."

Oh, how you want me to ask, don't you, Denny? Rose tilted her head. "How tolerant of them to allow you time off to listen."

Denny blinked, then backpedaled. "Well, of course I haven't actually *heard* anything."

"Indeed. Of course." The parlor doors opened and the Sergeant beckoned her in. She sent a sweetly innocent smile toward Denny. "Do remember to hang my shawl properly, will you, Denny? It landed on the floor last time I visited." She had the small pleasure of seeing the Sergeant, who took the quality of service very seriously, send an affronted glare Denny's way before she entered the gates of purgatory. Denny, irritating as he was, was the least of her worries.

In the parlor, Rose found Sir Simon, Lord Etheridge, and his wife, Clara, who sent Rose an encouraging smile. Rose had expected to see Lady Agatha as well. Then again, Lady Raines didn't get about much now, since riding in the carriage made her ill.

"I pop like a bottle of bad wine after half a block," she'd told Rose regretfully. Rose wrinkled her nose at the thought. Yes, that whole childbearing lot could wait. It was too bad, for Lady Agatha might have weighed in on Rose's side. As it was, there was no denying the disapproving tension in the room. Rose sat when invited to but refused tea. Her stomach was right tight enough, thank you.

"Where is Collis?"

Rose folded her hands to hide their shaking. "He is outside, on the walk."

"Doing what, pray tell?"

"Flirting." Rose was surprised by the snap in her own tone. She amended her comment. "Talking."

"Hmm. Knowing our Collis, I suspect *flirting* is the better description." Lady Etheridge stood to pull the bell rope for the Sergeant. "Sergeant, would you kindly drag Collis away from the ladies? We're ready for him now."

"Might I pull him by the ear?" The Sergeant was crisply eager.

Clara considered his request for a moment. "No. I fear he's too old for that."

"Pity," the Sergeant said without rancor. "Likely I couldn't reach it anyway."

Rose watched this interplay with interest. Clara rose from the arm of her husband's chair and patted Rose's arm on her way out of the parlor.

"Not to worry, dear," Clara whispered. "But . . . be polite. And don't fidget." Clara's gaze flickered back toward her husband and Sir Simon. "Good luck . . . anyway." She walked from the room, leaving Rose more disconcerted than before.

Oh, fry it. If Clara was worried, then there was indeed something to worry about. She'd tried to be a good student and she'd mostly succeeded, if one didn't count firearms. Her sex, now—this could cause issue.

Although Lady Raines and Lady Etheridge were part of the Liar's Club, they were not quite considered to be actual Liars themselves. She would be the first, and she knew that the verdict was not yet in on her induction.

They *did* need her. She felt it deeply. They needed her, and even more girls in training, for there was an entire side of life that the male Liars were excluded from. Rose knew that a wife, a sister, a daughter, could be every bit as involved in traitorous activities as a man, yet who would see those activities but another woman? Especially an invisible woman like a housemaid.

So much depended upon her success within the club. Her deeds would decide a great deal for the women behind her, and she felt the weight of that keenly. It wasn't fair, nor even especially sound, but it was true all the same.

So it was with knee-knocking dread that she waited for Collis to join them.

Chapter Five

❖

Collis tossed his coat and hat to Denny, then turned to face the parlor doors. The Sergeant stood at hand to open them for him, as if he were a stranger in his own house.

When he entered to see Rose's pale face among the others, he wished he'd come in with her. Her usual saucy bravado seemed quite snuffed out. He ought not to have made her face the lion's den alone.

He felt a vibration against his hip and looked down to see his dead hand trembling slightly at his side. Perhaps he was a tad nervous as well. Smoothly he clasped his hands behind his back, although he usually tried to avoid the strange sensation of feeling only half his own handclasp. He smiled winningly at all concerned. Full gallop forward, even over a cliff.

"I do hope I didn't keep you all waiting?" He went on without waiting for a response. "Good. Now, what may I do for you all this afternoon?"

Simon, at least, wasn't impressed. "You may sit. And if you are capable, you may listen."

Collis debated answering that one back, but the glint in Simon's blue eyes decided him against it. Though Simon was a bastard born, a child of the streets even beneath the level of Rose herself, he wasn't impressed by the Prince Regent, much less Collis Tremayne, former soldier and future—

Future what? Ah, that was what was being decided today, wasn't it?

Collis bowed briefly and seated himself near Rose. She continued to regard him gravely, only turning her attention away when Simon began to speak again.

"I could waste our time with a recitation of the offenses the two of you have committed on the school, but I think we've all heard enough about that. What I am concerned with is what you two intend to do about it?"

Collis didn't answer, but he saw Rose glance his way before she ventured to reply. "Clean," she said slowly. "And sew a new mat . . . but I have no idea how to replace the chandelier."

Simon's lips quirked, and Collis saw his expression ease as he looked at Rose. At least it didn't look as though she was in as much trouble as he was. Collis was grateful for that. He turned back to Simon. "Why don't you tell us what we are to do, sir?" He threw one arm back over his chair and crossed his ankles. "I'm sure you've thought of something suitably nasty."

Collis felt the growl coming from his uncle more than heard it. *Conduct unbecoming an Etheridge.* The familiar words thrummed inside his mind. He'd certainly heard them enough in the years since his parents had died and left him to the care of his mighty lordship.

Simon only smiled. "Dismount that high horse, Collis. You'll like this, I promise."

Dalton spoke at last. "Actually, I'm quite sure he'll hate it. Not that I mind, of course." He left his stance at the mantel. Collis felt as if he were looking in a mirror of himself in ten years, if he were still whole and if he were decidedly more grand.

Many would only see the cool and distant outer demeanor, but Collis knew well this uncle who might as well be a brother. They shared more than the Etheridge darkness and the Etheridge eyes—they also shared that inborn sense of distance from others, one even deeper than the reserve of the average Brit.

Dalton had overcome it after he'd found Clara—or at least after he'd lost her and found her again.

But there was no brilliant and spirited society lady waiting in the future for Collis. None that he'd care to expose his weakness to, at any rate. Half a man made half a husband, if his mathematics were correct.

Simon cocked a brow. "Your assignment is to make your way into a house of my choosing in any way you can, and to obtain evidence that would prove them to be traitors to the Crown. All previously arranged, of course."

"I was in the wrong, there's no doubt about that," Collis protested. "However, I don't see the point in making me—us—prove ourselves through some arranged test. Give us a real mission if you want to see what we can do."

Simon crossed his arms. "I have seen what you two

can do—in the cellar of the school. One ruined mat and ten rotted dummies later, I was not impressed. It was *not* a worthy effort."

"So we're off on a scavenger hunt for Papa?" Collis matched Simon's expression, right down to the narrowed eyes. "Will there be milk and biscuits after?"

A small choking sound came from the general direction of Rose. She either was appalled or was trying very hard not to laugh. Wouldn't it be intriguing if it was the latter?

Obviously exasperated, Simon threw up his hands in an *I give up* gesture and gave an assenting wave toward the spymaster before he turned away. Dalton nodded, then bent to murmur something to Rose, who turned to bustle down the hall and into Dalton's study. Simon followed her to the door to shut it on Denny, who was lingering in the hall.

Collis watched this with unease. If he was not mistaken, they were ridding the room of witnesses. "This looks ominous. Are you bringing out the big guns?"

Simon came back to take a turn holding up the mantel, giving Dalton the floor. Dalton folded his arms. "Why yes, as a matter of fact we are. You're a special case, Collis. As the heir to a major seat in the House of Lords, you stand to someday hold some power in the government. There has been some . . . discussion as to whether or not you are an appropriate candidate for the Liars. That perhaps we should not be endangering a man we could better use elsewhere."

"God forbid. Bloody boring, the House." Collis tried for an easy grin. "At any rate, I may be your heir,

Dalton, but you have Clara now. The way you two carry on, chances are I won't be heir for long."

Simon snorted at this. Dalton tightened his jaw and shot his quasi-partner a glare. "You should talk," he muttered to Simon. Then he turned back to Collis. "I am not the one you have to convince, Collis. Nor is Simon," he added when Collis turned to protest to the head of the Liar Academy.

Collis blew out a breath. "Then who? Liverpool?" The Prime Minister would be a tough nut to crack, but perhaps he could have his good friend Prince George work on old Liverpool a bit—

But Dalton was shaking his head. Oh, hell. That could only mean one thing. Collis swallowed. "Not the Royal Four?" he asked, appalled. At Dalton's all-too-serious nod, Collis felt his mouth go dry.

The Royal Four was a secret cadre of the four most influential men in the land, traditionally selected for their intelligence, their ethics, and their unwavering loyalty to England, beyond even loyalty to any one ruler. The Cobra, the Fox, the Lion, and the Falcon. Each was carefully groomed and selected by his predecessor, as Dalton had been by Lord Liverpool.

Until he'd begun training with the Liars, Collis had not even known his uncle had belonged to that intimidating crew and that he had stepped down to take over the Liar's Club upon the retirement of Simon Raines. Collis still didn't know who the new Cobra was, nor who the other three were.

The idea that those mysterious watchdogs of the kingdom might have their eyes on him made him uneasy. After all, even the monarch was not able to ignore the power of the Four. Look at what had happened to King George! Certifiably mad, locked away for the rest of his natural life while his son ruled the land as Regent.

Collis let out a gust of air. "I see. Well, it appears I will take that mission after all."

Dalton's lips twitched, but Collis didn't think humor had anything to do with it. "I apologize for putting you in this position, Collis. To be truthful, it never occurred to me that you would find training objectionable, or that you would not do well."

Collis flinched at that, although he fancied he hid it well. He was getting bloody good at hiding.

Dalton went on. "That said, I will add one thing. I am disappointed in you. You have so much potential, yet you persist in wasting your energies—"

"I tell you, last night was an accident!"

"I wasn't referring to your rivalry with Miss Lacey. Quite the opposite, in fact. If not for vying with Miss Lacey, you wouldn't have come as far as you have."

He pierced Collis with that damned unnerving silver stare. "A Liar needs passion—an obsession for espionage, if you will. So far, I have only seen that passion directed toward another student."

Collis blinked. "Passion for Rose? Are you mad?"

Dalton did smile slightly then. "So much protest, Col. If I didn't know better, I'd call it . . . *passionate*."

Rose made her way into the spymaster's study. Although she knew where the room was, she'd never been in it before. It was an undeniably masculine room, as richly elegant as its occupant. She gave a silent whistle. *Posh.*

"The Wentworth file," his lordship had said. "On top of the pile on my desk."

The room was dark with the draperies drawn against the day's glare, doubtless to protect the carpet from fading. The desk was not to be missed, being large enough to double as a bed should the house ever run out of rooms. As if that were a possibility.

Even as she reached the desk and stretched out her hand to take the top file from the stack there, her toe hit the leg of the desk and she stumbled. She caught herself, but the files slithered apart, some going over the side of the desk and landing on the floor.

"Bloody rotten hell," she hissed. With a sigh, she knelt to the floor and gathered up the files.

She'd have to peek now, to find the right one. The names were written only on the documents inside. Quickly, for surely his lordship was waiting on her, she untwisted the short bit of string that looped the first file closed around a disk sewn on the front like a button. "Name, name, blast it, where's the name?"

She peered at the first page. *Jackham.* Oh, my. She'd heard tales about him. He'd run the business side of the club for years before betraying the Liars to the French. He was dead now, found floating in the Thames, recognizable only by his waistcoat. Apparently it didn't do to betray the Liars.

Curiosity made her fingers itch to take the page from the file, but she sternly repressed it. Clara had said to watch her step, and she would watch it.

She reached to open the next file. *Porter.* Another

name with a tale attached. Poor Ren Porter, beaten
nearly to death by Lady Winchell's thugs, suspected
of being nigh crazed by the permanent damage done
to his body and mind. The last Rose heard, he'd disappeared, possibly wandering mad through England.

Secret, these are secret, you nosy creature! Oh, but
what she wouldn't do to be spymaster and have all
this lovely information at her fingertips!

She heard voices raised down the hall. She'd best
get out there before Collis ruined his chances forever.
She didn't for a moment believe he didn't care. She'd
been beside him in class after class, session after session. He wanted to be a Liar nearly as bad as she did.
If anything, he needed the Liars *more.*

Hurry. She grabbed the next file and fumbled at the
string, then pulled the top sheet out a few inches. *W—*

This was it. Wentworth. She stuffed the sheet back
in, shoved the stack back into a pile more or less re-
sembling the one it had been in, and scrambled for
the door.

"Collis Tremayne, just shut it until I get back out
there!" she muttered to herself as she made for the
front hall.

Rustling skirts behind Collis and Dalton indicated
Rose had returned. Dalton held out his hand. "This
file contains the basic amount of information we
might be able to obtain on any subject. Many Liars
have accomplished their missions armed with less."

Rose stepped forward to hand a leather-clad
dossier to Dalton. Collis intercepted the file with a
smooth motion. His uncle raised a brow but let it pass.

"The target's household has been informed of the mission, but not of your identities. All they know is that they are to go about their business as if they had nothing to hide, but to do all possible to keep anyone from finding the object."

"The targets are?"

"A family long friendly to the Liars. That is all you need to know."

Need to know. Collis really hated that expression. "And the object of this assignment is?"

Dalton smiled. "Something that would entirely expose them as traitors, of course. Your mission is to learn what that might be, how it can convict them, and where it is concealed." He nodded to the dossier in Collis's hand. "All other information is right there."

The file felt altogether light to Collis. Wasn't that just like the Liars? "Sending us out with two clues and a handshake? Is that handicap quite fair, do you think?"

Simon stepped forward. "Be off and don't come back to the club until you've gained your objective. Get in, get the evidence, and get out—*together.*"

Collis swallowed hard, turned to Rose and shot her a rueful grin. "Looks like we have a mission to plan."

Simon cleared his throat. "Aren't you two forgetting something?"

Rose sighed. "Yes, sir. We have some cleaning to do back at the Academy."

Collis snorted. "Apple polisher," he muttered to Rose.

He felt her heel come down on his instep, and he

grinned. Then she grabbed his hand and tugged him into the hallway. "Say goodbye to the nice spymasters," she hissed at him.

Collis blinked, then sent a casual wave back to the two men in the parlor. "Goodbye, Simon. See you at dinner, Dalton?"

Dalton shook his head in amused resignation. "See you at dinner, Collis."

With Collis in tow, Rose kept going until they were at the door and out of sight of Sir Simon and Lord Etheridge. Then she plunked both fists on her hips. "Are you trying to get us thrown out of the Liars?"

"Ease those reins, Briar Rose. It's only Dalton and Simon, after all."

Rose took her shawl from the Sergeant with a *thank you*. Collis took his hat and gloves with a grin and a punch in the arm for the dapper military man, who sighed deeply at such irreverence. Rose couldn't agree more. She tilted her head. "I despair," she murmured to the Sergeant, who was no taller than she.

"Yes, miss," he replied. "I fear it is contagious."

From his great height, Collis apparently caught on that he was being disparaged. "Ho there!"

"Never mind, Collis," Rose said. "Now, what to do first . . ."

"Plan," Collis said decisively.

Rose folded her arms. "Clean."

Collis matched her stance. *"Plan,"* he said more firmly.

Rose narrowed her eyes. "I get the feeling that this is going to be a very long mission."

Behind them, in the doorway of the parlor, Simon

and Dalton watched the two best students they had come to a stand-off before they'd even begun. Simon covered his face with his hands. Dalton leaned one broad shoulder on the doorjamb and heaved a great sigh of resignation.

"Do you believe they'll ever be able to work together?" Simon asked.

Dalton watched the argument before him with a frown. "Not a chance in hell."

Chapter Six

◆

Rose managed to keep her seething temper contained all the way back to the school. Collis had stood his ground like a bloomin' mule, insisting that they plan the mission until Rose had simply turned and left him behind. Once she was back at the Liar Academy, the younger students watched her with guarded curiosity.

The cellar was a stew of char, musty straw, and water. Quickly taking command of her fellow students, Rose worked hard at setting it to rights.

The job of clearing the destruction of the arena was overwhelming. Rose rolled up her sleeves and hiked the skirts of her oldest dress to tuck into her waist, then she and the other students dug in. There was simply so much!

After two exhausting hours, there was still a pile of wreckage in the middle of the floor and the water-soaked straw and canvas mess that used to be the mat was only partially lifted.

Rose was doggedly mopping a corner of the arena where the lowest level of the uneven floor had col-

lected the most water. This corner had held the rack
of dummies that she had just carried out to be carted
outside of London and burned. Around her the other
students attempted to tug the mat aside, calling con-
flicting commands to one another and getting
nowhere. Then a familiar deep voice among the others made Rose turn her head.

Collis strode into the mucky arena in his pristine
suit of clothing and with his kingly air and took over.
Perhaps Rose ought to have been irritated by his easy
assumption of authority, but she was just so bloody
glad to have his help that she didn't care a whit.

Within moments, he had the male students organ-
ized into a line that went up the winding cellar steps
and the shattered wreckage of the chandelier was
hoisted bit by bit, hand to hand, clear to the alley behind the school in a matter of minutes.

She watched him with reluctant admiration as he
directed the younger men. He didn't simply hand out
commands, but he tossed his jacket and waistcoat
aside and dirtied his elegant shirt carrying the sooty,
charred, soaked debris tucked into the crook of his
bad arm. It didn't take long before he was as dirty as
the rest of them.

It only made him more handsome, damn it. His
thick dark hair fell over his brow in a mess that made
Rose think of running her fingers through it. His fine
shirt was soon streaked and wet and it clung to his
broad shoulders and muscled chest like a lover's
hands.

Distracted from her mopping, Rose watched him
as he passed his burden up the line, making those

muscles ripple and flex before her eyes. Her mouth went dry. He didn't look like a lord now . . . and yet he did, more so than ever.

She could imagine him at the Etheridge estate, right out in the fields with the cottagers, or perhaps doing something highborn and manly with elegant long-legged horses . . . or something tiring and heated that would require him to doff his shirt on a summer's day.

The sun would shine on him—the sun always shone in the country, at least in her imagination—and his skin would glisten golden in the light and he would call to her—

"Rose?"

She jerked back to the moment, blinking rapidly and, yes, fry it, swallowing the saliva that had collected in her mouth at her stimulating thoughts. Collis stood before her, the real Collis, who would tease her mercilessly should he ever discern her thoughts—or, worse yet, would pity her impossible, inappropriate yearnings. She cleared her throat. "Um, yes, what?"

He grinned. "Woolgathering? You? Can't be."

"No! I was . . . I was thinking of a way to get the mat out to the alley as well." She had been earlier, anyway. "I think we ought to cut it up and stuff the lot into sacks, so we don't drop straw throughout the school."

He nodded. "Good idea. I'll send someone for sacks. In the meantime . . ." He reached one hand toward her. Bemused, she watched it come. What—?

Collis took her mop from her grip, tucked it under

his bad arm, and reached for her hand with his other one. He turned it over and frowned. "I thought so."

She ought to snatch her hand back. She ought not to let him touch her, it interfered so with her thinking. Instead, she left her hand where it was, cradled in his as he peered down at her palm.

"You've given yourself blisters," he said accusingly.

"I have not!" Now she snatched it back. "I don't get blisters. My hands work hard."

"Not anymore," he pointed out. She looked down at her own hand. There were three blisters in the crook of her thumb and fingers, sure enough. Apparently, her light kitchen duties and weapons work didn't cause the same wear as dawn-to-midnight cleaning had. She looked back up at him in surprise. "I haven't had a blister in years."

"You're not a housemaid anymore," Collis reminded her. "You're a spy, and far too good a one to ruin your hands mopping." He thrust the mop behind him when she reached for it. "No, your swabbing chores are over for now."

"I have to help with all this. I'm half to blame!"

"Well, then consider your half mopped. I'll do the rest."

She gaped at him. "You?"

He nodded. Then his eyes began to twinkle and the corners of his lips curved up. Her toes curled up as well.

"I do think you ought to change, however," he said with a knowing grin. "You'll catch your death."

Mystified, Rose followed his glance down to see that her bodice was soaked through from wringing out the filthy water collected by the mop. The elderly fabric clung to her breasts even more tightly than Collis's shirt clung to his muscles. To make matters worse, the chill air—it had to be the air, because if it was her vivid daydream of Collis she was going to have to die *right now*—had crested her nipples into diamond points that left nothing to the imagination.

"Oh!" She folded her arms tightly over her chest, giving him an angry glare. "Why didn't you say something sooner?"

He leaned close. "You're lucky I ever said anything at all," he whispered with a deep chuckle in his voice.

Then he stood back and hefted the mop. "You can hunt down the sacks and direct the stuffing and hauling. I'll clean behind you all."

And he did. She watched him closely for the next hour as she commanded the clearing of the tattered, burned, soaked mat. Properly covered by a dry apron, of course. He mopped industriously and very, very badly—holding the handle like a knight at a joust, with the butt tucked under his bad arm—but he mopped.

Finally, the room was cleared. Cleared did not mean clean, however. There was a sooty grime over every surface and the floor had gone slimy with it. There was a great deal more to do in the arena, but Rose felt the kitchen needed doing first. The students had to eat, after all.

Perhaps they didn't blame her, for no one said a word, but if they didn't, she certainly blamed herself aplenty. Especially after suffering through the bland and awful porridge that was all that could be managed for dinner.

But everyone was exhausted. So she bid them all good night and reassured Collis that she was going for a hot bath as soon as she'd put away the last bucket. She frankly wanted him gone, for he was flustering her to no end with his wet clothing and his disarming helpfulness.

It wouldn't do to be disarmed by him. She mustn't forget who he was, nor who she was.

No, that wouldn't do at all.

Alone, she threw herself into the restoration of the kitchen itself. She stayed there, taking out her remorse and confusion with scrub brush and vigor until after the others had long gone to bed.

Finally satisfied that she had removed the last of the smoke damage from the plaster walls, she hung her pail over the now-shining copper sink. The kitchen would be usable tomorrow, and the fresh whitewash could go up as soon as the plaster had dried. Penance accomplished.

She treated herself to a cup of chocolate, melting the rich-smelling shard of waxy cocoa in the steaming water from the kettle, stirring slowly and wearily as the chocolate liquefied and swirled beneath her spoon.

Chocolate was a recent passion of hers. She'd never tasted it before coming to the club. Cocoa came dear enough to be reserved for those with silver to spare and certainly hadn't been for the likes of Rose-the-housemaid, at least not in the Wadsworth household.

Kurt kept her supplied with it, through Ivory Coast sources it was best not to ask about, and she shared it with the other students on occasion. Only the girls truly seemed to like it—the boys were much more interested in tea and coffee.

She poured her bitter concoction into a sturdy mug and washed her pot efficiently. Then she filled a pitcher with half-hot, half-cool water for her washing, put it on a tray with her mug, and left the kitchen at last.

The arena beyond was bare now but for the lonely rack of swords. Even the cork target had been ruined by the soaking and had been pulled from its tacks and disposed of.

The students had been assigned the job of stitching and stuffing the new mat from sailcloth to be delivered tomorrow. Rose fought down the relief she felt at leaving them to it while she gallivanted off on her first mission. She ought not be so eager. Honor though her first assignment ought to be, she knew it was truly a test. A test she could not pass without Collis Tremayne's help.

The stairs were many to her room in the gables and she felt every one as she had not since her days in the Wadsworth household.

Rose entered her small attic room and set her tray aside. She didn't see anyone, for her head was bent as she untied her apron and began unbuttoning her bodice. A quick wash from the bowl on her washstand would do for now. As she turned to hang her apron on a peg, a hand came down on her shoulder.

Her apron fluttered up with a damp slap to cover her assailant's face. "Wha—oof." A kick to the stomach knocked him nearly to his knees. "Oh, *crikey*, that hurt," he gasped through his muslin mask, clutching his midsection.

"Collis?"

As he staggered, fighting for his breath, Collis was gratified to hear surprise in Rose's voice. At least this attack hadn't been personal.

Of course, the fact remained that she had unmanned him in seconds. Again. He peeled the clinging apron from his face, forcing himself to stand upright despite the ache in his gut. Rose stood before him, eyes wide and concerned. He couldn't help it. His eyes dropped to the parted placket of her bodice and held there.

Smooth, fair skin, elegant collarbone, and that lovely secret valley between her small, high breasts, just made for a man to rest his head . . . and her nipples were hard again. His throat closed and heat swept him. He raised his gaze to meet her curious hazel one.

Collis's eyes were like hot coal. The storm-cloud gray had darkened like the threat of lightning. The thunder came from her own heartbeat as it suddenly occurred to her that they were alone together in a room, in the dark of night. The last time that had happened, they'd nearly burned the school down. This time, Rose wondered if it were she who was due to combust. He was so close to her, in this tiny attic room with such a conveniently available bed and everyone else in the place sound asleep—

Her thoughts went to places she'd sworn she'd never go with Collis Tremayne. Maybe with someone, someday—someone like her—but not him, not perfect, highborn, unattainable Collis. Try as she might, she couldn't forget his body on hers last night, the feel of his golden skin beneath her hands, his hard chest pressed to hers, his muscled thigh pressing between hers—

Feels like me heart's fit to burn through me ribs.

Or perhaps a bit lower . . .

Damn him. Damn Collis with his teasing eyes and his wide shoulders and his perfect taut rear.

And damn her body for betraying her like this. She'd sworn never to let a man put her in such a state again. For all these years, she'd managed to keep her vow. Not since those few eternal weeks during which Louis Wadsworth had turned her inside out with his twisted attentions had she been even slightly interested in a man. She'd suppressed her earthier feelings completely and successfully.

Until Collis Tremayne had swaggered into her life. Now she was prone to fits of unseemly imagination and inclined to embarrassing displays of bodice . . . well, *displays. May as well hand 'im the keys to me safe box and play 'im a tune whilst he unlocks it.*

The bloody hell of it was, part of her truly liked that idea. Part of her, an animal creature she'd not acknowledged in so very long, wanted to drop her shield, beckon to Collis, and let him in. That dizzying possibility kept her breathless for one long moment. Naked Collis in her bed. *Oh, crikey.* She was fairly sure Collis knew his way around a woman, and even more sure that she'd enjoy every moment of that journey . . . but then what?

He was a charmer, a rotter, a man who went from woman to woman like a bee in a garden full of flowers.

Well, she for one refused to be just another forgotten bloom.

Collis was trying very hard to ignore the sudden awareness of Rose's scent. The room was full of it, a subtle blend of woman and flowers and . . . soap? Strange and luring and oddly, perfectly Rose.

Rose—who wanted nothing to do with him and made no bones about it. And truly, did he want anything to do with Briar Rose? Sharp as one of her own thorns and as cutting if you let her.

No, she was simply a female in a too-small room and it had been far too long since he'd been this close to a bed and a woman at the same time. Especially not one with her bodice undone. Shaking himself like a dog shedding water, at least inwardly, he closed off those longings.

No, he was simply sadly in need of a rogering, that was all. He took a deep breath anyway. She truly did smell good.

"Are you all right, Collis? Did I hurt you?"

"Not at all." He would not gasp in front of her. He would not. To hide the way his chest rose and fell, he crossed his arms, then delivered a naughty grin. "Your . . . ah . . ."

She remembered her buttons then and quickly did them up, looking away from him. Collis averted his gaze as well. He tilted his head to indicate her mug. "Is that chocolate? Having trouble letting go of childish things, are you?"

"Is it childish? Perhaps it is, to you." She looked away. "If you're all right, then why don't you leave? I've had all I can stomach today."

Collis grunted. "Do you think I'm here for the view?" All right, perhaps not the best retort, considering what he'd been viewing. "We've something to sort out, you and I."

Taking her cup, Rose sank to sit on her cot. She looked bored. "I've an idea. Let's sort it out tomorrow."

"No. Tomorrow I will be occupied with the first steps of infiltrating the target's house. That's why I must make this very clear to you now." She was slumping further every moment. Not the usual reaction he received when alone in a bedchamber with a woman. "I am in charge of this mission."

She gazed up at him, her usually serene brow furrowed innocently. "Why?"

He stopped. "What do you mean, why?"

"Why are you in charge? I think we ought to be equal partners." She folded her hands neatly in her lap. "After all, my induction depends as much on this mission as does yours."

"But—"

Rose had had enough. The last person she wanted to banter with that night was Collis Tremayne, charming, difficult, and all-around confusing gentleman. The last place she wanted to see *anyone* was in the tiny haven of her room. Yet there he was, looming and ridiculously handsome. Appalling as it might seem, she was going to have to forge some working relationship with him in order to graduate.

An idea bloomed. Anything to make him leave. "I'll make a wager with you, Collis," she said enticingly. "The first of us to infiltrate the house by any means necessary will take command of the mission."

Collis hesitated, obviously intrigued. "By any means necessary?"

She nodded. "Any means. You can bribe your way in for all I care."

He snorted. "And the loser?"

She raised her hand as if making a vow. "The loser follows the winner's orders."

"Without question," he prompted.

She placed her other hand over her heart. "Without question."

He smiled cockily. "Well, that will be refreshing."

Still he hesitated. She tilted her head and narrowed her eyes. "I double-damn dare you."

He sucked in his cheeks and narrowed his own gaze. "I believe I'll take that wager." He held out his hand.

She shook it quickly, trying very hard not to relish how large and warm his hand felt wrapped around her own. "Very well." She held out her hand. "The dossier, if you please."

He crossed his good arm over his chest, the leather-clad folder held prisoner behind the wall of his stubbornness. He grinned. "And give away my advantage? You did say 'by any means necessary.' "

Fry it. She had. Rose reached for patience. Patience wasn't home, so she had to make do with sheer will. *I won't toss him over my shoulder. I won't toss him over my shoulder.* "Then, might I have the address, please? Or will any man do?"

"Any man?" He grinned at that, a flirtatious flash of teeth that likely melted apart the knees of many a barmaid. "Why, Rose! Such a saucy question!" He moved closer. "Are you sure you want the answer?" His voice was low and coaxing. She knew very well he didn't mean it but was only trying to discomfit her.

She really, really wanted to toss him. That resounding *thud* he made when he landed was fast becoming her favorite sound in the world.

"Don't wear yourself out on me, *Collis.* I'm immune." She held out her hand. "The address?"

He tipped the file to his forehead in salute. "Very well." He opened the file and read aloud. "Our gentleman 'is thirty years of age, lives at Eighty-seven Milton Crescent. Wife, no offspring. Spends his days at his factory in the East End District, unless he is at his club'—of which you don't need to know, since you could never get in—'and he likes to dress very well indeed.' " He paused, then smiled. "I believe that part is in Button's handwriting." He snapped the dossier shut. "We'll begin tomorrow at dawn."

"Dawn?" Dismayed, Rose realized that was only a few hours away. "But people of that sort don't stir before noon, or ten at the earliest!"

"Ah, ah, ah." He waved a scolding finger at her, mockingly. "Assumptions again, Briar Rose. You won't truly establish their habits until you've observed them, now will you?"

Rose's hand tightened around her mug. That phrase was straight from day one of training. Fry it. She wished she'd had the chance to use it on him first.

Hard floor. Big man. The thud would be so very satisfying. . . .

Collis, clearly feeling that a strategic retreat was in order after winning the last fray, waved cheerily at her as he ducked out her low door. He didn't even hit his head.

Pity.

The next morning didn't dawn at all, at least not as far as Rose was concerned. She stood indifferent to the damp, partially hidden behind the corner of the last house on the opposite side of the street from 87 Milton Crescent.

She eyed the dark gray sky and calculated how long it would be before the rain came. There was little wind at least. That meant the storm wasn't immediately in the offing. If she was fortunate, the day would merely remain horrible and damp throughout.

Lovely. In a few hours, Collis would probably be jollying up to the master of the house in some gentlemen's club, drinking fine brandy by a roaring fire, being served delicacies on silver trays, while he finagled an invitation into the house.

Luckily, her goal wasn't to meet the mistress socially. Her goal was to get into the house! " 'By any means necessary,' " she quoted softly to herself. "Now, how does a young, hardworking servant girl get into a stranger's house?" Grinning wickedly, she gathered her shawl and dashed across the empty street.

The service entrance was down a short flight of stairs to one side of the front door, as in most terraced houses. She trotted down the steps to end up before an unadorned wooden door. "Why, she knocks, of course," she whispered to herself with a giggle.

The sour-faced cook who answered only glared at her suspiciously. "State y'business!"

Good. Sour was much better than jolly. Rose put on an earnest face. "I've come t'fill the housemaid position. The agency sent me."

The woman squinted at her. "We've no—"

Rose interrupted with a hand to her face and an expression of wide-eyed idiocy. "This is Number Eighty-five, isn't it?"

Rose could see calculation crossing the woman's face. Wrong number, dim-witted agency maid, bitter, overworked cook. Recipe for a bit of cheating in any household. The only person to suffer from such a mistake would be the servant sent by the agency, once the mistake was discovered. In the meantime, this household would enjoy the services of one able-bodied servant at no charge.

The door swung wide enough for Rose to trot in from the cold like a lamb to the wolves' den. "Am I to tend the bedchambers or only abovestairs?" She hung her shawl on a nearby peg and turned around—

To find a grimy apron shoved into her hands. "You'll see abovestairs only when you've cleaned up after the day's bakin'," the cook barked. "You mind those cheeky ways when you do go up. The master of this house is no ordinary bloke. Not him what dines with the Prime Minister himself!"

Well, that might very well be true, if the family was associated with Lord Etheridge. Meekly Rose tied the crusted apron on and went to work on the giant bread bowls. More cleaning, of course. She released a small sigh of regret but then rallied when she remembered that it wasn't yet nine in the morning and she was already inside the house! She felt a glow of satisfaction that she only usually achieved when she gave Collis a toss over her shoulder.

"Take that, Collis Tremayne," she whispered to the crusted bowl.

Thud.

Chapter Seven

─────────── ❖ ───────────

Collis had spent happy moments over his leisurely breakfast, picturing Rose on her pre-dawn surveillance. It was a nasty morning out. Perfect. She would be as mad as a wet cat by the time the lady of the house awoke and went about her day.

His conscience nagged, but he defended himself. It wasn't an entirely useless effort for her. She'd likely make her way into the house eventually. She was a smart one, his Rose.

He pulled the open dossier closer to his breakfast plate. The information within was so skeletal as to be embarrassing for an organization as thorough as the Liars. There was nothing at all within regarding the man's wife, other than the fact that the target was married. Basic information-gathering such as Rose was doing was necessary.

Still, to ease his own eroding principles, he decided it was time to get to work on their "case" himself. Time to go dangle a worm before his prey. The target was a very wealthy man with decidedly middle-class roots. In Collis's experience, such people who stood trembling on the edge of high society couldn't bear to pass up a chance to reach higher.

He stood and gathered up the flimsy file, tucking it under his bad arm and looking down at himself. "Not sufficiently wormy," he said to himself. He wasn't dressed for fishing. He ought to go change into something more dandified.

Denny had laid something nicely flashy out in Collis's bedchamber upstairs, but when he got there he saw that someone had left his bedchamber door slightly ajar. "Oh, no," he breathed, then pushed the door open slowly.

"Damn." It was worse than he'd thought. There was his finery, laid upon the pristine coverlet like a paper cutout of Collis himself. And there, in the center of his fine shirt, was the Beast from Hell.

"Mrowww." It wasn't a greeting. The huge street-scarred orange-striped tabby that went by the deceptively sweet name of Marmalade never greeted Collis. No, that deep and hair-raising sound was a warning. *Don't make me angry. You wouldn't like me when I'm angry.*

Collis held both palms up and slid sideways through the door, frantically trying to come up with a plan. "Denny?" he hissed over his shoulder into the hall. "Sergeant? *Sergeant!*"

The Sergeant popped up from nowhere. Collis would swear the man had magical powers. "Yes, Master Collis?"

"Quick, come help me!"

The Sergeant stepped forward smartly, as Collis

imagined he had through every battle he'd ever seen. The man was a decorated veteran, a proven paragon of valor and experience—

At the sight of the cat on the bed, the Sergeant gasped and jerked backward, automatically pressing his back to the opposite wall as if he could blend into the cheerful paper. "Oh, no, sir! I have special dispensation from his lordship! I need never have anything to do with That Animal!"

"Coward," Collis accused, though he had to admit, he himself wasn't going to take a step further without some backup. "Where is my aunt?" Only Clara could tame the creature. Marmalade turned into melted candy when Clara was about. Of course, that meant that Clara didn't believe a single word said against her beloved pet. Beauty and the Beast.

"Milady is out."

"Oh, hell."

At that moment, Dalton ambled down the hall, putting the final touches to his own day's ensemble. "What's the panic?" he asked amiably enough as he tugged at his cuffs, although Collis noted a certain sideways look concerning himself. Well enough, he would deal with his powerful and demanding uncle later. Right now he had bigger problems.

"The Devil Incarnate is getting hair all over my shirt."

Collis was gratified that even Dalton's eyes widened at that. "Oh." He cleared his throat. "I don't suppose you have another you can wear instead?"

"I am surrounded by cowards," Collis muttered.

"But I just got dressed," his uncle said plaintively.

Collis narrowed his eyes. "No shirt, no mission."

Dalton sighed. "If you insist." He turned to his majordomo. "Sergeant, if you would please see to putting out some fresh clothing for me—and perhaps . . . some ointment and bandages?"

The Sergeant went pale and mournful. "No, my lord! Please, wait for Milady!"

Dalton shook his head, resolute. "No. It must be now." He clapped the Sergeant on the shoulder. "Don't take on so, old man. I'll be fine."

Collis didn't think he sounded any too sure. Come to think of it, he wasn't at all sure himself. Dalton removed his frock coat and Collis put his file on the hall table. They poised outside the door.

"You go down. I'll go up," Dalton whispered. "On three." They took position. Dalton held up one finger, two, three—

They leaped from their hiding places. Collis jumped to the back of the settee by the fire. "Hyah!"

Dalton went in low and deadly while Collis held the enemy's deadly emerald-eyed attention. With his frock coat rolled around both forearms, Dalton managed to extract the hissing cat from her nest atop Collis's bed.

Dalton carefully carried her out at arm's length, then returned to the room a moment later at a run, slamming and locking the door behind him.

"Safe at last."

Collis was holding up his shirt to the light, peering ruefully at the damage. "I can see through these holes. Can you see through these holes?"

Dalton sighed. "So charge a new shirt to me. I'll pay for it."

Collis held up what had once been a lovely brocade waistcoat. "I want another weskit while you're at it. Denny will never be able to get these stains out."

"Fine." Dalton folded his arms over his chest and leaned against the door. "What are you still doing here? Don't you have a mission?"

"Which I am trying to dress for." Collis couldn't help smirking at Dalton. "Everything is 'need to know.' "

"Where is Rose?"

"Surveillance."

Dalton raised a brow, visibly impressed. "So the two of you have come to some sort of accord?"

"Of course." Collis smiled sweetly. *I'll soon be in charge and she'll do as she's told. Perfect accord.*

"Well then, I'll leave you to it." He frowned at the new waistcoat Collis had come up with. "That's hideous."

"Yes. It's exactly what I need." He held it up over his loose linen shirt. "Do I look rich and useless?"

Dalton hesitated. "Oh, no. That sounds like one of those female inquisitions. 'Does this make me look fat?' Is there a safe answer to that question?"

Collis shrugged. "I shan't insist on it."

Dalton nodded. "I'll leave you to it, then. There's just one thing. . . ." He hesitated.

Hesitation wasn't in Dalton's nature. Collis frowned. "What is it?"

Dalton examined his cuffs. "We've never had a female Liar before. There's some concern that sending a man and a woman out together could have some . . . well, consequences."

"Me and Briar Rose?" Collis snorted. "Don't worry, Dalton. That couldn't be farther from a possibility."

"As long as you are prepared against it, then." Dalton left, after carefully checking the hall for feline occupation.

"Not bloody likely," Collis murmured to his uncle's back. He firmly extinguished memories of a strong, supple creature writhing beneath him. *No.*

Once he was dressed, he headed out. At the door, he took his hat and coat from Denny with a quick nod. "Ho there, old man." Keep walking, or he'll twist your ear—

"Sir, if I may have a moment?"

Collis turned with exaggerated patience. But of course, Denny would never choose to see such subtle signals. One had to dunk the fellow in ice water to get him to see past the end of his haughty little nose. "Denny, I'm on my way to—"

"Yes, sir. That's what I wish to talk to you about."

Collis braced himself. If Denny thought he could complain about Rose, he was sadly mistaken. Rose might be disagreeable and, well, unbearable, but she was a good spy. She deserved to be in training. Collis wouldn't hear another word from Denny about it. "Well, what is it?"

"If you would tell me where you're off to, sir? I might need to reach you."

Collis snorted. "Hardly. Anyway, I'm not going anywhere important. Simply trying out a new gentlemen's club."

"What club would that be, sir?"

Denny had a tendency to mind business other than his own. "Nothing special about it. Simply a lark."

"Will anyone be accompanying you, sir?"

"No." Collis was abruptly tired of Denny's questions. "I must go. Thank you, Denny."

Denny nodded, clearly not satisfied that he had given gossip his best. Collis rolled his eyes as he left. Denny needed something more to do, that was obvious. To be frank, Collis didn't know what had possessed him to take the little man on.

Oh, he performed his duties well enough. Collis simply didn't need a valet. He'd been dressing himself for years and didn't need anyone holding his drawers for him.

It had been pity, he supposed. When James Cunnington had confessed that his betrothed had an aversion to Denny, Collis had felt sorry for the little man without a place in the world.

Collis ordered his uncle's most anonymous unmarked carriage, the one he'd used to pose as Sir Thorogood, to take him to the club mentioned in the dossier. Yes, he was definitely feeling sorry for Denny. Being a servant was a difficult life in itself. Collis was sure he could never bear the constant insecurity of needing to find a good master and get himself hired on—

Servant. Hired.

Rose.

Collis let his head fall back onto the carriage cushions in dismay. Here he'd been thinking himself ahead in the race. He'd completely forgotten that all Rose had to do to get into the house was get herself hired by the target!

He pounded one fist on the ceiling of the carriage. "Hawkins! Hurry!"

He was late for a one-sided appointment with a certain Louis Wadsworth, proprietor of Wadsworth & Son, Munitions.

Louis Wadsworth's pale blue eyes gazed at Rose from the life-size portrait like an arrow shot from the past. She stood there in the gallery, frozen in her memories with the dust rag dangling from her limp fingers and her heart beating in her ears.

Louis Wadsworth. She was in Louis Wadsworth's house.

In an instant Rose was back in the past. A girl again, proud of her first position in service to a fine household. She'd tried so hard to do well and the housekeeper seemed mostly inclined to approve of her.

Rose had been determined to succeed in Mr. Wadsworth's house, no matter how strange and lonely it all was. The master seemed a cold man, and the mistress spent her days locked quietly away in her luxurious rooms with what Rose suspected was a barrel of laudanum.

The housekeeper, Mrs. Pool, kept things running smartly nonetheless and Rose was beginning to feel comfortable with the routine. She ran the dust rag around the spindles of the banister once again, just in case she had missed some. Dust was very hard to see, although Mrs. Pool didn't seem to have any trouble spotting it.

Rose had just finished up the railing when she heard a smooth voice behind her.

"It shines like a new penny, but not as brightly as do you, my girl."

Surprised, she turned to see a handsome young man smiling at her. Louis Wadsworth, the master's son, was twenty years old, with white teeth and eyes that twinkled with what she originally believed was kindness.

All too soon, of course, she had discovered that Louis Wadsworth, scion of the Wadsworth manufacturing empire, had not a dust mote of kindness within him.

Collis Tremayne was having a nice glass of brandy by a toasty fire. From his comfortable chair he could see the front hall and any new arrivals. The surroundings were reassuringly masculine and expensive. Not a single female presence penetrated the smoky atmosphere of this particular club.

Unlike the public portion of the Liar's Club, this establishment was a place of quiet masculine escape, a place of genial business and low-voiced toadying, if one aimed to climb higher. Of course, this was a few steps below the level of Collis's own usual membership, which his target could never aspire to.

As he waited for Louis Wadsworth to arrive, Collis ran over what he knew of the man. The owner of several very profitable factories, the man was married, with no children. His wealth made him a valid player in the industrialist party of the government, although his role seemed more of quiet contributor than campaigner for the conservatives.

Wadsworth had never been accused of a crime. He worked hard, ran his factories with a tight hand, and frequented only the most respectable of private clubs.

How utterly boring.

Trust Dalton to give him the dullest assignment possible. Collis gazed into the cheery flames, nearly asleep. If chatting up conservative factory owners was the best the Liar's Club could come up with for him, perhaps he'd be better off pissing away his life at court. At least with his dry wit and bottomless bottles of wine, the Prince Regent was excellent company.

Hadn't there been a Wadsworth associated with that dust-up a few months ago when Dalton had met Clara? Yes, that was right, a man named Wadsworth was killed while trying to stop that circle of traitors, the Knights of the Lily. Was this Louis Wadsworth related to the heroic Mr. Edward Wadsworth?

If so, the file said nothing about it. There was nothing about Louis Wadsworth's parentage at all, now that Collis thought on it. That alone was curious.

A somberly liveried footman passed Collis by and gave him the prearranged signal with one gloved hand. Ah, the quarry had arrived. Looking casually to the door, Collis spotted a slender dapper fellow handing his hat and—oh, for pity's sake—a *walking stick* to a servant. The man couldn't be more than thirty years old!

Lovely. Boring *and* pretentious.

Collis waited. When he'd arrived, he'd lubricated relations with the staff with a bit of pocket change—very well, rather a lot of pocket change—but Rose had said by any means necessary.

Now to await the result. He casually raised the news sheet he wasn't reading to see the doorman pointing out the attractive prospect of the heir to a title in the club—himself. Rather like shooting hares in a cage, putting himself out to bait the slavering social ambitions of a man like that one. God only knew why everyone wanted a title. Collis would give his away if he could.

From his paper hunting blind, he watched the hare hop hesitantly forward. He could almost hear the thoughts in the man's head.

Cannot introduce myself, too forward. But if I wait, someone else will grab him. How can I induce him to speak to me first?

Collis decided to put him out of his misery. He closed his paper with a snap and folded it neatly. "I've finished with this. Have you read it yet?"

"No, I have not." The fish took the worm carefully, with a nod of thanks. "May I repay the favor with another brandy . . ." His voice trailed off, obviously hoping for further introduction.

Collis rose to extend his hand. "Collis Tremayne, sir, of Etheridge. And you?"

Something flashed in the hare's pale blue eyes, probably pure social greed. He clasped Collis's hand in an enthusiastic grip. "I am Louis W. Wadsworth, sir, of Wadsworth Munitions."

Chapter Eight

———◆———

Rose couldn't breathe. She was in Louis Wadsworth's house. Worse yet, she was a servant, a maid, in his house. Old fears, old nightmares, seemed to tingle across her vision like a mist. Out of ancient habit, she backed away from the portrait until she stood in shadow.

She'd lived in shadow before. She'd been like a mouse, keeping always to the edges, peering carefully around corners, starting at a footfall in the hall. Yet Louis had found her, again and again, in that month before he'd moved to his own establishment in what was probably a more interesting part of town.

For Louis had simply been bored. She was convinced of that. A bored young man trapped in a dull house, who had made up a little game to pass the time.

"It's called 'Hunt the Maid,'" he'd whispered to her once when he had her pinned against the bookcases in his father's study. "I am the hunter and you are the doe." He'd slipped his hand beneath her apron bodice to fondle her breast. She'd cringed but not cried out, for who would come to her aid against the master's son? She'd escaped eventually, her stomach roiling but her body twanging discordantly in response to his liberties.

The game went on, a pursuit combined of dark seduction and blatant intimidation that kept her mightily confused in her innocence. She did not imagine herself in love with him, yet he filled her days and worried her nights until she thought of nothing else but when he would next appear.

Until the day he'd shown her the man he truly was.

Mrs. Pool had gone to the master in a rage after finding Rose hiding in a cupboard in the kitchens, her uniform torn and her face and body bruised, and had accused the master's son of rape. Mr. Wadsworth had fired the housekeeper on the spot, simply turning her out without references. He probably would have done the same to Rose had not something more urgent caught at his attention. Days went by before she realized that he had apparently forgotten the entire matter.

There was something wrong in the house after that. Up until that day, every servant had received a day off, even the scullery. But the butler seemed to have his own way of running things, one that didn't seem to agree with the higher quality of servants in the house. One by one, the better ones left. The worst of it was they had Rose to blame.

What bit of friendship she'd managed to win from the other servants was lost from that day. She was ignored to despair even while she was discussed to shreds.

"She orta kept them knees locked," the cook opined with a sniff.

"Weren't so bad here afore *that one* got the young master worked up," the butler agreed.

As much as Rose tried to remind herself that she'd done nothing so wrong, time and disdain wore her down. With no one to bolster her against the blame, she came close to believing in it herself. Perhaps she *was* shameless, for hadn't Louis made her feel things?

She would have fled from it all, if she could have.

Yet where would she go? No other house would have her now, once they heard about her and the master's son.

So she stayed and kept to the darkest shadows, and out-waited Louis and the butler and all the other servants who came, only to leave again when the abominable conditions continued.

Finally, there were only the crooked and the desperate left who would work for the Wadsworths. The new butler who was skimming from the top of the housekeeping budget, the cook who sold half the food she bought and served little but gruel belowstairs, and Rose, the desperate, who had nowhere else to go.

Until she'd been plucked from the mire of her desperation and sent to the Liar's Club.

Until she'd found a home.

Louis Wadsworth could not hurt her now. She was not the lonely, desperate maid of the past. And she was on a mission, directed by the spymaster himself to—

No. His lordship had said the family was named "Wentworth." He had sent her to fetch the file from his study. *"The Wentworth file. On top of the pile on my desk."*

Wentworth. Wadsworth. Oh, God. Rose covered her face with her hands. She'd bungled it when she'd stubbed her toe on the leg of the desk and sent the files slithering out of their pile.

She'd sent herself to the wrong house.

She turned and hurried back down the long gallery. She had to get away—away from that portrait, away from this house. Away from Louis. Crikey, it was as if she could feel his breath on the back of her neck!

"I am not afraid of Louis Wadsworth," she muttered to herself. "Not anymore."

Oh? Then why are you fleeing?

She wasn't fleeing. She was staging a sensible retreat after realizing that she was in the wrong house.

Then why are your hands shaking?

She looked down. It was true. Her stomach was shaking as well. That was beside the point, however. The point was that she was in the wrong house and ought to skip right back to the club to report her mistake.

Leaving Louis in peace.

That thought stopped her in her tracks. Why was Louis Wadsworth living in peace? Why had he not been swept up in the circumstances that had finally disbanded his father's traitorous Knights of the Lily? Why was he living unworriedly in Mayfair, wealthier than ever, and dining with the Prime Minister?

The Liars didn't know. They couldn't know, or they would never suffer it.

She knew. She knew things about Louis Wadsworth that likely no one else on earth knew.

Memories swirled in her mind. The day Louis had

left the house was not the last time he'd visited, simply the last time he'd lived there.

No, he'd been back many times over the intervening years.

There had been many secret meetings, those she had been present for when no one else wanted to serve the late-night gatherings. Meetings between her own master, Mr. Wadsworth, and his group of anti-Crown French collaborators, the Knights of the Lily. And in the midst had been the scion of the industrialist's empire, his son, Louis—every bit as guilty as his father.

Mr. Edward Wadsworth had died for his crimes. For reasons of their own—probably to keep their own part secret—the Liars had allowed him to be publicly lauded as the hero of the piece. Harmless enough, she supposed, since the man was far too dead to get up to more treachery. Louis, however, was all too alive and apparently not under suspicion.

Louis was very wily. Rose had no doubt that he'd been clever enough to emerge clean from the debacle of the Knights of the Lily.

"The master of this house is no ordinary bloke. Not him what dines with the Prime Minister himself!"

Louis had indeed become a powerful man if he was associating with the likes of the Prime Minister of England.

Lord Liverpool was not a man Rose wanted to cross. He'd objected to her entry into the Liars on the grounds that she was too common and too female. He would not want to hear anything she would have to say about one of his friends. After all, it would be her word against Louis's.

Louis would win that battle, as always, unless she came armed with more than memories and accusations. She knew what would happen if the Liars heard Louis's version of events. She'd been shunned before and had barely survived it with her soul intact. No, she could only go to the Liars with something so damning, so concrete, that no one would ever take Louis's word again.

Hot excitement began to tingle through old chilly memories, burning them away in the flame of realization.

She was here, in Louis Wadsworth's house. She was a spy, trained to seek out treason, honed to fight for England . . . and the day was wasted anyway. She'd never manage to get back to the club to report and be able to make any progress on her actual assignment.

Which would be embarrassing. Clumsy housemaid makes mistake. Unless she went back with something in hand to remove the sting of failure. Unless she found something on Louis to prove his French allegiance, something that would set the Liars on him full-force. Something other than her opinion versus the friendship of the Prime Minister.

And maybe something that would prove to herself that she was no longer afraid of Louis Wadsworth.

Something niggled at the back of her mind. Oh, no. *Collis!* He was even now stalking Louis Wadsworth to cadge an invitation into the house, where he would be looking for falsely planted evidence of treason.

She hesitated, tapping her chin with one finger. Surely Collis's plan would not bear fruit in one day?

She could tell him about her mistake tomorrow before he got any farther.

She hoped.

Louis Wadsworth *was* a traitor, and if she could prove it, she could bring him to some kind of justice at last.

She only hoped Collis Tremayne would stay out of the way in the meantime. Not only might he muck up her single chance—he'd never let her live it down.

Collis followed Louis Wadsworth into Louis's desperately grand house with a smile. He hoped he could see Rose's face when she found out he'd walked right into their target's house only half a day into the mission.

It was probably some kind of Liar record, come to think of it. He'd enjoy telling Dalton about it as well.

"I hope you don't mind if I excuse myself a moment, Tremayne," Louis said. "I'll have the staff bring you some tea if you like."

Collis nodded genially. It would be a relief to get rid of his host for a breath or two. There was something repellent about the man. Louis's smile was friendly, but his eyes were always cool. Uneasily Collis wondered if he'd given himself away already. Dalton had said the family would know something of the assignment—had he said or done anything to make the man suspect him?

No, he decided. Other than his own casual overture with the news sheet, he'd ensured that Louis had made all the invitations.

Collis was led to an overdecorated guest parlor,

typical and worthless. As soon as the butler was gone, he stepped back into the front hall to gauge the lay of the land. The house was very fine and modern, as was the Wadsworths' wealth.

If they'd had the slightest clue how to get on in Society, they would have tried to mask the newness of their importance with the acquisition of a fine old property, perhaps one that still retained the impression of the highborn blood that had built it. Etheridge House was nearly as new, of course, but the Etheridge line had no need to mask a thing.

The carpets were a bit too bright, the portraits all in the style of the last decade, the fireplaces a tad too obvious in scale.

"Almost, but not quite, Louis." Collis grinned. Moving quickly through the house, he found a little-used room with a back garden window view. He unlatched the window with a quick motion. The likelihood that this latch would be checked before he came back was quite slim. He looked down into the garden. Lovely. There was even a trellis near the window.

He returned to the room he'd been assigned. While waiting for his host, Collis took a halfhearted look about the parlor. It was a very standard sort of chamber, perhaps a bit less tasteful than most. It seemed Mrs. Wadsworth had a taste for the baroque.

A maidservant bustled in, her cap-covered head bent over her burden of loaded tea tray. Collis scarcely registered her at first, until she glanced up at him past the lace edge of her mobcap. Hazel eyes widened in evident surprise.

In a few brisk strides, Rose had one hand wrapped about his arm and the other pushing shut the open door. She towed him to the opposite end of the room and to the hearth. Only then did she speak. "What the bloomin' hell are you doing?"

"Having tea," he said. His first surprise had worn off. He grinned. "And yourself?"

"Damn it, Collis!"

Her eyes flashed green fire. He badly, abruptly wanted to kiss her, but her stubborn chin was raised high. She'd likely smack him right back, and this was neither the time nor the place for him to get into a wrestling match with his tempting nemesis.

Then he froze, realization striking hard. She *was* in the house. First.

Damn.

She didn't smile, but the tiny quirk of the corner of her mouth was all the more riveting for it. "I've been here since before dawn," she said. "You've been here for perhaps . . . two minutes?"

He couldn't answer her. His jaw seemed cemented with dismay, which only grew worse when her gaze softened.

"Collis, don't take it hard." She leaned forward in sudden eagerness, which eased her grasp on his arm somewhat. "Oy, that means I've won and you must obey!"

Rose's breath caught as Collis stepped closer, using his height to loom over her. He had the additional advantage of being deadly attractive. It truly wasn't fair.

Nothing new there. Besides, this round she had the upper hand. So she merely cocked her head at him and waited for him to back away once more. To her surprise, the irritated flair in his gray eyes suddenly shifted to something equally hot and far more threatening.

Collis was having a bit of trouble remembering why he was riled when all he could think of was the scent of her hair. His body remembered the feel of her beneath him all too well, having been reminded in his dreams last night. Supple, energetic bundle that she was . . . would she be a lively partner? Would they pass hours away in happy animal coupling? Or would she be chill and slow to warm, only to explode at his hands at last?

He stepped closer, then again. His fingers came up to trace the neckline of her maid's livery, only allowing the tips to touch the silken skin just below. Her eyes flickered away from his, then back. Her hand came up to cover his, but instead of pushing it away, she slid it a few inches down and pressed his palm over the mound of her small, full breast.

The shock of her beneath his hand sent Collis into a full second of immobility. She filled his palm with yielding, satisfying woman. God, he wanted her so much—

"No, sor, playse!" she cried out abruptly, her common accent shrill and panicked. "Oi'm a good girl, Oi am!"

Collis snatched his hand back and stepped away from her in shock. She ducked under his arm and recoiled a few steps, holding the empty tea tray protectively before her face and emitting small terrified sobs.

A light laugh came from behind Collis. He turned

to see Louis Wadsworth in the doorway with a tolerant grin on his face. "Well, Tremayne, one can't fault you for speed from the gate! I can see I won't be able to let you alone for a minute."

Collis forced a lazy smile to his face. "Sorry, Wadsworth. Forgot myself."

Louis shrugged. "No matter. Will you be long then?"

Collis managed not to snarl at the man's careless attitude toward his dependent. "If you don't mind, I'll be all done in a moment." Louis grinned again and left, pointedly closing the door behind him.

Collis turned to Rose. "What kind of master knowingly leaves a young woman alone with a man with evil on his mind?"

She dropped her fearful pose and sighed. "You really are naïve, Collis. Why should he object, when he has a long history of accosting his own dependents?"

"What?"

"Hush. He'll hear you. Now, hold this." She plunked the tray into his hands. Then she pulled her cap askew, tugged several strands of hair down over her face, unbuttoned the top three buttons of her dress behind her neck, and pulled the neckline of her uniform to twist slightly over her breasts. Collis pulled his attention away from those breasts with difficulty. He knew why she'd done what she had.

It didn't change the fact that one brief touch had ignited his desire like a torch to paper. He gave his head a slight shake. It had been far, far too long.

After briskly damaging her respectability, Rose took the tea tray back from him and turned toward the door. "That ought to be long enough, don't you think?"

Collis ignored the slur on his masculinity for the moment. "Rose, we need to talk about this."

"I agree. Make your farewell as soon as you can. Meet me behind the mews at dusk. We can talk then." She gave an extra tug to her bodice. Creamy flesh welled. "I'll just rush out crying, shall I? He'll be directly across the hall. I wouldn't want him to miss anything," she said with sour satisfaction.

Distracted by her casual exposure, Collis merely turned to watch her go. Just before she touched the latch, she looked back over her shoulder with a frown. "That was your injured hand that you—that I used, wasn't it? The one that cannot feel?"

Though his entirely healthy and sensitive palm still burned from the softness of her breast, Collis nodded soberly. "Absolutely."

With a quick nod of relief, she was gone, running sobbing from the room and down the hall. Collis took a tip from her and twisted his waistcoat a bit, then ran a hand through his hair to disarrange it. It wasn't until he was across the hall, greeting Louis Wadsworth with a satisfied smile, that he realized he was now following orders. Her orders.

Damn, but she was good.

Chapter Nine

❖

Collis was waiting behind the mews well before dusk. He'd spent a half hour too long in Louis Wadsworth's company, dawdling over sherry and talk, before he finally declared another engagement for the evening.

At first it hadn't been too bad, as conversations go. Louis was an intelligent fellow, if given to waiting for his guest to express an opinion before actually daring one of his own.

Not that Collis had done anything but toe the conservative party line. Hell, even Dalton would have choked at hearing some of the stuffy declarations he'd made tonight in the interests of drawing Louis out.

Then he'd abruptly realized that Louis was very subtly and skillfully questioning *him*. That had been disconcerting, to say the least. Why would the head of a family "friendly to the Liars" be so interested in the doings of the Prince Regent and the Prime Minister?

Especially when Louis claimed to know Liverpool so well himself. He'd even proudly shown off his father's posthumous award for allegiance, received by

Louis directly from His Royal Highness George IV. It didn't seem to Collis as if Louis needed any help at all moving upward socially. He was already very nearly atmospheric.

Yet, for all his high connections, there was something about Louis that left Collis ill at ease. Perhaps it was simply his disregard for his dependents. To allow a guest to molest a housemaid was contrary to everything Collis believed in. To encourage it, yet?

Simon must not know this about Louis Wadsworth, Collis decided. Simon was well known for his stance on taking advantage of women. But Louis Wadsworth might very likely know something about *him*. It hadn't occurred to Collis that Louis might know of the connection between Simon and Dalton—and therefore to him. . . .

No. It really wasn't likely. Simon had nothing to do with Dalton in public, and Clara and Agatha did all their socializing in the secret rooms of the club.

All in all, not what he'd expected from a candy-coated test assignment. Simon was up to something here. Collis leaned against the stone wall surrounding the back garden of the Wadsworth house, studying the problem.

The garden gate next to him opened without the merest squeak. A dark shape, barely discernible in the growing dusk, stepped through, carefully and soundlessly closing the gate behind.

Collis couldn't resist. He clapped a heavy hand on her shoulder, intoning, "You there!" in a rough accent.

A moment later, he was lying breathless on the grimy cobbles of the alley, looking up at the pale oval of Rose's face peering at him from the depths of her shawl. She straightened, then kicked him lightly in the ribs with the toe of her shoe. "Don't *do* that!"

She held out her hand. Collis took her offer, for his breath hadn't entirely returned to his lungs. "One day, I'll learn," he gasped. He stood, grinning down at her. "Unless you want to keep tossing me on my back?" He leered playfully. "Or I could practice on you."

She didn't retort sharply, as she usually did when he teased her so presumptuously. Instead, she took his hand and dragged him farther behind the odd stacked crates and barrels that always seemed to end up lining the alleys of London. "I only have a moment before the cook will miss me," she hissed at him.

Unseated by her refusal to engage, Collis groped for a way to deal with this new, brisk Rose. "Aren't you taking this all a bit seriously? It's not as if you truly work here."

"I don't know about you, Collis, but I am indeed working at the moment." She regarded him closely. "What are you wearing?"

Collis spread his hands so she could see his version of the common man's tailoring. "Something more appropriate for lurking in an alleyway. Do you like it? I nicked it from one of the grooms at Etheridge House."

"You look . . ." Rose hesitated. He looked wonderful, actually. His broad shoulders filled out the rough jacket tightly, and the breeches weren't nearly as baggy on him as they ought to be. Aristocrat he might be, but no one could accuse Collis Tremayne of being a pasty weakling. In the workingman's kit he looked manly and slightly dangerous and—this was not a welcome thought—entirely attainable.

For one eternal fraction of an instant, her heart brought forth a full-blown fantasy of a world where this man before her was an ordinary man. In the blink of an eye, she saw them happy and poor and mad for each other, with fat laughing babies crawling underfoot in their humble, cramped, blissful abode.

Then reality snapped back into place with a sickening jolt and she promptly buried that fantasy in a plot marked "Things That Will Never Be."

"You lost," she said slowly. He wasn't going to like this. "You lost the wager, Collis. Go home." She only had to get rid of him for the night. So far, the cook was working her like a drudge and watching her every move. She still had not had the chance to do more than learn the lay of the house. Yet soon the staff would go to sleep, readying themselves for another early day. Then she could begin her search. Just a few midnight hours—that's all she would need.

Then, tomorrow she would confess everything, to Collis and to the Liars. *After* she had her evidence.

He grinned. She could see the flash of his smile in the dimness. "What, and let you have all the fun?"

"I'm quite serious. You shook on the wager. I won fair and square. My orders are for you to give me one day's head start. Go home. Go drink with your highborn friends. But tonight is mine."

He straightened to his full height. She couldn't see him well, but she could imagine his face. "We are supposed to work together, remember?"

Rose folded her arms. She had to get rid of him.

"What is the difficulty with giving me one night? It isn't as though you could get back in tonight. You've already been a guest, so you can't very well pose as a servant now."

He only looked intrigued. "Well, actually, I think that could be done—"

Rose could faintly hear the cook's voice shouting for her through the window of the kitchen. Her urgency surfaced as annoyance. "Collis, *no*. Now keep to your word! Are you a gentleman or are you just a rakehell?"

She felt the shot go deep, felt it in her own belly as he flinched at her words. Drat. She hadn't meant to wound him.

Vengeance tonight. Apologies tomorrow. She tightened her shawl over her shoulders. "Now go home," she ordered coolly, "and let me work."

With that, she turned back to Louis's house, leaving Collis standing in the grimy, darkened alley.

The royal private quarters of Carlton House, situated beautifully on Pall Mall in the heart of all that was fine and aristocratic in London, were something to behold. When Prince George had designed the rooms, he'd given free reign to his trained eye and profound love of beauty and fine architecture.

Not to mention comfort. Collis lounged deeper into what had to be the single best drinking chair in all of Christendom. Apparently nothing was too good for the royal arse. Collis's bones sighed in pleasure at the deep cushions meant for the gradually sinking posture imposed by the serious partaking of far, far too much superior wine.

At his feet was poised a small hassock, primed and ready for the moment when he was as nearly horizontal as a man could be without a girl and a bed.

Thinking of girls led one to think of breasts. That was fine. Collis had spent many happy hours of his life contemplating the divine miracle of breasts. Now of course, the thought of breasts led him to remember one certain breast in particular. One sweet, round, high breast that should have been altogether too small to be tempting. How could it be that it had felt so perfectly enticing in his hand?

And then of course, thoughts of that breast led one to wonder about the other half of the pair and what it would be like to see them, together, naked—to touch them both, together, naked—

Collis snorted into his wine, which really was too fine a vintage to deserve such treatment. *Two breasts require two hands, don't they?*

"And then what did you do?"

Collis raised his glass to peer through the wine to see the fire flickering in its ruby depths. "I left. What else should I have done? She'd won by getting into the house first."

His companion shook his head in amusement. "Giving up so easily? Pity. Seems a waste. What I would give for a chance to live so adventurously!"

Collis snorted. "Yes, I cannot imagine why everyone isn't doing it."

"I am referring to the excitement and danger of being a Crown spy. Beats the bloody hell out of my life, I'm sure."

Collis slid his eyes sideways, too drunk and too lethargic to move his head. Time to check his companion's mood. They were alone in the Prince's private sitting room. The considerable cadre of menservants and royal attendants, some more highborn than Collis himself, had been summarily dismissed after supplying them with more wine than any two men should sanely drink.

Still, such intimacy with royalty came with problems of its own. It didn't do to misinterpret the humor of George IV, Prince Regent and ruler of England.

Although Collis counted the Prince among his friends, George could be unpredictable. Half-filled with drunken ramblings, half with piercing insight, time spent with the Prince was rarely comfortable but always stimulating. Once very handsome, he had not aged well due to dissipation and overindulgence.

George was thought by most to be so vulgar as to be stupid, but Collis knew his friend to be a sensitive and intelligent man who had no compunction putting on his worst face when met with prudery and prejudice. The fact that the prejudice was highly merited never seemed to bother the Prince one jot. He liked sleeping with women, he liked eating and drinking and gambling, and he saw no reason to not do all with enormous energy.

Perhaps Collis understood the Prince's rebellion better than most, for he faced a very similar lot in life. Dalton Montmorency, the great Grand Oompah of Etheridge, might not cast a shadow as deep as a king's, but Collis knew well the burden of being heir.

George would have been happiest working as an artist or architect, married to his dear Maria Fitzherbert, an ordinary man with extraordinary talents.

The Prince emitted an enormous belch. Yes, George was drunk, although not as drunk as Collis. George was eye-bright-and-restless drunk. *Damn.* Collis was sure the Prince had matched him swallow for swallow. He sat up and set aside his glass. Rubbing both hands over his face to hopefully rouse himself to matching alertness, he sighed. "I'm not the man I once was."

George waved his glass airily. "Who said you ought to be? You were a poisonous little snot until you turned twenty-five. Vain and self-important. Now, you're much more amusing. Life and humbling disfigurement have given a nicely dry twist to your personality, rather like a hint of sour lime. I much prefer it."

"So happy to oblige." The Prince's offensive statement slid over Collis's wine-soaked mind, leaving only the truth behind. But what of it? He'd once had every right to be proud and every reason to be vain, hadn't he? Then he frowned. "You hardly spoke to me when I was twenty-five."

The Prince shrugged. "Ergo the poisonous-snot comment." He rested one gloriously clad leg on a hassock and propped his other across that knee to rub one stocking-clad foot. "I love those shoes, but they are bloody tight."

Collis's wavering gaze took in the offending but beloved shoes, a pair made of pristine white kidskin and embellished with gold buckles. "They do appear a bit small."

George nodded woefully. "But small feet are so fashionable right now."

Collis pondered his own booted feet blankly. His feet hadn't been small since he was five years old. "Damn," he swore mildly. "Looks like I'm on the outs, then."

George snickered. "Never mind, my boy. You've got other assets, from what the ladies at court say."

Collis eased himself back into his chair slowly. Only the asset of being highly ornamental, unfortunately. He'd not confided that to George or to anyone. Everyone made the obvious assumptions, keeping his roguish reputation intact.

Rose's eyes hovered before him in the flames. He saw disappointment and disdain rise in them, just as he had so many times. Had even intentionally caused, when she had provoked him too often. Grave hazel contempt.

I pity the waste. Suddenly his flirtations with the ladies at court seemed pathetic. Collis drained his glass. He would not ride that horse tonight.

"What are you thinking?" The Prince wasn't even looking at him but sat staring into the fire. Too damn perceptive by half.

"I am pondering the mystique of the female bosom."

"Ah. A favorite topic of mine as well. And how go your musings?"

"I'm working my way round the matter." He recalled the sensation of Rose's soft feminine flesh cradled in his palm. He smiled wistfully. "I'm still grasping the full import, so to speak."

George issued an appreciative snort and raised his

glass. "Would you like to hear how I spent my day? First I sat through six hours of incessant whining and begging—I refer to the Royal Audiences, of course— then Robert stalks in with the usual poker up his arse about how I'm spending too much time and money in Brighton. The man is clearly the stiffest Prime Minister England has ever seen."

George sniffed. "The only vaguely diverting thing that happened today was that I was presented with an example of a very pretty carbine I commissioned to award every soldier who has served his five years in my service. Which entertaining incident lasted scarcely five minutes before some old stick pattered in, complaining of yet another old-stick crisis."

George tossed back his wine. "Let me tell you this. If I were free to be a Liar, I would never let anyone stop me. I would go, this very moment, to ride every league of that race and beat her to the finish."

"I hardly think my target would welcome such a late visit."

The Prince tsked him sadly. "I thought you had a better mind—and more spine!—than that. Be creative, man! Change horses! Do the last thing she expects!"

Rose had expected him to wander off to play. His sodden mind began to turn slowly, like a wheel lodged in mud.

"She wouldn't expect me to change tactics. She wouldn't expect . . . a midnight housebreaking!" He stood abruptly. The room slid a bit sideways and his stomach churned, but he was proud to find that he was not as incapacitated as he had thought.

The Prince's face brightened. "Now? Like a parlor

thief in the night?" He sighed longingly. "How absolutely thrilling."

"Would you care to join me?" Collis blinked in surprise. Had he said that? What a terrible idea.

"What a marvelous idea!" The Prince was on his stocking-clad feet in a bound. "I'll just go change, shall I?" He was gone in a flash.

Collis was left standing in the middle of the room, bemused. Though stout with his lifetime goal of premeditated overindulgence, the Prince was surprisingly swift when he wanted to be.

How was he to talk George out of this appalling plan? A mission to break into a nobleman's house would put the Prince into inexcusable danger—

If it were a real mission. But it wasn't real, was it? A spun-candy farce of an operation designed to test his skills, wasn't it? One that Rose had likely already passed?

"Rose is going to knot her knickers over this," he murmured to the empty room with a smile.

"I'm ready!" The Prince bounded back into the room, dressed dramatically in all black. "We can use the tunnel beneath the palace to get out without my men seeing us." He waved an enormous square of black silk in his hand. "What do you think?" He held the silk across his face below his eyes. "Highwayman? Or thief?" He wrapped the scarf around the top portion of his face. "Of course, I'll have to cut eyeholes."

Collis laughed. Feeling suddenly buoyant and reckless, he bowed to his madly accessorizing prince and ruler. "My lord spy, your mission awaits you."

Chapter Ten

———◆———

Rose moved carefully through the dark house, trying to be undetectable and yet simultaneously look as though she were on a legitimate late-night task. She still didn't know the house as well as she ought before attempting such a thing.

She could not risk staying here another day. The cook would suspect such stupidity, first of all. Then there was Louis Wadsworth to contend with. She'd been careful to stay out of his path—but for that incident in the parlor. So far Louis apparently hadn't recognized her with her head bowed beneath her cap, but she had noticed him looking at her oddly, as though he was searching his memory.

As for her own memory, Louis was as fastidious and well groomed as ever. Still, she shuddered to think that she'd ever—

Then was then. Now was now. And now she was going to prove that Louis was in thick with the French, just like his father.

The study was on the ground floor at the back of

the house, overlooking the rather unimaginative gardens. The house gave forth a few nighttime creaks. Nothing suspicious about that, but still Rose's heart jumped. Should she blow out her candle? She could use his lordship's special friction matches to relight it. Yet there was a part of her that didn't want to give up the reassurance of the light, even for a moment.

If she was caught, she could not expect to be rescued by the club, especially since she was not acting on orders. She would be treated as any servant would who was caught with her hands in the master's safe box. Imprisonment would be her best hope. More likely she'd be pulled dead from the Thames. Louis was every bit as ruthless as his father. She had no doubt that he would prefer to enact his own brand of justice upon her.

Dare you risk this? Risk everything? It wasn't too late to back out, to go back to the club, admit to the mistake with the file, to be sent back out on her arranged mission to the Wentworth house.

Louis was too dangerous, too crafty, for her to face alone. This was a matter for the Liars to handle, not her.

Only they weren't handling it, were they?

"Stop tryin' to talk y'self out of it," she muttered in the comforting accents of her childhood. "Keep y'mind on y'work."

She was safely in the study. The door was shut, the draperies were drawn . . . now to find the safe box. Louis had a great deal to hide, and he wasn't a stupid man. He must have learned a few things from his father's downfall—such as where to conceal your guilt so that prying servants could not find the evidence. . . .

The safe box was plainly situated behind a large painting that hung over the desk. Rose didn't bother breaking the box. Louis was sly and very twisted of mind. He would keep his secrets somewhere unexpected, somewhere that amused him.

Yet she doubted he would put them anywhere else in the house. This study was his territory, safe from most daily intrusions by the others in the household. She stood in the middle of the room and turned slowly, trying to think like a twist-minded traitor.

Being inside Louis's head for even a moment made her feel ill, but she forced herself to remember back to how, for her own preservation, she'd learned him so well that she could almost predict where he'd be at any given moment and what he'd be doing.

Louis-now was more sophisticated than *Louis-then,* she had no doubt, but a rodent couldn't change its tail. The nasty, warped young man was still inside him. She could get inside him as well, if she was willing to return back there.

She gritted her teeth. "I am going to take a long, boiling bath when I get home," she muttered. Then she opened her memory fully.

Louis liked contrast, she recalled. Whatever she had been experiencing, he would turn it around. If she was content, he would disturb her. Once he'd caught her humming at her work. When he'd finished describing what better uses he could think of for her mouth, she'd been sickened and agitated. And yes, forcing herself to recall it fully, darkly intrigued.

He'd known her so well. He'd known when to stop before repelling her completely, had known when to turn the encounter light once more, so that she was even grateful to him for the reprieve. But in return, she had grown to know him as thoroughly.

Contrast. Rose opened her eyes to look around the room, turning slowly. Something sour would be disguised as sweet. Something evil would be portrayed as good.

Something secret would be . . .

In plain sight. *Yes.* Excitement flowed through Rose, sharpening her mind, returning her focus.

Earlier today she had inspected this room, albeit more quickly than she would have liked. The pinchpenny cook had been determined to get every unpaid, exhausting chore out of Rose by day's end, and she had only been able to spare a moment to investigate the room while she brought in coals for the fire.

It was a study like any other but for one thing. In the niche of one of the paneled walls there stood a plinth, the sort used to display an open book, atop of which rested a mahogany and glass case obviously designed to display something precious.

The case held only one object, a gold medal resting on a bed of velvet. The engraved plate on the case read: *Medal of Allegiance, awarded (posthumously) to Edward Wadsworth (1750–1813) for his ultimate sacrifice in the name of the Crown, by His Royal Highness George IV.*

How Louis must love the high irony of this award.

Rose approached the case with an eye to any sort of inappropriate seams or cracks. The mahogany-

framed glass lid was locked, but only with a tiny decorative latch that a child could undo with a hairpin.
The case was also quite flat, not much deeper than a
picture frame.

She wrapped her fingers around both sides of the
case to lift it carefully. For all she knew, Louis had
the folds of the velvet lining memorized. Best to keep
the entire thing level while she checked beneath it—

It didn't budge. The case was firmly attached to the
stand beneath. Curious. Rose dropped to her knees to
investigate.

The plinth was an ornate mahogany piece, waist-
high and carved to resemble a column from Roman
times. "Very expensive," Rose murmured as she ran
her hands carefully over every inch. "And hardly
even a little bit ugly." She found nothing. She sat back
on her heels to ponder the stand for a moment. It was
large enough to hide a great deal within, unlike the
case above.

The case. Rose went up on her knees to examine
the case at eye level. How was it attached to the stand?
There seemed to be nothing holding it there from the
outside, which meant that a certain amount of thought
had gone into concealing . . . something.

She was on the right track, she knew it. Closing her
eyes, she thought back to what she had learned when
their studies had covered secret compartments. Lord
Etheridge himself had taught that course and had
brought in several examples, from tiny slot drawers
built into desks to a mechanism that had come from a
false wall.

"The most secret compartments are often the most

obvious, once you know what to look for," he'd told the students. "Something that is loose, or something that is unusually solid. Most amateurs still believe in the sanctity of their safe boxes, or the common false-bottom drawer. It is the professional who will have put real thought into his concealment—thought that you will have to follow if you want to reveal it."

Lovely. Back into Louis's filthy mind she must go.

Collis stepped in something noxious but didn't bother mentioning it. The tunnel from the royal chambers was dry and dusty but had long been occupied by royal vermin. Royal vermin scat looked and smelled very much like common vermin scat, Collis noticed.

He had been led downward from the Prince's chamber on a spiral stairway made of stone that looked little used. "Built right into Carlton House," George had shared informatively. "In case of another riot. Just like those leading from the palace."

He seemed casually proud, rather like a host showing off his home. "The whole city is riddled with tunnels, you know. Old rivers that were built over, drainage sluices from the streets, sewers—you can access nearly every district in the city from here. Although I recommend we avoid the sewers, shall we? These royal escape tunnels are more pleasant . . . well, for the most part anyway. I haven't used these for years, although I tore a path through them enough when I was young. I wasn't fond of princely duties."

Collis grunted. He wouldn't be prince if his life depended upon it. His *and* Dalton's. 'Twas enough being heir to Etheridge. "And are you now?"

George raised the lantern they had brought with them to brighten the arches above and the webs festooning them. "I suppose I simply realized one day that there is no escaping one's fate," he said thoughtfully. Then he turned to Collis with a piratical grin. "Where's this house? I'm absolutely itching to do something rife with danger and crime."

Collis laughed, but he was beginning to regret this whole venture. Or perhaps he was merely regretting the wine. Either way, his head was pounding and the swaying of the lantern light was making him feel a mite sick.

Still, it was only a play mission with likely enough safety nets wrapped around it to keep a tot safe. "Milton Crescent," he told the Prince.

"Ah, east it is then!" The Prince charged down a branching tunnel. Collis sidestepped another pile of rodent pellets and followed him. The Prince seemed much enamored of excitement.

Collis hoped that tendency wasn't going to get them both into trouble.

For lack of any better ideas, Rose had finally reached for the set of picks strapped to her thigh and selected the one that fit the best. The decorative lock on the case gave way instantly.

She opened the case on her knees with her eyes level to the hinges. She didn't see any traps that would be triggered by the lifting of the case. That didn't mean they weren't there, of course. Then she gently ran her finger around the rim of the medal.

The medal didn't budge beneath her touch. Curious. She tried twisting it gently, but it wouldn't move. She tried harder, inadvertently pressing *down* on the gold disk.

Click.

A panel in the side of the plinth popped open a fraction of an inch. "Lovely," whispered Rose, and she reached carefully inside.

Later, Rose still sat tailor-fashion on the floor of Louis Wadsworth's study in the wee hours of the morning, trying to make sense of what she had found within the display plinth.

Diagrams. Perfectly legitimate drawings of perfectly legitimate muskets, at least as far as she could tell. Damn, she must have stumbled onto Louis's hiding place for his manufacturing secrets.

She chewed a nail pensively. She wasn't entirely sure about these plans, but she was absolutely sure of Louis's nature. He'd been an evil lad and he was an evil man. She would simply have to look further.

She rolled the plans up carefully, returning them to the narrow leather tube she'd found them in. There was nothing remarkable about the case, either. She'd examined it most carefully. Why keep it so secret?

She was about to open the secret compartment once more when she heard a soft slithering sound from the hall. Then came the unmistakable sound of metal in the lock of the study door. There wasn't time to return the case. Rose blew out her tiny candle and dived behind the desk even as the door opened.

Chapter Eleven

❖

Collis pushed the Prince into the study and shut the door quickly. He'd lived a lifetime in the ten minutes it had taken him to get George up the trellis, through his unlatched window, and into the study.

The Prince seemed determined to live out every moment of some parlor-thief fantasy and had even insisted on fumbling about with the lock on the study door before Collis had snatched away the picks and manipulated the catch open with one swift flick of his wrist.

"Sorry, Your Highness, but these are exceedingly chancy picks of mine." Collis whispered the balm to the Prince's notoriously prickly pride out of habit, even as he searched the room with his eyes.

Simon would never allow the test to be too easy. There would be some tricky element. It could be that the target didn't even keep the evidence in his study. Still, it was likely everything would be somewhere in this room, although not someplace predictable.

"Damn, we could be here all night," he muttered as he gazed around the study. It was crammed full of manly ornaments such as globes and model ships, and books that looked largely unread.

A crash sounded behind him. Collis whirled to see the Prince standing over a fallen pedestal and presentation case that lay shattered over it. Glass sparked in the lantern light like diamonds. George sent him a shame-faced shrug.

"So sorry," the Prince said.

"We'd better go, quickly!" The last of the wine fogging Collis's mind dissipated with the realization that if he were found here with his prince-at-large, his career would be over forever. How could he have been so stupid?

"How could you have been so *stupid*?"

Rose came out of nowhere, rather as if she had bobbed up from underwater. Collis took an involuntary step back as she charged at him with some sort of leather tube held in her hand like a club.

"You brought a friend along? On a mission? A clumsy friend at that!" She moved to the door and listened with her ear close to the wood. "Oh, crikey. They're coming."

She shoved the tube into Collis's stunned hand. He automatically tucked it under his bad arm. "Go," she urged. "Take it and hide. I'll try to buy some time, although I don't think anyone is going to believe I was simply doing a bit of pre-dawn dusting."

George stepped forward grandly, in full royal mode. "No, my dear." His fruity, formal, oft-mimicked tones were unmistakably Prince George's. "There is no need for you to take the blame for my blunder. I shall merely explain—"

Rose, who had been gazing at the masked, black-clad George with impatient mystification, suddenly clapped a hand over her mouth. "Oh!" She raised a shaking finger to point at George. "You're—you're the Prince Regent!"

Collis thought she was taking it awfully hard. Then again, housemaids didn't often happen onto monarchs. George had apparently come to the same conclusion, for he bowed deeply, then stepped forward with a soothing smile.

"Oh, *bugger*!" Rose's horrified, breathless curse stopped them both in their tracks.

"Really, Rose," Collis said uncomfortably. "Such language—"

The study door crashed open. Several hastily dressed footmen blundered through to blink at the three standing before the smashed case and stand. "Got you!" the lead man growled. "Thought you'd make off with the plate, did you?"

Resigned, Collis stepped forward with his hand out peaceably. "No need to worry, good sirs. If you'll simply wake the master, we can explain—"

"Collis, catch!"

Collis spun at Rose's cry, instinctively snatching out of the air the iron poker she tossed him. She flung the ornamented coal shovel to the Prince and brandished the fire tongs like a short sword. "Now!"

She charged at the group of servants like a small

mobcapped jouster. George sent a confused shrug at Collis, then followed her, wielding his shovel like a cricket bat at the scrambling servants.

Collis saw the leader raise a skinning knife high in the air, his vicious eyes intent on Rose. Collis let out a great roar, rushing the man.

The knife came down in a shimmering arc. He wasn't going to be in time! Collis threw the poker like a spear and it thudded into the man's chest. Rose dodged, the man went down, and the last servants still standing scrambled out of Collis's way. A fortunate thing, as he had no intention of stopping.

Rose and the Prince ran ahead, escaping the house by the simple expedient of flying out the front door. Collis chased after them into the night.

After turning the street corner, Rose slowed finally. She waited for the puffing prince and Collis to join her. "Quickly, we must go to ground!" She was pale and kept looking behind them urgently.

"Enough." Collis stopped in his tracks. "Rose, we've already failed the test. We were ordered to obtain the information without being discovered. It's a bit late now to worry, don't you think?"

"Damn the test! There is no test!" She shook her head. "Or there is, but not at that house." She sent another worried look behind them. "Collis, we must go! We must get His Highness to safety!"

Collis narrowed his eyes. "If you're worried that you'll be blamed for the Prince's presence, don't. I intend to take full responsibility."

George, who had been saving his energy for inhaling and exhaling, waved a pudgy hand. "No need, no need, my boy. I'll own up to wanting a bit of a holiday."

A distant shout sounded behind them. Rose squeaked and tugged at both their sleeves with surprising force. "Run!" she barked.

Collis found himself running. Stupidity now lending itself to imbecilic. Why were they running? Still, the cries coming from behind them sounded anything but sham. Perhaps the servants hadn't been informed of the test. If so, then deservedly angry footmen could quite possibly do damage to George before matters could be sufficiently sorted out.

Yes, running was sounding better by the moment.

They raced down the deserted street. It was so late that some of the lamps had burned all their oil already or else had blown out in the gusting dampness. The air hung heavy with storm as it had all day and night, making it seem oddly dense to run through.

George was puffing loudly now, drowning out any sounds from their pursuers. Collis kept an eye on him, but so far he seemed well enough, if winded. Rose darted ahead, seeking out alleys to dash down and deserted streets to follow. They weren't fast enough, weren't going to make it free of their hunters—

"Aha!" George suddenly surged ahead of Rose and dashed down a side alley. Rose and Collis followed. The alley turned twice before ending in a wall that glistened damply in the pre-dawn haze. Rose turned immediately to run back, but Collis caught her arm.

"No, you'll run right out in front of them. We'll have to climb those drainpipes."

As one, they turned to eye the maze of drainpipes that snaked down the buildings on all three sides. Heavy pipes of iron meant to keep water from collecting on the rooftops, held on by brackets bolted into the mortar, they could provide a ladder of sorts for Rose and Collis. But George would never make it.

Collis shuddered at the thought of losing the Prince to a fall to his death. "Never mind. We'll simply have to take our chances with the house lackeys."

"No." She couldn't let it happen. God, how could she have been so stupid? Rose took the Prince by one arm and dragged him into a shabby doorway. "Stay very still," she hissed. She snuffed his lantern and left him in the dark.

Then she grabbed Collis and pulled him with her into the only other opening available, a coal chute. The iron door creaked when they lifted it down, though Rose pressed her apron to the hinges to mask the noise.

They scrambled feet-first into the steeply angled chute, leaving the iron door hanging open. Hopefully, it would not be obvious in the darkness.

The chute was a tight fit for two. All the better to keep them from sliding all the way to the cellar, but Rose wished she had thought about the fact that Collis would be very nearly on top of her.

Every inch of where his body pressed to hers began to glow like embers ready to flare. She could feel his breath on her neck like a torch on her chilled skin.

She couldn't help a tiny shift of her head, just a slight tilt to the side to expose more of her flesh to him.

She told herself it was necessary in order to hear better, but the fact was, she was scarcely listening anyway. The only sound she was attuned to was the thunder of her own blood through her veins and the matching beat of his racing heart near her ear.

The chute was like a world within the world, the filthy walls a shield of timeless power that made them the only two people in the universe for that one endless moment.

"Rose." His whisper was nearly a growl. Her body pulsed from within at the animal ache she heard in the simple vowels of her name. He wanted her as much as she wanted him. And what was so wrong with such wanting? She couldn't remember anymore.

Whatever her reasons for denying her longing, they seemed paltry and weak and entirely ignorable. With a slight shift of her body, she bore into his strength, pressing into his hard and solid body as if she wished to sink within.

His hand came up her side, slowly sliding up the curve of her waist. He paused when he encountered the side of her breast. She stopped breathing, but he moved on after a single timeless beat to cup her shoulder in his large hand.

"Rose." He shook her slightly. "Rose, I think they've gone past us."

She blinked. Gone? Who?

Then the horrifying icy rush of reality deluged her. She was smearing herself all over him! And he hadn't been whispering her name in mutual lust, he'd been practically begging her to stop! She jerked back, nearly writhing in horrified embarrassment. They clambered from their hiding place, and Rose moved quickly away from him.

Thank God it was dark in the alley, or she'd have to die right here on this very spot. Her heated flush was hidden, as were the excited points of her nipples and her no-doubt dewy-eyed expression. "Do try to make less of a target next time," she hissed at him. "God knows you're a hard bloke to hide as it is."

Collis didn't say a word. Well, he couldn't reply, could he? Not until his towering erection faded and his blood returned to feed his brain with something other than white-hot images of Rose naked and sweating and crying his name. What was his name again?

"Collis." Rose's irritated whisper cut through the darkness to remind him. "Move it along, will you?"

"Coming, Mummy," he whispered back, desperate to regain his jesting equilibrium. Whatever the hell that moment of animal insanity had been, he didn't want Rose to know about it. She'd likely never let him forget it.

And forgetting was good. Especially when the woman he was having badly timed daydreams about wasn't interested in breathing the same air as him, much less sharing the same sheets.

Please, someone run me through. I've gone and fastened my passions to a woman who would just as soon have me fall from the Tower onto a pile of rocks.

There'd be no dealing with her if she knew. She'd

lord it over him until he took his pistol and put himself out of his misery.

George had emerged from his own hiding place and was bending to peer at the grimy cobbles paving the floor of the alley. They slanted downward from each side, so that a small valley formed in the center for drainage, now traced by a thin trickle of water shining silver against the black cobbles. "I know it's here somewhere. . . ." He began to run back along the way they had come.

Collis and Rose followed. "Where's your poker?" she asked him. She still brandished her tongs, and George still carried his shovel as well as his lantern. Collis clapped his good hand to his side, relieved to find that his bad arm still pinned the tube to his side. "I, ah, threw it away," he said weakly.

Rose rolled her eyes. At least, he was sure she had, despite the dimness. She turned away from him to catch up to George, who was squatting in the alley, tugging at something with both hands, his shovel and lantern on the ground beside him.

"What is it, Your Highness?" Collis was trying to be patient, but the sounds of pursuit were definitely growing louder. The footmen had found the alley.

"Help me lift this grate," George gasped. "Tunnel."

Collis and Rose bent swiftly to help. The grate was cemented in place with years of accumulated please-don't-ask, and was cast of heavy iron to boot, but they managed to shift it after Rose thought to dig the Prince's shovel into the seam as a sort of lever. In turn, they all dropped through, only to find that the fall was far longer than they'd thought.

When the footmen finally scouted the alley, they found nothing but a bent shovel and an open grate. When they cast the light from their lanterns into the hole, they could see nothing but darkness below.

Louis Wadsworth stood in his dressing gown and slippers in the middle of his luxurious study, regarding the mess of shattered glass and mahogany that had once housed his masterpiece.

Many men, finding their dreams in pieces on the floor, would have ranted, raged, even wept. Louis made it a practice to never raise his voice. He never allowed anger to sweep him up the way it had his father.

Acting in the heat had killed the senior Mr. Wadsworth. Louis much preferred acting with cold. He hadn't lost his temper in years. No, not since the incident with that silly housemaid when he was not much more than twenty. Of course, that sort of thing scarcely mattered, but it had taught Louis a valuable lesson.

So there were no bellows, no shouts—no words at all. Behind him, he could feel his loyal retainers becoming more and more concerned for their skins. Shuffling stances, rustling clothing, even the occasional daring whispered question to each other—he let their fear wash over him, soothing him. They expected rage. Why satisfy their expectations? It was much more droll to turn and smile at them all. He did so.

If anything, the tension in the room was heightened by his action. Worry crystallized into terror. Louis would have laughed, if he ever laughed. Still, the shrinking of his sturdy crew did much to set his mood to rights.

"I wonder," he said softly, and watched half of them start at the sound of his voice. "I wonder how someone entered my locked house, entered my locked study, discovered a very secure hiding place, wreaked havoc in my innermost domain, and then absconded with some very important materials without you lot getting so much as a good look at him."

"Them, sir."

Louis focused on one of the steadier examples of the lot. "Them . . . how many?"

"Two," said some.

"Three," said others. The group was about divided in half. Louis waited, imagining his patience stretching like a victim on the rack.

"There was two men, sir," said the first one to speak. "A tall one and a fat one. The fat one were masked, like a highwayman."

"Three," argued another. His voice quavered, however.

Louis tilted his head, examining the protester as if he were a not very interesting insect. The man continued, blurting out words as if he spoke against his will.

"There were the fat one, the tall one, and the wo—" The man next to him coughed sharply. The speaker hesitated, then continued. "The wee one."

One of the others made a slight noise at that, then shut up. Louis breathed in deeply. "Tell me about the tall one. The one without the mask."

The first and bravest speaker nodded. "He were

right tall, sir. And black-haired. Youngish, or at least, not old."

Louis exhaled smoothly. He had met a man such as that this very day. Had brought him to the house, although not to the study. A man with very interesting connections—connections that had done Louis's family rather astonishing amounts of harm. Still, he himself had profited nicely from that harm, so he hadn't been inclined to take it personally.

Until now. Louis eyed the first speaker for a long moment. The fellow regarded him warily, but without the abject fear of the others. A strong one. He could be useful.

"I have a little job for you." Louis waved a gentle hand at the others. "You lot can go. Have a pint of beer and charge it to me. Not too much now. I may have need of you later."

The stupid louts relaxed, blinking at him in surprise and pleasure. They left with much crude clomping of boots, leaving tiny traces of the street on his priceless carpet. Louis pondered the meager streaks for a long moment. His chosen man waited patiently, hands clasped behind his back.

The fellow was obviously of better make than his fellows. More intelligent, more stalwart. Perhaps capable of actual independent thought.

"Yes, you'll do nicely." Louis described his wishes to the fellow, who took it all in without requiring a word of simplification or explanation.

He nodded. "Yes, sir. I'll take care of it immediately."

Louis smiled serenely. "Excellent. Oh, and tell the butler to have this carpet taken up and burned, will you?"

The man nodded briskly and set off on his mission. Louis watched him go with satisfaction. The perfect man for the job. Independent thought, indeed.

Of course, once the fellow was successful, Louis was going to have to have him killed. There was no place for independent thought in this household. No, none at all.

"See? I told you I knew the tunnels." The Prince's pleased voice rang oddly through the tunnel, bouncing off the stone walls to boom and fade in their ears.

"This is hardly a royal passage, Your Highness."

"No," chortled George. "Merely an access to one. This way now." His lantern and his good spirits were lit once more.

Rose, on the other hand, seemed none too happy about being below the city to Collis. She walked a few steps ahead, between him and the Prince. She'd said nothing since her first gasp when they'd dropped into several inches of chill water running down the tunnel. The tunnel smelled like hell, of course, so perhaps she was merely busy mouth-breathing as much as possible—but Collis didn't think so.

She was breathing very fast, in halting little gasps like a child trying very hard not to cry, and her grip on her weapon of choice, the fire tongs, caused grotesque shadows as it shook with her trembling.

George, however, was in his element. He danced ahead of them with the lantern for all the world like a boy skipping out on his tutor. "I learned these tunnels at my father's knee—well, actually, I snuck the plans from his royal office. But in my day I used them aplenty. Oh, the mischief I got up to!"

"Mischief, my foot," muttered Rose, so low Collis could scarcely hear her. "Little rotter playing treason on a schoolboy holiday."

That startled a laugh from Collis. "What are you talking about?"

He saw her eyes flicker up to his, then away. "Did I say that out loud?" she squeaked. "I wasn't talking about anything—no, not a thing! Silly twit, whistling in the dark, that's me." She walked faster, her head bent so Collis couldn't see her face. He thought he heard another whisper—"Bloody stupid, you'll get yourself hanged, see if you don't!"

Apparently, Rose talked to herself . . . at least in the dark. Interesting theory. Collis couldn't wait to hear more.

"Why will you get yourself hanged? And what did you say about treason?"

"Shut it. Shut it. The walls have ears." The words hissed faintly back his way.

He laughed out loud, the sound ringing hollow in the tunnel. "Rose, the walls don't even have *walls*!"

George paused in his role as jolly leader. "What are you two going on about back there?"

"I'm frightened of the dark," Rose blurted. "Can't bear it, not one moment longer. Please-may-I-carry-the-lantern?"

George seemed surprised that anyone else would want it but handed it over willingly enough. Rose held the wire handle for a long moment, then handed it back. "No, no good at all. It isn't the dark. It's the underground part."

In the circle of sickly yellow light, Collis could see how large and profoundly frightened Rose's eyes had become. Seeing her this way, he felt bad for teasing her. He took her cold little hand in his again. "Rose, we're safe as houses. These tunnels have been here for decades, or even longer."

"Then they're due to collapse, to my way o' thinkin'!"

Odd, Collis couldn't remember the last time Rose's speech had slipped so badly. She truly must be nearly out of her wits with fear.

He ought to be enjoying her discomfort, since this was the first time he'd ever seen her without her customary air of superiority. But the childish cling of her fingers to his made him sorry for her fear and made him want to reassure her.

To Rose, it was as if the past months of security and learning had never happened. The school, the training, even the ache of her shoulder where she'd taken a blow from one of Louis's footmen—everything seemed to fade away, muffled and cut off by the tons of earth above and around her.

To be underground meant burial, and burial meant death, and all the study, all the rationality of thought, all the learning, was swept away in a wash of deeply bred superstition.

She was never going to see the sunlight again. She was going to die down here. She could taste the death in the very air. Her heart was beating like a frightened rabbit and her eyes were so wide open they ached. She felt as if the dank air was too thick to breathe and her lungs could not draw it in.

Collis and the Prince began to fade away, their lantern going dim. She could hear them talking to her, but the words made no sense. She could not catch her breath—

The sharp crack of a hand across her face brought her to just as she'd been about to fade completely. She blinked to see two worried faces staring at her in the circle of lamplight. Her cheek stung and she rubbed it, glaring at Collis despite the fact that she was grateful for the distraction of anger.

He held up his hand to fend off her glare and sent his eyes sideways to indicate the Prince. George stood there with the lantern raised, but Rose could see that he was shaking his other hand as if to relieve a sting.

Forced to draw back her sharp rebuke—for who was she to rebuke a royal slap?—Rose merely dipped a very slight curtsey. "Thank you, Your Highness." Still, a perverse little spirit slipped a few extra words in. "If I may ever repay the favor, it will be my pleasure, Your Highness."

Chapter Twelve

❖

Collis was glad to see Rose returning to her usual dry humor. Not that she was a jester in any way. He had only seen her smile once in a great while, and never at him. Why was that? The other students could sometimes coax a flash of light and life from her, and he had heard rumors that Phillipa Cunnington had even made Rose laugh out loud on occasion.

Unfathomable. Rose laughing. He itched to hear it, if only to fulfill his masochistic curiosity. Bah. He didn't believe it anyway. Rose Lacey wasn't human enough to laugh.

He wondered if her laugh had the husky edge that her voice carried when she was annoyed with him. He liked that edge, liked the way it worked upon his hunting instincts like a stimulus. That slightly deeper, wilder tone brought to mind the chase, which of course brought to mind the capture . . .

And the, ah . . . completion.

Now is not the time, old man. Now is the time to

*worry about your neck—and the Prince's—not other
parts of your anatomy.*

George had led them into an older segment of
tunnel. The hundred-year-old stones of the arched
wall and ceiling were fitted without mortar. Collis
tried to convince himself that that was a good
thing—that walls built so were sturdier against the
press of city above—but the decreasing height of the
tunnel only made him feel the weight of every cobble
and every shop above their heads.

The monotonous *splash-splash* of their steps had
been the only thing they could hear and the few feet
of tunnel ahead all they could see for so long that
Collis was beginning to feel as though they were
treading in place, never advancing. If they had been
wading against the current, he would have been sure
of it, but as it was, the flow of rank water pushed
steadily against the backs of their calves. They were
definitely on their way somewhere.

At least the smell was improving; that or his
senses had failed him completely. Terrible thought,
that. No more smelling the aroma of roasted venison,
no more scent of roses . . . no more sweetly perfumed
women. Not that he could do anything about them
now anyway.

"But the sniffing part was still good," he muttered
to himself. He saw Rose's profile against the lantern
for a moment as she turned her head at his words. He
didn't bother explaining himself. She'd only think
him mad for worrying about something so trivial
when all their lives were in danger.

Rose heard Collis's mutter clearly enough. If he was worried about losing his sense of smell, she could reassure him. She'd cleaned enough chamber pots and privies to know that after a time the smell simply stopped registering, leaving the nose in perfect working order.

Her shoulder throbbed with every beat of her pounding heart, but there was no time to worry about it now. She must not slow them down. The Prince must reach safety.

George looked over his shoulder at her, his plump cheeks glistening in the light of his lantern. "I knew I remembered this! There is a royal tunnel just ahead!" He splashed ahead with renewed enthusiasm.

Rose halted in dismay. Had there been a doubt?

Collis came close behind her. "Please tell me that he knows where he's going," he begged softly.

Rose could feel the heat of his big body through her damp dress. She longed to lean into him for warmth and strength, just for a moment. Of course, Collis would only stare at her oddly, but at this moment she was quite willing to be a fool if only he would warm and reassure her.

"Rose?" He touched her shoulder. "Are you all right?"

The concern in his voice made her knees weaken—and she could not afford to weaken. She brushed his hand away. "Good Lord, Collis, will any female in the dark do? Mind you keep your hands to yourself, if you please!" She forced her knees to turn to steel and stalked forward, her manufactured anger lending her force she hadn't had moments before.

Collis stared after her. His open palm closed to save the warmth of her.

A voice within reminded him that she was cold and frightened. He gave that voice a swift uppercut and left it unconscious on the ground. Miss Lacey still had some explaining to do.

She isn't the one who dragged the Prince Regent along on what appeared to be anything but a candy-coated test assignment, is she?

Damn. The little voice had returned. Well, at least he had company back here in the dark.

In an office high in the attic of the slightly left-of-respectable gentlemen's establishment known as the Liar's Club, Dalton Montmorency took a moment out of his busy spymaster's morning to roll his neck from side to side. His cravat and collar dug in at such an uncharacteristic motion. Bloody hell, he was tired. The first of the trainees had yet to graduate, and the Liars were still severely short-handed. Twice the operatives wouldn't be enough. Something was brewing on the other side of the channel. Dalton just knew it.

And then there was the double-damned Voice of Society. The tattle column had already leaked vital information to the public—information that no one could possibly know.

Except somehow, someone did.

It didn't matter which news sheet the Voice appeared in. When the government would try to put pressure on one publication, the Voice would simply disappear, only to emerge again at another paper.

No editor had ever been able to pin the Voice down to an agreement. There was no pay. But if one got the chance to publish the Voice, one took it. Whoever had the Voice sold more papers than all the others put together.

More papers giving away more of the Liars' secrets.

The acrid scent of painting spirits wafted under the door, bringing pleasant associations despite the reek. Clara was painting. Or, at least, trying to paint. She was such an accomplished sketch artist that Dalton tended to forget how untrained she was at her oils. Still, she was most diligent in her practice.

So diligent, in fact, that Dalton suspected she was submerging herself in her art to forget other, less pleasant regrets.

He wished she wouldn't worry so about conceiving a child. Although it was the dearest wish of both of them, it would be impossible to love her less, no matter if she was as barren as she feared. And anyway, it might be his doing. In his past he'd always been supremely circumspect—all right, very nearly monkish. At any rate, he'd never had any bastards lain at his door. It could be that he was not able.

Not for lack of trying, however. And they'd only been wed for a few months, he reminded himself. Just because she'd never conceived in her previous brief marriage—and just because she was nearly thirty years of age—well, it was preposterous. They'd yet have the large family of their dreams.

Still, it was fortunate he had Collis as his heir.

Collis. Now there was another drama in its first act.

Dalton rubbed his neck. If Collis would only come around—if Collis could manage to tie his talents together with Rose's gifts—

Dalton certainly hoped Simon's hare-brained "assignment" was going to work. As for himself, he was running fresh out of ideas.

A knock came to the door of the office, then Stubbs stepped inside without waiting for a reply. Dalton hid a sigh. He missed the days when the office had been secret from all but the select few. Now it seemed as if his doors never stopped swinging.

Stubbs was panting from the climb. Well, too bloody bad. Dalton refused to install a bell so he could be rung up like a butler.

"My lord—sir—he's come!"

"Oh, for pity's sake, Stubbs. Who is come to put you in such a piffle?"

"I am." A greyhound-lean man entered. Lord Liverpool, Prime Minister of England, was not a tall man, but still he managed to fill a room with his presence, especially one as small as Dalton's not-so-secret office.

Dalton stood and bowed. His rank and holdings were equal to Lord Liverpool's, but he'd always deferred to his mentor's age and greater experience. *Well,* he thought as a fresh wave of paint spirits entered the room, *perhaps not* always.

Thoughts of Clara revived his energy and he waved Liverpool to a seat with interest. "What has brought you here so early, my lord?" Or at all? Liverpool was not fond of the egalitarian nature of the

Liars and oft threatened to disband them when they didn't perform to his exacting standards. He usually only appeared in Liar territory when doom was about to strike.

"Oh, damn," Dalton muttered. "Which is it, George or Napoleon?" He passed a hand over his face. "Pray, tell me it's Napoleon."

"I'm afraid your first guess is correct." Liverpool sat in the chair as if it were a throne, or perhaps a chariot. His spine didn't bend in the least.

"What's he done now?" The Prince Regent had seemed so settled since taking over for his father, mad King George. Then again, perhaps the Prince was simply a dam waiting to break. Since George had already had a secret marriage, run off to play revolutionary, and spent his way right out of the palace vaults, Dalton shuddered to think what his reluctant ruler had done now.

"His Royal Highness has disappeared. Apparently voluntarily."

"Oh, hell," Dalton said weakly.

"There's more." Liverpool crossed his hands over the silver top of his walking stick and gave Dalton a supremely sour glare. "The last person seen in his presence was none other than our very own Collis Tremayne."

"Oh." Dalton sat opposite the Prime Minister, his knees weak at the thought of what the two of them could get up to together. "Oh, bloody hell and damn."

One corner of Liverpool's mouth twitched without humor. "My thoughts exactly."

. . .

The royal tunnels were a vast improvement over the storm drain, as far as Rose was concerned. Hardly damp and not a bit smelly. The arched ceiling was high enough for even Collis to stand erect, and the lantern's light seemed to go much farther when reflected by the elegant creamy stone walls.

Very nearly cozy, if not for the fact that it was still under the bloomin' ground. At last the three unlikely tunnel occupants came to an open area, in a sort of nexus of several tunnels, with carved relief work decorating a band of darker stone at eye level. Knots and spirals and stylized animals twined intricately together. It must have taken many hours of skilled labor to create.

Wasn't that just like the aristocracy? Rose snorted. "Why make it pretty when no one's going to see it?"

George came closer to her and held the lantern up to brighten the stonework. "It isn't only beautiful. It also tells where each tunnel goes, if you know the symbols used."

Rose turned to look at the Prince Regent meaningfully. He chuckled at her expression. "Yes, dear lady, I know the code." He yawned and turned away.

It must have been her imagination that made her think he muttered something as he turned away. Something that she was very much afraid sounded like, "Mostly."

George puttered around the chamber, lighting a few of the torches that stood ready on the walls. "These are dry as ash," he told Rose and Collis. "They won't last long, so rest while you can."

Rest? Under the ground? Not likely. Yet the floor here was dry and clean. George stretched himself out and closed his eyes in relief, pillowing his head on his crooked arm. He was snoring within seconds.

Rose tugged on Collis's hand. "Let me explain. Then we can decide what to do." She led him to a far corner, taking the lantern with her.

Independent Rose wanted to confer with him? Surprise mingled with concern. This did not bode well. He sank down beside her on the dusty stone floor. "Explain, then."

She sighed. "You are going to be furious, I fear."

She told him an appalling tale, from her first mistake in choosing the wrong file to her attempt to discourage his own participation.

"But why didn't you simply tell me?" Her silence stung, more than he wanted to admit. "I could have helped you."

She looked down. "It was my mess. I was only trying to lessen my error."

Collis had the distinct feeling that he wasn't being told everything. "Instead, you compounded it."

She sighed. "Yes, I did. With a bit of help from you, of course."

He held up a hand. "Oh, I know I did my part. I can't believe I let George tag along. Dalton's going to have cat fits over that one."

They both went silent as they imagined the magnitude of the spymaster's disapproval. It wasn't heartening. Liverpool's fury didn't even bear thinking on.

After a moment, Rose went on. "I only needed one

night. I knew I could find something and I did. At least, I think I did."

"Yes, the prize," Collis remembered. He pulled it from where he'd stuck it into the deepest inner pocket of his frock-coat. It was making a most unsightly lump in the fabric. Collis could almost hear Denny's moans of anguish.

He was really going to have to do something about Denny.

They uncapped the leather tube and spread the plans out in the circle of lantern light. Hunching over them, their shoulders touching, they tried to discern if there was anything suspicious contained in the detailed drawings.

"Well . . ." Collis scratched his ear. "It's a musket."

She slid him a low-lidded glare. "I gathered as much."

"And you think Louis Wadsworth has nefarious plans for this alleged musket?"

She chewed her lip. "I know he must have. I simply don't know what they are."

Collis had his doubts. Rose seemed to be leaping to some very far conclusions. "Yet the file contained nothing suspicious. Do you truly think that the Liars could be so ill-informed about Louis Wadsworth?"

She turned pensive. "I did find that hard to believe, actually. But the men have been stretched so thin for so long now. . . ." She shrugged. "They were so focused on his father's treason, I suppose Louis didn't seem like much of a threat."

Collis blinked. "But Edward Wadsworth was a

hero! The Knights of the Lily would have never have been revealed had it not been for his loyalty."

"Edward Wadsworth was a traitor. He was the leader of the Knights of the Lily. I should know. I worked in his house for years." She began to roll up the benign-seeming diagrams.

"Then you're the maid that Clara posed as!" He felt rather stupid for not realizing it before. Of course, he'd never asked, had he?

Rose nodded. "When Clara moved in next door, she asked to exchange places with me in order to spy on the master."

"Which is where she met Dalton, who was posing as a thief. I know the story, believe me." He'd heard it repeatedly, until all he needed to hear was, "Remember in the attic?" before his eyes glazed over.

"The two of them reminisce over dinner nearly every evening," he informed her. "One could toss one's lamb chops, the way those two carry on."

Rose looked a bit misty-eyed. "I think they're sweet."

Collis grunted. "Try living with them. You'd think they invented love."

She turned that sea-green gaze on him. "Don't be cynical, Collis. They're so happy."

Her eyes seemed to lock onto his, for he couldn't tear his gaze away. She was so close, shoulder to shoulder. If he wanted to, he could duck his head slightly and kiss her soft mouth.

The silence stretched on for two breaths, then three. Collis could feel heat rising under his collar, despite the chill of the tunnel. Rose's eyes sparked gold lantern light. Her lashes were very long, he noticed. Thick and dark, like her hair.

What did her hair look like down? He'd never seen it. She always wore her practical braids wound tightly around her head like an ebony crown. Suddenly, he wanted to see her hair. His fingers twitched with the impulse to pull the pins from her braids and comb free her tresses for his enjoyment.

Rose's hair, spread across his pillow. Spread across his chest—

"Collis?"

"Hmm?"

"Can I have the case?"

"What?" He swallowed, shook himself back to the moment and handed her the case. He'd been holding it in his bad hand. Mysteriously, it was quite crushed. Rose frowned at him but didn't say anything as she worked the stiff leather open again.

What had happened to him? He felt as though he'd stepped off the curb to the street, then found himself falling a great distance.

There was definitely something odd going on with him. Probably far too much wine last night.

Probably.

"Very well then. I'll take your word for Edward Wadsworth's guilt, but how can you be sure that Louis was involved?"

"Oh, he was involved, never fear."

Collis didn't think he liked the road his thoughts were traveling. "If Louis Wadsworth was a member of the Knights of the Lily . . . if he is a dangerous traitor . . . and if you once worked for his father . . ."

Rose looked up. "Oh, yes. That's all true."

"Then what the bloody hell were you thinking going in there alone?"

She said nothing, but only gazed at him with those bottomless eyes. Collis rose to pace before her, unable to contain his fury. "What if you'd been discovered? Did it ever occur to you that your rashness could get you killed?"

Her eyes narrowed and her chin rose. "If I had been apprehended—which I might point out I wasn't, despite severe interference on your part—I would have been sentenced as a thieving servant. That is all."

"What if Louis recognized you?"

She didn't look quite so sure of herself at that. "It wasn't likely. I stayed well out of his way."

An ugly thought slimed its way across Collis's mind. "You said Louis Wadsworth had a history of molesting his dependents. Did he ever . . . ?"

She put the cap on the leather tube with great concentration. "He never raped me, if that's what you're asking."

It was. The relief Collis felt was profound. The very thought—

But that wasn't the topic of the moment. The topic was—

"What the bloody hell were you thinking?"

Her lips twitched. "You're repeating yourself, Tremayne." She leaned her head to one side to look around him. "Keep your voice down, if you please. I don't want to wake the Prince Regent. I'm worried that he pushed himself too far last night."

Collis knelt before her, taking her chin in his good

hand. "Very well, then," he hissed. "You can quietly explain to me why you ignored every rule of the Liars to put yourself in gravest danger. I would have thought you had those rules written on your sleeve!" He released her, rubbing his fingers together. Her skin was so soft.

"That's silly," she retorted. "I keep them in my shoe."

He stared at her. She sent him an impish pursing of her lips. His anger was no match for the laughter boiling up from within.

When he was done, he sighed. "Oh, Briar Rose, you are going to die young. You know that, don't you?"

She shrugged. "Most Liars do, Collis. It's the nature of the vow we took."

That was true—but somehow, no longer such an easy prospect.

Glad that Collis had gotten over his anger, Rose busied herself tearing strips from the cleaner portions of her petticoats.

Collis frowned. "What are you doing?"

"Bandages," she explained. "For my shoulder."

Collis went ice-white. "You're *bleeding*?"

Chapter Thirteen

◈

"You're *wounded*?" Collis wasn't prepared for the icy jolt of fear in his gut. He dropped to his knees behind her. "What happened?"

Rose stretched her chin as far as possible but could not see her own shoulder blade. "Knife, I think. Blast it, I could have sworn they only had blunt weapons." She shuddered to think that she had led His Highness through such a gauntlet. What had she been thinking?

"I thought it missed you."

Even in the light, it was difficult to see the blood staining the heavy black fabric of her maid uniform, but there was no hiding the four-inch slit. Collis swallowed hard. He reached out and tried to peer through it to see the damage, only to snatch his hand away at Rose's sharp gasp. "Sorry. I think we ought to get you to a physician."

Rose shook her head. "We can't."

Collis frowned. "But you're bleeding!"

"It isn't so bad. I didn't even realize it until a moment ago."

Rose began to twist one arm behind her. She appeared to be trying to undo her gown with one hand.

He well knew how difficult that could be. He crossed the chamber and reached into the comatose prince's waistcoat for the scrolled silver flask he knew was secreted there, then he returned to her. She stopped her efforts to look up at him warily. Collis held out his hand. "You're no cat, Rose, though you may fight like one. You cannot reach. Let me."

Kneeling behind Rose, he tugged carefully at the row of small plain buttons that ran down the back of her uniform. She aided him by pulling aside the softly curling wisps of hair that had fallen to the nape of her neck. Her head bent, she sat vulnerable before him— a position that neither of them were at ease with.

The buttons parted far enough for him to pull the fabric aside, and he slowly dropped his hands from them. Carefully he lifted the gabardine away from her wound. They hissed simultaneously when the sticking cloth tore the drying scab anew.

Blood seeped from a long slice in her white skin. The sides did not gape, which meant that the cut was shallow, but the sluggishly flowing blood still alarmed him.

His own handkerchief was still dry and clean in his breast pocket. "This will sting, I fear, but there is no water here." He soaked his handkerchief with the contents of George's flask and dabbed tentatively at the wound.

"No," she said, her jaw clenched around the words. "Press. Press hard."

He did so, flattening his hand over the port-soaked linen with his fingers curling over her bare shoulder. She cried out softly but leaned hard into his touch, adding her own strength to the pressure. They remained thus, silent and intense, until finally Rose retreated with a gasp that told Collis she had been holding her breath.

"Is it bleeding still? Kurt told me that would stop the bleeding." Her voice was husky with pain and, if he was not mistaken, unshed tears.

Collis wiped carefully at the wound, then watched it. "No, only a very little."

"Oh, good," she said faintly. She lifted the strips of torn petticoat over her shoulder. "If you wouldn't mind . . . I would much appreciate your help."

Her polite request stung. Was he such an ogre that she suspected he needed to be asked—to be importuned to help dress a wound?

He took the strips silently. The handkerchief he folded into a sort of pad, which he meant to tie across her shoulder with the strips. Her gown defeated him, however.

"I'm afraid we must remove this," he said, tugging gently at the opened placket. Rose cast him a long look over her wounded shoulder, then nodded. Collis, fingers shaking inexplicably, undid the rest of the buttons to her waist, then eased the dress off both her shoulders. She managed to pull her uninjured arm from the sleeve, but stopped with a small involuntary noise when she tried to manage the other. Silently

Collis reached his arm around her to pull gently at her cuff, tugging the sleeve down to her wrist without further raising her arm.

She gathered her bodice to her front and leaned back toward him trustingly. She didn't seem fond of underthings, for she wore nothing beneath the dress but her petticoat, not even a chemise. How was he ever going to look at her again and not remember that arousing little fact?

Her upper body was as bare and gleaming as a Grecian sculpture in marble. Faint marks seemed to cross her back, some pale, some darker. No, it was likely only the uncertain light. The curve of her spine distracted him. He wanted to trace it with his fingertips down to where the parted gown clung to the swell of her buttocks. He remained frozen for only a moment, then recalled himself to his task.

The only way to fix the pad was to wind the binding under her arm and across her chest, then back around. Collis put enormous effort into not touching her breasts, but there were a few unavoidable moments. The soft weight of one sat warmly on his exposed wrist for a long moment that was drawn out by the fact that his hands began to shake rather severely.

A sonorous rumble rent the tension. George's snores were deafening in the confines of the stone chamber.

Holding herself quite still with her eyes closed, Rose said nothing, allowing him to regain his hold on the linen without interfering. Trusting Collis not to press his advantage was a bit like trusting a dog not to lick, but there it was. She trusted him.

Her shoulder burned so that tears began to press against her lids, demanding exit. Or perhaps she was simply weary. It could not be the tender way he handled her wound or the profoundly respectful way he navigated her near nudity, could it?

Oh, but to let her guard down for one blissful moment . . .

His hands were warm despite the pervading chill. How was he so warm? Did shining brilliant men like Collis simply burn hotter? He was melting her. She was wax set too close to the blaze. *So close.* She could feel his breath on her exposed nape. If only . . .

Collis was very upset at the damage to her flesh. He'd never realized how delicate she was, how fine boned. Her skin was pure ivory silk but for the slash profaning it. He cared for her silently, marveling at her bravery and her sheer dog-rotted idiocy. Finally, he tied the binding off and helped her pull her dress back on. After buttoning her up, he sat back on his heels.

"What are you doing in the Liar's Club?" His voice was soft. "What were you thinking? You shouldn't be putting yourself in such danger. You should be—"

She looked at him over one shoulder. "Toting chamber pots, like I was before?" She turned fully to him. "I'm no lady, Collis Tremayne. Don't forget that. Servitude can be as dangerous as espionage in some settings. At least with the Liars I have my pride."

Rose and her pride. "I'm quite sure you had an apronful of pride as a servant, as well, for you've much to spare now."

She was silent for a moment, then shook her head. "No, I had no pride. There was no depth that I was not sunk to in the name of the master." She shrugged. "I know there are proud servants. I've met the legendary Mr. Pearson. But where I was there was no time for pride. There was only survival."

She turned to look at him, pulling the dress back over her shoulder. The faint pale streaks upon her skin flashed slightly in the lantern's light. *Scars.* Collis felt sick. "You were whipped? But that is illegal!"

"Yes," she said dryly. "What a comfort to know that when your back is being torn to strips." Her tone was light, but her body was so tense Collis thought she might shatter from it.

His own behavior came back to haunt him now. His teasing, his competitiveness. "I'm sorry, Rose."

He didn't have to explain what for. She gazed at him, then nodded. "You should be. You can be rather foul, you know."

"I know. I always have. It's a sort of gift of mine, to be able to know precisely what will upset someone the most. I don't use it, mind you. At least, not usually."

"It's a powerful weapon. I suggest you keep it unloaded."

He grinned. "Or I might shoot myself?"

She almost smiled. "The possibility exists."

He cocked his head at her. "You do speak beautifully, you know. One would never doubt that you were a lady."

She actually blushed. "Thank you."

Praising her felt very good. Collis gave it another

try. "If it wasn't for your direct gaze, you'd pass as well-born."

"Direct?"

"One would think there was a map of the world on the carpet for the way ladies stare at it all the time."

She looked away. "I didn't know."

"Now you're doing it. Ladies do tend to look away a great deal—I wonder why—"

"So you can't see your own foolishness reflected in their eyes, you young lout," came a rusty voice behind them. The Prince was awake.

Chapter Fourteen

―――――――◈―――――――

They were holding a mission discussion, Rose realized, except that instead of Lord Etheridge, there was the Prince Regent of England—and instead of the well-equipped environs of the Liar's Club, she and Collis stood before the seated Prince in an underground audience chamber. A rising giggle threatened to interrupt His Royal Highness. She bit down on her tongue, *hard*.

"Now, thanks to our dear Miss Lacey—how are you feeling, my dear? Better now? Good—we have in our hands the diagrams for the commemorative carbines that I was telling you about, Collis."

Rose nearly held up her hand like a good student. The Prince must have noticed her aborted gesture, for he nodded at her like a teacher. "Yes, Miss Lacey?"

"Do you mean to say you've already seen these diagrams?"

The Prince frowned slightly. "I have seen sketches and I have seen the finished product . . . but no, somehow I missed seeing these particular drawings before."

Collis crossed his arms. "Would you necessarily

see the manufacturing diagrams, Your Highness?"

George shrugged. "Sometimes, perhaps. If I'm not too bored."

Collis glanced at her. She returned the look. There was no respectful way to respond to that statement, was there? Collis settled for clearing his throat instead.

"Isn't the arms market very competitive now, Your Highness? What is so unusual about a manufacturer keeping his designs locked away? I would think it the norm, rather."

"That is quite true, Collis. The plans do not seem odd. The fact of their concealment is not odd. In fact, nothing about this case seems odd—except for the fact that Miss Lacey suspects that Louis Wadsworth is not what he seems."

Knows he is not what he seems, Rose wanted to say, but she held her tongue. So far, George seemed willing to listen to her. She would not correct him.

The Prince continued. "The fact that Louis was concealing these plans at home does seem slightly odd. I have toured his factory. He has a perfectly good vault in it that is good enough for his money . . . so why not good enough for these plans?

"According to information collected by the Liars, there is nothing suspect about the actual operations of the factory. It has produced thousands of guns over the last few years that are already in use defending England." George smiled at them both. "Yet the fact remains that I want this looked into. That's the lovely part about being the ruler. I can."

He paused, looking at them both. Rose could very

nearly hear the royal gears turning. His gaze flicked to her. "Miss Lacey, are you sure you are not in need of a physician?"

She shook her head. Despite his reputation and royal stature, she found him rather sweet. "It takes more than a scratch to put me out, Your Highness. I was a housemaid, a *real* housemaid, before I joined the Liars."

"Yes, my dear. I know. Collis speaks of you often."

"He—he does?" Oh, fry it. That couldn't be good. Collis shuffled uncomfortably next to her.

The Prince stood and stretched. "Do you know, I never wanted to be King," he said lightly, in what seemed to be an odd change of subject. "They say I couldn't wait to seize my father's power. I suppose it's hard for people to understand. It *seems* so lovely, being the ruler." George sighed. "Yet all I ever wanted was to live my own life. Dream my own dreams. Love my own love."

Rose didn't know how to respond to that confidence. Of course she knew about his strange marriage to his first cousin, Caroline of Brunswick. The story had it that they had never met until three days before the royal wedding and it was loathing at first sight for the both of them. Even legendary lecher George had never managed to get more than one child with his despised wife, and had eventually banished her to roam Europe, where, according to gossip, she was doing everything possible to shame and disgust her husband. And knowing what George was capable of, that likely meant going quite far.

Rose wasn't one to collect royal gossip, but this was all common knowledge. Every blacksmith and baker knew the story. Many even rooted for Caroline, since George had never made the least effort to become beloved by his subjects.

Still, Rose felt for him. Perhaps if he'd been allowed to remain married to his beloved Maria Fitzherbert, he would not be the madly unhappy man he was now.

Perhaps being King was not so free, after all.

"I—I'm sure you will be a great king, Your Highness."

"I'm sure I will be a great joke." George smiled. "Still, you and Collis remind me of myself and my dear Fitzherbert. 'A rose by any other name would smell as sweet.'" Then the Prince smiled indulgently at her. "You look puzzled. Forgive me, my dear. Of course you wouldn't recognize the reference."

She and Collis? Romantic? She heard Collis make a strangled sound beside her. She was *not* going to look at him. Ever.

"Oh, I recognize the line, Your Highness," she said quickly. "I simply can't see how you could compare the situations. Collis and I could never be considered to be from 'two households, both alike in dignity.'"

Both men blinked. Reaching the limit of her patience, Rose rolled her eyes at their stunned expressions. "Good Lord, do you think I have wasted these last months?"

Collis looked uneasy. "But—but I was told that when you came to the Liars you could barely read."

"True, but I was able to catch up very quickly. Lady Raines has been teaching me etiquette and mathematics, while Lady Etheridge has been teaching me literature and history."

Collis looked absolutely dumbfounded. *"When?"* He peered at her. "You've been in every class that I have, and a few that I have not. You work in the school to earn your keep, and you said you work extra hours with Kurt in the arena."

She shrugged, uncomfortable. "There are sometimes fewer hours in the day than I would like, but truly, it isn't like real work at all. When I was in service, I was up well before dawn and sometimes worked well past midnight."

Collis thought uneasily of his own efforts. Here was a girl who had lived her days working out of fear of a beating or a sacking. Here was someone who truly knew the meaning of survival.

"If not for vying with Miss Lacey, you wouldn't have come as far as you have." Dalton had been entirely correct. Bloody hell.

The Prince tapped the leather case against his thigh impatiently. "Now, if we've all our history out of the way, I want to tell you my plan."

Collis and Rose blinked at the Prince. "Your *plan,* Your Highness?"

George folded his hands across his girth and smiled benevolently. He looked rather like Humpty Dumpty perched on the wall, a drawing in one of Collis's old picture books. The image did Collis's peace of mind no favor. Humpty Dumpty hadn't gotten on well at all.

"My plan is that we take these drawings to a man I

know. These tunnels will take us directly to him. He'll know if there is anything interesting about these guns. Then we can decide what to do about young Louis."

"We?" Collis swallowed. Shattered prince filled his mind. "Oh, no, Your Highness. *We* are going to get you straight on back to the palace! Then we are going to take our suspicions to the club." He was glad to see out of the corner of his eye Rose nodding vigorously.

George tilted his head. "You and whose army?"

All the king's horses and all the king's men . . . Panic welled. "Your Highness, you can't be serious—"

"I am most serious. I've been in need of a holiday. Well, I'm going to take it. I like you two, or I did, and I fancy a bit of adventure." He casually studied his nails. "Of course, if you don't wish to tag along . . ."

Collis stopped breathing. Rose squeaked and sent him a look of pure panic. But what could he do? Refusing to accompany the Prince on his "holiday" would be disastrous! Obviously knowing this, George sighed happily and smiled sweetly at them both. "I expect we'll have great fun. You'll like old Forsythe. He's not terribly social, but he can hold more liquor than a barrel."

Rose visibly swallowed. "And then—after we see Mr. Forsythe—you'll go back to the palace?"

George shrugged broadly. "Where else would I go?"

Collis noticed that the Prince didn't precisely promise—but again, what could he do? George was his own man. He listened to no one anyway, except for—

"Liverpool!" Yes. "What of the Prime Minister, Your Highness?"

"Robert will go on running the nation, as usual. I'm sure he'll be able to come up with some way to excuse my absence for a day . . . or three. Don't you two want to prove Louis Wadsworth guilty? I'm quite sure I do. Poisonous fellow."

"But—in that case, why don't you simply overrule Liverpool, have Wadsworth investigated?"

"Gainsay my Prime Minister on your word? Liverpool is valuable and very powerful. Even I would not do it without good reason. Don't let my adventurous nature fool you, Collis. I am not a political idiot."

Collis was going to hyperventilate. And then he was going to faint like a tightly corseted dowager. And when he woke up, he was going to hyperventilate some more. He glanced at Rose. She didn't look any better off. She was as white as paper, with a rosy spot of sheer panic on each cheek. She gazed at him like a deer that knew very well it was about to be shot.

"Well, at least we're going to go to hell together," he murmured to her. As soon as possible, he would hire a likely boy to carry a note to Denny. A street boy wouldn't be able to get within a mile of the Prime Minister, but Denny had been used as courier before.

Rose shook her head repeatedly. "No. This is a very bad idea, Collis."

"Do you want him wandering around alone? Look what nearly happened at Wadsworth's!" Collis didn't really care if George could hear their hissed conversation. Serve him right, the spoiled old scoundrel!

Rose pressed both hands to her stomach. "If we get him back safe, maybe they won't hang us." She didn't sound any too sure.

"Oh, don't worry. The Liars don't perform public executions."

"What about private ones?"

Kurt's flashing knives shimmered dangerously across Collis's mind. "Well, that I don't know. But I do know that if we allow him out alone, we'll face much worse."

"I suppose."

They turned to George, united in their dread. "Very well, Your Highness. We'll go show the plans to your Mr. Forsythe."

The Prince rubbed both hands together with glee. "Lovely. I'll lead the way, shall I?"

Collis's hopes of sending word to Liverpool were dashed by the fact that George was able to negotiate the tunnels all the way to and into the Tower environs. How the Prince held the map of this odd, disjointed system in his head so well was a mystery, but Collis knew that when Dalton learned of it, he would covet it powerfully.

They made excellent time through the relatively open, airy dry passages that looked as though they had been built last year, they were so unworn. It would take five times as long to navigate London's twisting, traffic-clogged streets. Collis felt he could happily use this system every day.

Rose, however, suffered silently enough but Collis could tell she was unhappy about being underground. Her cool fingers would reach for his in the shifting dimness behind George and his lantern, sometimes just for an instant of contact before she would march forward.

Finally, they climbed an interminable iron ladder up to a more elderly tunnel. "We're just under the White Tower," explained George. "Only a little farther now."

"Just who is this Forsythe, Your Highness?"

Collis was glad to see Rose recovered enough to be curious again. It seemed she wouldn't be holding his hand for a while. Pity.

"He's an inventor," George said. "Explosives, primarily. A true man of science, not one of those posturing mystics floating around London these days prattling to old ladies about Electricity."

"But 'tis early morning, Your Highness. Are you sure he will not be asleep?"

"Oh, Forsythe doesn't sleep. Says it's a waste of time." George knocked on a plain wooden door. Rose expected him to walk directly in—after all, he was the ruler of the country, was he not?—but George waited patiently with a small smile on his face.

Eventually the sound of multiple bolts sliding from their locks came through the thick wood. The door opened a tiny slot. "What?"

"Why bother locking if you simply open the door?" George grinned. "You have callers, Forsythe! Put your drawers on and let us in."

The door opened slightly wider. "Who's that? Georgie? Bloody rotter, I've got my drawers on. I just don't have any trousers. Can't think where I put them. . . ." The voice wandered away. George pushed the door open and strode in.

Chapter Fifteen

❧

The Prince disappeared into the tower chamber. Rose glanced at Collis, who shrugged. They entered a few respectful feet behind the Prince. After three steps, they stopped, for there was nowhere to go in the cramped room.

It was a large room, enormous even, for it used an entire open floor of the Tower. Only pillars supporting struts broke the openness, yet there was hardly an inch unused. Or unpacked. Books, mostly, although there were open crates of metal objects here and there as well. Collis whistled. "It's like Portobello Road in here."

"Ha!" A frazzled gray head popped up not ten inches from Rose's elbow. "I've more books than those wankers! I've more books than anybody!" A man bustled out, clad in shirt, waistcoat and, yes, baggy, dingy drawers. He wasn't a bit taller than Rose, but that was likely caused by his incredible stoop, which almost merited the term *hunchback*. His head was as large as Collis's, and if his bent back were straightened, he would be nearly as tall. Rose had the impression that the bent back was the result of a lifetime of neglecting to stand up straight rather than an accident of birth.

He wore two pairs of spectacles, one perched on his nose and one perched atop his wild mop of hair. "I," he said with great dignity, "have more books than the King himself."

George grunted. "These are my father's books, Forsythe."

"Mine now. But you may borrow one if you like. As long as it doesn't leave this room."

Suddenly the man seemed to notice Rose for the first time. He halted, blinked, then swept her a tottering bow. "Georgie, where are your manners? Introduce me to the lady!"

Rose stepped forward. "I am Rose Lacey, sir. I am—" She cast a questioning glance at the Prince. Did this man know about the Liar's Club?

"She's one of Etheridge's trainees, Forsythe."

"Etheridge! Is he still playing spy at that boys' club of his? Oh, well, at least they're using their heads for something besides holding up their hats." Forsythe swung on Collis. "Ha! That's why you look so familiar. You're Etheridge's heir, aren't you?"

Collis nodded. "Collis Tremayne, sir, at your service."

"At my bloody service, eh? Not likely. No one comes up here unless they want something. Even you, Georgie. No time to visit an old friend anymore? You used to hang about here by the hour. Couldn't get rid of you for anything but a meal or a pretty girl."

"Sorry, old friend. It's that damn Regent thing I do. Takes all my bloody time."

"Ha! That Jenkins boy does all the work and you know it."

Rose slid a glance at Collis. *Jenkins boy?* she mouthed. Collis nodded. *Liverpool*, his lips said.

Robert Jenkins, Lord Liverpool? Mr. Forsythe called the Prime Minister of England "that Jenkins boy"? He was either entirely mad or the bravest man she'd ever met. Even Lord Etheridge said "my lord."

While she'd been pondering that, Mr. Forsythe had wandered away. They found him puttering about the other end of the room where a series of tables had been set up. Rose eyed the scorch marks on the nearby walls and stayed well away from the bubbling beakers and coils of copper tubing, but Collis and George approached the table to exclaim over the apparatus assembled there.

She watched in horror as her two companions poured something from one of those dangerous-looking containers into two smaller beakers and toasted each other. They raised their "glasses" to drink. "Stop!" She rushed forward. "What are you thinking?"

George sipped. "I'm thinking it's a bit young, but it's been a long night. What are you thinking, Collis?"

Collis sniffed his first. "I'm thinking it's best tossed back quickly."

"Agreed." They quaffed their potions, gasped, and choked—then laughed at Rose's look of horror.

"It's a still, my dear," said George. "Gin. Forsythe

makes it himself." He patted back a belch. "Pardon me!"

Forsythe looked up, blinking through the fog that had collected on his spectacles from the boiling pot he was watching. Rose stepped forward warily to peek. Stew?

"Are you still here?"

"Yes, Forsythe." George seemed to have all the patience in the world for this old man. "We're still here."

Forsythe sighed. "Oh, very well. If the rudeness isn't working, I might as well give it up. Very tiring, you know."

"I know." George clapped the man on the back. "And I hate to bother you in the middle of your . . ." He sniffed. "Lamb?"

"And leeks."

"Ah. Well, in the middle of your, um, breakfast. We must ask your help deciphering some designs."

"Ooh. I like designs. What for?"

"The George the Fourth Commemorative Carbine, I believe."

"Well, give! Give!" Forsythe nearly danced in anticipation. The Prince handed him the battered leather case that Rose had stolen from Louis. Forsythe spread the plans out on a table, disregarding George's and Collis's attempts to clear it first. He picked up a candle to peer closely at the plans. "Hmph. Heavy-handed with the stock decoration, I'd say."

"Yes, Forsythe. I thought so as well. Do you see any reason for someone to hide this away, anything wrong—or hidden?"

"I'll say I do. Lousy proportions, for one. A well-made musket is a lost art, if you ask me. Ever since that upstart Manton came up with his ridiculous percussion cap—"

"Now, Forsythe—just because he got his design before the Board of Ordnance first."

Forsythe made a noise and peered more closely until his untidy mustache trailed on the paper. "Oh, my! Oh, my, my, my. . . ."

George, Collis, and Rose stepped forward simultaneously. "Yes?"

Forsythe grunted. "Well, either Mr. Wadsworth is the worst musket designer in the world or . . ."

"Or?"

"He's not on our side." Forsythe tapped a portion of the drawing. "See this?"

They all peered closer, although of course the symbols were meaningless to them.

"The boring, you see." He looked up at them, but they obviously didn't see. He sighed, as if teaching a group of very slow children. "The bore is the hole, if you will, through—"

"Through the barrel, yes, we know, Forsythe. Go on."

"Well, this bore is tapered, just a fraction. You wouldn't even see it in the design if you weren't looking. But if the barrel is machined to these specifications it will swell with heat. It will tighten—well, you see what I mean!"

He looked at them and sighed. "If you built this musket, per this design, using these materials . . . I give you two, three firings before the bloody thing blows up in your hands."

Rose saw Collis flinch and then rub his damaged arm. George pursed his lips. "So," he said, "I hand out these weapons, with my name and image upon them—"

"But why?" Rose demanded. "It wouldn't work, not really. After a few incidents, the lot of them would be discarded. They wouldn't do that much damage."

"They would do enough," Collis growled. He'd gone pale and tight-lipped. "How many men would lose their hands? Their sight? Die? Even one makes him a murderer."

George nodded thoughtfully. "And me by association, I assume."

Rose gasped. "He wants you blamed!"

Forsythe was examining the plans again. "How many of these crackers did you have made?"

"We upped the order," George said faintly. "Louis gave us a wonderful price. The commemoration was his idea. We'd thought to replace a large percentage of the weapons now in use. Some of them are so old. We had them made for cavalry and infantry. The gleaming damascened barrels, you know. Reflecting the sunlight on the battlefield. 'So intimidating,' Louis said. 'The French will be half-beaten at the sight.'"

George closed his eyes for a moment. When he opened them again, he was no longer the jovial prince Rose had come to know in the last few hours. His eyes had gone cold and icy and his round jaw had attained a firmness that bode Louis Wadsworth no good.

George turned to offer her a deep, heartfelt bow. "My thanks, Rose of the Liars. It seems you have come just in time. The carbines aren't due to be shipped for another three days. You have saved me from a great burden of guilt, and many men from a terrible fate."

He kissed her hand. She couldn't do anything but nod in a short, panicky manner. The Prince squeezed her fingers lightly. "Now, my dears, we must end our adventure. To the palace."

"Georgie!" Forsythe looked up from his fascination with the plans. "Are you sure he actually *made* the guns flawed? Could be this design was accidental, then discarded. Not that I couldn't have done better, mind you. But if you chop off his head before you're sure . . ."

George thought a moment. "Could you tell me? If I find you some of them to try, could you tell me—without blowing yourself up?"

"Oh, too right I could. Let's see . . . to ignite and fire without actually touching the trigger?" He started to wander off again. "I could use a string . . . or a spring! Or a . . ." He disappeared among the chaos.

George nodded shortly. "Come, you two. We'll just duck down through the tunnels back to the palace." Before they managed to find the door, Forsythe appeared once more.

"Presents!" he cackled. He handed Collis a complicated contraption of hinged metal. "You push this release here and it snaps open to become a grappling hook." He scratched his nose. "I think. If I recall." He turned to Rose.

"A gift for the Rose of the Liars," he said, and pressed a small, delicate pistol into Rose's hand. She'd never seen a pistol so small. "It is decorated with the huntress Diana there on the lock plate, and the barrel is damascened with silver. A pistol fit for a lady," Forsythe said proudly. Indeed, it was incredibly delicate and ornate, nearly a shimmering deadly piece of jewelry in its own right.

Still, Rose could not help shrinking from it. "Oh, no thank you, sir!"

Collis shifted his stance. "Rose is afraid of firearms, Mr. Forsythe."

Forsythe wrapped her fingers about the pistol anyway. "It seems to me that when a lady needs a pistol the most, fear of a bit of noise would not be a problem."

Rose laughed shortly. "That is true, sir. But I cannot accept this. It is much too fine for me. If you must give me something, let it be another box of your amazing matches. I'll find them vastly more useful, I'm sure."

Forsythe squinted at her. "If you'll come back and visit me, I'll make sure you never run out."

She smiled. "You're flirting, sir."

He cackled. "You're correct, my dear."

She leaned forward to plant a kiss on his creased cheek.

"Ladies are born, Rose of the Liars," he whispered while she was near. "Born, not made. And you, my dear, are a lady born."

She pulled away to gaze at him questioningly, but he was gone, wandering through his stacks of books and other objects like a man lost in the forest.

"Now where did I put those breeches? I know I saw them last week. . . ."

The Prince's vow to "duck back down through the tunnels back to the palace" was an understatement. St. James's Palace was far from the Tower and would take much longer to traverse than their previous journey.

"I know a shortcut," George assured them, and led the way once more.

The carved designations to the tunnels made no sense to Collis, and he worried. "But they aren't supposed to," claimed George, "or just anyone could find their way into the palace! If you don't know the code, you'll just wander around down here until you die."

That was just what Collis was afraid of.

Rose set an exhausting pace. "Louis knows we have the plans," she insisted. "We need to get His Highness to safety and turn the Liars loose on Louis's factory." She'd taken Collis's hand, his left one, for a moment and gazed into his eyes. "I don't want those guns to reach our soldiers' hands, do you?"

So Collis followed. And he worried.

Especially when he saw George's "shortcut." They were stopped at a gaping break in the tunnel, their toes hanging off a ledge that dropped to darkness. Collis heard water running—nay, rushing—below them. He gritted his teeth. "What. Is. This?"

"The Tyburn," George said airily.

"There is no Tyburn any longer," Rose pointed out.

"Oh, it's here. It's merely been paved over, like the Fleet River turned to Fleet Street." George leaned out to hold the lantern over the water. Rose made a protesting noise and Collis grabbed the royal coattails before the royal drowning took place.

"See?" George held the lantern to one side. Collis and Rose could see large, heavy iron rings the size of dinner plates set horizontally into the stone, only a crescent remaining exposed like the rungs of a ladder. The whole thing reminded Collis of the bare ribs of some serpentine beast.

"You hold on, and step on them," George told them. "There's a ledge that runs alongside the water. We can travel due south, right to the palace." He sounded sublimely confident.

Collis wasn't so sure. "Why not stay in the tunnel?"

George handed the lantern to him and swung out into the river tunnel, his chubby fists clinging to the rusting rings. "Can't get there from here," he chuckled, and began to grunt his way down the line of rings.

They had no choice but to follow. "Can you manage?" Collis asked Rose.

She nodded wearily. "Just don't drop the bloomin' light."

Collis obediently hooked the wire handle of the lantern to his waist. Then he moved it slightly to the right—away from the "Etheridge jewels" as Rose called it. Despite his worry, he grinned at the memory.

At the bottom of the rings, there was indeed a ledge running alongside the water. It was raised not quite a foot above the waterline. George frowned. "I don't remember the river being so high before." He straightened his cuffs. "Oh, well, only a few more miles to go." He took the lantern from Collis and took the lead.

It may have been only a few miles, but to Rose it felt endless. She'd had only a few hours of sleep in the past few days, and her shoulder burned like fire. She wanted no more of tunnels and darkness. Especially dark, tunneling *rivers*. The ledge was no wider than a footpath, so she kept one hand trailing along the wall so she didn't misstep. The water rushing past alongside her reminded her very forcefully that she'd never learned to swim.

George, however, seemed to be having fun again. "I'm building a grand park just above us here," he informed them, his voice raised over the constant rush of water. "It will be surrounded by the finest homes and have an ornamental lake fed by this very river." He looked over his shoulder at Rose. "I haven't named the lake yet. Any suggestions?"

He wanted ideas from her? Now? "I—I'll have to think on it," she said faintly. That seemed to satisfy him and he trundled happily on. Princes were so odd!

An hour later, the river was so loud that Rose began to wonder if she'd gone deaf, for she could hear nothing else—not their footfalls or her own breathing or heartbeat.

Collis turned to say something to her, but she didn't hear. At that moment, she realized that her feet were wet from more than spray. There was an inch of water coming over the ledge!

Her horrified gaze shot up to meet Collis's equally appalled one in the dimness. Rose lost his next words in the rumble that slowly grew, traveling right through them, vibrating teeth and inner ears.

In front of Rose the Prince whirled to gaze back down the tunnel past them, his face slack with horror. "The rain!" His shout was a mere whisper. "The storm!"

Flood. Rose picked up her skirts and ran without a word, Collis right behind her. The Prince ran ahead, kicking up his thick legs like a carriage horse. The lantern wobbled, creating confusion and shadows in their vision, but it didn't matter. There was only one direction in which to run.

The only question was . . . how far until the next ladder?

The water, fed from a thousand streaming drains set into a hundred streets, rose so rapidly that it soon reached her ankles. Her skirts, sodden and heavy, wrapped around her legs under the water like some sort of subterranean beast, ready to pull her off the ledge and down into the depths for its tea.

Ahead, the glowing blob that represented the Prince stopped. Rose would have screamed at him to keep going, had she the breath to so much as whisper. Why had he paused? Was he ill? Heart seizure came to mind instantly. *Oh, bugger, we've killed the Prince!*

The answer came when she saw him rise from the water, his lantern drifting upward in jerking motions. Had he found a way up and out?

"The ring ladder!" Collis shouted back to her. "We can make it!"

He sounded so sure to Rose's air-starved mind. Who was he trying to fool? She was going to die sometime in the next five steps. Yet somehow she was suddenly there, clinging to a rusting iron ring that led somewhere blessedly up.

Collis clambered past her to take the lantern before George fell from his one-handed grip. With his bad arm hooked through a ring, he hoisted the Prince higher. Below him, Rose kicked her skirts aside to feel for the rings with her feet. The freezing water was past her knees, pulling at her heavy skirts like a winch.

So cold. Her mind felt slow, like a stream choked by swiftly forming ice. She could hear little over the rush of the water, but Collis and the Prince seemed to be having a bit of trouble with the climb.

The roar of the water suddenly swelled to nearly drown out her very thoughts. The current yanked her feet from beneath her and jerked her arms to full extension.

She watched with horror as her numb fingers began to loosen their hold on the gritty iron ring. *"Collis!"* She knew she was screaming, but she couldn't hear her own voice.

Oh, God. Which hand would let go first, the left or the right?

Ah, the left, of course. Always weaker, the left hand. Just like Collis, except that Collis's left hand was stronger than both of hers, for all the damage. Collis's left hand.

Her panicked ricocheting thoughts suddenly recalled the previous day, when she'd pressed Collis's hand to her breast. The left or the right? She watched her right hand's grip begin to slip. *The dirty rotter,* she thought with hysteria. That had been his right hand after all. She called for him, over and over. *Collis, Collis, Collis. Rose, Rose—*

"Rose!" Collis's bellow sounded over even the rush of the water. She blinked at him. The lantern must be fixed somewhere above them, for light was shining on his dripping hair like a halo.

"Rose, help me!" Collis was halfway in the water, hanging from the ladder with one hand fisted around a ring, muscles bulging beneath his wet shirt. His other arm was stretched out, his big hand clamped around her wrist.

"Rose, I can't hold you! Wrap your hands around my wrist!"

Poor Collis. Her thoughts moved like cold jelly. It was true. His left hand wasn't much good for holding. He dropped things all the time. He hated dropping things. So embarrassing. She understood that. She'd broken many a dish and vase during her days as a clumsy, nearsighted housemaid.

He didn't want to drop her. She saw her wet wrist emerging from his grip, one fragment of an inch at a time. Oh, no. He was going to be so upset.

Poor Collis.

Chapter Sixteen

———————— ❖ ————————

Collis was close to panic. He was losing her. Oh-dear-God-in-heaven, he was losing her! He'd tried pulling her to him, but his bloody hand couldn't seem to hold and pull at the same time. He'd almost let go.

He willed himself to tighten his grip, no matter if he broke her wrist, but he couldn't feel her, couldn't even see their hands in the rising water. She went under, her dark hair disappearing beneath the darker water. For one eternal fraction of a second, he couldn't even be sure he still held her. But then the agonizing pull on his other stretched arm assured him that he did. She emerged from the water, bobbing up with a gasp he saw more than heard. He watched in horror as her wrist emerged still farther from his grip.

"Rose, you have to help me! Help me, Rose!"

She turned dull eyes to his, blinking sluggishly against the drops hitting her face. Her lips moved. *Collis.*

"Rose, snap out of it, damn it!" Collis cried, his

voice hoarse with fear. "Are you a hothouse flower, to give up after a little chill?"

A spark lit her eyes for a moment at his taunt. Good. "Common as a weed, isn't that the way of it?" He watched her struggle to draw her other hand against the current to grip his. It slipped away, circling his wrist like a delicate manacle, then falling away. He was losing her.

"Come on, Thorny Rose!" he shouted. "What, can't you handle a bit of water without a mop in your hands? Poor little Rose, has to struggle so hard," he mocked viciously. Her hand rose again, creeping toward his. She faltered. He'd thought he couldn't be more afraid, yet every moment drove him deeper into panic. "I'll let the Liars know you gave up, Rose! I'll tell Clara you quit on her!"

Light flared in her eyes and he saw her hand wrap firmly around his wrist. He pulled again, and this time she came with him, closer, closer, until he could drag them both one rung higher on the ladder. Then another. Their feet free of the water at last, he crushed her to him with his aching right arm.

She hung limply, so cold—and nearly unconscious by the look of her. He pressed his face into her icy neck for the duration of one broken breath. *Safe.*

His precious, beloved Rose, by God, safe in his arms.

Rose awoke in a nest of warmth and softness. Soft bed, soft, warm covers, coals glowing on the hearth before her. She blinked and rolled her head on the pillow. She was lying in a large chamber draped in absolutely miles of sapphire-colored satin and furnished in gleaming black wood. The sensuous combination made her think of both fornication and sloth. Given time, she could probably come up with a few more sins.

What a singularly wicked room. Luxurious to the extreme, but wicked. Were those golden wrist cuffs hanging from the bedpost?

"It looks like a whore's boudoir," she muttered to herself as she propped herself up on her elbows. Her head pounded.

"It is. Mrs. Blythe's Palace of Pleasure, to be exact."

Collis unfolded his long self from a purple upholstered chair by the fire. He was dressed in black trousers that made him look lean and dangerous, topped by a flowing shirt made of silk that draped over his broad shoulders and clung to his flat stomach. She didn't know where he came by such clothing, but as her throat went dry, she abruptly decided that he shouldn't be let out in public wearing it. He came to sit on the mattress beside her, as familiar as a lover. Rose shifted uneasily away.

What could he mean by such an easy distance? She looked down to see that she herself was wearing a filmy nightdress that looked perfectly at home in this den of sin. Were those her nipples showing through? Hastily she sat up to grab the linens and hide what the gown failed to cover.

A large warm hand came up to cradle her jaw gently for a moment, then her forehead.

"No fever," Collis said softly.

His touch was so soothing. She wanted to lean into him, give herself up to his care . . . but this was Collis. She didn't dare. She pulled her spine straight with effort, belatedly remembering to cover her front with the bed linens.

One thing at a time. "Mrs. Blythe?"

He allowed his hand to drop away slowly. Then he grinned. "Do you mean to say there is something about the Liars you don't know? Our patroness, of sorts. Mrs. Blythe is the proud owner of this fine establishment, and has previously been of aid to the Liars. James and I came here once in pursuit of a missing prostitute."

Click. "Oh, yes. Fleur."

"Mrs. Blythe has since been useful to Dalton's search for French recruiting agents." He frowned at her worriedly.

"You aren't going to lose consciousness again, are you?"

"Lose consciousness? Did I do that before?" She blinked at him. His gray eyes looked so . . . concerned? And close. Very, very close. "The only time you've ever been this close to me was when . . ."

"When you were tossing my arse to the mat," he reminded her softly.

"Well, yes." She drew in a breath, unable to look away from his eyes. "This is very odd."

He nodded slowly once. "And then earlier this evening."

She wet her dry lips with the tip of her tongue. "This evening?"

"Yes. You needed bathing, you know. We both did."

The tub by the fire. White-hot horror seized her. "You *bathed* me?" Various humiliating and titillating images flashed across her mind. Oh, no.

But she had undoubtedly been bathed. *Oh, yes. Sorry you missed it?*

His eyes narrowed and his smile became very wicked. "What, you don't think I could handle a flannel and soap and you, all at the same time?" He breathed a deeply satisfied sigh. "Good times, Briar Rose. Very good times."

She punched him hard, right in the pectoral. "I'll kill you if you ever breathe a word—"

He backed off and rubbed his chest with his good hand, his smile gone wry. "I didn't bathe you, if it makes you feel any better. A couple of the ladies here did that. I was only called on to help put you in bed when they were done." He smiled. "Still, a very nice time." He leaned closer and sniffed. "Fresh Rose. A favorite perfume the world over."

She snorted and made another fist. He grinned at her, but there was something in his eyes . . .

"The mission!"

Collis shook his head. "I sent word to Denny. He'll bring Lord Liverpool and some of the guard here. We can't take the chance of George being seen out on the streets." He smiled down at her. "And I, for one, do not want to see another tunnel for, oh, perhaps the rest of my life."

Rose relaxed slightly. But Collis still looked worried. About what? They'd made it free of Louis's men, free of the tunnels—she and Collis and George.

George. She sat up again in horror. "Oh, God. His Highness! There's something wrong, isn't there?"

Collis put a gentle hand on her shoulders and pushed her back down. "He's fine. He had his bath and his dinner and now he's being entertained by Mrs. Blythe herself."

"Entertained?" The mental image of George in the throes of entertainment—no, best not to dwell there. "Ew."

Collis raised a brow. "They've been at it for hours. Still going strong at his age. One must admire his stamina." He shrugged and leaned back to wrap his good arm around his raised knee. "Probably something in the air. This place is alive with Eros. I've heard no less than four orgasms in the last hour." He waved his hand around the room. "One from each wall. Mrs. Blythe does excellent business here."

A knock came at the door. Collis rose to answer it. "Food!"

He turned back to her with a tray. "I have tea and toast and ginger jam," he said brightly.

Rose wrapped herself in a blanket from the bed, feeling much recovered at the thought of food. She glanced askance at the tray and shook her head. "Spare me the aristocracy. All that money and no idea how to eat. Where's the meat? The mash? Crikey, no beer?"

He looked down at the ladylike fare arranged on the tray. It was the sort of thing his mother had always asked for when she was sick. "Damn, I wish I'd thought of beer."

She sighed. "Never mind." She snapped up the toast and bit down on it with predatory accuracy.

"Uh, Rose?"

"Mmm?"

The first piece of toast was gone. He handed her the second, mindful of his fingers. "Are you hungry?"

She swallowed, then snorted. "I am not hungry. I am famished. What's today?"

"Thursday."

"Ah. Well, let me ask you—if you had hardly eaten since Monday, would you be happy with tea and toast and bloody rotten ginger *jam*?"

He had eaten. He'd had a very fine meal in the bordello's kitchen while Rose was recovering. "Meat it is." He was nearly out the door when he turned back. "Do you fancy it cooked, or should I just drive the beast directly up the stairs?"

He shut the door on the flying toast and her reluctant laughter.

Rose stood in the center of the room after Collis left her, feeling strangely on edge. Her chill was gone, her strength was nearly returned—or it would be when she got a meal in her—and George was safe.

What was wrong?

Oh, dear. Collis. She sat down on the edge of the velvet chair by the fire, dropping her forehead onto her hands. Was Collis being kind to her now? The very concept turned her world a bit sideways. Her rivalry with Collis had become rather like a stone wall she had leaned on for months. Now that it was gone, what was she to think?

Was she expected to become his friend?

Impossible. You could never bear to be his friend.

But why not? Because he was male? She was friends with the other male trainees, wasn't she?

Then was it because he was highborn? Yet she was friends with Lady Etheridge and Lady Raines, wasn't she?

Because you are in love with him?

"Oh." She pressed her palms to her suddenly burning cheeks. "Oh, that."

Oh, yes. Her great, consuming unrequited obsession with Collis Tremayne. Quite. Of course, she'd tried to hide it, even from herself. Had almost succeeded, too, until this mad adventure of theirs. She ought to be surprised, even stunned, by the realization, but she honestly couldn't stoop to be so blind about herself. From the first flush of attraction, she'd eaten, slept, and breathed Collis and only Collis. His strength, his weaknesses, his every victory, his smallest defeat, all neatly cataloged in her memory, hoarded like a miser's pennies.

Well, she was simply going to continue to hide it. She could falsify friendship as well as enmity, couldn't she? And really, what was the chance that they would ever go on a mission together again? Collis was destined to work the highest end of Society, while she was slotted to use her servitude skills to gather information from the other side of the silver salver. She'd get through this mission and—

Someone knocked on her door. Rose dried her eyes swiftly, then answered to find a girl in familiar black and white garb outside. Good heavens, even whores had housemaids?

The girl entered, her arms laden with a rainbow selection of gowns. She spread each one lovingly on the wide bed, then turned to smile brightly at Rose. "Madame said thank you so much for coming and bringing your friend. Madame said since your dress was ruined you was to take your pick. Aren't they tremendous?"

"Ah . . . yes, tremendous." Tremendously awful. There wasn't one dress there that wasn't cut down to *there* or up to *there*. And that one—yes, it was both. Rose held one up to her. The fabric was fine, oh yes, but there simply wasn't enough of it. "I hate to trouble you further, but . . . do you think you might be able to find me something a bit more . . . demure?"

"What's that mean?"

Well, she hadn't known that word, either, until quite recently. "It means . . . seemly, or modest."

Comprehension lit the plain maid's face. "Oh, you is wantin' a virgin's dress!" She smiled brightly. "We have them, for when a new girl comes in. Them's the finest, anyway. The gents do love their virgins."

"Indeed," Rose said faintly. "I don't suppose you could locate one that hasn't been . . . used?"

The girl gathered up her charges and trotted away, soon to return with a dress that was only virginal in the sense that it was white. Rose held it up to herself, relieved at least to find it cut decently across the bodice and with no revealing slits in the skirt. "Thank you," she told the girl warmly. "This will do very well indeed." Unless of course she ever wanted to leave the confines of her room. Or look at herself in a mirror.

Still, it was better than donning her river-soaked gabardine. She put the dress on, a little disconcerted to find the maid performing intimate tasks such as buttoning the back and then adjusting her breasts within the bodice with swift, efficient hands. "Er, thank you. I can manage on my own now."

Except for one simple fact. How was she going to face Collis now?

Chapter Seventeen

———————— ◆ ————————

By the time Collis returned with her meal, Rose was dressed and the maid was gone. When he uncovered the plate this time, with a typical Collis flourish, it was to reveal a savory feast worthy of George himself. "Oh, heaven," Rose breathed, and fell to.

She was halfway to emptying the plate when she thought to ask him if he wanted any. She looked up to find him watching her with hooded eyes, one hand covering his mouth pensively. She put down her fork, abruptly aware of her manners or lack thereof. He must be appalled. After all, he was used to ladies, not trough-feeders.

She wiped her lips delicately with her napkin and straightened her spine. "How long do you think it will take for Lord Liverpool to come?"

Collis grunted. "He ought to have been here by now. Perhaps his attendants are giving Denny difficulty. Still, I gave him enough information to stop the shipments in good time. I don't know about you, but I'm in no hurry to face Dalton and Simon."

"So it's over, then?" The next bite was cut small with precise movements of the knife and fork. Forcing herself to chew slowly was agony, for the beef was tender and nicely seasoned, nearly as good as Kurt's.

"Seems so."

"Do you think we'll be in terrible trouble?"

His gaze didn't so much as flicker. "Hmm-mm."

It seemed nothing was going to distract Collis from watching her. Finally, tiny bite after tiny bite, she finished. With excruciating dignity, she refrained from licking her fingers to catch the last taste of that heavenly gravy. She looked at Collis again. His expression hadn't changed.

Her patience snapped. "What is it? Have I turned green?"

"Where did you get that gown?"

She raised her chin defiantly. "It was the most decent thing I could find in this place." She tightened the shawl over her shoulders and across her breasts. "Besides, I am well covered."

She stood, then turned to stride from the table. Collis nearly swallowed his tongue. Her torso might be shielded by the wool, but there was nearly nothing standing between his gaze and the rest of her. When she began to pace before the fire, the sheer gown very nearly disappeared altogether.

He ought to say something. He truly ought to. A gentleman would never . . .

She turned to pass before the flames again. Oh, he was going to burn for this. His trousers tightened and he shifted unconsciously, never taking his gaze from the lithe figure before him. She was perfect. It no longer mattered to him that her curves were not generous. Seeing her lean, limber form in motion belied her femininity in a way he'd never had the pleasure to see before. She was as graceful as a dancer, as fluid as a huntress. She was as supple and strong as a feline. If she suddenly developed the ability to leap to high places he would not have been at all surprised.

Oh yes, he was in love all right.

She must have caught a hint of something in his gaze, for she halted. Luckily for him and only him, she halted directly before the fire.

"What is it? Why do you look at me so?"

With great effort, considering the breathless need roiling through him, Collis waved a negligent hand in the air. "Only staring into the fire, thinking. Don't mind me."

With a puzzled frown only slightly marred by suspicion, Rose returned to her pacing. Collis nearly went down on his knees in thanks.

"Is George still occupied with Mrs. Blythe?"

"Hmm? Who? Oh, yes. He's having the time of his life, apparently."

"He'll be sorry to return to the palace, I imagine."

"I won't. George is having entirely too much fun with this mad gadabout. He's even taken to regaling the wh—ladies with tales of our subterranean adventure."

Rose laughed shortly. "Appropriately embellished, I'm sure. Or is he telling them about our near death in the Tyburn?"

"Why, Rose! Do you mean to say that you didn't

find the tunnels entertaining? I'm shocked." Collis
smiled at her. Once he'd managed to look away from
her . . . assets, he found himself surprised by the rest
of her. "What have you done with your hair?"

It was piled high, with curly bits on the side doing
interesting things to her wide eyes and sharp cheek-
bones. Even her lips looked newly lush and pink, as if
she'd been biting them. Or been thoroughly
kissed. . . .

"My hair?" She touched it self-consciously. "It
was the maid they sent me. It didn't seem wise to ar-
gue with her. She wielded a mean bristle brush."

"You look . . . very well, indeed." She looked confused. True, she wasn't used to compliments from
him. Perhaps he ought to change the subject. "How
old are you?"

The question came out more abruptly than he in-
tended. He'd always thought her his own age. Now
she looked soft and dewy, and he was going to get
himself in serious trouble if he didn't think about
something else. Now.

"I am four and twenty. How old are you?"

He was obscurely relieved. "Nine and twenty."

She nodded. "Oh." She sat in the purple chair,
hands folded in her lap.

Silence fell, a silence in which Collis fancied he
could hear her heart beating from halfway across the
room. Or was that his own throbbing in his ears?
*Don't think about throbbing, you fool! Think about
snow, and wet rainy London winters that go on and
on. . . .*

His blood cooled slightly. Excellent. Of course, he'd become a master of control in the last year, hadn't he? He hadn't been close to a woman in a long time.

None but Rose. She'd been close to him, had fought him and learned with him and depended on him when in danger. Abruptly, he was very glad he'd exerted that self-control. There was no one else in the world who suited him so perfectly.

"Do you have any family?" The question came out of nowhere, spurred by panic, not curiosity. Yet he did want to know more about her. Maybe talking would work better than silence. If he was talking and listening, maybe he would be able to keep from saying what he was very sure she had no desire to hear.

I love you.

The time wasn't right. She was used to seeing him as Collis the rival, Collis the flirt. Collis the charmer. Well then, he would attach her affections using the skills of a lifetime. He would *charm* her into falling in love with him.

She would never know what hit her.

Once she was wound up around his finger like the ladies at court—*then* he would declare his love. Pity she was far too sensible to faint. It would have put a nice finish on his fantasy. Oh, well. He wouldn't want her any other way.

She was looking at him oddly but answered willingly enough. She must be as uncomfortable as he was, of course for entirely different reasons, he was sure.

"Not anymore. My parents passed on some years ago." She played with the end fringe of her borrowed shawl, not looking at him.

"I don't have any siblings," he offered.

"I know."

"You do?" Collis frowned. "What else do you know?"

"Well, quite a lot, actually." She looked uncomfortable. "See here, Collis. I know more than I likely should. But people talk around me as if I'm not there, even his lordship and Milady Clara."

Collis narrowed his eyes to hide his glee. She was curious about him. It was a good sign. "What's my second name?"

"Clarence," she replied promptly. Her nose wrinkled. "My sympathies."

"What is my favorite pudding?"

"Blueberry Fool."

"Hmph. Everyone at the club knows that. What color is my bedchamber at Etheridge House?"

"Cream and green."

"What kind of dog did I have when I was a boy?"

"Wolfhound. Named 'Wolfie.' Not terribly original, you know."

Collis covered his face with his hands. This was far too good to be true. "Who . . . was . . . my . . . mother's . . . companion?"

"Hmm. That one I don't know."

"Ha!" Collis jumped up to point his finger at her playfully. "Gretchen! She was from—"

"Germany. I know. She came in Princess Caroline's entourage when George was to be married, but she left court because she was so fond of your mother. But I never knew her name."

Collis sank limply into his chair once more. She was perfect. "Is there anything you don't know?"

Yes. Why was it that they kept finding themselves alone in rooms with beds in them? Rose kept her gaze from flicking to the great sinful nest of pillows and silk, but that didn't mean that it didn't loom large in her awareness.

No, the bleedin' thing was like a magnet, pulling her mind to thoughts of happily sweaty exploration of every inch of Collis's muscled body. She rubbed both hands over her face. Stop it. Stop playing out those thoughts in your head. Stop thinking about him kissing his way down your neck until he gets to your toes—

Stop it!

Collis watched Rose cover her face and sighed in disappointment that her pert bosom was hidden by her forearms. Ah, well, back to those long legs perfectly revealed by the firelight. Elegant legs, trim and traced with supple muscle like a high-blooded horse. Long, elegant legs that led up to a firm bottom he knew well from Rose's many hours spent in boyish trousers.

Ah, those lovely, worn old trousers that had clung like the finest silk to her pert, curved rear. A man could learn to appreciate a less curvaceous form, it seemed. All it took was a bit of keen observation. An eye for the subtler signs of femininity—a taut, supple waist, a high, small bosom, and a pair of legs that went from here to Paris.

Those legs around him, wrapping tightly to his waist like heavenly bonds that no man in his right mind would try to escape . . . those lean thighs astride him, riding him athletically, tirelessly, forever . . . oh, dear God, he was in deep trouble here.

"There is one thing that I would like to know," Rose said slowly. "What is it like to be in battle?"

Chapter Eighteen

———— ◆ ————

Whatever Collis had been expecting, it wasn't that. The question hit him like a blow in the belly. With all she knew, didn't she also know about the silent agreement never to mention the war? Once he'd come home from Chelsea Hospital, no one in the Etheridge household had ever asked him about it.

But for Rose, of course. Too forthright by half. Perhaps it was time he acknowledged that last battle in his own mind. He rubbed the back of his neck, trying to find the words to explain.

"Did you hear about how I was wounded?"

"You fell from your horse?"

He laughed shortly. "I was blown from my horse." He rubbed the shoulder of his numb arm with his good hand. "The battlefield isn't like the stories, you know. It isn't grand. It isn't stirring. It isn't anything but awful, loud, and dangerous. Cannon booming, muskets firing, horses and men screaming and screaming . . ." He put his hand over his face. Then he raised his head, blinking quickly. "The first time I went into battle, I was worried about losing my favorite horse. Five minutes into it, I was worried about losing my friends. Then I forgot to worry about anything but losing my life."

"Yet you stayed and fought."

"I did. I made it through that battle, and the next, and the next. I lost count really, with all the big battles and minor skirmishes. . . . I don't even know how many weeks passed. I'm sure I was keeping count somehow, but I don't remember. There was a great deal of drinking going on at that point." He drew in his breath and tried to send her an impish grin. He was fairly sure it came out gruesome.

"And then the cannonball bounced this way instead of that—they bounce, you know. Just like great India rubber balls. They don't even look all that dangerous, as if they were too slow to hurt anyone. Yet one cannonball can take out twenty men and horses before it comes still." He sat up straighter and looked into Rose's sympathetic hazel eyes. "I woke up in a tented wagon, jostling my way off the line. I remember the hospital tent, and the surgeon, and then they started giving me the poppy syrup and things were properly blurred after that. I tried to tell them my arm didn't hurt, although my ribs were cracked and it hurt fiercely just to breathe. But I kept thinking, if my arm is broken, it ought to hurt.

"I woke up in the Chelsea Hospital, back in London, and the first thought I had was that they had cut it off, because I couldn't feel a thing." He laughed shortly. "Ironic, because when I spoke to a bloke who'd truly lost his arm, he claimed he could still feel his."

Rose was watching him still, her hands gone quiet in her lap and her eyes shining damply. She opened her mouth to speak. "I—"

From the other side of the nearest wall came a great moan. Then another, louder. Rose pulled back, alarmed, as the moans multiplied and amplified, accompanied by a great rhythmic slamming of the bed to the wall, culminating in a thunderous orgasm that shook the very flames in the candles.

Sudden silence descended, leaving only the faint tinkling of the settling glassware behind. Rose's expression was priceless. Her jaw hung open and her eyes were wide and a very hot flush had crept over her cheeks. Collis threw back his head to release a great shout of laughter, feeling suddenly freed from a black and choking darkness.

Rose put both palms to her hot cheeks. "I—I was going to say," she raised her voice over his laughter, "that I'm sorry for asking so many questions. I must be making you feel like an insect under a quizzing glass."

Collis let his laughter go with a relieved sigh and relaxed back into his chair. "Stop apologizing. You are damn clever at gathering information and putting together clues, and you've a memory like a poacher's trap, for God's sake! These are valuable gifts and you should be proud to own them."

"Gifts?"

He laughed. "Even that alleged invisibility of yours, if you like. Being ignored has definite advantages." He looked her over with a puzzled air. "Damned if I know how anyone could ignore you, though."

The remark was meant casually enough, in relation to his current state of semi-arousal, that he was surprised by the intense look of longing that came over her face. She looked so lost, so hungry—

He was on his feet in one beat of his heart. He was standing before her by the next one. "What is it?" Damn the betraying hoarseness of his voice. "What is wrong, my Briar Rose?"

She blinked once, hard, then again, but she was not able to fight back the sheen of tears in her eyes. "You never have, have you? You've never ignored me, not for a single moment."

That surprised a low laugh from him. "Never." Ignore that fire, that sizzling suppleness, that flash of shadowy rebellion within her that matched his own so well?

"Why you?"

"You and I—we are the same," he whispered.

With a swift duck of his head, he kissed her. Her lips parted in surprise. He could feel his own breath invade her with her sharp gasp. He turned his hand free upon her. That hair—that skin—

He would never get enough.

Rose couldn't breathe, didn't care, couldn't even remember the importance of breath—*Collis*. He pulled her close even as she stepped closer. She was quivering, still shocked into stillness under his assault. "Kiss me," he murmured into her mouth. *Please. Kiss me now. Kiss me back. Kiss me hard—*

She kissed him back. Her arms wrapped themselves around his neck and she threw herself into the kiss as if he were saving her from drowning once again. He stumbled, she followed, and they arrived together on the carpet as if by design.

He was hot to the touch, hot to the taste. Rose slid her hands beneath the open collar of his shirt even as his right hand slid to the nape of her neck. Her shawl fell to the floor, freeing her breasts to press to his broad chest with only two thin layers of fabric between. It was two too many.

She was not soft and pliant beneath him. She was supple steel on fire and he was her blacksmith. The taste of her mouth was wild and unexpectedly hot, as if all her prim competence was a shell around a molten core.

He had made her so. She had melted at his hand. Possessive satisfaction flooded him, like hot brandy over the fire of his need. The heat rose within him, burning up every thought but one. *My Rose. Mine.*

Then she uttered a small, broken noise. Unmistakably one of pain. Collis realized that he had embraced her with both arms, the good and the bad, and he was gripping her with bruising force. He released her instantly. Chagrin nearly doused his desire as he scrambled back from her. He stood and backed away, knees nearly shaking from interrupted desire.

"I'm sorry."

Chapter Nineteen

◆

Louis Wadsworth stood at the window, surveying the kingdom of his factory from the tower of his office. Wadsworth & Son, Munitions, was spread out before him like a feudal keep of old. His father, the unlamented Edward Wadsworth, had entertained delusions of nobility, declaring that if he had been born centuries ago, he would have been made a lord for the power and wealth he'd accumulated. It had been promises of just that sort of reward under Napoleon that had lured Louis's father into treason in the first place.

Frankly, Louis couldn't care less about such things. Oh, he admired Napoleon's initiative and sheer nerve and certainly considered the British aristocracy to be a vast pool of leeches. His own king and prince were beneath his disdain. All that rampant emotionalism—Prinny with his ladyloves and his art and music.

Louis truly respected only one thing. Money. There was only one reason that he'd bothered to continue his father's plotting. For the shipment of

"George IV Commemorative Carbines" he was going to be paid very handsomely. Twice.

He very nearly smiled at the thought. He only wished he'd had time to sound out other bidders. The Americans likely would have chipped in as well. Ah, well, his father had never possessed any real vision.

The thought of being caught had never entered the picture until he'd seen the mangled mahogany case on the floor of his study. But nothing had come of it yet. The men responsible could be mere thieves or might be holding out for some sort of blackmail.

Unless it truly had been Collis Tremayne in his study in the night. The heir to Etheridge . . . no, he was no common parlor thief. Etheridge was on the side of justice and right. Incorruptible, Louis's father had said. Louis wasn't sure. Every man had a price, after all. It was merely a matter of being willing to pay it.

A tap came at his door. Louis clasped his hands behind his back. "Enter," he called without turning.

"Sir?"

Ah, it was the minion with initiative. Louis exhaled. "Back so soon? Did you bring me something nice?"

"Yes, sir. I caught a boy just before he knocked on the door to the house. He had him a message from a gent what was staying at Mrs. Blythe's."

Mrs. Blythe? "How . . . coarse."

The minion didn't quite snicker. "Yes, sir. The note came in two parts. One for the manservant, and another for him what to pass on to Lord Liverpool."

Louis hungered for that second message. He closed his eyes and savored the anticipation. "And where are the two messages now?"

"I let the boy deliver the one to the valet bloke. It didn't say nothing but where the man was. I kept the other for you."

"And the boy won't talk?"

"Not anymore, sir."

"Excellent. You may put the letter on my desk." Louis didn't turn until he heard the man shuffle from the room and close the door. Then Louis turned to regard the folded missive with cool restraint and hot, avid eyes.

After a moment, he allowed himself to open the letter to Lord Liverpool and read. It was lovely. It was everything he'd thought it would be. Of course, it mentioned no names or definite facts, but when one knew more than the letter writer, one could read between the lines. After all, he was the one telling this story, wasn't he?

Mrs. Blythe's. Louis knew of her, of course, although he'd never entered her establishment. His tastes were much more refined now. So Mrs. Blythe had an influential guest, hmm?

With precise pleasure, he rang for his secretary. "That fellow who was just here—I wish him to be silenced. And send me someone else . . . someone thorough. I have a bit of work to be done."

"I hurt you," Collis blurted from his safe and lonely distance. "I'm sorry."

Rose was still sprawled on the floor, but now half-risen on her elbows. Her expression was part aroused smolder and part confused irritation, all directed at him. Her never-terribly-modest gown was rucked up to her knees and hung half off one ivory shoulder. Her hair was mussed and her lips swollen from his kiss.

She looked a proper mess. She'd never been more beautiful to him. He held out his hand to aid her to her feet. She batted him aside and rose on her own. "Don't be an ass, Collis."

"I'm sorry. I never should have—I should know that I can't—"

Something in his tone caught her attention. She looked up swiftly. "You can't?" Her fine brows drew together. "Does that mean you haven't, ah," she waved a hand vaguely at the floor where they had just lain, "since you were wounded?"

He shook his head. She had a right to know. "No."

For some odd reason, she smiled. It was a swift, happy expression, gone almost before he registered it. She then folded her arms over her barely covered bodice and regarded him somberly. "So all the flirting?"

He shrugged. "Smoke without the fire."

"No fire at all?"

He growled. "None! Satisfied?"

"Oh, not nearly." She tapped her fingertips meditatively. "I happened to have observed that all the pertinent equipment is in working order, yes?"

Her wording surprised a bark of laughter from him. "The equipment is working, yes." Oh, God yes. The way her crossed arms braced her pretty bosom was providing abundant fuel for the "equipment," even now. It was very nearly enough to encourage furthering the conversation, if only to continue the utterly delectable view.

"So the problem is?"

He drew his gaze from her décolletage with a sigh. "The problem, Rose," he clapped his hand to his wounded arm, "is that I cannot control this piece of dead wood enough to trust myself not to hurt someone." The last words were betrayed by his hoarseness. Damn his voice for breaking.

Rose crossed the distance between them in a bound. Her supple arms surrounded him, pulling him close for comfort he'd never dared ask for.

Rose closed her eyes when she felt his arm come around her. She'd embraced him impulsively, pulled by his pain. Too late, she had worried for her own. But he didn't push her away. Instead, he took that comfort, dropping his face into her neck with a gusting breath that warmed her skin and her heart.

"I would try for you," he whispered.

He was too tall to coddle, though she longed to heal the broken boy within him. He was a man, with a man's touchy pride and walls of stone around his vulnerability.

As their touching flesh warmed, she was distracted by her own still-tingling state of arousal. His body was so hard against hers, his muscles and broad chest like rock to her softer flesh. A man, indeed.

She wanted to be naked with Collis. Now. She wanted to see and touch and kiss and bite every inch of naked Collis.

He barked a short, hard laugh into her neck, making her realize she'd spoken aloud. "Your wish is my command, lady spy." He stripped off his shirt in a single nearly graceful movement, but for the way his damaged arm tangled the matter. She pulled the silk from him the rest of the way, too impatient to wait, and tossed it to the floor. He moved to take her in his arms again, but she pressed both hands to his chest.

"Wait. I want to look."

Emotions flickered in those gray eyes. Surprise, arousal, and . . . wariness. She must erase that. "This is not the first time I've seen you thus."

"True."

"I like your chest." She spread her hands wide over the thick muscles covering his torso. He sucked in a breath when she dug her nails in slightly. She'd wanted to do this for so long . . . maybe all her life. The gleaming flesh she had only allowed herself to fight, now she was allowed to love.

If she died tomorrow, she would be furious with herself for passing up this chance. He didn't love her, of course. She didn't mind. She loved him and that was enough for the moment.

It wasn't as if there was ever going to be another.

Both saddened and liberated by that thought, she stepped back from him. His hand rose as if to reach for her. His one hand.

In a flash, she had understood so much. All those "conquests," all those flirtations—lies. A mask, a fog, to hide his dark and painful insecurity. What a demon for a man to keep inside!

Ah, but then, she was a trained fighter, was she not?

She danced another step away. "Shh."

He obeyed, but dark warning flickered in his gaze. She liked him obedient, she decided. For now. He burned deep, she knew that of him. When he burst into flame—she shivered in anticipation of that erotic danger.

But there was something she must do first. She took the pins from her hair and let it fall. His lips parted at the rich blue-black cascade down her back. Then she pulled slowly at the tiny bows binding the bodice of her "virginal" dress. The silk parted easily, as it was designed to do, so that by the time she'd untied the last one at her waist, her breasts were fully exposed to his hot gaze.

The room was warm, but her nipples crinkled nonetheless as the air caressed them. She refused to shiver, however. Louis had liked her shy and shivering and cowering—she would not shiver with Collis. She would not play shy, pretending she did not want him as badly as he wanted her.

Neither would she declare her love. There would be no point in it, nor any profit. This was a one-night affair. She would not waste precious time with pretense.

With her chin high, she stepped forward once more to rest her right hand on his left shoulder. His left arm showed little difference to the right, thanks to Kurt's strengthening regimen. His flesh was firm and ruddy, his muscles thick and corded. Only his hand seemed different—lifeless and still compared to the flashing competence of the right.

She slid her hand down to entwine her fingers with his stiff ones. He watched this, making as if to pull away. She tightened her grip. "Shh."

She raised both their hands to press a kiss to his fingers. They jerked, a spastic movement that nearly crushed her fingers. She covered it gently with her other hand, as if capturing a wild thing. His gaze was guarded and unsure now, as if he actually feared her rejection. Bloody idiot.

She slid her fingers out from between his in a slow release, enjoying the heat of his hand captured in hers. She spread his palm over her bare breast and closed her eyes, letting the glow of manly warmth ease the ache in her aroused nipple.

"But I cannot feel you," he whispered.

"Selfish thing. *I* can feel *you*." She opened her eyes to smile at him. "Or don't you care?"

He made a confused, frustrated noise. "Of course I care, but how you could enjoy the touch of that dead thing—"

"Dead? When it is as hot as those coals?" She looked down at his sun-darkened fingers spread open over her paler flesh. Lovely. Louis had such soft, white, damp hands. "And this is not a thing. I see strength, and power. This is a warrior's hand. An artist's hand."

"No longer." He almost pulled away then.

She caught him back and pressed him tighter to her. "I like your touch, Collis. This is *you,* not some rock tied to the end of your arm. Perhaps it doesn't work as well as you like, but neither do my eyes. Or do you hold my spectacles against me?"

He smiled slightly, the old roguish Collis appearing for a moment. "I like you in your spectacles. You look so serious and studious. I used to fantasize about taking them off to kiss you."

"What a delightful thought."

He laughed, then gently pulled his hand away. The motion lacked his previous panic, though. "Now who's the selfish one? I'd very much like to feel you now."

"Another charming idea." She dropped her head back and closed her eyes, offering herself freely, delicious anticipation tickling her spine.

She felt the heat of his body as he stepped closer. His right hand came to rest on her other, rather lonely breast. So warm, like the other, but there ended the similarity. Collis Tremayne certainly knew his way around the female nipple.

"Oh, damn," she said softly to the ceiling. "I'm surely in trouble now."

His chuckle swept across her bare neck, awaking new tingles. He kissed them away, never ceasing his teasing, plucking caresses.

"Both hands," she whispered. "'Tis only fair. Two breasts, after all."

"I—I have no control," he protested. "I might hurt you."

"Am I a hothouse flower, then?" she asked, throwing his words back at him.

He laughed. "You remember? I thought you near unconsciousness."

"Touch me, Collis. I am a common weed, a briar, remember? You cannot hurt me."

His left hand came up to rest over her breast. He made no attempt at the subtle skills of the right but only cupped and warmed her with his palm.

"Not a weed. A briar rose. A survivor," he murmured as he tasted the skin of her throat. "Have you ever tried to kill briar roses in a pasture, Rose?" He kissed the spot where her murmur of denial originated. "Hack them, burn them—they grow back more beautiful than ever, blooming like mad, perfuming every breath, until you'd rather let them be than destroy them."

His words nearly brought tears to her eyes. Too close, too vulnerable. *Careful.* She snorted irreverently. "Are you trying to say I've grown on you?"

"I'm trying to say that you are strong, you are lovely, and you smell so damn good—" He wrapped both arms about her waist and slung them both bodily onto the mattress. His left arm held too tightly, but she would have died rather than say so. He growled into her neck, then pulled up to glare into her eyes. "I think you should shut up now . . . until I make you scream."

She gazed up at him saucily. "I double-damn dare you."

He came down upon her even as she rose to meet him. It was like a dance, an ancient dance bred into their bones, each of them exploring the other in a celebration meant from the beginning of time. His hands, both of them, stroked down her body beneath him as he kissed her. Subtle curves, subtle beauty, all the more precious for being his to discover.

"I love your hands on me," she murmured into his lips. "Play me. Let me be your instrument."

Smiling, Collis slipped to one side of her, pressing her body to his length. His left arm supported her and held those pretty breasts arched high for his hungry attention. His right hand was for her. He slid his dancing fingertips down her taut belly to her bare navel. Farther . . . and she shivered in his arms. He took her rigid nipple gently between his teeth just to feel her tremble again.

The quiver traveled through her body, leading his questing hand farther like an arrow pointing his way. The gown only parted so far. He flattened his hand and slid it beneath the fabric, seeking her secret like the spy he was.

Her hips leaped slightly at the touch of his nimble fingers combing into her silky nest. She was so ready to be played by him. He found her sweetly dampened and eager for him. He could drive himself into her now and he knew she would not object.

Later. He was too busy making soft and breathy music fly from her lips. The piano required a delicate touch, a way of sneaking up on the note and making it sound without ringing. Rose was more sensitive than any ivory or ebony keys. With the merest shiver of his fingertips, he found her note and made her sing it.

When her orgasm swept her, he pulled her close and kissed her, taking the music for his own. When he released her, she lay dazed in his arms while final tiny quivers visibly rang through her.

Eventually she caught her breath. Pity. He'd enjoyed watching her pert breasts heave. Then she smiled up at him and slid her hands up his bare chest. "I begin to see where you earned your reputation."

Then, quick as a wink, he found himself on his back on the bed and Rose above him. Laughing in surprise, he was soon sobered by the way she kissed his neck and ear.

Rose was still thrumming from her experience. Her body felt alive and shivery. More. There was more to come and she wanted it. Still, a little demon of competition would not allow her to lie back and let Collis do all the seducing.

She threw one thigh over him and straddled his body, trapping his erection beneath her, yet hiding everything with the skirt that still clung to her hips. His hands began to slide up her legs to her hips, but she pressed them back down to just above her knees. This was her turn. Bare-breasted as a Greek goddess, she pinned him down while she did her best to drive him mad.

His body was like rock and satin and hot embers. She spread her open hands across the breadth of his chest but didn't even begin to cover it. Wide, broad, and strong. On impulse she bent low and bit lightly at his muscular shoulder while she ran her hands between them to stroke his rippling taut stomach.

He grew beneath her, pressing larger and firmer to her center. She couldn't resist a small grind of her hips, just to hear him groan. He did. Satisfied that he was not the only one who could elicit hungry noises, she desisted. There was still so much strong, hard body to explore.

Her fingers encountered the waist of his trousers. *Now that won't do.* Slowly, she unbuttoned his placket while she watched his face. His gray eyes were shadowed and hotly intent and his breath came quickly. His hands tightened on her thighs, but he made no attempt to reroute her intentions.

Smiling, Rose slid back slightly to free his erection

into her hands. When her fingers closed about him, he arched involuntarily beneath her and his head tipped back, eyes closing. Submitting entirely to her whim.

She could get used to that. Then she fell to exploring his sex with all the curiosity of a woman all too tired of her own dreams. He was thick and hot and filled her two hands. When she tightened her curious grip, he flexed against it and grew yet more before her wide eyes. Her own body throbbed right back in response.

Oh, heavens. This is going to be interesting.

Abruptly she decided she was all done with her game of catch-me-if-you-can. Keeping one hand wrapped warmly about him, she leaned down to kiss him back to her. "Toss me," she whispered.

She was on her back before she could take another breath. Collis, freed from his polite submission, was a hungering beast. Hot hands, hot mouth, urgent body—

The remainder of their clothing took only a moment's attention. Then they were skin to skin at last. Collis took her mouth with his as he came to rest between her thighs. She responded fearlessly, her arms about his neck, her legs about his waist. "Come inside," she whispered, as if inviting him home.

Home. "I don't want to hurt you," he said softly as he rested the tip of his erection at her center. She only kissed him in answer. He drove steadily, deeply within her, every instant of the journey a torturous pleasure. In that instant, everything changed. Something like awe swept him at the feel of her around him. Yes, they were like two pieces of the same stone, broken apart aeons ago, then brought together at last, the fracture made whole.

Rose bit her own lip at his entry. He was large and so very thick. She ached at taking him fully, but he was being so careful that she briefly, poignantly, wished she was the virgin he obviously believed her to be.

He withdrew slightly and came to her again, driving away the ache with clenching pleasure. Again and again, she felt him expand and fill and claim her. *Yes, yours. Finally . . . only . . . yours.* Then all thoughts of the past left her, washed away by the renewing beauty of having the man she loved above her, inside her, surrounding her with demanding tenderness.

Right where he belonged.

Then the tenderness flared to passion, and the passion to combustion, until there were no thoughts at all.

Chapter Twenty

❧⟡❧

When the knock came at the doors of Etheridge
House, it was far too early in the morning for visitors.
So, of course, the new arrival was Liverpool, bran-
dishing what had to be a very early edition of a London news sheet. Dalton tugged the belt of his dressing
gown tighter and waved his guest to a seat in the front
parlor as he took the folded news sheet and read the
column displayed in front.

> *Button, button, who has the button? Or should
> your Voice of Society say, "Who has the Prince
> Regent?" Our dear Prinny missed his audi-
> ences yesterday, leaving more than one dis-
> gruntled supplicant without a promised word.
> Our source at the palace says no one has seen
> the Royal George since Monday night. Perhaps
> he's ill, and our Prime Minister doesn't want
> anyone to worry. Perhaps he's merely taking a
> tiny holiday from the worries and wearies of
> the royal schedule. Still, such an absence does*

remind one of those early days before King
George slipped away from us entirely, hmm?

Dalton's gut sank. "Oh, damn."

Liverpool pursed his lips. "You said that before. Yet the Prince is still missing. Perhaps these mongrels of yours are not as efficient as you claim. Where is Tremayne?"

"He and Rose haven't returned to the club since Monday morning."

"And Tremayne and the Prince Regent went missing Monday night." Liverpool fidgeted irritably with the head of his walking stick.

Dalton knew that was not auspicious. Lord Liverpool was made of ice. Ice men *never* fidgeted. Dalton overcame the powerful urge to scoot his chair a few inches farther back. "My lord, I have every man out looking for them now."

"I don't trust your lot to find their shoes in the morning. Get out there yourself and get George back before I have to go public with his disappearance."

Liverpool narrowed his eyes as he went on. "Trust me, George does not want me to go public with information of erratic behavior. There are too many rumors floating about already about 'diminished capacity.' If he returns at once, I can still provide a reasonable cover. If he doesn't—then I'm not sure I want to."

Dalton did not like the sound of that. "My lord! His Highness may be self-indulgent and lazy, but he isn't *mad*!"

"Isn't he? You cannot prove it by this latest circus! If he does not take care, he will spend his days locked in a room next to his father." Liverpool struck the tip of his walking stick on the floor for emphasis. "And in typical careless form, he has left me with so few suitable heirs! Charlotte is his only child, and she is a sickly creature. After her, we must take George's younger brothers into account, and every one is more worthless than the one before!"

It would be best to deflect Lord Liverpool from the topic of heirs. "We don't know that George is gone apurpose," Dalton said soothingly. "Perhaps he met with foul play." Although why that would be the more comforting alternative, he didn't know. Unless it was that it was more possible to be rescued from danger than from madness.

He leaned back in his chair, frustrated and weary. This whole mess was turned about. Rose and Collis were missing. The Wentworths reported no contact from either one. There had been no word to Denny, Collis's valet, or Clara, Rose's dearest friend.

"People don't simply vanish," Dalton said grimly.

"Of course they do," Liverpool snapped.

"Not my people," Dalton retorted, his patience overcoming his lifelong habit of respect to his mentor. "Not the Liars."

The Sergeant pattered in just then, still somehow militarily rigid despite his fuzzy wool dressing gown. "My lords, it's Denny! He's come back with a message from Master Collis!"

Dalton blinked. "Come back?" Why had Denny been out and about in the night? Then the sleep cleared from his brain. "Collis!"

* * *

Collis was quite delightfully stuck. Rose was asleep upon him, draped like a womanly blanket over his shoulder and chest. Her thigh lay over his groin and her hair spread across him, tickling nearly unbearably. Still, it had been so long since he'd enjoyed the privilege of being wrapped in naked woman that he refused to move an inch for fear of waking her.

A woman. Not his woman, despite his barbaric thoughts earlier. At least, not yet.

And what a woman she was. She was swift and fierce and intelligent and would be a credit to the Liars. She was also, he was surprised to realize, a friend, the like of which he had not had since before he went to war.

A good friend. A respected colleague. He stroked her hair with tender fingers. An enchanting lover.

He wanted more.

It felt odd to be in love for the first time in his life. He looked at her burrowed deeply into the sapphire covers of the sinful bed, with only her hair and the tip of her nose showing from beneath the counterpane.

The first time.

And the last.

Yet she'd never listen to him if he told her now. He knew what she believed, that he was only interested in bedding her. That he would never have the thoughts that he was having right now.

"I want to marry you," he whispered, so softly that even if she had been awake, she likely could not have heard him. "I want to shower you with luxuries that you've never known, and bring you chocolate every morning. I'll build a hearth in our room big enough for a half dozen fires, and I'll put up a target in our ballroom for you to practice your knives. I want to be your partner, your friend and your lover forever."

He leaned down to drop a feather kiss on the end of her nose. She snuffled and pulled her head deeper into the bed linens. Collis chuckled. "And then when forever is over," he breathed into her hair, "I want to start again."

She stirred, then yawned. "Collis?" Her voice was muffled by the covers.

"Yes?"

"Why now?"

He knew what she wanted to know. "When I think back, I realize now that I always wanted you."

She rose up on her elbows to gaze into his face. "You did not."

"Why else would I have fought so hard to drive you away?"

He could tell when she believed at last, when her body seemed to melt against his, as if all the tension and defenses had drained away and left only her. Only Rose. Only Collis.

She dropped her forehead to rest on his chest. He stroked her hair, treasuring the softness of every strand. To touch her, to truly be able to feel her hair, her skin, the taut, flexible firmness of her—he planned to spend the rest of his life trying vainly to tire of this woman.

"There is a story about a girl named Briar Rose," he mused aloud. "Gretchen—who became more a nanny to me than a companion to my mother—used to tell me all sorts of tales from Germany. Most of them contained ravenous wolves for some reason, so I always asked for more."

He felt a soft gust of laughter on his skin. "I know," he said. "Bloodthirsty little snot that I was, I loved them. But there was one about a princess, whose royal parents had angered a witch by not inviting her to the baby princess's christening. So the witch comes uninvited, and there is a curse, and the Princess Rose falls asleep in a castle surrounded by a wall of briars for a hundred years." He snuggled her closer and paused for a yawn. "Now, having some experience with briars myself, I have a lot more sympathy for all the questing princes who died trying to scale those thorny walls."

She bit him lightly at that. He chuckled, then went on. "Eventually, one especially handsome and noble prince comes along and the briars part for him like a sickly hedge, and he finds the Princess Briar Rose, as legend has named her, sleeping in her tower. And, this is the part that I found particularly fascinating, she isn't a day older than she was when she fell asleep a century before. So of course, being well versed in princely etiquette, he kisses her. She wakes up, falls madly in love with him at first sight, and they marry and live happily ever after."

He heard and felt her derisive snort against his skin. "What a load of night soil," she muttered. "Tell me one with wolves."

Collis laughed out loud. "Briar Rose indeed!"

She said something too softly against his skin. He chuckled. "That feels rather stimulating, but I didn't understand a word."

She raised her head. "I tried to drive you away, too."

He nodded. "It was probably a very good idea. I'm glad it didn't work."

"I am, too." She smoothed a hand over her hair to clear it from her face. He'd never seen her look so sad. "The lord and the housemaid. Hardly a suitable match."

"So I snarled."

"And I sniped."

"And here we are, after all."

She rolled into the crook of his arm, no longer looking at him. "Here we are."

The next question hung in the air, but neither of them was willing to speak it.

What do we do now?

The fire was dimming and the room was turning chill. Collis rose, drew on his trousers over his nakedness, and stirred the coals. Pulling his shirt over his head to hang loosely, he took the tasseled throw from the sofa to layer it over the sleeping Rose and climbed in behind her. She immediately turned to him, sleepily opening her arms to draw him into her warmth.

That seemed somehow unusually generous to him, that she would rather warm him than retain her own comfort. She wrapped her arms about him and pulled him close. He relaxed into her lithe softness, feeling rather alarmingly at home.

Then she kicked him. "Hot," she muttered, and shoved the covers down to her hips.

Well, then, perhaps not so very at home after all. He tugged the covers back up. The room was nearly icy in his view. He drew them up over both their shoulders, enjoying the warmth around his neck. Rose all but decapitated him when she yanked them away to push them down. "Oomph," she protested. Then she kicked him again.

Finally he gave up with a sigh. She was apparently much tougher than he was, and he was likely a good deal more spoiled. He left her half-covered and re-treated to the other side of the bed. But he took the throw with him.

There were unrealized benefits from this position. He could admire half-naked girl to his heart's content from here. The fire had regained some of its glow and it shone on Rose's skin like the evening light on snow. Curves and slopes, shaped into glory by nature . . . his own private Alps.

Collis's drowsy contemplation of the precise con-tour of Rose's naked hip was interrupted by the sound of a door crashing open somewhere in the house. Somewhere very close by—as in the next room, where the Prince Regent was.

In an instant Collis was up and pulling his weapon from beneath his pile of clothing. Rose's feet hit the floor only a split second after his. She whipped her gown over her head and made for her own weapons.

Too late. The door to their room crashed open un-der the blows of several large fellows. Collis couldn't be sure, but they bore a remarkable resemblance to ruffians he'd met before. They poured into the room in a flood.

Collis brought his pistol up just a moment too late. A massive hand covered his and his shot was wasted on the plaster of the ceiling. He tossed the useless pistol aside and took the fellow on by hand.

In one corner of his mind he was aware of the shrieks and commotion coming from the room next door, and in still another portion he was painfully aware of every rough hand now pinning down a viciously struggling Rose.

The majority of the players were in his court, however, and he took them on willingly enough. There were simply too many. He'd down one with a mighty right cross, only to find another taking the place of the first.

Someone had left nothing to chance in hiring enough louts to take down an army. Collis didn't have to stretch too far to think of who. Rose had been quite correct. Louis Wadsworth wanted his secret kept at any cost.

As he inevitably went down under a mass attack, buried under odorous bodies, Collis had the sinking feeling they were about to find out the hard way.

Collis was down. Rose could see him being hauled limply by the thugs from her position in the hands of two of their attackers. She struck out with bare feet at one, but he'd learned his lesson too well already and stayed just out of reach of her kicks. The two had her nearly stretched between them, one on each arm, immobilizing her with meaty paws that were more binding than manacles.

Collis was dragged into the hall. Rose wasn't far behind. When she passed through the door she saw Mrs. Blythe and the Prince Regent in similar straits. The Prince seemed nearly unconscious and nearly unrecognizable, for his face was rapidly swelling from the beating he must have taken. Mrs. Blythe, a stout but handsome woman, was shrieking foul epithets upon the heads of one and all. Finally one of the men cracked her across the face with the back of his hand.

"Where's the other one?"

Startled, Mrs. Blythe gulped back more shrieks. "Other one? What other one?"

The surprise on her face was too real to be feigned and the biggest man swore. "They must have split up. The bloke what sent us said there were three."

Someone had slipped up. These men thought they were after three men. Thinking quickly, Rose shot an urgent look at Madame. Then she burst into tears, wailing loudly. "I ain't done nothing. I was just supposed to give the gent a good tossing! I ain't done nothing wrong!"

She saw the madam's eyes widen. Then the woman joined in. "You let her go, you hear me! I paid good copper for her and she ain't worked it back yet!" Mrs. Blythe grabbed Rose by the sleeve and pulled. The two louts holding her shifted in their shoes and looked questioningly at their leader. Rose saw the man thinking hard, his heavy brows beetled and his eyes narrowed. He didn't look as though he practiced the art very often. She increased the volume of her wails. Mrs. Blythe matched her in curses. Finally the noise proved too much for the man and he stepped back.

"Let the whore go," he said disdainfully. The two men holding Rose let her go with obvious relief and stepped smartly away. Rose flung herself into her benefactress's arms and continued to wail loudly until the men had dragged Collis and George down the rickety stairs.

Then she pulled away abruptly. "Thank you," she said fervently, and dashed back into her room to pull on her shoes and shawl and to strap on her knife sheaths. She was twisting her hair up out of her way when Mrs. Blythe followed her into the room.

"Who told them we were here?" Rose asked as she sorted herself out. "Did anyone of your people know who your guest was?"

Mrs. Blythe shook her head. "I'm the only one who knows anything. It didn't come from my house."

Rose nearly asked the woman to take a message to Lord Etheridge, then halted. Could she be sure the woman wasn't an informant? Perhaps Mrs. Blythe was not as dependable as the Liars thought. Rose's recent realization of their fallibility furthered her caution. No, for now, she kept her own counsel in all things.

"What was that all about?" The woman looked worried and suspicious . . . as she might whether guilty or innocent.

Rose shook her head. "You don't want to know any more than you know already."

"But where are you off to?"

Rose hesitated, then decided there was no harm in stating the obvious. "I'm going to follow them, of course." With that, she was gone, flying down the stairs and slipping out the door into the rain.

Chapter Twenty-one

———— ❖ ————

Rose was able to follow the band of thugs easily enough, for they obviously saw no reason to fear being trailed. After all, they'd captured the *men*. No reason to worry about repercussions from a house of women.

The ruffians had tossed their prizes into a waiting cart and had set off at an unhurried pace. Rose followed them at a distance, keeping well to the shadows of the early-morning streets, using her shawl for cover. There wasn't much chance of them spying her through the mist of rain, anyway.

Still, the last thing she wanted was to call attention to herself while wearing a borrowed prostitute's gown. Fear for herself felt almost wrong, however, especially when she saw the cart pulling into a heavy iron gate placed in a high, intimidating wall.

The sign above the gate, picked out in black iron against a gray sky, said: WADSWORTH & SON, MUNITIONS.

Oh, no.

As the gates creaked to a close, meeting in a heavy crash of metal, Rose turned and ran. Help was only a few miles away.

Finally, the edifice of the Liar's Club loomed gray and lightless in the dim rain-swept morning. Rose pelted past the front door without truly recognizing the fact that Stubbs was not on duty there. Collis's position was growing more dangerous by the moment.

To the right of the main door was the short stair from the street down to the service entrance. There were eight steps. Her feet touched only two.

She pushed through the door so fast it impacted the wall behind her. The storerooms were dark and unheated, but then, they always were. Rose took the steps up to the kitchen at a run to burst hurriedly into the kitchen.

Into pitch-darkness. The kitchen was always occupied. Even when Kurt was out or on a mission, Liars were forever scrounging in the larder. Rose had never seen it fully dark, and never, never was it cold. The great stove seemed to burn eternally. "Kurt?" There was no answer.

She groped her way to where the stove was and felt in the darkness for the small wooden box kept there. The new friction matches were much prized and the Liars were urged to keep them for use only on missions, but Kurt lived a law of his own. He always kept a good supply on hand, and some of the Liars were known to barter theirs for an extra serving of Kurt's superb pastries.

Rose spared not a moment for her usual wonder as

she swiftly lit a twist of paper she pulled from where it waited for the giant stove. The weak yellow light flickered to show a room abandoned in the middle of cooking. Vegetables lay wilted on the table. An opened sack of potatoes had emptied itself across the floor. Kurt's favorite cooking knife lay stained and bloodied next to a graying slab of beef.

It didn't look as though there had been any sort of attack. It more seemed as if Kurt had simply dropped everything to walk out of the club—for days. And if Kurt was gone—

Icy fear lanced through her. She fumbled for a nearby candle and lit it quickly. With one hand shielding the flame from the draft, she ran back into the common room of the true club.

Deserted, as were the map room and the code room and his lordship's secret office, which she wasn't even supposed to know about.

They were all gone and had been so for at least a full day, perhaps longer. What disaster could have pulled them all from the club? What level of emergency? Only invasion by the French themselves came to mind, or some sort of royal crisis—

"Oh, God. *George.*"

Of course they'd depart in a panic! George must have seemed to disappear in a puff of smoke! Hadn't they received word yet from Lord Liverpool? "Oh, Collis, we've done it now."

She made for the tunnel to the Lillian Raines School, cringing at the necessity of going underground again. There was no one in the school, either. Everyone must be hunting the city like mad. Rose pressed her fingers to her temples. "Hunting the nation, no doubt. Oh, God, what am I going to do?"

Her own shivering chill finally registered. Quickly she rummaged for a set of her training kit, an old pair of boy's knee breeches and shirt. She found a pair of boots that would protect her better than Mrs. Blythe's satin slippers and grabbed a waistcoat and short jacket from another student's room. She shoved her hair under a borrowed cap and ran back to the main club.

Her first duty was to leave a message for the spymaster that the Prince and Collis had been taken by Louis Wadsworth. Her next duty was to go back to them. But alone? She'd be no more help than she had been before. To go back alone would only ensure that all three of them would be killed.

Rose banged on the door of Etheridge House until her fist throbbed, but it still took several minutes before someone opened the door. Denny stood blocking her way in, gazing at her sourly.

"Oh, it's you."

Rose didn't have time to play. "Denny, let me in. I need to see his lordship!"

Denny sneered. "Gone. Him and Sir Simon and even the Sergeant. All gone, leavin' me to answer the door like a bloody underfootman. I hope you're happy about what you done. They're all in a right tizzy about you kidnapping the Prince Regent."

"Denny, stop it. Tell me where they are. It's urgent!"

Denny folded his arms. "Tell you what. Give me your message and I'll see he gets it."

Message. Rose went still as she remembered. "Collis sent the message to you about where we were, didn't he? Why didn't you give it to Liverpool?"

That surprised him completely, she was sure of it. "Why would I? It didn't say nothin' about Liverpool. Just that you and him and Prinny was to be found at that brothel house."

Rose narrowed her eyes. "It didn't say anything like that. Collis would never be that explicit."

Denny gave her a superior smile. "I been around Liars since you was cleaning chamber pots, *Miss* Lacey. I knew right off that when Master Collis said he was with his uncle George, he was with Prinny. Master Collis ain't got an uncle George."

There was something else here. Rose knew it. Collis had sent that message yesterday evening. The spymaster and Liverpool should have arrived within a few hours at the most. "Collis sent you a message to take to Lord Liverpool. What happened to it?"

Denny looked genuinely confused. "I don't know. Cor, I could have done it, too. They know me around Westminster, they do!" Disappointment twisted his features. "You probably lost it."

"I never saw it, you idiot. Collis gave both messages to that boy he paid." The child might have dropped one. He wouldn't likely admit it when he reached his destination, would he? Of course, he probably couldn't read. The sort of children who ran the streets didn't come with educations.

Damn it, time was running out! "So his lordship has gone to Mrs. Blythe's?"

"Been and gone. They're all out in the city now, trying to track you lot. How'd you do it anyway?" Denny asked curiously. "How'd you go and disappear that way?"

She couldn't ask him to come with her. Rose wouldn't trust Denny with a dirty tea towel. "Spy secrets, of course. Listen, if you see his lordship, tell him I left a very important message for him at the club."

"I ain't your servant!"

Rose had had enough. She stepped forward and shoved the blighter once in the chest. "Denny, Kurt taught me everything he knows. Do you truly want to plague me off?"

Denny's eyes widened and he pulled back in alarm. "Right then. Tell him I will." Then he shut the door on her, leaving her standing outside.

On her own. Again.

Rose left Etheridge House and headed back toward the factory. Where to find help? She could fight her way back through the city to Sir Simon's house—but they'd have joined the hunt along with every able-bodied servant they had.

There was no time left to risk it. She must find help closer at hand. She closed her eyes and fought back her weariness long enough to *think.*

One name came to her. Someone Collis believed in completely. *"I've known Ethan Damont since school. I'm sure he is to be trusted."*

Ethan Damont, gambler and likely ne'er-do-well—her only hope. Dear God, would he be any better than Denny? Scowling through her dread, Rose ran from the fine square that held Etheridge House to run toward the only help she could think of. The rain had stopped. She could see the clouds lightening— moving west, driven by a fresh wind from the sea.

Ethan Damont, the "Diamond." Only dire panic would spur her to go to such lengths. That and the knowledge that Collis would do the same or more for her.

"Collis," she muttered to him across the miles, "I hope you're a better judge of friends than you are of valets."

Ethan Damont poured himself another brandy . . . almost. Only an unfortunate trickle flowed into his snifter to swirl sadly round the bottom. He threw back his head to call, "Jeeves, bring more brandy!"

The shout brought no response, of course. There was no such Jeeves. No valet, no butler, not even a charwoman. Such people would insist on being paid a fair wage or any wage at all, neither of which the Damont household could supply at the moment.

And no more brandy, either, unless he'd somehow overlooked a dusty bottle in a corner of the cellar. Unlikely, since he'd scrounged everything that was left to eat, drink, or sell. Lady Luck had spurned him a few too many times lately. His fortunes at the tables had been dismal.

Fickle bitch.

Ethan glanced upward. "I didn't mean that. So sorry. You're a beauty, a vision, a veritable goddess. I could go on for hours, if only you would knock on my door once more."

Knock, knock. There was no knocker on the door (good brass castings were worth nearly a week of grub, after all) so only the insubstantial tap of knuckles echoed through his empty rooms.

"Company," Ethan muttered to no one. He didn't feel much like answering. Likely it was only a creditor come to claim the last of Ethan's possessions. And he didn't much feel like giving up his shoes. Good thing he'd drunk all the brandy after all. He tossed back the last dribble, just in case. While his head was still tipped back, he smiled wistfully up at his neglectful lady.

"My princess, if only that was you at my door. Why don't you come calling anymore, darling? What did I do to offend you?"

Truth be told, he knew why. He'd lost the passion. One day he'd woken up without feeling the thrill of the chase, the hunger for the game. Cards were just pasteboard and ink. Green felt suddenly seemed bilious rather than filled with emerald promise.

The knock came again, along with a high querying voice. A female voice, calling him by name. Ethan blinked in surprise. "Is it you, my love?" Well then, he had best answer after all. He could think of no women to whom he owed anything, unless it was some old lover seeking either renewal or vengeance. Either way, it was a change from the bare walls and empty decanter.

He stood, wavered a moment, then shuffled to the

front hall. It was a fine hall, guarded by an even finer door. He wondered idly if it was worth anything. The latch was beyond him for a moment, but he mastered it at last. Bloody good brandy. Too bad it was gone.

Ethan opened the door and flinched from the bright light of day. "Morning already?"

Something shoved him backward as it pushed by him. "It is afternoon, Mr. Damont. Well past tea. You missed the rain entirely."

"Oh . . . tea." Abruptly, fierce longing seized Ethan. Tea and cakes, fresh from baking. "I like the ones with the little seeds."

"Oh, for pity's sake. You're drunk."

"Not willingly," Ethan protested, still blinking to clear the jangling glare from his vision. "Couldn't let the bastards get the brandy, you know."

"No, I don't know and I don't care." The door closed, shutting out the day with a crisp bang. Ethan sighed in gratitude. After a moment the after-glare receded and he found himself confronted with a very angry person in mismatched clothing. Angry or scared. Possibly both.

A woman—he was nearly positive she was female—in need of help, if he was not mistaken. He'd been a gentleman once, of sorts. Ethan reached deep to find if any shred of chivalry remained. Oh, there it was.

"Please, come in," he said gallantly.

"I am in." She folded her arms and glared at him.

She was pretty, if you liked them dark and pale. And thin. And rather scary.

Ethan found himself standing straighter, pulling

himself together as if in answer to some unspoken challenge. He swallowed and hoped his breath wasn't too brandied.

"How may I be of service, dear lady?"

She tugged her cap free of her hair, letting it fall halfway down her back. "I'm not a lady."

Chapter Twenty-two

———— ❖ ————

There was something about the cliché of being manacled in a dungeon beneath a castle that really annoyed Collis. Of course, it wasn't really a dungeon. More of a storage cellar, with a number of crates piled high along one wall, stacked so high they required brackets and chains to keep them from tumbling down.

Nor was it truly a castle, merely an overdecorated arms factory not far from the East India docks.

But the manacles were real enough, cast of cold iron and uncomfortably tight on his right wrist and his left as well, theoretically. He was hanging at arm's length from one of the brackets jutting from this wall. The Prince hung from another such bracket about six feet away, looking rather like a bloodied side of beef in a tattered and stained nightshirt. The Prince wasn't moving.

Collis peered at him again, trying desperately to note any sign of life through his own battered and swollen eyes. If he looked anything like George did, two black eyes were the least of his worries. George had been beaten beyond recognition. His face was bruised and bloodied, and Collis had been watching blood drip slowly from George's hair for the last hour. Head wounds could kill, or render the victim mentally damaged forever. Collis was very worried.

And Rose was not here. He knew he ought to be more worried about his monarch than his partner, but it was all he could do to contain the breathtaking fear he felt inside at thoughts of Rose's fate. The men who had taken them had been foul brutes, low hired scum who might have taken Rose for themselves as a sort of fringe benefit.

Ironic that he hoped mightily that she was being held prisoner by Louis Wadsworth instead, as he was. The fact that she was being held elsewhere might even mean that she was being treated better than they, perhaps even like a guest—

It was a fruitless fantasy, but he couldn't bear to think otherwise or he wouldn't be able to think at all.

While he waited for George to wake—perhaps yet another fantasy—he tested his manacles with all his strength, stopping only when he saw the blood begin to drip down his left arm from his own abraded wrist. It was difficult to care about injuring that piece of dead wood, but slicing a vein and bleeding to death would do none of them any good.

A chain clanked, not one of his. Turning his head, he saw George rolling his head and blinking his eyes. "Sir!" he didn't dare address him properly, for it was still possible that their captor knew not who he held. "Sir, are you well?"

George cleared his throat and tested his swollen,

broken lips with the tip of his tongue. "That ith a thtupid quethtion. Of courthe I'm not well." He shook his head and blinked rapidly. "I lotht a bloody tooth!"

Overcome with relief, Collis laughed aloud. George looked at him sourly. "Not amuthing. At my age, every tooth counth!"

"No, sir, it isn't amusing. But it is very good to hear that they didn't knock your brains from your skull, sir."

"Humph. Bloody well feelth like it." His speech was becoming clearer by the moment. And more recognizable.

"Sir, it might be wise if you try not to sound like yourself. I don't think Wadsworth—" He had to be careful. There was no way to know if they were being overheard.

"You don't think he knowth that you hired me to help you steal his planth?"

Collis snorted. "Exactly." Good old George, sharp as ever. Thank every god ever named. He'd even altered his voice, turning his refined fruity tones into something nasal and high.

"Where's our—ah—other friend?"

Collis ground his jaw. "I don't know."

"Are you sure that friend was taken?"

Collis closed his eyes, the image of an overwhelmed Rose going down fighting burned onto his inner vision forever. "Yes."

"Ah." The Prince fell silent. There was no need to say more. They both knew the fate that could befall a woman in unfriendly hands.

It seemed Collis had not been too far off to think

them overheard, for shortly they heard the sound of a key in the lock of the great double doors. Someone had been waiting for them to awake, it seemed.

The doors slid sideways along rails to stand alongside the walls. Collis flinched against the sudden brightness, the light shooting through his pounding head like a lance. He blinked rapidly, trying to clear his vision as if seeing what was coming would help him fend it off.

It might have been late afternoon, for the sunlight slanting along the hallway outside had that peculiar golden tint that indicated sunset neared. Through the shimmering bars of floating dust motes stepped a figure all in black—Louis Wadsworth, clad like a highwayman in head-to-toe ebony silk.

"Oh, dear. Did I look that ridiculous?" George whispered.

Very nearly, Collis wanted to say, but the man was a prince, after all. "Shh, sir."

Louis strutted toward them, his hand at his hip as if he fancied himself toting a sword as well. Collis would have rolled his eyes if they hadn't been nearly swollen shut. Then he remembered his missing Rose and became serious indeed.

The factory was well guarded, but Rose thought not impenetrable. She could just see over the wall from her stance atop Damont's shoulders. The main building was somewhat unnecessarily decorated in a rather medieval fashion, giving the entire establishment a castlelike appearance. This was reinforced by the many smaller brick structures that scattered at its feet like a small, grim village. The wall surrounded it all, enclosing a cobbled yard in the center.

Most important, there was a drain in the courtyard; she could see it from here. She jumped down to tell Ethan her plan.

"The sewer? Are you sure?"

"Yes. The storm drains run beneath the streets, mostly. If we follow the road into the factory back the way we came, we'll find another grate. We can walk right beneath the wall!"

He looked doubtful. "Then how will we get into the factory proper? The place is packed with workers. They won't leave until it is too dark inside to see."

"They won't simply use candles or lanterns?"

Ethan looked appalled. "Do you have any idea how expensive that would be, to light an entire factory?"

"Oh, true." She frowned at him. "You have surprising facets, Mr. Damont."

The corner of his mouth twisted. "Did you think I was born a gambler?"

"Sorry." She chewed her lip. "I hate to wait one moment longer, but I think we must. The sun will set soon. It will be much easier to get past the night watch."

"So you say." Ethan was looking stubborn. "Why don't we simply call the magistrate and tell him Collis is being held against his will?"

Rose waved her hand at the fortress behind them. "Do you know who owns this place? Louis Wadsworth, that's who!"

Ethan grimaced. "Wadsworth, eh? Nasty sort. Gets very mean when he loses."

"No need to tell me that. And he *is* the magistrate for this district, so it would do us no good to seek help from the law."

Ethan pushed himself off the wall with a sigh. "So we find the grate."

It didn't take long. Finding the grate was simply a matter of circling the factory in an ever larger spiral. Of course, the factory grounds were vast. Rose cast a look back at a lagging Damont. "You truly ought to get out more."

His answer was a gusting laugh and a wave onward. At last—though less than a quarter of an hour later—she spotted a likely grate in a small side street. There was still enough sunlight for Rose to see that the narrow stream in the bottom of the tunnel was flowing away from the factory. "This is the one." She looked around them.

The cobbled side street was deserted for the moment, although it might be filled soon with homeward-bound factory workers. "Quickly, help me pry it up."

The grate came up more easily than the older ones in the inner city had. She only hoped the tunnel below was correspondingly modern. "Down we go then," she said to Ethan.

He bowed. "Ladies first."

It was a short jaunt back up the tunnel to below the factory. This tunnel was purely storm drainage, fortunately, with very little filth in view. Rose halted when she saw daylight seeping through from above. "How do you know we're under the right grate?" Ethan wanted to know.

"Listen," she said. "We could hear the stamping mill from where we stood at the wall, remember? It's even louder down here." The rhythm of the heavy stamper seemed about to come down directly upon them, in fact.

"All right then. Now what?"

Rose sighed, frustrated. "We wait. The workers will be leaving soon. After that, there will hopefully only be a few watchmen left."

"So how did Collis anger this Wadsworth fellow anyway?"

Rose seated herself on a vaguely dry spot. "I'm afraid I can't discuss it."

Damont plopped down beside her. "You can't discuss much, can you?" Ethan sighed heavily. "Well, I'm hungry and I'm bored, so I'll talk, shall I?"

"I'm hungry as well, but I am not bored." She shot him a black look. "Yet."

"Well, then I'll talk about our mutual friend. Luckiest sod I ever knew. He shouldn't have been much higher than me, by his birth. His mother had connections, but his father was naught but a lieutenant colonel in the army, albeit a highly decorated one."

Damont leaned back against the grimy wall of the culvert and rubbed his head. "Yet there he was, heir to Etheridge and a title. Just the sort of *haute ton* snot my father sent me to school with—so I could make valuable connections, you see—and handsome and talented to boot." He chuckled reminiscently. "He was a right tool, he was. And somehow, it all seemed a bit unfair."

He didn't look at her, but she could feel his attention on her nonetheless. "Did you ever wonder how Collis could be in line for Etheridge from his maternal uncle?" he asked.

Rose shook her head. She'd thought it odd but had dismissed it as some part of the aristocratic world she was unfamiliar with. People had been conspicuously silent on the topic, now that she thought about it.

Now here was Ethan Damont, being deceptively casual, virtually panting to tell her. This ought to be interesting indeed.

Rational information-seeking aside, she was mad for word of Collis's safety. Word of his past would have to do.

"He told me once, when we were boys. Since his father was not aristocracy by any means, that meant his mother married vastly beneath herself. I've heard since that she was intent on having him for her husband. A real love match. Uncommon, that."

Not in her world. They seemed to shine all around her, like mirrors to show her what she would never have. Agatha and Simon, Dalton and Clara, James and Phillipa. Her lips quirked. What *was* Kurt putting in the pudding? "So you're saying Collis should have been the last one to inherit, correct?"

"Well, I suppose if you've been dangled on the Prince's knee since you were a tot, you rate a little dispensation. He used to tell me the most fantastic stories about the Prince when we were in our first years at school. I thought for the longest time that he was making them up. Then I suppose he didn't see him for a long while, for he didn't talk about him anymore. Anyway, by then we'd discovered the fascinating topic of females."

Rose snorted softly. "I can imagine."

Ethan smiled at her. "I wonder. Would you believe it if I told you that Collis was, at one time, the most absurdly romantic soul I've ever known? Addicted to Shakespeare, mad for poetry, inclined to spout rhyme about 'hearts entwined of lace and fire'?"

Rose narrowed her eyes at him. Here was another man full of malarkey. "Not one little bit."

"Every word of it truth, I swear it." He shook his head. "I don't know where that boy went. After his parents died, I think a part of him went into hiding. Or perhaps it was the army, or the wound. . . . I know he came back different, or at least it seemed that way the one time I saw him."

Rose wished she could have known Collis then. She could imagine him young and untroubled. He would have been a beautiful boy, whole in body and soul. How he must have shone, like a silver chalice unmarred by fingerprints or tarnish.

Damn, she would never stop being a housemaid, would she? Silver polishing, for heaven's sake. She'd best keep in mind that if Collis was a silver chalice, then she was a humble wooden spoon. A spoon with a mission, one she'd best be keeping her mind on. As soon as she heard a little more about Collis.

"You were supposed to be telling me about his inheriting Etheridge."

"Did I wander? Sorry."

She didn't believe his apology. He'd had some reason of his own for telling her that. But then again, he was a mad, drunk gambler. She ought not to listen to a thing this man had to say . . . except that she desperately wanted to hear. "So how did he come to be heir if his father was only an officer?"

"The way he told it, there are no other Etheridge men to be found. A search back along the line left no relatives of any kind, if you can believe that. Apparently they don't breed well at all. Lots of only children, lots of dying young, that sort of thing."

That didn't sound quite right to her . . . a bit convenient, really. Still, there was no accounting for the heights of snobbery enacted by the aristocracy. The proper heir probably farmed pigs in the north country or something unbearable like that.

"But can you simply pick someone to be heir?"

"To a title, no, not usually. But then, most of us aren't Collis, born with a golden horseshoe up his arse, either. A word in the ear of the Prince and a bit of mudgery-pudgery in the entail records and voilà! Instant heir."

"Seems a bit dodgy to me, but I suppose what the Prince Regent says, happens." George was capable of sudden and outrageous generosity, she'd heard. She could imagine him taking a fancy to little Collis and waving his royal hand . . . but he'd not been Regent then, had he? It must have been the King's wish as well.

"Of course, they treated him more like a royal heir than simply Etheridge's heir," Ethan went on. "Not spoiling him as much as smothering him. Etheridge, loyalty to Etheridge, devotion to Etheridge. Everyone telling him it was the most important thing in the world—but it meant nothing to him. And why should it, with his uncle being a young, hardy bloke? The odds of him inheriting have always been slight. No, his mistress was always music, even as a lad. The music master at school gave up teaching him after a bit. I think Col must have passed the fellow right up."

Rose sighed. "I've never heard him play."

Ethan blinked. "Do you mean to tell me he doesn't play *at all*?"

Hugging herself, Rose shook her head. "Never once since he was wounded. He played the drums for a while, I heard, but I think he was only trying to fend off all the sympathy."

"God save us, the Etheridge stiff upper lip. Bloody miracle any of them can speak at all." Ethan blew a sigh of amazement at the ceiling. "Not playing at all. Damn, he must be nearly ready to explode."

"Why do you say that?"

"Collis needs a mistress, a cause to serve—somewhere to belong, if you like. Not like me. I prefer being on my own."

Rose wasn't any too sure of that, but she didn't interrupt.

"Collis without music is Collis without any meaning at all, I imagine." Ethan looked sorrowful. "Damn. Poor bloke."

"He belongs," Rose said quietly. "Or rather, he will." If she hadn't ruined everything for him. She firmly pushed that guilt aside. No time for worrying about that now. "I do think he's searching, a bit. He seems so . . . lost, sometimes."

"The man after."

Rose frowned. "Who?"

"The man after. The fellow one becomes *after* life blows up in your face. My da used to tell me that it wasn't the man you were before trouble hit that counted. It was the man after."

"Your da sounds like a wise man."

"My da was a social-climbing shoemaker. He was talking about taking advantage of a bad situation to gain rank and status." He cocked a thumb at his chest. "I'm the one to put the philosophical light on it."

"A gambling philosopher?"

He shrugged. "Or a philosophical gambler. I'll take either."

She squinted at him. "Are you sure you're quite sober now?"

"Oh, heavens, no. Where'd you get that impression?"

"Hmm."

"You're a very nice lass. I like you." Ethan put his arm behind her shoulders. Rose allowed it, for there wasn't a great deal of room to be missish in their hiding place. He wasn't a bad sort, either, for a mad, drunk gambler.

"You'd clean up nicely, I think," she told him. "Burn the blinding waistcoats and shave the mustache . . ."

"The mustache? You don't like it? But it comes in

so handy as a distraction when I'm playing. The marks think they're reading me, you see. They think they can decode how I'm toying with my mustache in order to discern my true feelings about my hand." He petted the furry thing fondly. "I'd hate to deprive them of the fun of that."

"Well, think of it this way. They'll all go spinning off, looking for the new code. That ought to supply you with hours of amusement."

He laughed, his brows raised in surprise. "Do you gamble, my pretty Rose?" His hand came to rest on her shoulder. She peeled it off with an unoffended smile.

"I'm not your pretty anything, Mr. Damont. And I do not gamble . . . at least not with cards."

He dropped his flirtatious attempts to regard her with worried eyes. "Take care, pretty lass. If Collis Tremayne is the reason you won't be flirted with, then you are playing deep stakes indeed. His level is not for the likes of us, you do know that, don't you?"

She twitched her lips. "Mr. Damont, even you are completely out of my range. I know I cannot touch Collis."

He watched her, his eyes still somber. "But the question is . . . Does he know he has touched you?"

Rose didn't answer. The silence grew, punctuated by the *thump-thump* of the stamping mill over their heads.

Chapter Twenty-three

❖

Louis Wadsworth didn't seem like an outraged victim of theft, Collis realized. Rather, he seemed more to be playing the part for his own amusement, like a bored stage actor making up his own drama.

There was trenchant irony in the costuming and the elaborate dungeon scenario. All very flamboyant, all very riveting. Collis wondered what Louis was really doing it for.

Louis was parading now, pacing back and forth before his prisoners, his personal guard a stolid threat behind him. The swish of his walking stick, the click of his boot heels, was so very considered as to be laughable.

But if Louis wanted them to laugh, to discount, to underestimate . . . then it followed that there was more here than met the eye. Collis was a professional, and personal, expert on distraction techniques. He used them to keep others from seeing his own occasional despair.

What was Louis keeping under wraps?

Aside from the fact that he was bloody foaming mad, of course. Louis paused in his pacing to peer curiously into George's battered face. Abruptly Collis tired of waiting. "Louis, I'm tired and I have to piss. Hurry it on, would you?"

Louis turned to him, coming to a stop in front of Collis with his stick resting on his shoulder like a rifle. "So sorry, was I boring you?" He twitched the stick to the other shoulder, wrapping both hands casually around the knob. "I could provide a bit more excitement, I'm sure. That is, if you really want me to."

Collis didn't even have to force the weary tone in his voice. "Louis, even you don't believe this charade. Why don't you just jump right in with your reasons for committing treason? I'm sure we're all just panting to know."

Louis quirked a brow, as if he had not expected such a direct challenge and found it interesting. "Treason? How dare you, sir! It is I who have been betrayed. I, a peaceful man, a man of industry—I have been violated by thieves!" He ended his passionate speech with his arms flung open and his stick raised high for emphasis.

Collis didn't believe a word of it. "Thrilling performance, truly," he said dryly. "I might cry."

Louis shrugged. "Ah, well, mock me then. You will not be mocking soon." He shook his head sadly. "Tonight I shall be forced to shoot two masked intruders who will violate my home. Alas, it will only be afterward that I'll realize I have killed my new acquaintance Mr. Tremayne and his hireling."

Collis sighed. "Ah, now come the clichés."

That chipped Louis's armor, Collis could see. Something dark flashed in Louis's eyes and he stepped closer, tipping his stick under Collis's chin. "You are pressing your luck, Mr. Tremayne. What were you doing in my study, hmm?" His eyes narrowed. "Who sent you there?"

Collis grinned through battered lips. "The Worshipful Company of Gunmakers."

That made Louis blink. "The competition?" His eyes narrowed as he thought about it. Collis didn't have much hope of him believing it. His own link with Dalton, the man who'd killed Louis's father in the heat of committing high treason, pointed to a slightly higher authority than a lot of disgruntled gunmakers who'd been outbid by Wadsworth & Son. Dalton's well-known connection to Liverpool further damaged Collis's ability to hide any dire motivation. Damn. Louis had had him spotted from the first moment in that club, as a plant. And since Collis had been operating on misinformation, he hadn't had the opportunity to play the disenchanted heir, the bored Corinthian whose possibilities were hampered by an all too young and healthy uncle—which just might have worked. Too late now.

The cane tip dug into Collis's throat more fiercely. "Try again," crooned Louis.

"Ah, Mrs. Blythe? She heard you didn't like girls."

The first blow of the walking stick wasn't so bad, for it glanced off the meaty part of his right shoulder. The second one took him hard in the ribs. He would have doubled over but for the manacles trapping his wrists, so the third blow caught him full in the gut. He bent over as far as his arms would let him, trying to ease the pain. He breathlessly contemplated vomiting on Louis's shiny boots, but sadly, he hadn't eaten lately.

George rattled in his bonds, but Collis quelled him with a look. The more of Louis's attention that stayed on him, the less Louis would have to spare for George. If the man realized who he had in his grasp—there was no way to tell which way he would spring. Collis didn't want to push Louis to that level of desperation, not until George was safely back where he belonged.

The longer Louis amused himself by beating Collis like a back-alley hound, the longer the Liars had to come to George and Collis's rescue. Surely Mrs. Blythe would have told them something. And surely Dalton would follow their trail to Wadsworth's—except he hadn't sent them to Wadsworth's, he'd sent them to Wentworth's, hadn't he?

As Louis continued to apply the walking stick in all sorts of painful places, Collis began to realize just how helpless and alone they were. If only someone out there knew where he and the Prince were.

"No!" he cried out after a mighty blow of the stick. "Not my left arm, please! I was wounded—"

He drew a subtle sigh of relief when Louis began to work assiduously on his dead arm. Although the blows rocked his body, he felt nothing. It might buy a little time.

He only hoped it would be enough.

Ethan and Rose made their way into the factory just as she had planned. Louis Wadsworth was apparently very confident of the protection provided by his high walls, for there were only two watchmen whom she could see. Those two spent their time casting dice by the gate. Once the growing dusk could mask their movements, Ethan and Rose quietly pushed the grate up and slipped into the factory proper. Ethan quickly armed himself with a pry bar from a crating area.

Knowing Louis, he would have hidden his captives somewhere that amused him. A bell tower or an animal's cage . . . she looked up at the castlelike facade of the building . . . or a dungeon.

It didn't take long, for there was only one stair that went down. The massive door might have posed a problem, but the slack guards had left the key in the lock for their own convenience. God bless lazy men!

When she and Ethan eased into the great storeroom, Rose gasped at the sight of Collis and the Prince, hung from their wrists like prisoners of the Bastille. Collis rolled his head at the noise, blinking into the shadows.

"Who's there?"

Ethan whistled low. "Good Lord, Col! Whose wife did you kiss this time?"

Collis's eyes widened. "Damont! What are you doing here?"

"Your fiancée brought me."

"She's not my fiancée."

"I'm not his fiancée."

Their simultaneous denials had even the Prince chuckling. Ethan tilted his head and pursed his lips. "Good. I'll marry her then," he said lightly.

Rose pushed past him. "Not bloody likely, you sot." As much as she longed to go to Collis first, she knew her duty. She examined the Prince's manacles. There was no chain. The iron bindings were bolted directly into the stone.

The Prince was eyeing Ethan over her shoulder. "I've seen you before. Damont?" George narrowed his eyes. "You're not a Liar!"

Ethan blinked. "Oh, it comes and goes."

Collis spoke up. "Don't worry, Your H—ah, self. Ethan can be trusted."

George gazed at Collis for a long moment. "You trust him with your life?"

Collis smiled slightly. "More. I trust him with yours."

Ethan cleared his throat. "I really think we ought to get out of here." He placed the iron between the stone and George's manacles. "Watch your wrist there," he warned. Then, with Rose's help, he put his weight on the bar, trying to pry the bolt from the stone.

Rose thought they had it for a moment, but the bolt only bent a bit, making the pry bar slip and sending her and Ethan toppling to the floor.

"Ouch," the Prince said in a mild voice, but Rose heard Collis gasp. "You're bleeding, sir!"

In horror, Rose looked up to see a dark stream running down the Prince's bared arm. The iron had cut the flesh of his wrist. "Oh, no!"

Ethan stood, brushed himself off, and lifted the lantern to peer at the wound. Then he shrugged. "It'll scar a bit. But it missed the vein. You'll live." He turned to catch Rose's and Collis's glares. He blinked in surprise. "What?"

Rose pushed him aside to press a clean handkerchief against the Prince's wrist. "Are you all right, sir?"

The Prince nodded, a bemused expression on his face. "You know, I think I like him."

Ethan snorted. "Goodness me, I should hope so. I'm only about to get your pudgy arse out of this hole."

The Prince blinked. "Then again, perhaps I don't."

Ethan shrugged. "As though I cared a whit." He turned to Collis's manacles. "Let's see if these are any easier than your uncle's bindings."

"No," Collis ordered. "His chains first."

Ethan dropped his hands. "Who's doing this, you or I?"

Rose reached to take the pry bar from Ethan. "Really, Mr. Damont, we must do His H—his uncle's first."

"Yes," agreed the Prince mildly. "My pudgy arse first, if you please." He contemplated Ethan for a moment. "Simply out of curiosity, why do you assume I am uncle to Collis?"

"Same chin, under those bruises. I've seen Collie after a brawl or two, you know. Can't recognize a thing but that damn stubborn chin of his." Ethan grunted with effort, but the iron scarcely bent. He stopped to wipe the sweat from his eyes, then grinned at the Prince. "Besides, you look like the sort to enjoy his wine, women, and song, just like old Collis there."

Collis snorted. "According to Rose, the aristocracy is all but inbred anyway."

"Got it in one." Ethan tried leaning back instead, grunting. "Methinks you all look alike."

"Hmm." The Prince turned his head to gaze at Collis.

Ethan put all his weight behind the bar, Rose as

well. "Although Col is a good sight better looking." The bolt sprang free at last. He straightened and clapped the Prince on the back. "Off you get, old codge. You're free."

Rose was staring at George, brows drawn together. Ethan snapped his fingers before her eyes. "Might I disturb your brown study? I'd rather like to get free of this pit."

"Quite." Collis strained at his own manacles. His veins bulged, but there was no progress. Then Ethan stepped up with the pry bar. It was only the work of a moment to get the first manacle free. The second was more resistant. Even when Ethan and George put their full strength behind the pry bar, there was no releasing him.

The pit of Collis's stomach began to chill uneasily. "This isn't going to work. You lot go on. Get the—my uncle to safety, Rose."

"Shut it." She wouldn't look at him as she strained against the bar once more. "We cannot leave you."

"Rose," Collis said softly. "You must and you know it."

Her shoulders sank. She stepped back and let the bar hang limply from her hands. "You wouldn't leave me here."

Her faith in him warmed him inside. Despite the very real danger, he tossed her one of his old devil-may-care grins. "What's a bit of damp cellar, m'lady? I'll have a lovely kip while you call down the troops, all right?"

She raised her chin. "No." She jerked her head at

the other two men. "Get over here," she barked. They obeyed, surprisingly enough. With the three of them leaning on the pry bar, they tried from every angle and every lever point.

"Damn it, *pull*, you bastards," Rose hissed. She swung all her weight from the bar. Ethan and George were red-faced and puffing.

With a sound like a rifle shot, the bolt popped out of the wall and flew across the storeroom. Rose, Ethan, and George collapsed in a pile. Collis dropped to his knees, freed.

Collis slumped a bit when they finally got him on his feet. His vision tended to fog a bit around the edges. He blinked rapidly, trying to restore his equilibrium. He couldn't slow everyone down now.

George was standing watch by the door. He looked up when Ethan and Rose helped Collis to his side. "This is Wadsworth's factory, isn't it?"

Rose nodded. "Yes, sir. If we can get to the courtyard, there's a drain there. We can take the sewer under the wall."

George squinted at the shadowy factory beyond. "In a moment. First, we need to find one of the carbines for Forsythe to test."

Collis blinked. "But why? Wadsworth is now guilty of attacking and kidnapping you! That's enough to send him up forever."

George shook his head. "No. He attacked and kidnapped two men who broke into his house and stole from him. He yet has no idea who I am."

Rose nodded. "You do look really terrible, sir."

George tried to grin, then winced and put a hand to his split lip. "Precisely. I don't want any misunderstandings this time. I want a clear-cut case of treason. I want this man down and my name cleared."

Ethan cleared his throat. "I don't know about this treason and I don't much care at this moment. Whatever you must do, let's do it quickly."

George nodded sharply. "To it then." As the only one who'd ever seen the interior of the factory in the light of day, he led them to where the craftsmen put the final touches on the finished guns. "Louis gave me one yest—" He blinked. "Ah, two days ago. He said it was the first one off the line."

They looked all around. There were a great many rifles and muskets lying about in various states of assembly, but there were no damascened George IV Commemorative Carbines to be seen.

Ethan scratched his head. "I know I'm only a flunky in this play, but I do know a bit about factories. When something is finished, it's crated up and shipped. There isn't room to hang on to large lots, particularly if they've already been sold."

Collis nodded. "Yes, that's true."

George worked his jaw. "Louis included the shipping of the weapons in his bid. He said he would be proud to put his finest work into the hands of our finest men."

Rose nodded sympathetically. Louis would enjoy the irony of that statement.

Collis turned to the Prince. "Did you see a shipping office on your tour? Belonging to a foreman, or an overseer of some kind?"

George showed them the cramped and dusty office of Wadsworth's foreman. Rose and Collis quickly bent to search the files and records for a manifest of some kind. Rose pulled it out finally. "Here! It isn't labeled correctly, but just yesterday the foreman paid five carters to deliver a large shipment to the docks!"

George took the receipt from her. "Good God, do you know what this means?"

Rose and Collis nodded. "They're already on their way," she said softly. "The ship probably sailed at dawn."

Defeat. There was no way to send word faster than the guns themselves. Men would suffer, be maimed. Even die. Collis rubbed his head, then cast a thoughtful look at his dead hand. "No."

"Collis?" Rose was there, her eyes calculating in the dimness. He knew what she was thinking, for he was thinking the same.

He straightened, his pain washed aside by new urgency. "Let's go. It's time to rally the Liars."

It would have been impossible to help both Collis and George back under the wall through the narrow tunnel. Rose decided to try to pass the guards.

With her hair tucked under her cap, she walked with Collis, bracing him as if he were drunk. Ethan did the same with George. The four of them approached the gate as if they were workers who had lost track of both time and quantity.

"Here now!" One of the guards stepped forward.

"You lot ain't supposed to be hangin' about this late."

The four continued their exaggerated staggering toward the gate, although Rose suspected that Collis was not exaggerating very much. He had one arm draped around Rose and was using a broomstick—sans broom head—to brace himself on the other.

Rose worried that the guards weren't taking the bait. Sure enough, they raised their clubs aggressively as the foursome neared. "Oy, ain't them the blokes what was in the hole?"

"Looks like you're on," Collis whispered into her ear. "Are you sure you can take them?"

"Could you take them?" she murmured back. "Because I can take you."

He grunted a painful laugh and handed her the broomstick. "Do Kurt proud." Then he stepped back to join Ethan and George. "Ethan, get ready to jump in. She might need you."

Ethan blinked at him. "You're letting that dainty snip take on those ruffians? Are you mad?" He shook off George onto Collis and strode forward.

Only to stop cold when the first *swish* of the quarterstaff split the air.

It didn't take long. Collis tilted his head, watching Rose dance through the burly guards as if they were archway gargoyles. *Block. Strike. Strike. Block.*

Beside him, George grunted in approval. "Nice form."

"The best," sighed Collis in admiration. "She's the best."

Swish. Thud. Thud.

The guards were down. George and Collis moved

forward to join Ethan where he stood open-mouthed and completely untouched by the action.

"How'd you like that?" Collis still had plans for Ethan.

"Marvelous," Ethan breathed. "Where do I get one of those?"

Ha. Ethan was hooked all right. "A quarterstaff?"

"No. A girl like her."

Hmph. Perhaps Ethan would be better off elsewhere. Somewhere far from the Liar's Club. Like the West Indies. Or the moon.

Chapter Twenty-four

———◆———

The foursome got back to Etheridge House by the simple expedient of hiring a hack. There was certainly no danger of the cabbie recognizing George, for the Prince Regent was filthy, bruised, and gray with fatigue. Not the fastidiously elegant image of him that was usually portrayed. Therefore, they drove up to the house in style and stumbled from the carriage in all their damaged glory, manacles and all.

It turned out they were expected. Not only was Dalton there, but Lord Liverpool was as well. The Sergeant was speechless as he held open the door for them, nearly forgetting to bow to George. Then he caught himself, bobbed a quick dip of respect, and scurried to pay the hack.

Ethan Damont was directed to a front parlor with a wide-eyed Stubbs, who walked away with his head turned nearly reversed on his neck, gawking at the Prince Regent. Dalton greeted Collis with a brief nod, but his cool demeanor could not hide his immense relief.

Liverpool was not nearly so impressed. The door of Dalton's study had scarcely shut on the three of them and Dalton when the Prime Minister's temper burst. "George, you flaming idiot!"

George, who had gratefully sunk into Dalton's best chair, had only enough stamina to shrug helplessly. "It seemed like a fine idea at the time."

"Do you have any idea of the uproar you've caused?" Liverpool went on in this vein for a while. Rose sat pale and horrified as the Prime Minister carried on. Collis did think it was rather too bad of him to berate His Highness before others that way. Then again, the Liars were as safe as priests, weren't they? There would certainly be no gossip coming from this room.

Speaking of which—he cleared his throat loudly enough to distract even Liverpool's rage. "My lords, a more pressing issue is . . . how did the Voice of Society know His Highness was . . . ah . . . out and about?"

Even Liverpool had to admit that the entire affair would have been much less public without the gossip columnist. The leak had troubled them before, yet no progress had ever been made in the search for the informant. *Someone* knew too bloody much and wasn't shy about telling it.

"Well, you've done it now, George," Liverpool said with slightly more restrained ire. "That outrageous challenge to these . . . these amateurs! . . . to accompany you on your misadventure? Madness! Are you *trying* to have yourself committed?"

Dalton folded his arms. "That's a bit much, my

lord." He looked very uncomfortable with Liverpool's assertions. "It isn't for you to make that decision anymore."

No, Collis thought. Liverpool had left his seat on the Royal Four to take the appointment to Prime Minister—and only the Royal Four had the combined muscle to remove a king from a throne, a power they did not take lightly. Even then, King George III had had to exhibit undeniable madness before steps were taken.

Come to think of it, Liverpool had been a part of that decision at the time. . . .

Collis's drifting attention was caught by George rising. They all scrambled to their feet as well.

Rose hopped up quickly. It was odd, how comfortable she had become in the company of a prince. But their adventure was over. George was again "Your Highness," and she was again simply Rose Lacey. She must watch herself to behave properly now.

Before he left the room, George turned wearily to clap one hand on Collis's shoulder. "It was an honor and a pleasure to spend time with . . . with such lively young adventurers. I won't forget how you kept that maniac distracted from me, son."

Collis bowed his head in silent acknowledgment. From Rose's view, for just a moment, both Collis and the Prince Regent were in perfect mirror profile.

Perfect. Every turn of lip and dip of nose was identical, despite the bruising. Etheridge coloring aside, Collis could have been George's brother.

Son. The icy wash of realization kept her frozen

for a long heartbeat. George turned to cup her cheek briefly, then moved off with Lord Liverpool, his shoulders sagging in exhaustion.

"He called you son," Rose breathed.

Collis turned to cast her a questioning glance. "What's that?"

Dalton stepped between them. "Collis, Simon will debrief you. Miss Lacey, you're with me, if you please."

Rose turned automatically to follow Lord Etheridge to a small morning room. The cozy chamber and the roaring fire should have been welcome treats. She stood there blindly, scarcely aware of her surroundings. *Son.*

Like the stamping mill in Louis's factory, the clues came down upon her mind with numbing force.

The lengths that had been gone to in order to make Collis Tremayne a lord's heir and not a simple lieutenant colonel's heir.

"Gretchen—who became more a nanny to me than a companion to my mother—"

Lady Gretchen, from the King's court. What highborn lady would consent to be an ordinary nanny? A *royal* nanny, now . . . that was something else altogether.

"They treated him more like a royal heir than simply Etheridge's heir."

"Rose."

She was snatched from her stunning realization by Lord Etheridge's voice. Yes, the debriefing. She stammered a bit, her mind still spinning, then began to tell his lordship precisely how she'd come to be at Wadsworth's house.

She stood before him like a schoolchild repeating the lesson. Which, in a way, she was. She spared herself nothing. From her first foolish mistake to her final error in not reporting in, she told the spymaster everything. He watched her with cool appraisal, occasionally nodding encouragement.

When she finally wound down, he gestured for her to sit, then took the chair opposite. "Miss Lacey, you have been exceptionally lucky, but perhaps there is less luck involved than you realize. You have demonstrated a knack for information analysis again and again. Putting clues together is one thing. Putting clues together while on the run is something else altogether. The ability to think on one's feet is a rare and fine thing. Yet perhaps not surprising, considering your experiences in Edward Wadsworth's service."

She caught her breath to ask his meaning but stopped. He raised a brow at her small noise of confusion. "Is a servant not required to anticipate others in order to survive? In your case, I mean that literally. Living in constant danger is wonderful training for the espionage trade."

Could that be? All those years, living in shadow and careful silence? "You believe I gained from that, my lord?"

"Why not? It is the hard knocks of the hammer that shape the iron, after all. The question everyone must ask themselves is, How am I going to use what life has given me? You'd make a handy thief. Or a wildly efficient housekeeper." He did smile slightly then. "And, as tempting as it is to hire you to run Etheridge for me, I think I'll pass."

He was jesting with her, of course. Especially the comment about becoming a thief. Did he think her untrustworthy?

"It truly was a mistake, my lord, at first," she hurried to reassure him. "I thought I brought out the Wentworth dossier."

"I wonder. Simon believes in hunches, as he calls them. Intuition, I suppose he means, although he claims that the mind is always processing information, even when we are not aware of it. He would probably conclude that a part of you did know that you had the wrong file."

Intuition. It sounded like huggery-muggery to her. "I don't know about that, my lord."

He didn't smile, although the corners of his eyes did crinkle a bit. "Neither do I. I prefer to deal in facts. Something I would recommend you keep in mind, now that you are no longer one of Simon's students."

Oh, no. She *was* being sacked. "My lord?"

"Welcome to the Liar's Club, Miss Lacey."

She couldn't speak. Finally, she inhaled at last. "Thank you, my lord," she said faintly. Then she thought of something else. Collis . . . but what of Collis, now? If what she had surmised was true, then someone must know. Someone like Lord Etheridge.

"And Collis, my lord?" She watched him closely. "Will he be admitted to the Liars as well?"

"That remains to be seen." Lord Etheridge tented his fingers, tapping the tips to his chin. "Rose," he said finally, "one of the things that makes a good operative is the ability to know when to use information . . . and when not." He tilted his head. "I'd like to tell you a story."

She blinked at his casual tone but nodded obediently. "As you wish, sir."

"There was once a man who had a sister. She was a good deal older than him, so he did not know her well, although by all accounts she was a fine woman." He contemplated the carpet for a moment. "This sister married a good man, entirely her choice, but she wed quite young. Her husband was a military man and often gone from home for great lengths of time. Lord Liverpool took pity on her loneliness and brought her to Court. She was witty and very attractive, and soon made some . . . influential friends."

Collis's mother had been stunningly beautiful, from her portrait hanging in this house. Rose could see where his lordship was heading. George, with his eye for beauty, had been the influential friend. Pretty Mrs. Tremayne was young and flattered, Mr. Tremayne was older and patient . . .

It was well known that Prinny was fond of married women and, despite his regard for his "dear Fitzherbert," he had always been a dallying sort.

Dalton cleared his throat. "It was a brief period at Court and much regretted by this sister. She confessed all to her husband even before she knew she was with child. His patience and compassion finally won her love forever, I believe."

Rose noticed that his lordship had very carefully mentioned no names.

"Of course, she never told her brother of this. He learned it when he gained possession of their letters after they died. She loved her husband and son with all her heart. They were as happy as I've ever seen a family be."

"I'm sure they were, sir."

He still wasn't looking at her. How difficult it must be for such a private man to open locked doors of the past. His jaw worked. "Do you believe there is any point in Collis knowing of this?"

Rose studied his profile silhouetted against the flames. So like Collis, and yet so very different. He was nowhere near as cool as he seemed. His hand resting on the arm of the chair was posed casually, yet the tension in his fingers dented the taut fabric. His gaze was fixed nowhere in particular, yet his entire being seemed aimed at her as if she held his treasure in her careless hands.

"What of truth, then?" she asked quietly. "Is it not Collis's right to know who his father is?"

"Collis's father was Wallace Tremayne, in Collis's truth. But you could change that. Would you take his father from him, staining every memory he has with this other truth?"

Rose lifted her chin at the tone in his voice. "You wish me to believe that no political advantage holds your hand?"

That brought a wry sound from his throat. "Trust me, Miss Lacey. There is no political advantage to Collis in knowing the truth. It would change every-thing, and nothing. George would still make no claim,

Princess Charlotte would still take the throne, and all you will have done is bring Collis to the attention of anyone with a vendetta against the Crown."

Rose could see it clearly. The plotting that would ensue, the dark influences who would only too gladly try to use Collis as a sort of figurehead to take over the government.

His lordship was watching her now. "Rather makes Liverpool seem the lesser evil now, doesn't it?"

Convinced, Rose nodded soberly. "But the concerns of the Crown will not convince *me*."

He raised a brow at her and waited.

"I mean no disrespect, my lord, but I cannot agree to keep your secret. I must make my own decision on the question."

A corner of his mouth quirked. "Well said, and so I must allow it is so. You have come far, Miss Lacey." He smiled in earnest. "Indeed, if you managed to turn Ethan Damont into a useful example of humanity. What did you do to him, anyway?"

Remembering her behavior, Rose nearly laughed. "I made him get up from his drinking binge and help me get into the factory."

His lordship's eyes widened. "You *made* him?"

Rose nodded. "I fear so, my lord. I was most forceful about it."

A brief chuckle rumbled from somewhere deep in his chest, but he almost covered it with a cough. "I, ah, see. Well, I'm sure you did no lasting harm to Mr. Damont's reputation as a libertine."

"No, sir, I'm sure you're right. Still, he was very drunk. It required a certain amount of icy water."

Chuckling out loud, Lord Etheridge only shook his head at her. "You have no idea how intimidating you can be, do you?"

Intimidating? "Me, sir?" Rose could only blink at him. "But I'm just a—"

He held up a hand. "Don't. Don't say that you are only a maid, Miss Lacey. You are not a housemaid any longer. You are a trained and accomplished Liar and don't you ever forget it."

She took a deep breath, for the air had somehow grown sweeter. "I am a Liar," she said softly to herself. Then she pinned him with a sharp look. "When will you induct Collis? He deserves it every bit as much as I."

Lord Etheridge inhaled. "Miss Lacey, that is complicated."

A voice came from behind her. "That is none of your business, girl."

Rose turned to find Lord Liverpool and Clara standing in the doorway. The Prime Minister indicated Rose with a disparaging flick of his stick. "Not this one?"

Rose saw Clara stiffen. "You asked for Miss Rose Lacey, my lord. This is she."

Lord Liverpool's eyes turned to slits. If Rose had been standing in the arena, she would be bracing herself for attack. Then again, bracing herself seemed like a very good idea.

The Prime Minister walked toward her silently. He wasn't a big man, not much taller than her and spare of flesh, but he was a man of enormous presence. Rose felt that presence—that *disapproving* presence—like a force pushing her backward.

Pushing her down.

She stood as tall as she could manage for the shaking in her knees. He stopped no more than a foot away from her and tilted his head, considering her. "You're a plain, pale thing. I don't understand the attraction." He turned toward Dalton. "How do you propose to separate Tremayne from this opportunistic creature?"

"They were merely partners in the test mission, my lord," the spymaster said. "They are comrades. No more." He smiled slightly at Rose. "Miss Lacey is all business, my lord."

Ah. Rose thought that might be a very good moment to gaze elsewhere. There was a lovely vase on a pedestal table. Very fine, all cool blue and white—

"Miss Lacey?" Lord Etheridge's voice was impossible to ignore.

Rose swallowed. How much should she reveal? It all seemed so pointless now. If Collis had been out of her reach as the future Lord Etheridge, then he was very nearly invisible to her now. She met Lord Etheridge's silver gaze. "Yes, my lord?"

"Lord Liverpool is curious about the state of your relationship with Collis." He cast the Prime Minister an acid glance. "It is of course none of his bloody business, but be a good girl and reassure him."

The breath left her lungs. Oh, *bugger.*

Chapter Twenty-five

◆

Rose swallowed, stalling while her frantic mind flittered from lie to truth like a captured bird. The state of her relationship? As of now? "Collis is a much respected colleague to me, my lord." A scrap of truth won out. "And a very good friend."

"There, my lord, you see?" The spymaster waved a hand. "Nothing to worry about."

Liverpool was inspecting Rose as if she were an unwelcome insect. She clasped her hands behind her back—mainly to keep from shaking—and watched him warily.

"I'll bloody well worry if I like," the Prime Minister retorted. "Tremayne has enormous expectations. He could be very useful someday."

Useful. A handy item to keep around. Or throw away. Rose couldn't bear it. Collis was so much more than a tool for political manipulation.

Expectations, my arse.

Lord Liverpool's eyes narrowed. "What did you say?"

"Oh, *bugger*." Rose bit her lips shut.

The Prime Minister didn't take his predatory gaze from her. "Etheridge, is this how you teach your gang of ruffians to respect authority?"

Dalton folded his arms. "Miss Lacey, is there something you wish to say? You may speak freely."

There was a great deal she would like to say to Lord Liverpool, master manipulator that he was. Yet she held silent. Until she saw that flash of triumph in the man's colorless eyes.

Oh, now that is simply that. Collis was being held in reserve by this political shark, hanging lost and without his well-earned status as a Liar, because of this man's desire for power. Protective fury came upon her like a tide.

"You, with your plans within plots within schemes!" Rose burst out. "Did you think of this before or after Collis was born, Lord Liverpool? You always think so far ahead, don't you? Did you throw Collis's mother in the way of the Prince on purpose?"

Dalton jerked at that. Rose saw it from the corner of her vision but did not halt. "Is it not a sweet contingency plan? A half-prince, a spare—unsuspecting his power, yet close at hand in case George's future bride did not breed well. Or was it in case His Highness continued in his wild ways?"

Liverpool gazed coolly back at her. "I'm sure I have no idea what you are speaking of. You've concocted an interesting fantasy, but it has nothing to do with me, girl."

Clara lifted her chin. "Miss Lacey, my lord."

Liverpool's eyes slid to Clara. "She is a servant, a housemaid."

Clara stood firm. "She is a woman who has proven her loyalty to England and His Highness again and again. She deserves to be addressed accordingly."

Rose shook her head. "I thank you, my lady, but I do not care for his good opinion any more than he cares for mine." She threw up her hands. "Collis is a man, blast you! Not simply a contingency plan!" She held Dalton in her gaze for a moment. "Not even for you."

"Rose!" Dalton barked. "You endanger your place."

"No, she is quite correct." Clara moved to stand with Rose. "Dalton, make your own heir or let Etheridge go." She turned to Liverpool. "My lord, you have a perfectly good princess at hand. Charlotte is everything George is not. She'll make a marvelous queen someday, if you don't stamp every independent thought from her head."

"I have ever said so," replied the Prime Minister smoothly. "I cannot think where you lot have come across this fantastic idea."

Rose took a breath. "So you'll free Collis?"

"I've no need to free him. Collis knows his duty and his place."

Rose sighed and rubbed her forehead with one hand. "I'm sure he does. Every suffocating ounce of it."

Liverpool tapped his chin with one finger. "And what of you, Miss Lacey? Are you willing to free Mr. Tremayne?"

Rose eyed him warily. He hadn't believed her. Had the Prince revealed them? "I have no grip on Collis," she said truthfully. "The . . . partnership is dissolved with the end of the test."

"Hmm." Liverpool's expression of sour disbelief did not alter.

Clara interceded delicately. "If you have finished with Miss Lacy, my lord, she needs to get some rest."

"Oh, no, milady!" Rose protested. "There's no time to waste. We must stop the shipment!"

Dalton nodded. "And we will. I have already sent Feebles to the docks to track down the vessel used, and we're trying to bring in as many Liars as we can. Unfortunately, they scattered at dawn to continue the search for His Highness. When we have what we need, we'll move immediately." He gave her a short nod. "You've done well. Go and rest now."

Rose felt the urgent momentum leave her at his words. There was nothing more for her to do at the moment. Weariness stole up her limbs to weaken her spine and fog her mind. "Yes, my lord." *Rest. Oh, yes.*

But first, Collis. She simply needed to see that he was well tended to. And perhaps to wish a silent Godspeed to what would never be. She curtseyed to all and let Clara direct her out.

Back in the study, Dalton was trying to interpret the expression on Clara's face when she returned. She ought to have supported him just now. She of all people knew why he could not afford to release Collis from the burden of Etheridge. Now she was regarding him with what seemed to be repressed humor—or was it joy?

She met his eyes, then glanced downward. He followed her gaze to her midriff, where she casually clasped her hands just below her waist. As he watched, she spread both hands flat upon her belly in a gentle gesture. When she raised her gaze to his again, there was mischief and, yes, definitely joy. Dalton took a very deep breath. *At last.* He suddenly felt as if he could conquer worlds. He wanted to go to her, to pull her into his arms, to—

An irritated throat clearing reminded Dalton that his honored guest was still in the room. Liverpool regarded him sourly. "I know you encourage independence, Etheridge, but I do think you might have tried a bit harder to control that upstart housemaid. Tremayne is of no use if he's saddled with such an embarrassing attachment. What were you thinking, sending someone so valuable on a test mission? I told you from the beginning, this business of Liar training is nonsense. He can never be permitted to go into such danger."

Dalton couldn't stop looking at his beautiful Clara. "It kept him from eating his pistol," he said absently.

"Well, I hope you intend to divide him from these ruffian companions soon. Housemaids, bah! The next thing you know, he'll be wanting to marry that creature!"

Would the man never leave? Dalton folded his arms and regarded his leader and mentor with a supremely unconcerned gaze. "I'm sure I have no idea what you are speaking of. What a fantastic idea."

Rose found Collis in his quarters. He opened the door dabbing at his lip with a handkerchief, having just had

Denny tend his cuts and bruises and dress him in a shirt and breeches covered by a dark blue dressing gown that turned his eyes the color of slate. His hair clung damply to the periphery of his face and his bruises were much less frightening now that he was clean.

He smiled happily at her, then flinched when he pulled at his split lip. "Rose! Come in!" He stepped back to let her in. "You haven't had a moment to change, I see. Did Dalton make you go over every bloody thing three times?"

She had to step past him as she entered the outer sitting room of his chambers. The pull to put his arms around her was powerful.

"Hello." She looked confused and a bit wary. Collis gently pushed the door closed. She didn't object, but neither did she relax. She merely stood by the door as if she couldn't wait to leave.

"Rose, what is bothering you?" She seemed to pull even farther away, although he was not touching her. "If you don't want to tell me, simply say so. I won't pry."

She nodded shortly. "I don't want to tell you."

"Why not?" He sighed and offered her a smile. "Breaking my word already, aren't I?"

She didn't smile back. He felt as though the last week had never happened. As if he had never seen her smiling, never felt her warm skin on his, never been kissed in entirely surprising places by that solemn mouth. "Where have you gone, Briar Rose?" he asked her softly.

She actually flinched at the name. Collis began to

be very worried indeed. He dropped his casual pose to go to her where she stood so stiffly by the door as if she feared for her ability to retreat. She looked away as he approached, but he saw her raise one hand to her throat. Her fingers were trembling.

"Rose?"

"Yes?"

"What has changed?" He reached to stroke a finger down her cheek. Her eyelids dropped to cover her gaze, but he thought she leaned into the caress ever so slightly. He cupped her face in his hand—no, two hands for Rose, always—in his two hands, carefully. He tipped her face up to kiss her lips. For a long moment she did not respond, her lips cool and quiet beneath his. Where was his fiery warrior? He deepened the kiss. Desperation began to rise in him. He'd been so sure of his reception—what had changed? What had he done to turn her away?

"Why have you left me, Rose?" he growled into her lips. "What have I done?"

She pulled away in a desperate spasm. "Nothing! You've done nothing." She turned from him to tug at the door latch. "I should go."

Her back was as stiff as armor, her movements jerky and panicked. Something was wrong. He moved behind her to gently place his hands over her shoulders. She reacted as if his touch was icy cold, twitching as he held her. Determined to break through her inexplicable resistance, he lowered his mouth to that sensitive place behind her ear. "Stay," he whispered into those soft wisps of hair. "Talk to me."

She spun from him in a fierce motion, turning to face him at last. Her gaze was dark and unreadable, but he was glad to see that her color was high and bright once more. Her frozen pallor had been much too disturbing. Rose in a passion was someone he could reach.

He laughed, trying to keep his voice light. "You were ever hard to keep a hold on."

"Collis, I don't—I can't—" She shook her head fiercely, as if shedding water.

He rubbed his head. "I don't know what I've done, but I'm sorry. Please, don't punish me further without at least telling me how I've turned you away."

"I'm not punishing you, Collis."

"Well, it bloody well feels like it from my end!" He controlled his unease with an effort. "Rose, would you just sit down for a moment and talk to me? Just talk, I promise."

She sat, perching on the edge of the sofa cushion like a tightened spring, ready to unwind in a bound. He settled next to her, afraid to sit too close, afraid to sit too far away. "Will you answer one question?"

She didn't look at him, but she nodded.

"What of the night we spent together?"

She took a deep breath. "That was . . . very nice."

"Nice?" Unbearable. "You're lying."

"What if I am?"

"Well, I won't lie. That night was . . . it was my salvation, do you understand? I felt as though I was a man again, instead of a thing of wood and straw. You made me feel alive for the first time since . . ."

She shifted her gaze toward him at last. "Since?"

"Since I last touched the keys of my piano."

A tiny tilt occurred at the corner of her mouth, not quite a smile, but reward enough for the confession. "I'm glad," she said softly.

He touched that mouth with one finger, drawing it over the softness of her bottom lip. "Did that night change nothing for you?"

She took a deep breath, then turned and face him fully at last. "Collis, do you want to make love to me again?"

"Absolutely," he responded promptly. "But perhaps not just now. First I'd like to hear your answer."

She stood. "And I think I'd like to feel you inside me." She began to unbutton the front of her trousers in swift, efficient motions.

Collis blinked. "Rose—wait—"

The waistcoat dropped to the floor. She was wearing only a shirt beneath it. He could see the soft plumpness of her tidy breasts pressing against the worn linen. He cleared his suddenly dry throat. "Rose, now wait just a moment—"

Finally clad in nothing but the shirt, she smiled at last, a wide, reckless grin. Approaching him with a slow, languid stride, she put both hands on his shoulders and one bare silken knee astride him and pressed him back on the sofa. He resisted, despite the erection tenting his dressing gown. "Rose, this is not what I want—"

"Liar," she growled. Then she flipped them both neatly, him atop her. "You were ever easy to toss," she said huskily. She kissed him, her mouth hot and giving, her supple body writhing beneath his. "I want your mouth on me," she ordered. "I want your hands on me. Now."

"Rose—" He was the stupidest man alive, to be turning down such a goddess. He flipped her above him once more. "I want to talk to you." He didn't want to hold back anymore. He needed to tell her how much he loved her.

She backed off of him and stood, her chin high in challenge. "All right then, blueblood." She stood with her feet apart in readiness stance . . . which was quite a sight when she was nearly naked. Her shirt clung to her lithe body as she moved, and the sinuous muscles of her thighs flexed. Very distracting.

"Throw me."

He jerked his gaze away from where the soft linen outlined the vee of her thighs. "What?"

The corner of her mouth twitched. "Double-damn dare you," she said huskily.

Well, then. He had no choice at all, did he? They could talk later.

He stood and crossed slowly to her, tugging off his shirt as he did so. Her gaze slid over his body like hot hands, and his erection pulsed in response. He raised one hand in a slow arc, as if he were trying to move through water, or molasses. Her eyes narrowed in appreciation of his tactic, and she responded to his move with matching slowness.

Their battle became a dance, one of slow, sliding moves and sensuous, embracing holds. Hot skin to hot skin, she pulled him close. Instead of being rolled over her shoulder, he turned to press against her back, with his good arm crooked over her throat, his hand thrust into her hair.

She pressed against him for an instant, her head falling back onto his shoulder. His lips found her neck for a single long moment before she arced away from him again. With the grace of a long-legged bird, she kicked one foot high. Rather than striking him, she merely rested her bare foot on his chest for an instant, then rolled backward in a controlled flip that proved there was nothing at all beneath that shirt.

He followed her with a spinning low kick that tripped her gently into his arms. They fell together onto the carpet.

Altogether more satisfactory. Kurt had always stressed the importance of good floor work. Their bodies rolled like one being, erotically wrestling the last of their clothing free. Rose's shirt landed on the floor and was lost in the sensuous scuffle. Collis's trousers met a similar fate behind a chair.

Finally, he had her just where he wanted her. He lay flat on his back, pinned by her shapely knees on either side of his head. With both hands, he carefully cupped her bare bottom, pressing her forward for his kiss. His tongue slipped inside her, caressing the very center of her desire. He flicked, then stroked, then circled her in an ever-varying ride of ecstasy.

Gasping, breathless, Rose allowed the pleasurable shocks to roll through her undenied. There was no point in pretending that she did not feel what she felt, no worth in hiding her passionate response. She did remember to press one hand over her own mouth when she peaked, some scrap of sanity recalling that they were still in Etheridge House.

At last she collapsed upon him, falling back onto his chest and hard stomach. He untangled her weakened legs for her and caught her neatly when she rolled from him. "Where do you think you are going?"

"To the bed?"

"Pantywaist. Will there be beds on every mission?"

Rose giggled at the perfect mimicry. The remark was classic Kurt, only Rose didn't think she'd ever heard Kurt speak on this particular topic.

"Yes, sir," she said with mocking respect. "The floor it is, sir."

He pulled her down to him until she lay atop him, nose to nose, toes to toes . . . but for the fact that her toes dangled somewhat closer to his ankles. She stroked her toes down his manly, hairy ankles. She'd never thought to admire a man's ankles before, probably because she'd rarely seen any, but she had to admit that Collis's ankles were as perfect as the rest of him. She rolled her head to take a bite at his stone-hard bicep. "You are too perfect," she murmured.

He laughed, a low rumble deep in his throat. "Is that possible?"

"It is if you are you and I am me."

She hadn't meant anything by the comment, but something angry flashed behind his laughing eyes. He pulled her higher and bit her lightly on the chin. "You are perfectly you, Briar Rose Lacey, and I wouldn't have you any other way."

Too serious. Rose tossed him a challenging grin designed to change the mood. "Well, speak for yourself. I would have you—" She rolled him over her with a well-placed tug. His legs fell between hers, and she spread them willingly. "This way."

God, a willing, passionate Rose beneath him on the carpet, the firelight shining on her fine skin, her hair a tossed skein of dark silk across the floor. Her thighs came up to wrap about his waist with authority, and the rest of his poetic thoughts faded at the feel of her moist center pressing urgently to his erection. His brain slowed, with only dark and animal thoughts allowed.

Hot. Wet. Woman.

His woman.

Now.

Her throat arched and her head fell back as he took her hard. Each thrust rippled up her supple body as he watched her take him fully again and again. Then his vision glazed as the pleasure took him over. She was all around him, her arms and legs trapping him, her soft, tight dampness owning him. He was hers entirely and she was his.

They thrust wildly together, two strong and bestial creatures locked in the growing darkness as the fire died, as the room cooled, and finally the candle burned out. In full darkness at last, Rose allowed her soul to be entirely free. She came to him hard, repeatedly, without restraint, until he had to cover her mouth with his own to contain her raw cries of ecstasy. At last he growled deeply into her neck as he took his own satisfaction with a last forceful thrust that tore a husky gasp from her weary throat.

He collapsed beside and upon her, and she relished

his warm weight. She felt his heart pounding against hers, as if they were two more caged beasts fighting to get to each other.

But no. His heart was not for her.

She felt him reach high, then felt the warmth of the counterpane fall over them in a careless drape. He sighed and his body eased with sleep. With the last of her strength, she wrapped her arms about her lover, her charmer, her prince . . . and fell asleep holding him.

Chapter Twenty-six

❖

Rose opened her eyes to stare at her lover through sleepy eyes. Collis was stretched out on his stomach on the carpet beside her—minus any sort of covers. Hmm. She appeared to have taken complete possession of the bed linens. With a small, rueful laugh, she pulled the counterpane over his naked body.

Of course, she did it very slowly, for the view in the last glow of the coals was quite astonishing. His long, delightfully hairy, muscular legs were covered first. Then that magnificent rear. He shifted, moving toward the warmth, causing her to pause for a moment to admire the rippling muscles in his buttocks.

In truth, she'd always wanted a room with a view. Although currently, the rest of the view had a good many livid bruises in sight.

He mumbled and moved again, seeking the heat of her body. She kissed his air-cooled shoulder in apology, then covered him completely. He relaxed once more, going still.

It seemed she had some things to learn about sleeping with a lover.

Lover.

She'd come to him yesterday evening out of a need to see that he was recovering from his beating at Louis's hands, and to decide whether to tell him the truth of his parentage . . . and to say good-bye to any future they might have had together.

She'd found herself completely unable to talk to him. She had felt as though the secrets were simply piling up within her, choking off her words.

She couldn't bear to tell him the truth about Louis. She couldn't risk seeing that awful disdain rising against her again. From the Liars, it would devastate her. From Collis—she shuddered. *No.* That bit of the past was best kept buried. Besides, there was no need to tell anyone now. Louis need never even know she, Rose Lacey, had aught to do with his fall.

Collis being the Prince's bastard . . . that was going to require some thought. If she wasn't so sure that Collis would hate every moment of royal heirdom—as he now hated being heir to Etheridge—she would tell him immediately. She had no family, no parents living. It was a lonely existence. Collis had one who was mightily fond of him. He should be told he still had a father, shouldn't he? She still couldn't decide.

As for saying good-bye—that hadn't gone precisely as planned. She'd quite suddenly lost all resolve when faced with her actual Collis, although she had tried to keep her intent light and uninvolved. As happy as she was that he wanted her and that she had healed him of his fears of insufficiency, she dreaded the eventual breakage of her heart. Surely the pain would worsen the more nights they spent together.

She ought to go now, before he awoke. Perhaps if she kept from him for a few days—or years—or possibly decades—she would be able to save her even-now fracturing heart. Moving carefully, she began to slide from under the counterpane. She found her shirt and pulled it over her head, then bent to reach for her trousers where they lay next to Collis.

Even before opening his eyes, Collis moved like a striking snake. His sleepy mind was only aware of one thing. He wasn't letting her go. Ever.

He caught her hand to pull her to him. She resisted. Abruptly he gentled his approach. With tenderness, he twined his fingers through hers and brought her hand to his lips. "Stay," he whispered into her palm. He brought their twined hands to his brow as if to ease a pain there. "I need you."

His eyes were filled with a warmth that Rose could not resist. She moved an inch closer, then another. He simply waited, holding her hand lightly to his cheek, until she came close enough to kiss.

"Well," she said, as she pulled away and gave him a look of mock frustration. "Are you going to make love to me or not?"

Collis knew she was running away from the moment and he let her. She was still too shy of moments of real emotion, he reminded himself. He only hoped that keeping her in his bed would make her forget what she was running from long enough for him to secure her heart.

So he smiled and tugged on her hand. "Are you trying to seduce me, Briar Rose?"

She smiled, obvious in her relief at his tacit agreement to let the moment go. "How does one seduce the
Mighty Tremayne?" She put her other hand in his and
pulled him to his feet. "Do I merely need to trip you
and fall on you?"

"That will just about do," he said airily, and pulled
her into his arms. If he could not speak his need, then
he would show it.

Rose greatly feared that she was making the mistake of her life, but she could not leave him tonight.
Tomorrow, she would explain . . . if she could. This
night was her gift, and in the years to come, she
hoped, her solace.

When he reached for the hem of the shirt she wore,
she raised her arms to allow him to pull it over her
head. He tugged it as high as her wrists, then gave it a
small twist, tying her playfully. It was a useless
bondage, for she could free herself with a tug, but she
allowed it. The feeling of being vulnerable before
him in her nakedness sent small darts of heat through
her belly. Collis was her friend as well as lover. She
would trust him with her life. She knew she'd come to
no harm in his little game.

She let her hands drop behind her head and stood
before him like an offering.

He raised a brow, his expression amused but his
gaze hot. "I like you like that."

"I'll wager you do." She gave him a sultry look.
"But careful, I'm an excellent kicker."

He smiled slightly and trailed a finger over her collarbone. "Methinks the lady wants her ankles tied, too."

"Methinks the gentleman had best shut up and get busy."

"Is that so?" His large warm hands covered her hips and he bent to take her nipple into his mouth. She sucked in her breath at the sweet pain/pleasure as he allowed his teeth to gently bite. She didn't even realize he was maneuvering her backward step-by-step until her back encountered the cool wood of the bedpost.

With his hands pinning her there and her own hands restrained, she had no choice but to allow him to delicately torture her breasts and nipples with pleasure. Her knees were still weak from their first bout. Now they went to water as he made free with his imaginative mouth. She grabbed the slick wood of the bedpost with what little grip she could manage through the wound shirt fabric, just to keep from sliding down it to the floor. Her cleft swelled with wanting until she could feel her very heartbeat throb within it. He caressed her not at all but simply held her hips to the post and drove her mad with lips, tongue, and teeth. He brought his knee to press between her thighs lightly, teasingly, not nearly firmly enough—

She was going mad. The wanting was so good, but it went on until her entire body quivered for release. He was tenderly merciless, and she forgot all about that easy tug to free her hands. The control was his to serve, as ecstasy was his to give.

Finally, it occurred to her to beg. "Collis, I need you. Take me now. Please!"

In a heartbeat she was on her back on the bed and

he was naked above her. With a single wicked thrust, he was inside her. With another, she was in pieces, sobbing his name gratefully as the pulsating pleasure took her over.

He was ruthless, driving her up again and again, never allowing her body to still that inner vibration that kept her vulnerable to further stimulation. Finally, as she begged for release yet again, her voice gone hoarse and husky from her cries, he took her to the edge once more and fell over it with her. With a guttural cry of his own, he pulsated within her as she gasped for breath over her pounding heart.

He collapsed half upon her, with one leg still threaded between hers and his left arm most unselfconsciously slung across her waist.

As her breath began to steady at last, despite the lingering spasms of pleasure within her, she opened her eyes to stare at the forest-green velvet bed hangings above. "Collis Clarence Tremayne—what in hell *was* that?"

He chuckled weakly into her neck. "I think they call it 'making love.'"

"I think they call it 'the end of the world'!" She tried to untangle the shirt from her hands but dropped them back onto the pillow over her head, too tired to care. "Whew! My legs are shaking. I hope you don't plan on making me get up anytime during the next year."

He bit her earlobe lightly. "I think I could occupy you for about that long."

"Braggart."

"Vixen."

She yawned helplessly. He followed suit an instant

later and they laughed at each other. "I only need a moment to recover," she said. "Then I'll slip out."

He didn't answer, for he was very nearly asleep with his face tucked into her neck, but his disabled arm tightened around her waist. She gently eased his grip slightly, then allowed her eyes to close. Just for a moment.

The door to Collis's bedchamber opened. Dalton stuck his head in. "We've got the ship name! Time to—"

He halted, obviously dismayed at finding the two of them so. Damn. Collis hadn't precisely wanted their courtship announced until—well, until he'd had the opportunity to court her, for pity's sake! Collis blinked at his uncle, then shook himself awake. "Can we catch them?"

Dalton was very carefully looking at the floor and not at Rose's tousled and extremely nude state. Collis appreciated the courtesy in a grim sort of way. Of course, he'd have preferred the courtesy of, oh, say, *knocking*.

Rose was blushing furiously and pulling on what items of clothing she could reach without letting go her death grip on the covers pulled over her breasts. Collis turned to Dalton. "Why don't you wait in the hall? We'll be right with you."

Dalton hesitated. He did not look pleased, with either of them. Collis bristled. "For God's sake, Dalton, I'm not fourteen!"

Dalton frowned. "Evidently." He left, pulling the door closed with a decisive click.

Rose scrambled for her clothing. She kept her head down, her face hidden beneath the fall of her hair.

"Rose, I—he isn't mad at you."

She was pulling up her stockings with hurried tugs. "I wouldn't be too sure. Oh, God, what he must think of me! Especially now—" She stopped and bit her lip.

Collis dragged his own shirt over his head. He felt better after Rose's ministrations and . . . well, *ministrations,* and a bit of sleep certainly hadn't hurt. Very nearly himself, but for the fact that something seemed amiss with his left arm. Just clumsier than usual, probably, after the beating it had taken from Louis. He ordered his hand to make a fist, watching it carefully. It obeyed, somewhat. Good enough. It wasn't as if he were going to use it anyway.

He got his boots on while she was buttoning her own sturdy shoes. Being a gentleman, he tried not to be distracted by the glimpse of white thigh she exposed while propping her foot on the chair. He decided he was grateful that the rest of the world didn't seem to see her beauty the way he did. Selfish, yes, but all the better to have her offer up her secrets to him alone. Naked Rose was too much for any mortal man, anyway.

Ready, she stood, quickly twisting her amazing hair into something sensible and humdrum. Collis smiled. Just the way he liked it.

"Ready?"

He knew she meant more than simply being dressed. Outside that door lay the world, and that world had just pierced their lovely fantasy. Perhaps even fatally.

No. He wouldn't—*couldn't* allow it. The world

and Dalton were simply going to have to understand. He needed Rose. That settled the matter.

Dalton wasn't angrily waiting in the hall as they'd have expected. He was in the entrance hall, directing the gathered Liars to two large Etheridge carriages waiting on the street. Rose clattered down in front of Collis, and they both took their wraps from a visibly twitching Denny.

Rose stared at the valet, who wouldn't meet her eye. If she didn't know any better she would swear that Denny looked . . . guilty? What did Denny have to be guilty of, other than his usual obnoxiousness? It hadn't been his fault that the message to Liverpool had been lost, and it hadn't been his fault that his lordship hadn't received Collis's note in time to come for the Prince Regent—

But the note had been sent in good time. Even allowing for the delivery to go somewhat astray, Dalton should have made it to Mrs. Blythe's by midnight. Unless whoever had informed the Voice of Society had somehow interpreted the message first—

Oh, Denny, you ass.

Rose grabbed the valet's arm in a grip Kurt had taught her and marched him out of the general bedlam. In the nook beneath the staircase, she let him pull away from her with a grimace.

"What's this 'ere?" he protested. "You got your nerve!"

Rose leaned in close. "You got the note early, didn't you? You knew where we were, where the Prince Regent was, and you couldn't resist the chance to make trouble."

Denny tugged at his collar, his eyes sliding away. "Don't know what you mean," he muttered. "Crazy mop."

Rose poked him in the chest with one finger. "You went to the Voice of Society and you sold us out! Because of you, the Prince Regent was put in terrible danger!"

He slapped her hand away feebly. "Did no such thing. You can't prove nothin'."

"The Sergeant said you came home with the note early in the morning. Where did you go, Denny?"

He stepped back and tugged at his waistcoat. "That's my business and none of yours. I got the note as I was coming into the house, just like I told his lordship!"

Rose crossed her arms. "You're a dead man, Denny. How could you be so *stupid*? Don't you realize what will happen to you when I tell them?"

Denny paled but kept his chin aggressively high. "Why would they believe you? I been here for years, workin' for Sir Simon, and for Mr. Cunnington, and for Master Collis—you been here for a few months! D'you really think they'll believe you over me?"

He had a point. Then Rose shook her head. No, she belonged now. "Of course they will, Denny. I'm a Liar."

Red fury washed Denny's cheeks. Rose almost felt sorry for him. Until she remembered Collis and George hanging bruised and bloody in that factory cellar. Denny's days might very well be numbered. The Liar's Club was on the side of right, but they didn't shy from doing what was necessary to preserve their secret existence. "You've gone too far, Denny."

Denny lifted a shaking hand to brush a sandy lock from his forehead. "No, it wasn't like that."

Dalton was shoving Liars out the door as fast as he could. "Miss Lacey, come along!" he called from across the entrance hall. Rose hesitated. There wasn't time for the spymaster to deal with Denny right now. "He has to know, Denny. Perhaps . . . perhaps if you told him yourself, confessed . . . it might go easier on you."

He rubbed his hands down his waistcoat. "D'you think so?"

She didn't, not really. But she shrugged. "Perhaps."

Denny nodded shortly. "I'll do it." He peered around her at an impatiently waiting Dalton. "When this has passed."

Rose tugged her shawl tighter and tilted her head warningly at him. "Don't wait too long, Denny." Then she turned away. She carefully avoided meeting Dalton's eye at the door.

Outside, Feebles handed her into the waiting carriage with the respect he'd always shown her, and she took her place among the Liars seated there.

At last.

Collis stepped up to speak to Dalton privately for a moment. It certainly wasn't the time, yet he had to dispel the chill disapproval that shrouded Dalton's expression. His uncle-nearly-brother was the only family he had. Collis had to make Dalton understand.

But Dalton spoke before Collis could. "Clara isn't feeling well," Dalton said absently as he watched the Liars climbing into the carriages.

Collis blinked, surprised. "I hope it will pass," he ventured.

A sudden boyish grin broke over Dalton's face. He looked very nearly giddy. "It will," he announced with pride, "Until tomorrow morning."

"Oh?" Collis frowned. "Oh!"

Dalton pasted his usual cool demeanor over his joy as they stepped up to the first carriage, but Collis imagined he could see it shining through the cracks. He clapped Dalton on the shoulder. "Well done, you old sod!" he whispered.

Dalton nodded shortly. "Thank you. I thought you should know."

Indeed. Collis felt unadulterated relief rush through him, like a cleansing wave.

"I must congratulate you as well," Dalton continued. "I hear the Liars will be calling you the Phoenix. Appropriate, I'd say." Dalton's expression held mingled worry and pride. "You have risen from the ashes indeed."

Collis's breath left him in a gust. *The Phoenix.* Now that was a dashing alias!

The world was suddenly finer and more glorious than he ever remembered. He was a Liar. And he was free, free to be an ordinary man. A spy. A husband.

He couldn't wait to tell Rose.

Chapter Twenty-seven

◆

In the foremost carriage, Collis wanted to sit by Rose—*damn, he was like an infatuated schoolboy*—but she squeezed in between Kurt and Button. Probably a good idea to have the two smallest Liars sit with the largest, ballast-wise.

Impossible to be jealous of Button. The Liars' costumer extraordinaire was more puckish than roguish. Impossible as well to be jealous of scarred man-mountain Kurt—yet Collis managed, in a buoyant, reckless way. At the moment, he'd be besottedly envious of a butterfly lighting on her shoulder.

For pity's sake, man, keep your mind on your job. A rush of pride went through him. His job. He had a place in this mad crew now. An earned place.

He looked at Rose, his lover and partner, and all his odd lot of comrades, and all was right in his world for the first time in a very long time. He and the Liars would stop the ship, the muskets and carbines would be seized, and the nameless, faceless British soldiers fighting on the Peninsula would not face that particular horror.

Yes, by God, he and Rose had earned their places.

The flush of the hunt carried him for a while. Then, after the first hour, the tight quarters of the carriage became arduous. Dalton would not allow Hawkins to slack in speed once they were out of the city proper. With clean hard-packed road ahead, the coachman let the horses run full out, sending the coach on a jarring, careening pace.

The passengers within were forced to brace themselves however they could, a draining exercise that left feet trodden, arses weary, and even heads knocked.

After the umpteenth time Stubbs's elbow contacted his sore ribs, Collis could bear it no longer. He leaned around Stubbs to speak to Dalton, who was gripping the hand strap with white-knuckled determination. No undignified bouncing for his lordship, of course. *Dalton, you truly need to unbind your lordly arse.*

"This is too slow!" Even yelling at the top of his lungs, Collis wasn't sure Dalton could hear him over the jangling, creaking carriage. "We'll never catch the ship this way." It took time for a ship to navigate the Thames, but that time was running out.

It was true. Even now, Collis could tell the coach horses were slowing, losing their fresh edge.

"What do you propose?" Dalton shouted back.

Collis was about to propose dumping half the Liars by the roadside, Stubbs in particular, when he spotted a hostelry sign on a post by the road.

THE WHITE CHARGER INN AND HOSTELRY.

Horses. Ycs. He pointed silently at it as it flashed by. Fortunately, Dalton saw it as well.

With one fist, Dalton pounded on the trap in the roof of the carriage. Hawkins flipped it open but only glanced down, for he was keeping the four at a gallop. Dalton shouted for him to stop.

It took a long moment for the carriage to slack its speed. The momentum of the overloaded burdens could not be allowed to overrun the tired carriage horses. With one last arse-bruising jolt, the carriage pulled to a halt. The sudden lack of clatter left their ears ringing. Collis was sure he wasn't the only one subtly letting go a sigh of relief.

The carriage behind them was already slowing, Collis saw when he thrust his head out the window. Simon must have seen the sign as well. The coaches couldn't turn, of course, so the Liars piled out, right there on the narrow, dusty road.

"What are we doing?" Button yawned. Of all of them, Button had been the most comfortable, drowsing on Rose's shoulder. How anyone could have slept through that brutal jouncing was beyond Collis.

He took Button by one arm and Rose took the other. Together the Liars marched back down the road and up the deep U-shaped drive of the inn.

The burly leather-aproned hosteller went wide-eyed at the sight of twelve dusty and intimidating travelers marching en masse up his drive.

"We likely look like highwaymen," Collis muttered to Rose over Button's natty beaver hat.

"What do you call highwaymen who hold up ships?" she sent back with a flash of smile.

Collis grinned fiercely. "Pirates."

Whether the man was more impressed by their intimidating appearance or the pound notes waved by Dalton, the horses were brought out in very short order. Not all the Liars were experienced riders, something Collis thought Dalton ought to attend to.

Rose went up behind Collis, for "the closest I've ever been to a horse is fetching the bottles in from the milk cart."

Ethan Damont was fitted with a fine hunter, which he received with an ironic bow for the hosteller. The only horse in the establishment large enough to carry Kurt was a heavy-boned gray plow horse. Mounted on the great beast, which didn't look nearly so large with Kurt on his back, the club's premiere assassin looked like a knight of old on his destrier. "The Green Knight," Ethan said blandly when he noted Kurt's unusual pallor.

Button plunked himself behind Ethan, because, as he proclaimed, "he is the best dressed." Simon and Dalton took their own mounts, with a pale Stubbs clinging behind Simon, but there was no persuasion in the world strong enough to get Feebles on horseback.

"Sir, you can shoot me now if you like, but I won't do it. Not a bit of it. Anyway, someone orta stay here with the carriages, like."

The Sergeant looked very fine and martial on a sturdy mare, and Collis was reminded that the man had not always run a lord's house.

Rigg and Fisher were put up on careworn mounts that the hosteller assured them would simply follow the others. With a wave to the unmounted Feebles and a great whoop of, "To the river, lads!"—and a few startled cries as the horses responded—the eleven very unlikely horsemen laid a trail of dust down the road to the Thames.

A fine day, a grand mission, a fairly acceptable horse—and Rose behind him, clinging to his waist with all her supple strength. What more could a man want? Collis nearly laughed aloud at his own mawkish thoughts, yet truly, he was happy. It had been so long, he scarcely recalled the warm sensation that now grew within him.

The thundering herd—or was it horde?—passed through a few tiny river towns, which they galloped through too quickly to glimpse more than a number of startled faces and weathered alehouses. Then the hard-packed road began to follow the river itself, trailing up and down the uneven land that banked it. Barge road, Collis realized. Large barges without steam or sails were pulled by chains attached to draft horses on the banks. The hard-packed road gave the Liars' own horses excellent footing as the miles flashed by.

Along this route, the Thames seemed cleaner and less like a glorified sewer, although that might have been an impression given by the refreshingly grassy banks. Coming from London, the water itself was likely as filthy as ever.

The river stretching ahead and curving out of sight was dotted with ships and boats of all types, but the *Clarimond* was a double-topsail schooner. Ethan claimed he could spot the distinctive sails from behind the trees.

They had been racing for what seemed like hours,

but surely wasn't, when Ethan raised one arm and shouted out. Ahead, just past the last slow bend before the sea, was a schooner, double topsails shining in the sun. They pushed their mounts to run up the slope to the top of the rise of the embankment that had pushed the river to such a bend.

From there they could see clearly. It was the *Clarimond,* sails full, heading for the mouth of the Thames and the open sea.

Dalton turned in the saddle and shouted, "Hurry, lads!"

The ship picked up speed even as they did and bid fair to outrace their tired mounts. Rose pounded on Collis's thigh to get his attention.

He turned his head to hear her over the pounding hoofbeats and the wind rushing past his ears.

"Is this bank too high?" she shouted. "Could we jump in and swim for it? Surely they'd notice that and stop to help."

Collis looked down at the distance from the grassy bluff at his horse's feet to the turgid river below. It wouldn't work. The crew of the *Clarimond* had their faces to the sea, busy with their sails. A man could drown waiting for them to notice.

But the bluff just ahead was even higher—

Even as the idea occurred to Collis, he acted. Without a word, Collis grabbed Rose by the waist and deposited her on the ground. She landed on her feet, staggering a little. "What—"

Collis didn't hear the rest. With a fierce jab to his poor mount's sides, he raced directly through the galloping Liars to follow the barge road down and then up the farther swell. As his horse bunched powerful haunches to push them up the steep path to the bluff, Collis wrapped the reins around his left hand and reached his right into the bag slung beside him.

The grapple hook sprung open with a simple flip of his wrist—*thank you, Forsythe*—and the rope that was knotted to it came easily from its coil in the bag.

With an unruly yank of his left arm he stopped his poor hired horse at the highest point of the bluff. Using even his mount's added hands of height, he kicked free of the stirrups and swung one leg over to sit sidesaddle.

The *Clarimond* was nearly out of range. There was no time for fine aim. He made the hardest crude throw he could manage—

The hook tangled in the rigging. He only had an instant to wind the rope around his left arm and jump clear before the speed of the ship could yank him down and drag him over the edge of the bluff. Still, terrific pain shot through his bruised shoulder as his weight came full on the rope, but his wrapped grip held.

As he swung over the brown and dirty Thames, the wind rushing into his face until his eyes watered, he thought he heard Rose's voice call out to him.

"Collis, you ass!"

It occurred to Collis belatedly that he had no idea where he was going to end up. Smacking into the side of the ship didn't appeal, but the pitted and stained wood grew very large in his vision—

Until he landed, or crashed really, sprawling on the deck amid men and casks and coils of thick, smelly rope.

Impact. Pain. *Ow.*

Blackness quickly faded to light and his breath filled his lungs. He'd made it! Now he must persuade the captain quickly, likely an impossible task. Rolling onto his left shoulder, he reached into his waistcoat and pulled free his pistol.

With breathtaking swiftness, he found himself the center of a thorny hedge of bristling firearms of every make and era.

Lying breathless on his back, with a riveting view up at his circle of righteously suspicious captors, Collis broke out in a gust of laughter. "Stand and deliver?"

Chapter Twenty-eight

───────◆───────

The ship was halted, its anchor dropped against the river's current. After Collis had convinced the vastly disgruntled captain that his keepers were waiting on-shore, Dalton and Simon had managed to convince the captain that Collis was only slightly mad and not really dangerous. In addition, they had persuaded the man to give up his cargo. With a written receipt and Lord Etheridge's personal financial guarantee, of course.

The crew wasn't so sure, especially after the Liars began to break open the crates to account for every last firearm. "Cor, what a pretty thing!" they said when the first musket was lifted to the daylight. The crewmen were obviously dazzled by the brilliant damascening and the intricate lock-plate castings. It made Rose wonder if that had been part and parcel of the plan, to make the guns irresistible to the British soldiers.

Rose thought the crew would riot in earnest when the first of the weapons hit the river, where they sank until the brilliance disappeared beneath the churning silt.

"What you do that for?" cried the most belligerent fellow. "I coulda used a pretty musket like that!"

"Bad guns, lads," growled Kurt, and that put paid to further protest, although the shocked grumblings continued until the last of the carbines and muskets went to the bottom of the Thames. Dalton held back a few random samplings from the crates for Forsythe to test and for evidence against Louis Wadsworth.

It was over. As she stood with her feet braced on the mildly rocking deck, the fresh breeze making the rigging slap and ring above her, Rose felt the burden of responsibility slip deliciously off her shoulders. For the first time since she'd recognized Louis Wadsworth's portrait, she felt the muscles of her neck relax. Her fine leaders were in charge at last, and she could go back to being an ordinary soldier. Her eyes found Collis, wanting to share the vast relief.

He was standing to one side with wind-tousled hair and his clothing much the worse for his careening impact with the grimy deck. He didn't meet her glance but stood there rubbing his shoulder with a curious expression of dismay on his face.

She was at his side in an instant. "What is it?"

He blinked at her. "I'm not sure. When I was swinging, I think I—or perhaps it was when I landed—but it hasn't been quite right since Louis beat on it. . . ." He trailed off, then took a deep breath. "At any rate, I can't move it at all now."

There was quiet panic in his gray eyes. He made no

move, but Rose could feel the terror shimmering from him. "Oh, no," she breathed.

He forced a sickly grin. "Never thought I'd wish it to be the way it was, but at least I could move it. Now—" He swallowed. "Now, they may as well cut the blasted thing off."

She wanted to reach for him, reassure him. A cry from nearby them cut her off.

"My lord! Sir Simon!" Button was scrambling up the main companionway to the deck waving a sheaf of papers in his hand. The ship's captain followed him up at a more leisurely pace.

Button ran to where Simon and Dalton stood not far from Rose and Collis. "My lord—sir! I think you need to see this!"

Dalton took the papers and flipped through them. "Copies of the manifest and shipping orders? Yes, thank you, Button. We'll add this to our evidence."

Rose started to turn back to Collis, but Button was not done.

"No, my lord—*this*!" Button extracted a sheet from the pile and thrust it beneath Dalton's nose. Dalton took it and held it a few inches farther away. Simon leaned over to peer at it.

"What is it?" Simon asked.

Dalton read it. "It looks like a special undocking dispensation for the ship to leave ahead of schedule." He looked up and grinned. "Wadsworth sped up the order. He shipped the crates as soon as possible after the break-in occurred." He looked down at the sheet again, his eyes scanning rapidly. "Oh, bloody hell," he breathed, then handed the sheet to Simon.

Rose was startled at Lord Etheridge's horrified tone of voice. Sir Simon's quiet curse wasn't reassuring. "Signed by Lord Liverpool himself," Simon said slowly.

Rose was stunned. *Liverpool?*

"Are you positive it's Liverpool's signature?" Simon asked.

Dalton rubbed his neck. "I know it like my own."

Rose couldn't believe it. She might personally find the Prime Minister ruthless and unpleasant, but she simply couldn't imagine the man as a traitor.

"What would be the point of such a thing?" she asked, stepping away from Collis.

Dalton shot her a *don't-be-presumptuous* look, but he answered all the same. "Well, we thought before that the plot might have something to do with discrediting George . . . but the only ones to benefit from the removal of George would be those within the British government who find him to be an obstruction."

Well, that did make sense. "Does Lord Liverpool consider him to be an obstruction?"

Dalton sent Simon a look she couldn't decipher, but she recalled the Prime Minister's very vocal doubts in the study about George's sanity. Dalton seemed to be thinking along the same lines.

"If Liverpool is trying to have George declared mad," Dalton mused, "then this sort of capricious negligence might be just the sort of thing to win his case."

Rose shook her head. "But Lord Liverpool is fanatically loyal to the Crown, isn't he?"

Another one of those looks between the two men.

What were they thinking? They couldn't truly suspect Lord Liverpool, could they?

"Fanatical . . . yes," Dalton said quietly. "Precisely."

"We've always wondered when he might go too far," Simon said quietly, as if reminding Dalton of something they'd previously discussed.

"Indeed." Dalton's expression was grim and—she was horribly afraid—quite convinced.

No. Her mind spun. There was more here. What had Lord Etheridge said a moment ago? *"The only ones to benefit from the removal of George would be those within the British government."* Yet who would benefit the most from the removal of the most powerful and masterful Prime Minister England had ever seen?

Why, Napoleon, of course.

Rose felt the devious hand of Louis Wadsworth at work here. That was what he did, after all—tie one's mind in knots until one doubted one's own motives and sanity!

Confidence rang through Rose's next words. "My lord, that signature is a forgery. This is all part of Louis Wadsworth's plan to rid England of the Prime Minister."

Collis clutched his wounded arm, lost in his thoughts. Images crossed his mind. His arm, being truly dead now, turning to rot while still on his body. In the hospital, he'd seen the gangrene take healthy, strong men, turning them to rotting corpses while still breathing.

He felt lost, spinning off-center. Turning quickly, he scanned the ship with desperate eyes. He needed Rose.

There she was, arguing with Dalton and Simon. Even that stunning sight could not distract him from his breathless dismay. *Rose.* He moved toward her like a compass needle turning north.

Rose's voice was raised above the crew's noise, above the wind and the water. "I'm telling you, I know Louis Wadsworth! He had this all mapped, a plan within a plan. He knew you would find the manifest! He forged it. He planted it here!"

Simon folded his arms. "Dalton, what if she is right about Wadsworth? If this is a plan to make *us* act against the Prime Minister, then it very nearly worked. Think about it. I know you suspect Lord Liverpool tried to have Clara eliminated a few months ago, but there were logical reasons at the time. What would be the profit in declaring George mad? If nothing else, you must agree that Liverpool is eminently logical."

Scarcely listening, Collis wanted Rose away from them. He wanted her alone. The argument before him scarcely penetrated his disorienting fog. His arm was swelling. He could feel it under his right hand. It was already nearly filling his sleeve. He'd have to cut his sleeve off.

Cut it off. The thought wouldn't stop running through his mind. *Cut it off.*

There was something wrong with his vision—the world had turned sharp and glassy. . . .

"Rose." Was that his voice? It sounded rather far away.

She turned to him with relief. "Collis, tell them! I *know* Louis!"

Louis. Louis who? The traitor. Yes, that was it.

When he didn't answer, she turned back to Simon and Dalton. "You must listen to me. Lord Liverpool is *not* plotting against His Highness. That's what Louis wants you to think!"

Dalton frowned. "That's a bit of a stretch, Miss Lacey. What would be the profit in such an intricate plan? How could Wadsworth know that we would see this manifest?"

Rose threw up her hands. Her frustration penetrated even Collis's sickened fog. "The profit is that now you wish to put the Prime Minister on trial for treason!"

Dalton and Simon glanced at her, then exchanged a look, as if to say, *What trial?* Of course. The Liars didn't try their targets in public. If the Liars decided that the Prime Minister was a traitor, it was a sure wager the man would meet with an accident in the next week that would never raise a single suspicion.

"God. You'd do it, too, wouldn't you?" Rose looked from one to the other in horror. "Don't you think you ought to at least *consider* my suspicions first?"

Dalton narrowed his eyes and lifted his chin. "Miss Lacey, I certainly hope you can supply me with some reason to excuse such insubordination. We have no evidence to support your accusations of a man whose father you served many years ago—"

"I *know* him," she burst out.

No. It couldn't be. Not his Rose. *No, Rose, don't say it. Don't say what I think you're going to say.*

"I experienced his convoluted planning more times than I can recall!" Her furious voice rang out over the entire ship. "Louis Wadsworth and I were lovers!"

"No!"

Rose flinched from the anguished tone in Collis's voice. He looked terrible, she realized, from much more than simple bruising from his impact with the deck. She reached a hand to him. "Collis? My God, what's wrong—"

He only stared at her. "That's—that's *disgusting.*"

"Collis." Lord Etheridge's barked command must have reached Collis, for he visibly pulled himself together, though he still swayed where he stood. Then the spymaster turned to her. She recoiled from the judgment and disappointment in Dalton's eyes.

"We," he said in a cool, level voice, "do not allow our past . . . dalliances . . . to rule our reason, Miss Lacey. You are obviously too close to this case. I'm afraid your assessment of the situation may be unduly influenced."

He thought her no more than a scorned woman, taking revenge on her former lover. Rose felt her belly turn to ice, black spikes of ice that threatened to pierce her lungs. "You do not trust me, my lord?"

He raised a brow. "I do not trust your emotional state, no."

All activity near them had ceased, she realized. Liars and sailors alike openly gaped at the four of them. She didn't need to look at her fellow Liars to know what she would see. She'd seen it before. She wouldn't look at Collis. She *wouldn't.*

She took a step back. "I see. I will not put you

through the distress of having a Liar in the club you cannot trust, my lord."

She took another step. She would *not* look at Collis. She should never have done so in the first place. Never should have raised her eyes so high, never should have reached—

She turned and ran down the length of the ship, away from curious and accusing eyes.

She ran to where the Liars were preparing the small boats to return to the bank. Kurt was there, doing the work of two men, as usual. She reached for his huge, hard hand. "Help me," she whispered.

He didn't question. With a barked order, he had the small boat pulled close, and lowered her into it as if she were a child. With a careful drop, he joined her. He pushed off with a giant heave at the oars and they were at the bank in a matter of moments. So quickly her new life was left behind.

When she leaped from the boat, Kurt said only one word. "Careful."

She turned to him, the silent killer who had taught her more than all the others put together, and smiled tightly at him. "Do you mean careful on the bank or careful in the world?"

He nodded. *Both.* Then he turned the small boat with a few deep strokes of one oar, turning his back on her, turning back to the Liars.

Rose walked back to the barge road and stood for a moment in the dust. Stubbs was back down the path gingerly holding the horses. But riding one herself . . . no. She turned to face the road back to London. She didn't belong with Collis. She didn't belong with the Liars. She felt as though the light that had shone on her these past months had suddenly gone out.

To be invisible again might very well destroy her.

If that was so, then by God she was taking Louis Wadsworth with her.

Chapter Twenty-nine

Collis's confused gaze followed Rose as she hurried down the length of the ship. Then he blinked as his sight seemed to narrow and the ship began to tilt dangerously beneath his feet. "Oh, *bugger*—"

Dalton caught him as he fell. "Collis!"

The dimness receded to the edges of his vision, but the ringing increased. He was lying on the deck, looking up at the sky through bound sails and rigging, and wheeling seabirds. It wasn't the ship then. It was him.

How odd.

Dalton's voice faded in and out of his hearing. He felt his coat being pulled from him and tucked under his head.

"Collis? Good God, Simon, look at his arm!" Dalton sounded genuinely appalled.

Simon swore softly. "He must have broken it when he landed on the deck. I think he's gone into shock."

Dalton shook him, then rapped him across the cheek. It took Collis a moment to focus on his uncle.

Dalton looked bloody well panicked. "Where is Rose?" Collis asked him.

"Collis, you have to stay awake." Dalton turned away to shout over his shoulder. "Simon, get a small boat ready! Captain, do you have any stimulants—"

The bustle went on about him. Collis noticed that the gray edges were creeping back. The *Clarimond* and the Liars all seemed very far away. Collis's last thought before he passed out was, *Where is Rose?*

Collis came awake suddenly, with no dreamy edging toward alertness. His eyes opened instantly, his vision focusing clearly on the tester above his own bed at Etheridge House. How had he come home?

Then the various aches and complaints of his body made themselves heard. From the shoulder of his numb arm to his knees, he throbbed. He felt as though he'd been dropped from a great height to smack on the cobbles like a thrown egg.

His swing from the bluff to the ship came back to him. In a sense, he had been dropped, hadn't he? Now he felt every plank of that decking as if it had imprinted itself onto his very bones. Rose was right. What an ass he was.

Rose. Rose and *Louis.* Unbearable.

He struggled to sit up, only to find his left arm immobilized in a splint from armpit to wrist and bound to his chest with strips of linen.

"Broken," came a voice from beside the bed.

He looked up to see Clara sitting there in his chair, silhouetted against the gray light of dawn coming through his draperies. The hell-cat was draped across her lap, purring like the orange-furred shedding mechanism it was. It opened one baleful green eye.

"*Mrow,*" uttered the beast.

"I love you, too," muttered Collis, then turned his attention to Clara. In the dim light, he could see the alleged resemblance to Rose that had allowed Clara to pass as a housemaid in Edward Wadsworth's house.

Of course, Clara was prettier and softer and most definitely friendlier. Rose was prickly and defensive and no one would ever call her merely pretty—in fact, she reminded Collis very much of Marmalade.

Like the cat, she had survived much and had the scars to show for it. Like the cat, she stood her ground in the face of the enemy, claws extended.

Clara leaned forward to plant her elbow on the arm of her chair and grin at him. "Yes, you broke your arm again—in at least two places which may have healed badly from your first injury—and dislocated your shoulder joint as well, according to Dr. Westfall. He seemed to think it was already broken when you leaped off the bluff."

Dr. Westfall was Lord Liverpool's personal physician and one trusted implicitly by the Liar's Club. They didn't use him often, especially with Kurt knowing so much of human anatomy and Button so handy with a needle and thread, so for the great doctor to be called, the situation must be quite serious.

Collis swallowed and reached to grip his left shoulder with his right hand. "Will I keep it, then?"

She took his hand in hers and squeezed. "Yes, you

are to keep it. You may have to start over with your recovery, but he says you ought not to be any worse off in the end."

Breathing deeply again, Collis nodded. He never thought he'd be grateful to have one good arm and one numb arm, but he was. He sat up carefully but experienced nothing more than the soreness he expected in the rest of his body. Then the events on the ship came back to him fully. "What is Dalton going to do about Lord Liverpool?"

Clara pursed her lips. "Thanks to Rose's protest, he isn't entirely convinced of Liverpool's guilt yet. He and Simon have set up a dinner tonight with Louis, Liverpool, and the Prince Regent. Only George knows the situation fully. Dalton's hoping to stir something up that will expose the truth."

A dinner with the five cagiest men Collis had ever encountered? "That sounds positively explosive. I'm very glad I won't be there."

"I, too." Clara sat back, watching him, her fingertips disappearing into the cat's thick orange fur. The off-key purr increased in volume.

Collis glanced around his bedchamber. "Where is Rose?"

Clara raised a brow and tilted her head at him. "Rose is gone. She disappeared from the ship about the time you collapsed. Dalton didn't even notice she wasn't with the Liars until he had you halfway home."

"Disappeared?" In instinctive response to a call to action, he reached for the covers to leap from the bed. "Was she kidnapped?"

Clara stayed his hand. "According to Kurt, she walked off under her own power."

He slowly leaned back on the pillow. "She left me?"

"She left us all," Dalton declared from the doorway, where he now stood with folded arms and one shoulder leaning on the door jamb. He shook his head. "I can't believe we were all so thoroughly duped by an illiterate gold-digger."

Despite his confusion, Collis glared at Dalton. "She is no such thing!"

Dalton blinked. "But she virtually admitted it. First Louis Wadsworth, then you. You sent her off packing, don't you remember?"

Icy horror twined through him. "I did *not*!"

Clara tilted her head. "According to everyone who was there, you pronounced her 'disgusting' with deepest revulsion."

Oh, God. *Oh, Rose.* Collis brought a shaking hand to plunge into his hair. "No—no, I meant that Louis—that molesting one of his own servants was disgusting." His stomach turned. Oh, God, what she must think!

Clara blinked. "Oh, drat."

Obviously unconvinced, Dalton raised his chin. "There remains the fact that she tried to attach herself to you."

Collis let out a bitter laugh and eased himself to the edge of the bed. "No, she didn't. I tried to attach myself to her." He slid one foot to the floor. "And I fully intend to try again."

"What are you doing?" Dalton moved forward as

if he were going to bodily force him back into bed. Clara stopped her husband with one small hand to his arm.

"Let him be," she ordered.

"But he's—"

"Dalton, I love you to bits, but you can be such an ass sometimes." She shook her head. "Can't you see that he is in love with her?"

"He can't be. I won't allow it!"

Collis stood, his bare feet cold on the floor. He shot a glance at his aunt. "Do you see what I have had to put up with all these years?"

She folded her arms. "Liverpool shadows you still."

"Ah!" Dalton protested. "I am nothing like Liverpool! I only mean that he can't—"

"And I only mean that he can. You must let him go, Dalton." She put both hands on her hips. "Both you and Liverpool."

Collis flicked his gaze back to his uncle, who was in true sweat, caught between his love and his allegiance. Poor slob. Collis knew which one he would choose.

He'd choose Rose.

"I'm going, so any discussion you want to have about letting me go will have to wait for me not to be gone any longer." Collis shrugged into his shirt and glanced apologetically at his aunt. "Clara, would you mind?"

Clara tugged at Dalton. "You can spin in circles just as well out in the hall, darling." She pushed him through the door and tossed a gamine smile back at Collis. "Go get our Rose," she ordered.

"Yes, milady," Collis promised with a salute. "I could use another hand," he added. "Would you mind sending Denny up?"

"I'll have to call the Sergeant," Clara said. "Denny is gone. His things are missing from his chamber and he told the Sergeant he'd had the offer of a better position."

"Better?" Collis froze. "But if he—"

With a rueful expression, Clara nodded shortly. "Precisely. Dalton has already ordered that he be . . ." She hesitated. "Ordered him found. There is a great deal we would like to know about Denny's activities lately. Especially regarding the letter you sent about being at Mrs. Blythe's. We now suspect that Denny was the leak to the Voice of Society all along." She smiled sadly. "Actually, it was something overheard from a confrontation between Denny and Rose that made Dalton realize it."

Collis paused to regard her seriously. "There is no need to pursue Rose like we must pursue Denny. You know that Rose would never carry tales about the club."

She nodded. "You and I may know that, but Dalton must consider the larger issue."

"Damn Dalton. He'd kill a dog to rid it of fleas." He grabbed up an acceptable suit of clothing. "Then I must get to her first."

Clara smiled and he realized that had been her goal all along. "Well, then. If you're determined to go." She turned to leave him in privacy, then stopped at the door. "Collis," she began casually. "I happen to know that Louis hadn't lived in his father's house for the past ten years." She cast him a meaningful glance over her shoulder as she left. "You might want to think about that."

Ten years? Collis froze with his shirt in his hands. Ten years ago, Rose had been a mere fourteen. A slender and defenseless girl. Oh, dear God, that sick bastard! What had Louis done to her?

Disgusting. Hot horror welled up within him as he remembered his own words to her.

"Oh, Rose," he said aloud to the empty room. "What have *I* done to you?"

Chapter Thirty

◆

Morning was just breaking over the soot-stained rooftops of London when the kind carter who had given Rose a ride into the city proper handed her down like a lady from her barouche. Then he tipped his shabby cap to her and drove off, his ancient draft horse moving at the same plodding pace that had taken the entire evening and most of the night to reach their destination.

The Liars had made much better time than she. This she knew because she had seen them race past in the Etheridge carriages. Something had put them into a tearing hurry. Rose had reminded herself that whatever it was, it was no longer her concern. She had hidden behind the lumpy bags of onions in the back of the cart as the carter had pulled to one side and waved the fine carriages onward.

By now, Collis would have been home for hours. She could see him, sleeping in that great wide bed in that lovely green and cream bedchamber. Was he thinking of her at all?

She snorted with disbelief at her own reckless longing and turned her feet toward the one man who might aid her. Someone unconcerned with Liar business—someone unconcerned with anything but his own pursuits. Nonetheless, he'd helped before. She was hoping she could convince him to help again.

Some parts of the city never slept, so she was careful in her passage through. Keeping to the shadows, slipping around spots of trouble, she made her way to certain areas from memory as the dawn lightened the gray smoky sky to silver.

She was cut off from the Liars. She was cut off from Collis. There was nowhere else to go.

Except one place.

Ethan Damont poured himself another brandy. His decanter was full of smoky liquid goodness. In addition, his cellar was full of coal, his kitchen was full of delicious smells due to the efforts of his hurriedly re-hired cook, and his house would be full of furnishings by the end of the week.

Apparently that uncle of Collis's had a very generous, very grateful streak. The most excellent fellow had sent him a sizable cheque yesterday evening, with a note signed only "The Codger."

"Nice old Codge," Ethan mused as he swirled the brandy in his glass and waited for his lovely breakfast. Drinking before breakfast didn't count if one hadn't been to bed the night before.

Then his lovely morning was interrupted by an urgent pounding on the door. "Ah, that's right," Ethan recalled aloud. "I must remember to hire myself a

Jeeves." In the meantime, there was no one to answer it but him. Padding to the door in his stocking feet, he swung it open upon a desperate-looking Collis Tremayne.

"Oh, balls, it's you." Ethan began to shut the door. "You ass."

Collis shoved the door open with one hand and pushed past Ethan. He looked bloody awful. Ethan found himself much pleased by that.

"Is Rose here?" Collis's voice was rough with urgency.

Ethan smiled nastily. "Absolutely. She came right over after she finished rogering the regiment." Ethan poked Collis hard in the chest. "You really are a bastard, you know that, Tremayne? How could you do that to her?"

In an instant, Ethan found himself pressed against the wall of his own front hall with Collis's fist tangled in his shirtfront. Blast it, he really was going to seed. Taken apart by a man with one hand tied to his chest. "I must take up pugilism," Ethan gasped.

"Is . . . Rose . . . here?" There was a truly threatening note in Collis's voice. Dangerous and desperate.

Ethan began peeling Collis's fingers off, one by one. "No, you supreme and utter ass—yes, *ass* will do until I think of a better word—she is not. The last time I saw her she was marching back down the Thames barge road to London with her chin high and her spine like a poker. I looked for her all the way back yesterday evening, but I never saw her."

"You saw her leave and you didn't stop her?"

"Why should I have? You humiliated her before

the entire ship! My God, I think even the gulls were laughing at her."

Collis shut his eyes and let Ethan drop. Ethan tossed back the last swallow of brandy. Heavens, he'd almost spilled it. He waved the empty glass at Collis. "If you'd like to drown the memory of your vast and endless stupidity, I've an entire cellar full of this vintage. Although I doubt it will be enough."

Collis grunted, his expression veering toward hopeless. "I thought she might have come to you for help. She did before."

Ethan tilted his head to regard his old friend with no sympathy whatsoever. "If she did, and I actually told you—which she didn't and I wouldn't anyway— what could you possibly have to say to her?"

"She must return with me. I—we need her."

Ethan pondered this. "No, not convincing."

"What do you mean?"

"As far as I have gathered, you took her to your bed without bothering to marry her first. Then, once she was utterly and entirely in love with you, you called her disgusting and rejected her in front of . . ." He paused to count on his fingers. "In front of no less than fifty witnesses."

"Do you truly think she's in—" Collis flushed. "It wasn't like that."

Ethan folded his arms and waited.

Collis rubbed the back of his neck with his unbound hand. "All right, it did *seem* like that. But I didn't mean it that way!"

"So, now you're going to chase her down—even

though she was quite right to leave your sorry arse on the dim horizon—and do what precisely?"

"The most important thing is to find her," Collis insisted. "I can't explain why, but—oh, hell, Ethan, she's in danger!"

Ethan straightened. "She is? From whom?"

"From Louis, who is still loose—and from others."

Ethan forgot about his rather envious tormenting of his friend. "She didn't come to me—what other friends does she have in London?"

Collis looked haunted. "I'm not sure there is anyone else she can trust."

"What about the Codger? He seemed to like her well enough."

Collis blinked, then shook his head. "No. I doubt she could even get in to see His—the Codger. He's well guar—he's quite reclusive."

"Well, then who? She must have gained someone's friendship in her life, other than you lot." Ethan scowled. "Who are you lot, anyway?"

Collis waved a hand absently. "Just a sort of boys' club—" Abruptly his eyes went bright. "Ah." He turned to go so swiftly he was halfway to the street before Ethan realized it.

"Where are you going?"

Without so much as slowing his stride, Collis turned back to grin fiercely and wave. "To the Tower!"

As before, the Tower drainage tunnel allowed Rose to approach Forsythe's workshop in the White Tower undetected. Oddly enough, being underground did not upset her in the slightest this time.

She gave the workshop door a brisk rap with her knuckles. Then a solid blow with her fist. Then she took off her shoe and pounded the door for several minutes, not stopping until Forsythe answered from the other side, "Who is it?"

"It's Rose, Mr. Forsythe. I've come for—"

The heavy old door swung open. "You've come for more matches," said Forsythe with a wrinkled grin.

"No, sir." She would not be charmed. "I've come for the pistol you offered me before."

His smile fell. "The pistol? But I thought you didn't like firearms."

"I like them better than I like a traitor."

He peered at her carefully. "It's that Wadsworth sod, isn't it? Didn't you tell Jenkins what I told you?"

"Lord Liverpool is not being kept abreast of the entire matter," Rose said stiffly. Then her shell cracked a bit. "Louis has them all convinced—" She forced herself to stop. Mr. Forsythe had his own place within George's domain, but she had no idea how secure that place was. She would not endanger Forsythe by including him in her plan.

"Please, trust me, Mr. Forsythe. I know what I am doing."

"Hmm." He seemed doubtful, but he let her in all the same. The pistol was right where she had left it, a mite dustier but still gleaming in the dim recesses of Forsythe's cave of wonders.

Rose hefted it in her hand. "Do you have the balls and powder?"

Forsythe patted his pockets absently. "I put them somewhere. . . ."

Rose narrowed her eyes at him. "Mr. Forsythe, if you are trying to stall me for some reason, I wouldn't recommend it. Besides, wouldn't you rather I use one of your fine pistols than some cheap thing I might obtain in the city?"

He shuddered. "You'll blow your lovely hand right off with that rubbish." He sighed, giving in. "Oh, very well." He handed her a doeskin pouch that held everything she needed.

She thanked him and turned back to the door. He followed her nervously. "Are you sure you know how to use it?"

"Yes, Mr. Forsythe, I've been trained by the best."

"It's pretty, but it's still a very deadly thing."

Rose wrapped her fingers around the carved butt. It settled into her palm, nestling there like a part of her hand. A perfect fit. "Not as deadly as I am," she murmured.

Chapter Thirty-one

———— ◆ ————

As Rose left Forsythe's workshop, she turned to close the door carefully behind her. She paused to rub her tired eyes for a moment. Her spectacles had been lost in the flood. Even though she'd managed without them for most of her life, she missed them dreadfully now. Perhaps when all this was over, she could obtain new ones—

Of course, there was a very real chance that when all this was over, she'd be quite beyond the need of spectacles ever again.

So be it. Louis Wadsworth must be stopped. If the Liars weren't up to the task, then someone must clean up the mess. Who better than a housemaid?

When she dropped her hands and turned, she saw Collis leaning insouciantly against the far wall, watching her.

He had his left arm tied beneath his shirt and open coat and his right hand on his hip, looking for all the world like a beau tolerantly waiting for his lady to finish her shopping.

He smiled at her wryly, but with hesitation in his gaze. "Hello, Rose."

Disgusting. The word lashed through her memory like a whip. Collis thought she was disgusting, nothing more than a whore.

She covered her surprise with a slowly indrawn breath and the act of folding her arms over her breasts. "Nice work, Collis. Did it take you all night to figure this out?"

He straightened, raking her with a shadowed gaze. "What were you doing at Forsythe's, Rose?"

She laughed bitterly. "Something dangerous and illegal, of course." She raised her chin. "You needn't bother to try and stop me, Collis. You know I'll only toss you."

To her astonishment, he grinned, a fierce flash of white in the dim passage. "If you are talking about eliminating Louis Wadsworth once and for all, I have no intention of stopping you." He stepped forward until she could see the approving light in his gray eyes. "In fact, I am here to help."

The ice that she'd wrapped her heart in threatened to melt. No. She could not allow herself to believe in him. She stepped back slightly. There was still room to maneuver, if she didn't allow him to get too close.

Never, never would she be close to him again. If she weren't made of ice, she'd be finding it very difficult to breathe at this moment. "Why would you do that? Why would you risk your precious place with the Liars to help me?"

"Because I—" He stopped. He seemed oddly cautious. Rose tried to read his face in the shadows. She wished she had her spectacles.

Collis could scarcely bear the suspicion etched into the delicate planes of her face. Yet a mere apology seemed so worthless. "We are partners, you and I, remember?" he said in a low voice. "Because I trust you more than I've ever trusted anyone in my life." He wanted to drop to his knees and beg her forgiveness, but he was fairly positive she wouldn't believe a word he said. Words. His gift—but words had always failed with Rose. More substantial proof was required.

So he ignored his yearning heart and simply favored her with that cocky grin of old. "Besides, *I* know where Louis Wadsworth will be having dinner this evening."

Rose followed Collis through the service entrance of Etheridge House. He breezed through the kitchen with a flirtatious word to the cook, who slapped at him playfully with a plump, floured hand. Then he led the way up the service stairs to the servants' passage outside the dining room.

"Why don't you give me that pistol?" he whispered to her when they had paused at the plain door marked only D for dining room.

"Why don't you take a flying leap over the Thames?" retorted Rose. She pressed the catch and allowed the door to open a tiny slit.

There, at a lovely table set with the finest of everything Etheridge House had to offer—which was finer than anything Rose had ever seen—sat the Prince Regent, his bruised face highly powdered, the Prime Minister, Lord Etheridge, Sir Simon Raines . . . and Mr. Louis Wadsworth.

"What's your plan?" Collis whispered in her ear.

"Plan?" She was watching Louis with disbelief. He was laughing carefully at something the Prince Regent said as the Sergeant, resplendent in his military-style livery, bent to offer him something savory and expensive from a salver.

Louis was being *feasted*?

That was beyond all she could bear. Rose brought the pistol from her dress pocket and stepped forward. Leveling the barrel directly between Louis Wadsworth's eyes, she stopped within a yard of him. No chance of missing at this distance.

"Confess," she said.

"Wh-what?" Wadsworth nearly choked on his beef.

The royal guards in the room leaped forward but dared not touch her while she held the pistol. Collis waved them back.

Liverpool jerked in shock. "Dare you pull a weapon in the presence of His Highness?"

George burped delicately and patted his royal lips with a piece of snowy monogrammed linen. "What weapon? I see no weapon."

Wadsworth flicked a gaze from the barrel of the pistol to the Prince Regent, then back to a now-silent Prime Minister. Dalton moved to stand but halted when Simon shook his head.

"Confess," whispered Rose.

"You're mad," Louis sneered. Then he blinked and looked closer. "Who are you?"

"I'm no one." Rose smiled. "No one at all—with nothing left to lose."

"I'll have you brought to justice for this! You'll be hanged!"

Rose tilted her head. "You won't be there to see it."

"You're dead already."

"Am I? When it is I who hold the pistol?" She waggled it. Wadsworth's eyes followed the movement and his jaw worked. He let his eyes flicker around the table, but Rose guessed he saw no help there.

"What was it you said the other day, Louis?" mused George. "Ah, yes." He leaned back, the fingers of one hand gingerly exploring his bruised mouth. "You are pressing your luck, Mr. Wadsworth."

Louis's eyes flicked to the fading bruises on George's face, to the more battered Collis, then back to the hole in the barrel of the disturbingly pretty pistol aimed unerringly at his brain.

"Confess," Rose sang softly.

Louis, obviously still hoping to salvage something, shrugged ruefully. "It was my father who made the deal with Arch-Chancellor Talleyrand. Wadsworth Munitions was built with Napoleon's money. Then the favor came due. I was only afraid—they threatened me! I had to fulfill the bargain, don't you understand?" He turned insistent eyes on the Prime Minister and the Prince Regent. "They said they'd break me!"

Liverpool narrowed his eyes. "You're a fool, Wadsworth. A bit of bankruptcy is nothing next to treason."

"No! Not treason—you can't prove that!"

Rose cleared her throat. "Pardon me for the interruption, but I should like to point out that I needn't prove a thing. All I need to do is tighten my finger the slightest bit. . . ."

"Rose. No." Collis's voice was just a breath, but Rose closed her eyes momentarily at the sound of her name on his lips. Then she eased her trigger finger.

She turned her head to gaze at Liverpool. "He ought to pay. He tried to have us assassinate you."

Liverpool slid his gaze sideways to take in Dalton and Simon. "Interesting."

"He forged your name on a manifest, to make it seem as though you were behind a plot to have George declared as mad as his father."

The Prince Regent also raised a brow at Dalton and Simon. Dalton managed a cool smile, as if he'd never believed a word of it.

Lord Liverpool's gaze flicked back to Louis. "Did he now?"

"Who *are* you, woman?" Louis snapped.

She tilted her head and regarded him without emotion. "I wasn't a woman when we met. Don't you remember seducing the housemaid, Louis? Don't you remember twisting her up in knots to get her into your bed, only to beat her nearly senseless when your own equipment eventually failed you?"

Shock paled his features. *"You?"*

She nodded calmly. "Me."

He stuttered for a moment, then his gaze sharpened. "Then—then, Your Highness, my lords—this is simply a bit of female vengeance—"

"This isn't revenge, Louis. I don't care one way or

the other about you anymore." She let the candlelight shimmer from the lovely pistol, reflecting it into his eyes. "I could kill you, I'm sure. I'm quite capable of it now. However, I don't *yearn* to kill you." She gazed at him serenely. "Unless you force me to."

Louis appeared to be close to breaking. Rose could almost hear the panicked, plotting thoughts swirling through his mind. It would be best not to let him think overlong. "Louis, confess. My hand grows tired. I daresay my finger will slip soon."

"Very well," he spat. "I forged the manifest!"

Rose eyed the other four men at the table. "Do you gentlemen have any more questions for Louis? He seems to be in a talkative mood."

Dalton gazed at her appraisingly. "Thank you, Miss Lacey. I believe we can take it from here."

Wadsworth protested. "You cannot put faith in a confession at the point of a pistol!"

Rose shook her head. "I don't give a rotten fig, Louis." She glanced toward the Prime Minister. "Do you?"

Lord Liverpool quirked his lips. "Not particularly."

Rose released a breath. Then she carefully handed the pistol to the Prime Minister. "It's a very nice pistol, my lord. I recommend its maker highly."

"Indeed." Liverpool regarded it for a moment before training it quite purposefully on Louis Wadsworth.

George leaned back from the table and bent a kindly smile on Wadsworth. "Louis, dear boy. It seems the responsibility of such an important industry has become too much for you. Might I recommend an

extended stay in the Tower? At His Majesty's pleasure, of course. No need to worry about your factory.
I'm sure the British government would be happy to
confisc—relieve you of such a tremendous burden."

Rose faded back, away from the table. It was over at
last. Louis had cost her dearly, but it was finally over.

Wadsworth was spilling everything in a rush, obviously desperate to get back into his patron's good
graces. Collis stepped up to corroborate the facts of
the matter.

Rose saw Collis turn his head to look about the
room. She ducked quickly behind a fascinated footman and calmly escaped the dining room.

It was time to disappear.

As Rose made her way through the fine halls of
Etheridge House, heading out a side garden door she
was fairly sure would be unguarded, it occurred to her
that she had nowhere to go.

Perhaps she could work at Mrs. Blythe's, she
thought wryly through her pain.

Then she heard Collis calling out to her. Quickening her pace, she ducked down the heavily carpeted
gallery. High, wide windows punctuated the length of
the chamber along one side, and life-size paintings of
past Etheridges hung upon the other.

A hand came down heavily on her shoulder. "Rose,
please—"

Thud.

Rose squatted down next to a prone and panting
Collis, shaking her head. "You never learn. Did that
hurt?"

"Yes," he wheezed.

She eyed his splinted and bound arm worriedly. "Did I jar your broken bones?"

"Probably."

"Good." She stood to gaze down at him in exasperation, her hands on her hips. "You deserve it for spoiling my perfectly good clean getaway."

"So sorry." His breath seemed to be coming back to him. "But I must talk to you."

She folded her arms. "I can't imagine what we have to talk about."

He sat up slowly, wincing. "I don't think I can stand at the moment. Would you mind terribly coming down here?"

She couldn't help a short laugh. Damn him for making her laugh when she hated him so! Dropping to her knees next to him in the hall, she made sure there was more than an arm's length of floor between them. "I'm listening."

He took a deep breath. "You cannot leave m—us. You cannot leave the Liars."

The Liars. Of course. "Watch me." She moved to stand again. "If I don't want to be found, no one will find me. Kurt and the others trained me as well as you, you know."

"No!" He reached out his hand to stay her. "Wait. It isn't simply that. You *need* the Liars, Rose. And I . . . and they need you." His gray eyes beseeched her so earnestly that she actually considered it for a moment.

If she stayed, she would be in dire trouble for what she'd just done, if Dalton's expression had been any sort of clue, but surely it would pass eventually. She could stay with the Liar's Club, be the first lady Liar—

And spend the rest of her life desperately trying not to love a man who didn't love her. Could she see Collis every day, possibly even work with him, as if she'd never loved him at all? Could she be his *friend*? She shook her head with involuntary rejection. "Collis, you don't know what you're asking of me."

Collis couldn't bear the pain in her eyes. Pain he'd put there. "I'm asking you to stay, that's all. Stay and see this through. Be the Liar you were meant to be, the woman you were meant to be."

She dropped her gaze to her hands resting on her thighs. "No. That isn't enough." She stood.

Collis scrambled to his knees in hope. Not enough? What would be enough? Him?

Certainty shot through him like a bullet.

Oh, yes. I finally found her, Mum. My Briar Rose.

"Marry me!"

She froze in place. Only her gaze shot to meet his, her eyes unreadable. "What?"

When he needed it the most, his glibness failed him. "*Bloody hell.* Rose, I love you and I want you and I admire you and I need you and I *must* marry you."

"Hmm. All that?" she said faintly.

Fool! "I can do better," he blurted in a panic. "Let me try again!"

She held up one hand. "No! No need. My answer is no."

No. He couldn't breathe. "It's because of what you thought I said about Louis, isn't it?"

"Bugger Louis!" Rose threw out her hands in frustration. "Look, Louis is a right wanker, I won't deny that. But I survived him. He's behind me, like a shadow that I don't even pay mind to anymore. My answer isn't about Louis, it's about me."

She sighed and wove her fingers together as if she didn't know what to do with her hands. "Collis, I can't be your lady."

"But—"

She held up a hand to halt him. "I know I could pass as one if I tried—Lord knows I've been trained for it—but to take a pose for one mission isn't the same as lying for the rest of my life."

"Rose, I never asked you to be Lady Etheridge. I asked you to be mine, for always."

Her face crumpled and she looked away. "That sounds lovely," she whispered.

His chest ached at how unhappy he'd made her. How could he undo what he had done? Unsay what he had said? "There are no words," he blurted. "There is no apology I can make to erase my stupidity."

Amends, my darling. Oh, heartfelt amends. "Can you not forgive me?"

She shoved her hands into her pockets. "I already forgave you. I'm simply having a little trouble forgiving myself."

He blinked at that. "Forgiving yourself for what?"

Her gaze went somewhere over his shoulder. "For loving you anyway."

She loved him. She loved him *anyway.* His aches and pains disappeared before a tide of pure joy. He stood swiftly. "But that's wonderful!" He moved to take her in his arms—well, arm, at any rate.

She backed two steps away, holding up her hands. "No, Collis. No. Nothing has changed."

"Everything has changed! I love you! You love me!"

She laughed, a bitter, damp sound. "Collis, not everything is that simple! You cannot wave your aristocratic hand and make these obstacles disappear! I am a butcher's daughter!"

"And a spy."

Frustrated, she waved assent. "Very well, a butcher's daughter and a spy. You are a lord's heir!"

"And a spy." He tilted his head to smile at her. "I won't be the heir for long, you know. Clara's increasing even now."

She blinked. "Oh. She must be so happy." Then she frowned. "That changes nothing, Collis."

"Of course it does! Even if this one is not a boy, the next may be, or the next! Should we wait ten years, waste ten years, until we know? I want to live now. Not for the future, nor for the past."

She smiled at him then, a truly proud smile, through damp eyes. "I'm very happy you have come to that decision." Then she shook her head again. "But the answer is still no."

"Why? I want to marry you. I want green-eyed daughters and black-haired sons. I want to grow gray with you, and be buried next to you under an oak. I want—"

She laid her fingers over his lips, unable to bear

his aching pleas any longer. "You have a fine and worthy heritage to live up to. I would only be in the way of that."

"Are you so sickeningly honorable, so selfless, as that, Rose, that you think the world owes you no happiness at all?"

She shook her head sadly. "No, I am not so sickeningly selfless as all that. But I do not think the world owes me anything but air to breathe. The rest must be earned, for such as me."

"And how do I earn you, Briar Rose? What sacrifice must I make? What kingdom must I give up?"

Her hand jerked within his and she blinked. "What did you say?"

He frowned slightly, then kissed her hand. "Did I wax too melodramatic? Sorry, I didn't mean to be theatrical. I'm just so bloody tired, Rose. Bone-deep and down-to-my-boot-heels tired, and I simply don't know what else to do. How can I let you walk away? I'll be losing half of myself!"

Rose felt his love fall upon her upturned face like the first sunlight of spring. She closed her eyes against it, fighting to keep out the awareness, but it sank into her skin and through to her heart like sweet poison that she would never survive.

Her resistance melted. Her resolve faltered. Even her knees weakened. She sank against him for a moment, needing to draw on his strength and solidity. His arm came around her and she melted into him. It felt so good to give in. She knew the weariness he spoke of. To resist was costing her far too much.

To give in to him would cost him more.

She pushed away. His hand clung, but she was determined. "I am who I am, Collis. I am not a lady. Do you truly want to tie yourself down to a wife like me?"

He smiled. "I would be honored to have you as my lady."

"I cannot pass in Society, not really. Nor do I wish to." She gazed at him, trying to see into his eyes, into his future. "Ethan said you were looking for 'the man after.' Well, I have found the woman after and I intend to keep her. I will not lose her again in order to pretend to be your lady." She opened her arms wide, displaying her stained male attire, her trained fighter's figure, her plain, uninspiring face. "This is the bargain, Mr. Tremayne. Your world will not forgive you easily. You might want to think what it will cost you."

"*You* might want to think what it will save him from." The voice came from behind them.

Rose started at the unmistakable fruity tones of George IV, Prince Regent. She turned to see him several yards down the gallery, lounging against a window embrasure, accompanied by two stone-faced guards and a very repressed-looking Prime Minister.

In fact, Lord Liverpool looked as though he were about to "shit diamonds," as Stubbs might say.

George's words swirled through Rose's thoughts. *Save him from.*

Could she save him? If a prince's bastard—but acceptably well-born—son married a butcher's daughter, one with a distinctly tarnished past yet, would that union not remove him from royal consideration?

Rose eyed the Prime Minister. By the fury on Lord Liverpool's face, that answer would be a resounding

"Yes." The man looked as though he could slit her throat on the spot, just for receiving such a proposal.

Oh, blimey. To have her heart's desire *and* score one off the heartless, manipulative Prime Minister? She sent Lord Liverpool her sweetest smile.

Then she turned to Collis, dropped to one knee, and said clearly enough for all concerned to hear, *"Bloody hell.* Collis, I love you and I want you and I admire you and I need you and I *must* marry you."

He gaped at her.

She grinned up at him and tilted her head. "I can do better."

"No need," he breathed, laughter and love shining from his storm-cloud eyes. "My answer is yes."

Chapter Thirty-two

◆

Rose Lacey stood with her eyes clenched shut tight and her hands held fast in the grip of her closest friend—a woman who was soon to be her family in truth. "Clara, please, let go. I have to—"

"You aren't going anywhere, Rose. Let him be. You don't want to get blood on your beautiful gown."

Rose sighed and forced herself to relax. "You're quite right. I know you're right. Besides, it's damned hard to fight in a floor-length veil." She twitched her nose and fought off a faceful of the webby stuff. "But why did he have to come in here now?" she wailed. "Did the Prime Minister truly think he could talk me out of marrying Collis *today*?"

Clara chuckled. "Well, he only had minutes left, didn't he? After you and Collis make your vows, his cause is quite lost."

"He'll do something dastardly, I know it. He wants the ceremony stopped—what if he sets fire to the chapel?"

"Oh, I expect you'd spit twice and put the flames

right out," Clara said admiringly. "You were as cool as brook water just now. *'I'm sure I have no idea what you are speaking of,'* " Clara quoted. " *'You've concocted an interesting fantasy, my lord, but it has nothing to do with me.'* " She chuckled. "I'll treasure his expression always. I wish I'd had a pencil and paper to sketch it."

Rose snickered. "Don't you dare!"

Clara sent her a wicked look. "Are you sure you wouldn't want a copy? 'Twould make a lovely bride gift."

"Absolutely not!" Rose arranged her voluminous skirts. Then she snickered again. "Oh, very well. Slip it to me later."

A knock came on the door. The Sergeant's voice came through the wood. "Miss, His Highness is waiting!"

Clara shook her head with wonder. "To be walked down the aisle by the Prince Regent himself! What a tale to tell your children." She patted her still-flat stomach idly. "You could be the toast of London Society, you know."

"I know," fretted Rose. "I couldn't turn him down, of course, but at least I managed to talk him into a private ceremony. How would I ever be of use to the Liars if I became notorious?"

"You'd manage." Clara kissed her cheek. "You have more to offer than a housemaid's skills, dear one." She stood back and held Rose at arm's length. "Perfection." She shook her head. "Remember when I found you in the attic?"

Rose smiled through incipient tears and sniffed. "My nose was running then, too."

Clara adjusted the veil and pushed her toward the door. "Be happy, dear."

Rose stepped into the church proper with her hand on the arm of the Prince Regent of England and gazed down the aisle at Collis Tremayne, tall and fine in wedding gray, his left arm slung in silvery silk. *Happy* didn't begin to describe it.

Around him stood her Liars, every one, for none would agree on who would stand up with Collis.

Rose smiled at George through her joy. "I'll take good care of him for you," she whispered.

He smiled and patted her hand on his arm. "You're a good girl, my dear." They took the first step to the rising strains of music. "But I'm sure I have no idea what you are speaking of."

Epilogue

❖

The room was dark and so silent that the merest rustle of Rose's skirts sounded in her listening ears.

She twiddled her picks to tumble the wall-mounted safe box securely locked once more, her heart pounding with excitement. She'd found it!

At last there was proof of treason against Lord Maywell, whom the spymaster had long suspected of collusion with the French. Several forays into Maywell Manor by the Liars had produced nothing solid to back up Lord Etheridge's suspicions. Maywell's study was clean, his bedchamber cleaner.

Fortunately, Rose had flirted an interesting detail out of a young footman only too willing to impress the new maid with his superior knowledge of the house.

There was a room, he'd claimed, that no one went into, not staff or family. A small room, out of the main wing, that from the outside seemed no more important than a closet for linens. A room Lord Maywell had been overheard to refer to as the "hidey-hole."

And Rose had found it. She'd entered the room using the master key she'd nicked from the Maywells' butler's ring a short while ago as the man was distracted by the preparations for the upcoming ball. Then she'd tickled open the safe and found all the evidence Lord Liverpool could ask for, and then some.

Now to get it out of the house. She stuffed the packet of betraying documents under her skirts and made for the hall. She tugged her mobcap low and adopted a busy shuffle back to the main wing. If she could get back without being seen—

"Oy there! You!" She'd been seen. A burly footman strode toward her, suspicion on his face.

Rose didn't hesitate. She ran.

Somewhere down the third twisting corridor the man fell behind. Rose ducked into a dark room and quickly made her change. Off with the dull maid's uniform. Underneath she wore shimmering beaded silk. Off with the floppy mob-cap. Beneath it, her hair was wound with crystals and ribbon.

Rose wadded her useless uniform into her apron and tossed it from the room's window into the shrubbery below. She'd best have Feebles fetch it later. Then she pulled her evening gloves from her bodice and tugged them on while she listened at the door. When she was sure all pursuit had passed her by, she sucked in a deep breath.

Then, with a pat to her hair, she flung open the door and strode confidently out.

The burly footman passed her once as she made her way back to the ballroom, but his gaze was focused on housemaids, not guests. He merely bowed perfunctorily as he went by. Rose didn't acknowledge him at all, but only continued down the hall, her expression serene, her heart pounding.

The ball was in full crush. It was a mad rout, a frantic display—one of the last balls of the season. Rose made her way around the outskirts of the dancers to the gentlemen's card room off to one side. She could have found it by the smell of smoke alone, even had she not known the house so well. She dawdled in the doorway until she caught Collis's eye.

With a tiny lift of one brow, he asked. With a smug pursing of her lips, she answered. Impressed pride flashed across his features, then he turned his attention back to the game he played with Lord Maywell. "I fear I must fold, my lord."

Lord Maywell, a bushy-browed man of middle years and impressive girth, grunted in disapproval. "You're not going to let a few bad hands stop you? You young lot—no fortitude!"

Collis stood anyway and bowed. "Ah, but my lady awaits, my lord," he said with a smile.

Lord Maywell cast an incurious glance toward Rose, who tried to appear highly decorative and useless. "Didn't know you'd married, Tremayne," he grunted. "Someone forgot to tell Lady Maywell, I'll wager. I'm fairly sure you were only invited so she could try to pawn one of my daughters off on you."

"Oh, yes, I'm wed." Collis smiled dangerously at Rose. She felt her toes curl.

Lord Maywell turned to one of the other players at the table. "I suppose you're leaving as well, since you came with Tremayne," he said sourly.

Ethan Damont, who could scarcely see over the immense pile of winnings before him, sighed regretfully. "I fear I must, my lord." Then he blinked hopefully. "Unless you care to extend an invitation—"

At Lord Maywell's growl, Ethan nodded and swept his plunder into a precarious two-handed pile. He stood and bowed, amazingly without dropping a single coin. "Until we meet again, my lord."

Collis and Ethan joined Rose in the ballroom. She grinned at Ethan. "You were only supposed to occupy him, not beggar him!"

Ethan blinked innocently. "Is it my heartache if his lordship is the worst player I've ever seen?"

Collis clapped his friend on the shoulder. "It's good to see you taking an interest in a bit of good, honest cheating again."

"Oh, I'm quite recovered," Ethan claimed roguishly, but Rose wasn't convinced. The gambler hadn't wanted any part of the plan until they'd told him that Lord Maywell was a very unsavory member of Society. These days, it seemed to her as if Ethan Damont was less interested in gambling for gambling's sake and more interested in somewhat higher motivations.

Ethan excused himself. "I'm off. I can't very well dance with my hands full," he said with a wink. He sauntered away.

Collis pulled Rose close to whisper in her ear. "You did it!" Pride swelled within him. His magnificent, talented bride!

"*We* did it," she whispered back, then bit his earlobe lightly. "But you had better dance me to the door.

I can't keep carrying the evidence strapped to my thigh!"

"Lucky evidence," he replied with a chuckle, then swept her into his arms. They waltzed gracefully through the crowd with nary a trampled toe, then arrived at the terrace doors with a last breathless spin.

She was so bright tonight, her hair a gleaming crown, her supple body elegant in moonlight-colored silk. The Unicorn, they'd dubbed her at the club. It suited her. Bright and clever and his.

The mission was accomplished. Now there was only the remains of the evening and his lovely, charming spy.

"Mrs. Tremayne," he murmured to her, "would you care for a turn in the garden?"

"Why, Mr. Tremayne! In the dark? Alone?" She fluttered her eyelashes at him. "I cannot, for I doubt your intentions entirely, sir!"

Collis leaned closer until the tips of her breasts brushed his chest. Her sea-green eyes flashed at him as she cast him a saucy look. With his left hand, the one out of sight of the crowd, he slid his grip from her waist up to the side of her breast.

He put his lips to her ear. "I double-damn dare you."

Turn the page for an excerpt from
the first book in The Royal Four

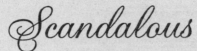

Nathaniel "The Cobra" Stonewell,
Lord Reardon's Story

Now available from St. Martin's Paperbacks

Every ruler needs a few men he can count on
to tell him the truth
—whether he wants to hear it or not.

Created in the time of the Normans, when King William the Conqueror found himself overrun with "advisors" more concerned with their own agendas than with the good of the whole, the Quatre Royale were selected from the king's own boyhood friends. Lords and warriors all, bound by loyalty rather than selfish motives, these four men took on the names of ruthless predators while acting as the Quatre, keeping their lives and identities separate from their true roles . . .

. . . to act as the shield of deceit and the sword of truth in the name of the king.

> Courageous as the Lion
> Deadly as the Cobra
> Vigilant as the Falcon
> Clever as the Fox

The appointment is for life—the commitment absolute. Bonds of family, friends, and even love become as insubstantial as a dream when each hand-selected apprentice takes the seat of the master. All else is merely pretense, kept for the sake of secrecy and anonymity. For it is true that the iron bars of duty cage the hearts and souls of . . .

. . . THE ROYAL FOUR.

BUT SOMETIMES LOVE PREVAILS.

Willa hummed cheerfully, if somewhat out of tune, as she foraged in the meadow for a few greens to round out their noontide meal. Traveling with her husband suited her absolutely. Even with Nathaniel's strange aversion to staying at inns and his tendency to monosyllabic conversation, she was determined to enjoy his company.

Besides, she was seeing places she'd never seen before. Even though the new stone-walled sheep fields greatly resembled the previous stone-walled sheep fields of her experience, they were *new*. After a lifetime spent in the same tiny village and its monotonous environs, anything new was delightful.

Furthermore, marriage was *new*. Spending her days with such an attractive man was entirely new, and there was no point in denying the purely female pleasure she took in watching Nathaniel ride, walk— oh, heavens, that leonesque stride!—and basically breathe in and out.

Of course, she'd imagined that by now she and her

husband would have managed to put that silly consummation requirement behind them . . .

Willa picked up her sack of found treasure and decided to cross the beck further down to look for watercress. There were many small trails leading through the meadow to the beck, and Willa chose a likely spot. The bank was steeper here, which meant the water was likely deeper as well. Watching her feet on the damp slope, Willa didn't look up until she reached the water's edge.

When she did, her heart stopped beating, the breath left her lungs, and her mouth went dry.

He was beautiful.

Nathaniel knelt in the beck only a few yards away. With his back to her and her arrival masked by the chuckling water, he was entirely oblivious to her gaze.

He was also entirely wet.

And entirely naked.

The water was shallow, and there weren't enough bubbles in the world to cover the sheer expanse of naked man that rose from the beck.

Willa couldn't breathe. Her knees went weak at the sight of the sudsy water streaming down his broad back into the crease of his powerful buttocks. She had never seen anything so unbearably delicious in her life.

His back rippled with muscle as he soaped his hair, the cloudy afternoon light doing nothing to dim the sleek shine of soap and water on his male perfection.

Nathaniel bent to duck his head in the water, and Willa could not control the moan that escaped her at the view.

Instantly Nathaniel whirled, one fist pulled back in

instinctive defense while his other hand frantically wiped soap from his eyes. Damn, he should have known he was too vulnerable here. He hadn't been thinking with the mind of a spy but had let thoughts of Willa's sumptuous thighs distract him.

His vision cleared and he saw her. The impulse to fight eased, only to be replaced by another equally ancient instinct.

It was her eyes. They were wide and hungry, with a shining ache in them that he knew from his own soul. She wanted him. He could see it in the way her chest swelled with heavy breaths and by the sheen of perspiration gilding her face and neck.

His own need rose in response to her hungry gaze, and he saw her gaze drop and her eyes widen in surprise. Then slowly, her gaze traveled back up him. Nathaniel straightened and stood motionless for her perusal.

He was the most magnificent creature she had ever seen. She knew that the thrumming within her was because of his male attraction, but the ache in her heart was from his sheer lonely perfection.

I could have her. The thought ran through Nathaniel's mind like the animal it was. He could take her now, on the bank with their legs tangling in the stream edge and her hair spread across the moss. She would accept him hard and fast, he could see it in her eyes, and he could make her like it.

They would be wild creatures, naked and rutting, smeared with mud and bits of grass. He could empty himself in her, here in the daylight, in the dappled green shade that smelt of peat and lust.

He was going to take her, Willa could see it in his eyes. Her knees shook from mingled desire and apprehension. There was so much she didn't know. She wanted him to show her, to feed and foster and answer the ache growing within her by the moment.

With shaking hands, Willa began to unbutton the bodice of her dress without ever taking her gaze from his. He didn't look in her eyes, but followed the course of the open front of her gown as it grew.

Nathaniel began to walk toward her, wading through the water with a slow implacable stride, his erection jutting mightily before him.

Her hands began to shake too much to handle the fastenings, and she dropped them uselessly to her sides. The time was now, and she wasn't sure she was ready.

The female beast within her wanted it and wanted it now. Wanted something untamed and unloving and undeniable.

The female heart wept warning, but the heat and rush of her animal blood drowned it almost beyond hearing.

Her breath coming so hard it almost sobbed, Willa closed her eyes and waited for him to overwhelm her. He stopped before her, so large she could sense him blocking the light from behind her eyelids.

She quivered in response, and felt a first startling burst of pleasure between her thighs. God help her, he hadn't even touched her yet.

He stepped closer, so close that she felt cold water drip from him onto the tops of her breasts. The drops should have hissed on her hot flesh, but they only rolled to meet one another and trickle down between her breasts.

She was hot. Hot and throbbing and aching, and exceedingly nervous, all at the same time.

Willa stood before Nathaniel like a pagan sacrifice, her breasts bared and her eyes shut tight, helplessly offering herself to his worst bestial impulse.

Consequently, he had them. Oh, he wanted to do terrible, wicked, pleasurable things to this simple country girl, this flowering weed plucked from the side of the road. He could teach her such dark and sinful things, and make her beg for more.

Slowly, Nathaniel reached out and took the shoulders of her opened gown in each hand. He could bare her in one horrific rip, tear her clothes from her sweetly offered body and splay her on the ground for his consumption.

His aching lust pounded through him, driving him to do just that, to own and possess this ripe willing female and to the devil with the consequences. His hands fisted in the fabric of her gown, tugging it tight and pulling her toward him.

She swayed forward unresisting and let her head fall back, baring her throat in an ancient instinctive gesture of submission.

Nathaniel could taste her already, taste how salty and sweet she would be, the salt of her skin and the sweetness of her virginal untouched nipples in his mouth. . . .

She believed herself to be his wife. To take her now, to consummate a marriage that wasn't real—it would make him everything they said he was. He had no feelings for her but desire—that and a rather consuming vexation, which was all the more reason to stop now.

He must keep his secret vow. There must be no children to bear his tarnished name. He was very much afraid that if he allowed himself a taste of Willa, there would be a child. He glanced down at her overflowing breasts.

Perhaps several children.

Nathaniel pulled the neckline of Willa's gown together once more, then placed her hands upon it to hold it closed.

She opened her eyes and blinked at him, her gaze thoroughly confused. He bent and retrieved the sack she had dropped.

"Go back to the horses," ordered Nathaniel softly, and for once, Willa blessedly offered no objection to his commanding tone.

With a dazed expression, she took the sack of greens from his hand. Nathaniel put his hands on her shoulders and gently turned her. Pointing her back to the camp, he gave her a little push.

"I'll join you in a moment. I need to dress." And somehow he must cool his throbbing arousal.

As Willa stumbled out of sight, Nathaniel picked up the bucket and dumped gallon after gallon of freezing beck water over his head.

Easier said than done.